They came together
in a tumultuous Australia—
the captive and the free...
the brash and the beautiful.

THE PRISONER—
Sara Dane, exquisitely blonde and beautiful. She was born to enflame men's hearts; she was destined to lose her own.

THE LIEUTENANT—
Andrew Maclay, bold and handsome. He defied convention to take a convict bride; he had to conquer a continent to keep her.

THE ENGLISHMAN—
Richard Barwell, dashing and domineering. He chose wealth over Sara's love, but he found he couldn't stop desiring her.

THE FRENCHMAN—
Louis de Bourget, dark and mysterious. He wanted all the riches of New South Wales as his own, and he wanted Sara by his side.

THE RIVAL—
Alison Watson, refined and elegant. Her inheritance could steal the one man Sara treasured; her secrets could ruin Sara's life.

SARA DANE
The bestselling saga of Australia from
CATHERINE GASKIN

D0823493

Bantam Books by Catherine Gaskin
Ask your bookseller for the books you have missed

FAMILY AFFAIRS
I KNOW MY LOVE
SARA DANE

Sara Dane

Catherine Gaskin

BANTAM BOOKS
TORONTO · NEW YORK · LONDON · SYDNEY

SARA DANE
A Bantam Book / published by arrangement with the Author

PRINTING HISTORY
First published in 1955 by William Collins Sons & Co., Ltd.
Bantam edition / March 1983

All rights reserved.
Copyright 1954 by Catherine Gaskin.
Copyright renewed © 1982 by Catherine Gaskin.
Cover art copyright © 1983 by Elaine Gignilliat.
This book may not be reproduced in whole or in part, by
mimeograph or any other means, without permission.
For information address: Bantam Books, Inc.

ISBN 0-553-23286-X

Published simultaneously in the United States and Canada

Bantam Books are published by Bantam Books, Inc. Its trade-
mark, consisting of the words ''Bantam Books'' and the por-
trayal of a rooster, is Registered in U.S. Patent and Trademark
Office and in other countries. Marca Registrada. Bantam
Books, Inc., 666 Fifth Avenue, New York, New York 10103.

PRINTED IN THE UNITED STATES OF AMERICA

O   9 8 7 6 5 4 3 2 1

Author's Note

The story of Mary Reibey has become something of a legend in Australian history—it is the story of a woman, who, sentenced to transportation for what can have been no more than a child's prank, overcame the stigma of her conviction, and rose to a position of wealth and prominence among the citizens of early New South Wales. This novel is *not* her story, but is based on the assumption that what one woman can do, so may another. The broad outlines of the lives of Mary Reibey and of Sara Dane are similar—the details differ sharply. This book is meant in no way to be a portrait of Mary Reibey, but simply a novel of her times.

In only one instance am I conscious of not having kept to the exact dates of the principal events in the colony. In Part II, Andrew Maclay takes up his grant of land on the Hawkesbury River about a year before the Historical Records show that the first settlers established themselves there.

Lastly, I should like to express my sincere thanks to Dr. G. M. Mackaness, of Sydney, for his advice and many suggestions on the early chapters; to Ian Grey; to Katherine MacDougall and George Naish, of Greenwich Maritime Museum; also to my sister, Moira, for whose help with research, and in editing the manuscript, I am deeply grateful.

C. M. G.

PART ONE

Chapter One

"I am the resurrection and the life, saith the Lord, he that believeth in me, though he were dead..."

There was very little movement among the crowd that packed the *Georgette's* deck. They listened to the words recited at the burial service, seeming frozen by the unemotional calm of the captain's voice. Only a few of the more curious pressed forward for a better view of the stitched bundle of sail cloth, partly hidden under a Union Jack.

It was noon of a June day in 1792. The *Georgette*, a sixty-four gun, two-decker, of the East India Company, was ten days out of Rio, headed for Cape Town. On leaving the Cape, her orders were to turn south into the Antarctic and then eastwards following a track that only a few ships had ever taken before her. Her destination was the settlement established four years ago on the shores of Port Jackson, in the new colony of New South Wales. It was hardly yet known by its proper name of Sydney—the familiar name, the name that rang through the courtrooms and prisons of England was that of Botany Bay. This was the dreaded settlement raised to house the overflow of the prisons, a prison complete in itself, from which escape was impossible, and the hope of ever returning to England almost futile. The *Georgette* was a convict transport, and the thought of Botany Bay stirred somewhere in the minds of most of those who listened silently to the captain's words.

"Man that is born of woman hath but a short time to live..."

They made a strange sight herded round the flag-draped sailcloth. All about, there on the upper-deck, the quarterdeck,

1

and the poop, the crew was arranged in orderly lines, bare-footed and dirty; they stood with faces arranged in careful solemnity; indifferent faces, because the identity of that roll of sailcloth meant less than nothing to them. One or two, making a gesture towards the occasion, had braided his greasy hair into a pigtail, much neater than the careless efforts of the rest. They were unwashed; they looked it, and they smelled vilely.

Four officers, the master, his mate, and six midshipmen, stood in a stiff line behind the captain. The ship's surgeon had taken his place at the end of the row—his attitude suggesting that he did not belong to that little hierarchy, because he was not, as they were, wholly a seaman. Each face in the row bore that same frigid look which found its echo in the crew about them; eyes were mostly fixed on the horizon that tilted steadily with the movement of the ship; bodies were drawn up in disciplined rigidity. The words of the service fell on inattentive ears; they had all heard it many times before, and only the midshipmen were young enough and fresh enough to the life of the sea to be greatly impressed. The youngest midshipman, a lad of fourteen, on his first voyage, now and then shot quick, nervous glances towards the sailcloth. But the rest wore an expression of patience, and an acceptance of the monotony, struggle, and death to which their long, slow voyaging had made them accustomed.

A man and a woman, with their two children, stood behind the officers, and a little to the side of them. They were grouped closely together, looking ill at ease, as if they were well aware that their servant, whose body lay under the flag, was no concern of the crew; she had been an ordinary woman, leaving no impression with these men who might have passed her on deck a dozen times in a day. The wind played with the long bright skirts of the woman and her young daughter; it played among the fringes of their shawls. The colour and the movement of the soft materials was a touch of frivolity thrust among those erect lines.

The convicts stood by themselves, farther away from the captain, their armed guards making a sharp division between them and the rest of the crowd on the upper-deck. There were two hundred and seven convicts aboard the *Georgette*, an ill-assorted mass of human cargo, housed down in the darkness between decks, waiting without hope for the arrival in Botany Bay. They were sullenly submissive while the words of the burial service droned over them. But heads kept turning, eyes wandered to the masts and the riggings stretching above, to the endless

2

horizons. They blinked constantly in the strong light; the distances of sea and sky were painful when they had looked at nothing for weeks but the bulkheads, dark with age and damp. The wind sported pitilessly with the rags they wore. They were a wild-looking lot—men and women; long hair, matted with filth, hung on their frowning brows; their eyes, screwed up against the hard glare, were fierce and unrepentant. There was scarcely an adequate pair of boots or shoes among them, and the flapping of their tattered clothes gave them the appearance of a collection of scarecrows. They shifted gingerly from one foot to another, savouring the relief of stretching their legs and filling their lungs with fresh air.

"We therefore commit her body to the deep, to be turned into corruption . . . ."

All heads craned in curiosity as the sailcloth bundle was raised and slid forward through one of the open gun ports. The flag was drawn back, and the body fell with a splash into the sea. The shock of the sound registered briefly on a few faces. There was a strange, choked-back cry from the midst of the convicts, and a child of eleven suddenly bent her face into her grimy hands. No one took any notice, except a woman standing behind who gave her a half-affectionate pat on the shoulder. The child's sobs continued, soft little cries which the captain's voice easily overrode. As though afraid of the noise she made, she ceased weeping abruptly, and raised her head. The tears had made fresh tracks in the dirt on her cheeks.

Finally the captain lifted his eyes from the book he held, reciting the last words of the service from memory.

"Amen." The crew mumbled the word in a chorus. They waited for the order to dismiss.

Among the convicts there was a sense of tension as they formed up to go below again.

Andrew Maclay, the *Georgette's* second officer, watched them go below, a tattered, barefoot mob. They were a miserable-looking lot, he thought. There wasn't even a picturesque quality about them—just a collection of thieves and ruffians, some of them lucky to have escaped the gallows. They murmured among themselves as they bunched around the hatchway, waiting to go down. A guard's voice sharply ordered them to silence. Andrew watched only a moment longer, thinking that it would take more than the sort of punishment New South Wales meted out to

3

reform the greater part of this sorry crowd. He turned, starting to make his way to the companion-ladder leading to the cabins. But he was halted suddenly by a woman's voice, rising high and indignantly from the midst of the waiting convicts.

"Here, mind what you're doing! You'll have the child down that ladder on her head!"

"You mind your words, you . . . !" The sentence finished in a stream of oaths.

Andrew wheeled. The group round the hatchway parted at his approach, and stood silently watching to see what would happen. The guard, made aware of an officer's presence by the quietening of the crowd, turned swiftly. He jerked his thumb backwards at the convict-woman who had called out.

"Causing trouble, sir," he said. "Holding up the line, she was."

The woman had her hand on the arm of the child whose sobbing had broken into the burial service. She drew herself up very straight, looking from the marine guard to Andrew, and for a brief moment the filthy remains of the gown she wore seemed to stir and quiver with the force of a barely controlled anger.

She burst out! *"You* saw what happened!" The words were fairly flung at Andrew. "He," pointing to the guard, "almost threw her down there!"

"Sir . . . !"

The guard made a savage movement with his musket towards the woman. The circle of convicts closed in, heads craning, tongues loosened with excitement at the prospect of a set-to. In those dulled eyes Andrew saw a flicker of interest build up within a second. This crowd was spoiling for a diversion, eagerly waiting his order for punishment for the woman. He was sickened by the sight of them, the sharp, watching faces, without a trace of pity for one of their own kind, or even for the child.

"Enough! Silence—both of you!"

He addressed the woman then. "Get below—at once!"

She looked back at him for only a moment longer, and then she urged the child towards the companion-ladder. The guard, relieved, began to hustle the convicts forward again. The babel of talk increased.

"Keep them in order, there!" Andrew commanded curtly as he turned away.

"Aye, aye, sir!"

Andrew made his way below, and he found himself thinking of

4

the incident. It was all over in a few seconds—it hadn't even attracted the attention of any other officer. It was no more than the smallest point of discipline, something which happened constantly when the convicts were bunched together in groups on deck. Yet his mind lingered on the scene. The eager, pitiless faces revolted him; he had seen their quick willingness to turn upon one of their own. And the woman herself—there had been a fierce kind of spirit in the way she sprang to the defence of the child. He tried to think what she had looked like; but she was no different from any of the other young women who clutched their indistinguishable rags. All he could clearly recall was the angry flash of an extraordinary pair of eyes when she had first turned to him.

With his hand stretched towards the knob of the wardroom door he halted, remembering, with a sense of shock, that her voice had been that of an educated woman.

II

As readily as any other member of the party, Andrew had accepted Captain Marshall's invitation to eat dinner with him after the burial service. This was a diversion from routine for which they were all thankful; these meals at the captain's table, lengthy and rather boisterous, made up for a whole week of monotony in the wardroom. He settled back in his chair, drowsy, contented, and watched the man opposite, their passenger, James Ryder. Ryder had been a prosperous East Anglian farmer, who now, for some inexplicable reason, was determined to settle and farm in New South Wales. Andrew privately thought this revealed a man of incredible eccentricity, and yet his appearance was perfectly normal, He carried the marks of his class and type—well-cut coat and immaculate linen. Ryder's pretty, frail wife had also been pressed to join them at the table, but the ordeal on deck that morning had tired her, and she had gone directly to her cabin. Also absent was Howlett, the purser, and young Roberts, the fourth lieutenant.

It was mid-afternoon and the meal had not yet finished. They had eaten well; the madeira was good and plentiful. Their spirits were high, though their talk had turned for the second time to the subject of the scene they had witnessed at noon that day.

Brooks, the surgeon, addressed Ryder.

"I'm afraid your wife, sir, will be greatly inconvenienced by the death of her servant. Most unfortunate . . ."

Ryder nodded agreement. "I'm afraid she will, Mr. Brooks."

Andrew's eyes flicked from one to the other of the company, watching their expressions change as the topic was reintroduced. The men's ages ranged from Lieutenant Wilder's twenty-four years, to the captain's mid-fifties. It was a party of six—the captain, Harding and Wilder, his first and third officers, Brooks, James Ryder, and Maclay himself.

Ryder fingered some breadcrumbs on his plate, then he looked directly towards the captain. He cleared his throat. "My wife has been wondering, Captain Marshall," he said, "if it's possible that you have a woman among the convicts called Sara Dane?"

A silence followed the words. The captain tilted the decanter carefully over his glass. The wine had been brought aboard at Teneriffe by Ryder, and it was uncommonly good. He sipped, raising his eyes to his passenger.

"What name did you say, Mr. Ryder?"

"Sara Dane, sir."

The captain glanced at his first officer. "Mr. Harding, can you recall that name on the list?"

Harding shook his head. "There are sixty-seven female convicts on board, sir. I can't, at the moment, remember if this person is among them." He turned to Ryder. "You have some special interest in this woman, sir?"

Ryder took his time in answering. He was frowning; his leathery skin was dark and lined, rough against the smooth white of the linen at his throat. "My wife, as you know, is a bad sailor. She is so often confined to her cabin that I honestly don't know what is to become of the children now that Martha Barratt is gone. She was quite excellent with them, you know."

Harding nodded, waiting to hear the rest.

But it was Brooks who spoke. His voice was cold and rapid. "And is that your reason for seeking this woman, sir? Are you thinking of making her a nurse for Ellen and Charles?"

Andrew saw that Ryder stiffened at the tone.

"Have you any objections to such a scheme, Mr. Brooks?"

"Well . . ." The surgeon hesitated. "She isn't known to you, is she?"

"Not personally," Ryder replied. "By hearsay."

They had all become interested by this time. Andrew noticed

that the captain was leaning forward, his elbows on the table, his glass clasped between both hands.

"Before we embarked at Portsmouth," Ryder said, "my wife received a letter from a friend who lives in Rye. The lady writes of Sara Dane, who was servant to a parson's family there—and sentenced to transportation about twelve months ago. My wife has hopes that this young woman may be on board. And, if so, as she is domestically trained, she would probably be of great help to her for the rest of the voyage."

He went on, "The doubt is, of course, whether she survived her imprisonment in England." Then he lifted his shoulders slightly. "She may already have reached New South Wales. Or, again, she might still be awaiting a transport."

Brooks spoke again. "Sentenced twelve months ago, you say? Then I should be surprised if she isn't dead. The gaols are filthy, and crawling with vermin—and the dogs in the street wouldn't eat the food the prisoners are given. When gaol-fever gets going the poor wretches die off like flies"

Captain Marshall looked round at his guest. "I once visited a gaol, gentlemen—not, of course, of necessity." Here he waited for the laughter which dutifully followed. "The place was in a state of ruin and the gaoler hadn't received any money for repairs. So what do you think the fellow did? He simply chained the prisoners to the good walls, and let the others tumble down about them!"

Andrew listened with interest. He had never seen the inside of the gaols where the gaolers acted as a kind of landlord, and the prisoners were treated according to their means.

"The sight you saw was not an unusual one, sir," Wilder put in. "It often happens. After all, what else can these gaolers do? They've got to live on what the prisoners can pay. They can hardly be expected to run their places like inns."

"Inns!" Brooks laughed. "There's not much chance of that! Believe me, gentlemen, you've seen nothing until you've been inside a woman's prison. Sometimes they cram thirty or forty women into a ward scarcely big enough to hold ten. I've seen them almost naked, and the few rags they do have are crawling with lice. Most of them haven't even the money to treat the gaoler to a pot of beer, so they're simply left to rot—and rot they do!" He added quickly, "If I ever have the bad luck to be sent to prison, I trust it will be after I've stolen a large enough sum of money to let me pay my way out again!"

No one spoke immediately; they seemed content to let Brooks's words sink in. The trouble was, Andrew thought, they were all, excepting James Ryder, half-asleep—the heat, the heavy, drawn-out meal and the plentiful wine were not conducive to purposeful conversation. But Wilder bestirred himself. Andrew, glancing at him, noted the nonchalantly-raised brows, the slow, studied smile, and wondered if Ryder allowed himself to be irritated by this young man.

"In view of what we've just heard, Mr. Ryder, do you really think it's a good idea to have one of these creatures to wait on your wife and children?" Wilder eyed the company with a slight smirk. "We all know what these women are. It's no secret that they pay their gaol fees by prostitution."

Ryder was immediately on the defensive. "I'm quite satisfied that my idea is a sound one, Mr. Wilder."

"Inadvisable, sir, surely," Wilder murmured. "These women are felons."

Andrew looked quickly at Ryder. Here was a man of solid worth, a farmer of considerable wealth and education, and the *Georgette's* officers still passed time amongst themselves wondering at the nature of his attraction to the struggling colony for which they were bound, why he should choose to drag his wife and children on this interminable voyage to set them down finally among savages and convicts in a penal colony.

"These felons are what the Governor will assign to me as servants when we reach New South Wales," Ryder replied, regarding Wilder coldly. "I am prepared to take a risk on whatever type of woman I choose from this ship. My wife must have someone to take care of the children." He turned to the captain. "Captain Marshall, have I your permission to see if this woman is aboard?"

"Oh, certainly, Mr. Ryder! Certainly!" the captain answered, scarcely taking the glass away from his lips. The top of his head, bald, and ringed in greying fuzz, was as pink and shiny as his cheeks.

The old fool, Andrew thought. Captain Marshall was more than half-drunk, and not at all concerned with the problem Ryder faced. But, to merit his passenger's generosity—for the madeira was indeed excellent—he would give all the help he could. The unwelcome job of routing the woman from the stink-hole between decks would fall to one of his luckless officers. Andrew felt it likely that Brooks would be chosen; it was the surgeon's duty to visit the convicts' quarters each day on a tour of inspection. And then it suddenly occurred to Andrew that he himself might be the one for the task. God forbid! He desperately hoped the captain's wandering glance might finally pause on Brooks.

But the captain was leaning towards Ryder again. "Yes, my dear sir, I quite agree with you. If you must have one of these women as a nursemaid, better to put her into service now—get whatever good you can out of her while you need her most."

Andrew put in good-humouredly, "You might not find her so bad a proposition, Mr. Ryder. They're not all desperate criminals, you know. We have poachers and dissenting preachers down in the holds. One could hardly call *them* criminals."

"Then what is one to call them?" Wilder asked.

"Well . . ." Andrew began. "I wouldn't call a man a criminal simply because he preaches another way to worship —or because he steals a chicken or two."

"Rash words, Mr. Maclay!" Harding said with a smile. "An odd preacher here and there—what does it matter? But think of hundreds of preachers and thousands of poachers and poultry thieves, and it becomes a different story altogether. Why, if these people were left unpunished they'd soon fancy themselves as good as their masters. It's that same feeling which produced the revolution in France. From what I can make out, it all started because the King was weak enough to call these fellows together and give them the idea that they had something to contribute to the Government. They, of course, seized power the first opportunity they got—and now the Royal family is imprisoned in the Tuileries, and from the temper of these Frenchies it looks as if they might all end up on the guillotine." He paused, and then said firmly, "And where did it all begin—with nothing more than letting an odd poacher off punishment, and permitting a few men to roam about the country stirring up trouble!"

Ryder nodded his agreement. "*I* like to see justice done. Sometimes the laws *are* severe on the poor. But rebellion breeds in the masses—and they must be taught that they can't break the law and expect to go unpunished. These agitators are dangerous men. Given half a chance they'll pull down King and Government. That rascal, Tom Paine now . . . His *Rights of Man* is as treasonable a document as ever yet hung a man."

Brooks, risking a rebuke for Jacobin sentiments, said, "All

Tom Paine wanted was representative government and old-age pensions."

"Tom Paine wanted to see the monarchy and House of Lords abolished," Harding said. "He wanted the poor educated above their stations—and he'd be happy to have us ruled by a gang of labourers, as they are in Paris."

"Look at the effect Paine's gospel and the French Revolution have had in Ireland," Ryder said. "Wolf Tone is a mad hothead! And the Irish have far from finished with rebellion yet, believe me!"

Andrew said thoughtfully, "I don't think it's altogether fair to blame the French for the agitation in Ireland. In my opinion the Irish simply don't like having their country ruled by English soldiers. And, as for England herself—wouldn't you say, Mr. Ryder, that the Enclosures Acts, driving the peasants out of the land into the factories, is the real cause of the trouble? Many of them who were happy and contented before, can't even earn a living wage. So they steal and poach."

The captain roused himself at that. "Yes, they steal and poach—and are very rightly sent to Botany Bay for their trouble. Once give them the idea that they can do that sort of thing and get away with it, and it's the end of decency and order."

"True enough, sir," Andrew said, "I don't say they ought not to be punished. But I can't see the decency and order in laws that hang a murderer, or give him life transportation to Botany Bay, and then deal out exactly the same sentence to a man for poaching a rabbit or two. It just doesn't make sense."

Harding chuckled softly. "You talk like a Whig Member of Parliament, Maclay! Will you speak for Law reform when you're sent to Westminster?"

There was general laughter among the group. Andrew answered amiably, "I only become a reformer over a bottle of wine, gentlemen. I'm afraid at other times the state of my fellow-man doesn't worry me much."

"Well," Wilder drawled, "one can't really expect much in the way of politics—or reform—from a Lowland Scots farmer-turned-sailor."

Andrew, not in the least put out, turned to him. "Perhaps Scottish farmers don't know much about politics—at least according to Westminster standards. But that doesn't make me altogether wrong in saying that not every man among the convicts is a criminal and not every woman is a slut. I think if

10

Mrs. Ryder is prepared to take a chance with one of the women, then it's more than likely she'll find someone to suit her.''

Captain Marshall seemed to think they had spoken long enough on an unpleasant subject. He rose to his feet. The others followed.

"Excellent wine, Mr. Ryder," he murmured, bowing.

Ryder also bowed.

The captain gazed round his assembled officers. He was smiling slightly. The tips of his fingers rested on the table as he leaned forward.

"Well, Mr. Maclay, you seem determined to champion the convicts. In which case, I think you'd probably be the best person to find out if this woman, Sara Dane, is on board with us.''

Andrew stiffened, and his face was suddenly hot. "Yes, sir!''

"And in the event of her not being with us," the captain went on, "I'm quite sure we're safe in entrusting the choice of a female to you. Isn't that right, gentlemen?"

Andrew saw the covert grins and heard the chorus of assent. "Yes, sir," he said.

The captain bowed again towards Ryder. "My compliments to your wife, sir. I'm sure Mr. Maclay will do everything possible to accommodate her." He pushed aside his chair and stepped back from the table. "Good-afternoon, gentlemen.''

An hour passed before Andrew sent one of the midshipmen for the list of the women convicts aboard. He was in the wardroom, a litter of maps and papers spread on the table before him. He was busy, but the captain's orders couldn't be kept waiting any longer, no matter how he cursed his luck in being the one to receive them. Damn old Marshall!

The door opened and he looked up. The youngest of the midshipmen entered, a leather-bound book under his arm.

Andrew reached out for it. "That's right, Williamson. Thank you.''

"Aye, aye, sir!''

The boy went out again.

The other two occupants of the wardroom, Brooks and Wilder, came over to the table.

Andrew pushed aside the maps and opened the book reluctantly.

"I wish to hell the old man had picked anyone else but me to do this.''

Wilder smiled. "I'll be interested to see what you produce —to see your idea of a virtuous woman."

Discipline on board the *Georgette* was strict. Captain Marshall had never turned a blind eye to fraternisation between his crew and the convicts. Andrew had little doubt that Wilder would be one of the first to consort with the women if the rule were relaxed. He recalled tales of other transports where the captain was lax, and the crew and convicts mixed riotously, making the voyage one long carousel. Wilder, he felt, was airing his contempt from the safety of his position on the other side of Captain Marshall's fast and set codes of conduct.

Andrew turned the pages distastefully. Feeling ran high among the officers of the East India Company that it was beneath their dignity to accept the contract to transport convicts to Botany Bay. The Company had of late made a number of contracts of this kind, and Andrew, at times, was doubtful that he would ever be transferred to a regular Indiaman run again.

Wilder leaned across his shoulder, looking down the list. He said idly, "Can't imagine why Ryder should want to go out there. And taking his wife ... You know, she's a damned pretty woman! And the fool proposes to set her down among a bunch of savages!"

"Ryder will probably make a fortune for her in New South Wales," Brooks remarked. "That's good enough reason for any man to want to go there.'

"A fortune, he says!" Wilder nudged Andrew. "I shouldn't think there was a hope in the world of that! What's to be gained from a penal colony? It hasn't any trading advantages like China and India. It can't export anything, and the natives are savages. It wouldn't have been settled at all if the war with America hadn't stopped the Government from sending convicts there. From all accounts Botany Bay is nothing more than a clump of huts—it'll never be other than a dumping-ground for the overflow of the prisons."

Brooks's brows were lifting slowly while Wilder spoke. He put his hands in his pockets, and threw one leg lazily across the corner of the table.

"Your opinion is interesting, Mr. Wilder," he said. "But I have a different one."

From Brooks's expression, Andrew knew that he was about to enjoy turning Wilder's second-hand views inside out. Brooks had sailed as surgeon with the second fleet of convicts to Port

Jackson. He was a quiet man, and didn't talk much about any previous voyages he had made. Andrew looked at him inquiringly.

"It's like no other place I've ever seen," Brooks said, half to himself, not looking at the other two. "And I've spent quite a few years of my life in ships, and there aren't many ports that I haven't seen. It's a mystery, the whole place—it's desolate, but it's fascinating. Captain Cook charted the east coast first about twenty-two years ago. He made only one landing, at Botany Bay. But when the First Fleet went out five years ago, Governor Phillip found Botany Bay impossible to settle. He moved his fleet to Port Jackson, a few miles along the coast. What a harbour that is! He landed and settled at a place he called Sydney Cove."

"And out of all that, where do you get your idea that Ryder has a chance of making a fortune?" Wilder asked.

"Because I agree with Governor Phillip," Brooks said, studying the amused set of Wilder's well-shaped mouth. "Phillip has great ideas for his prison-colony. And by God I don't care what anyone says, I think he's right!"

"What sort of ideas?" Andrew put in. "Is the land fertile?"

Brooks hesitated. "That's a difficult question, Maclay. At the moment they can get almost nothing out of it in the way of crops. They're perpetually on the point of starvation. They depend solely on England for supplies—and you know how precarious that is. The convicts die off in dozens, because if the ships are delayed they just haven't enough rations to keep alive. But Phillip thinks that the place can be made to produce when they learn to manage the soil and the climate. So far there doesn't seem to be a man among them with any real knowledge of farming—and the convicts aren't concerned for the future of the country." He finished earnestly. "That's why I think, Ryder has a fortune waiting out there. He has the right knowledge, and he has the money to push ahead."

Wilder's good-looking young face wore an expression of boredom. "Well, all I say is that it'll be a damned nuisance if Port Jackson becomes a regular call on the way to the East. I, for one, won't have a care if I never see the place after this trip."

Andrew turned again to the book in front of him. He flicked the pages impatiently. "Sara Dane...Hmm..." Suddenly he looked up. "God, how is one expected to tell these women apart? There aren't even papers sent with them to tell us what crimes they've committed."

Wilder laughed. "Perhaps we're consigning the gentle Mrs. Ryder into the hands of a murderess!"

"The whole position is absurd," Andrew said, frowning down at the book. "The Government has sent these people to the end of the earth without papers of any description. No one has the faintest idea why they were convicted. What's to happen to them when they reach New South Wales? How does Governor Phillip decide when their sentences have expired?"

"That's his affair, my dear fellow," Wilder said lightly. "Now, let's get on with the problem in hand. Let's find the fair damsel in the darkness below!"

"I'll warrant she's not on . . ." Andrew broke off, jabbing at a page with his forefinger. "Here she is . . . Sara Dane! . . . and no punishments marked against her. This is a piece of luck for Ryder!"

"Well, off you go, Maclay!" Wilder said good-humoured now. "I wish you joy with your task!" He gave them a half-salute, and, adjusting his coat with care, sauntered out of the wardroom. He paused before he pulled the door behind him, looking back over his shoulder. "A thought has just struck me."

"Yes?" Andrew said.

"I wouldn't," Wilder continued, "for all the wealth in the East, change places with the Governor of New South Wales!"

Chapter Two

Andrew was never free from his feeling of distaste whenever he was forced to visit the convict quarters. With a curt order he summoned a Sergeant of Marines to accompany him, and went quickly down the companion ladder, trying to stiffen himself for the ordeal facing him. Service with the Navy had hardened him against undue squeamishness, but this was something quite different. This was human cargo carried in worse conditions than the livestock—in fact the livestock was cared for as something of value, while the death of a convict was of no importance to anyone. As he reached the gun deck, where the prisoners were kept, the confused babel of voices reached him—the women's voices distinct and shrill above the lower tones of the men. He felt the sweat start in a prickle all over his body, and he longed

14

with a kind of desperation to turn again and mount the companion ladder.

He kept his ideas about the convicts to himself—except for the few times, as at dinner today, when he had been rash enough to voice his contempt for the chaos of English law which lumped murderers and petty thieves together in a transport bound for Botany Bay. Men of his class were not expected to feel pity for these prisoners—never once among the officers in the wardroom had he heard a word of sympathy for them. Listening to the way in which they talked of the convicts, he knew that he was quite alone in his feeling for them, a feeling that there was something personal to him in their sufferings, as if, even though he was completely removed from their world they still had the right to claim his attention and thoughts. Among British ship-owners, and from the men who campaigned against slavery, he had heard descriptions of the slave ships which plied between Africa and the West Indies; it seemed to him that the position of the convicts on the *Georgette* was hardly less terrible.

He hated the crowding, and the struggle for survival which went on among them; he had seen it all before in the crumbling houses in the alleyways of London and Edinburgh. His father had been a Scot with a lucrative practice at the English bar, who had lived only long enough to give his son a distaste for law as a profession, and the kind of reckless, purposeless courage which could let him stake his life on the turn of a card, or the throw of the dice. Andrew remembered his gambling father only dimly; he had been brought up by his mother's brother, who owned a small estate near Edinburgh. The only discipline he had known in his life was in the Navy, and after that the milder rule of the East India Company. He grew up with a horror of the crowded swarm of the great cities, and for anything which threatened to put a shackle upon his liberty. A kind of sickness crept over him sometimes at the thought of the packed gloom of the *Georgette*'s prison quarters, of the irons which still remained on some ankles.

Down here the gun ports were closed, and it was dim and airless. In the near-darkness it was always the stench which came first; the overpowering smell of unwashed bodies, the smell of rancid food, and of water, green and half-still with living things. The stench of the prisons had come aboard with the convicts, and Andrew imagined it would be a long time before the ship was rid of it.

The prison quarters had been made by running a bulkhead across the width of the ship, with square openings for the guards' muskets. He made his way reluctantly through the gloom; the guards were both bent with their faces to the holes. When they heard him they came to attention quickly, and one of them produced keys.

Andrew stood before the heavy door; through the grille at the top a confusion of shrill cries and the sounds of scuffling and falling bodies reached him.

He gestured towards it irritably. "For God's sake hurry yourself, man! What the devil's happening here?"

The guard fumbled with the locks. "Couldn't say, sir. It's just started—some sort of fight. They're always at it."

"Well, it's your duty to see that they're not always at it. Why haven't you made some attempt to stop it?"

"Stop it, sir?" The man straightened and threw Andrew an astonished glance. "Why, it does no good, sir. And besides I shouldn't like to go in there. They'd tear me to pieces!"

Andrew pushed him aside impatiently, rattling the key in the lock until it yielded. "I shall take care that the captain hears how you attend to your duties."

He swung the door open, and stepped inside. With noticeable reluctance the sergeant followed.

Inside, when his eyes became accustomed to the half-light, he could make out the mass of lying, sitting, and standing women. The noise was terrible, and in the centre of the space four or five women rolled together in a frenzied struggle. All the others had drawn back from them, watching the contest with vicious interest, lending their own threats and encouragement to the general noise. The combat was desperately unequal; even from the mass of kicking heels and waving arms Andrew was able to tell that one of them, lying so completely beneath the bodies of the others that he could hardly see her, was fighting alone. Judging from the size of the women who opposed her, he imagined that the struggle would have been brief, even if he had not come along.

"Silence!" he roared.

The women in the centre of the floor took not the least bit of notice. Around them, the others became gradually aware of his presence, and their cries faded away. In the growing quiet he could distinctly hear the grunts and sighs of the struggling women.

Suddenly one of them, kneeling on the legs of the woman beneath that incredible pile, was warned by the inexplicable stillness about her, and glanced round. She stared at him for only a second, with a trace of fear on her face; then she tugged at the shoulder of the woman nearest her.

"'Ere, Peg! Look!"

The woman she addressed looked up. Her expression altered immediately. She grinned toothlessly at Andrew and made a sort of flourish with her hands. Her harsh Cockney accent rang out over the fading sounds of the others' voices.

"'Ere's the 'andsome young officer come to visit us, dearies! Get out the tea-cups!"

Wild shrieks of laughter greeted the remark.

Andrew felt his face grow hot, and he cursed inwardly.

"Silence!" he rapped again. "What's the meaning of all this?"

The last murmurs died away completely. He knew that no one would answer him. They stared at him solidly, appearing to draw strength from their numbers, while he faced them alone. He watched the stirring of rags as they moved, the cracked, filthy hands plucking at garments which were no more than barely decent. The faces, under their coating of grease and dirt, were indistinguishable. And all the eyes were alike—watchful, shrewd. He looked them over, noting that even the ones who lay ill had raised their heads to see him better. The strongest among them had fought their way to the sides, and had at least the support of the bulkhead, their few possessions were grouped about them like the riches of a kingdom. While he watched them, the three in the centre gradually released their hold on their prisoner. Kneeling where they were, they watched him eagerly, while their victim sat up slowly, holding her head in her hands.

"You all know what the punishment is for fighting!" he said, fixing his gaze on the four culprits. He gestured towards the one he imagined was the ring-leader. "I seem to remember you've been punished before. Isn't it time you learned to obey orders?"

She answered him with another grin. "Yes, sweetheart, but I'm an old dog to be learning new tricks!"

He flushed, and in the laughter that followed her sally he turned towards the sergeant.

"See that Mr. Harding has these women's names."

"Aye, aye, sir!"

They quietened again at his words. A change at once ran through the crowd. They had been hilarious and cheeky, now they seemed hostile and resentful. There was nothing they could

17

do about it, he thought; they were defenceless against authority. If they once guessed his sympathy for their position they would fasten on it like vultures, and his life on the *Georgette* would be hell. From that minute every appearance he made among them would be the signal for outbursts of wit and insubordination.

He cleared his throat and said firmly, "Is there a woman here called Sara Dane?"

There was no response.

"Sara Dane," he repeated. "Is there anyone here by that name?"

The victim of the three attackers suddenly stirred and lifted her head.

"I'm Sara Dane."

She struggled to her knees, and then stood up. She began to push her way through the tightly packed bodies towards Andrew. As they moved and shoved to let her through, the suffocating odours reached him more strongly. She reached him at last, stumbling over a prostrate body as she came. This called forth a stream of angry blasphemy such as he had never heard bettered even in the Navy. But the woman moving towards him seemed completely indifferent to the abuse. She was tall; she had to stoop to avoid the low beams of the deckhead.

"Are you Sara Dane?"

"Yes—I am."

In the dimness he could make nothing of her—what sort of woman she was. But the voice he knew instantly. It was the same one that he had heard raised in protest over the treatment of the child, when the convicts had been sent below after the burial service—the voice which had troubled and puzzled him, He looked at her sharply.

"And what have you got to do with this disturbance? You should be flogged for being disorderly."

"Disorderly!" She swept the loose hair away from her face to look at him fully. For some reason he felt suddenly intimidated. "Do you call it disorderly to fight for what belongs to me? Why should I let this scum get their filthy hands on my things?"

"What were they trying to take from you?"

"This!" She raised her hand and swung before his face a dirty handkerchief knotted at the corners and weighted. "My rations."

Andrew looked around the sullen faces and fervently wished that he were out of this place. He was faced squarely here with the thought that was for ever at the back of his mind—the hunger

18

of the convicts. They lived mostly on salt pork and weevily ship's biscuits. Brooks, who worked among them daily, had told them that the rations were far less than was needed to keep them in health—there was always the fear of scurvy breaking out. There seemed nothing that he, or the captain, or even the East India Company itself could do about it—they were paid a fixed rate to transport the convicts, and it did not stretch to luxuries. In spite of what Brooks tried to do for them, there were frequent deaths. Andrew had heard tales from other transports of the convicts hiding the dead for days, in order to draw the extra rations. As always, where there was hunger, the bullies rose from the mass to take what they could get by force.

"Is this true?" he asked her.

"Of course it's true!" She gave her head a slight toss—an action that was oddly youthful, and didn't seem to fit her appearance. "Why do you think they . . . ?

He cut her short. "You've got too much to say! I'll deal with this."

He turned to the circle of faces about them. "One more instance of this—just one more—and I'll see that you're all punished. All of you—do you hear?" Then he addressed Sara Dane again. "And I don't want to hear any more from you.

"Well, would you stand by and let them . . . ?"

"*That will do!*"

He wheeled, motioning her to follow. "Come with me!"

As the guard swung the door wide for them to pass, the raucous Cockney shout rang out again,

"Have a nice time, sweetheart!" Be sure and tell the officers there are plenty more of us where you came from!"

Andrew stopped abruptly and faced them.

"Another word out of you," he said, "and you'll be stopped deck exercise for ten days!"

The guard pulled the door closed with a crash, but the stifled laughter followed him along the passage to the companion-ladder. He motioned the woman behind him to hurry.

When he reached the upper deck he turned to watch her as she emerged into the clear light. She staggered a little, as if the sudden sweet air and the sunlight were a shock to her senses. He half-reached out a hand to support her, and then, glancing at the sergeant, he let it drop lamely again. She regained her balance, looking about her with an air of ease and composure that mixed sadly with her rags. His lips parted faintly in a smile of amusement to see there was even a touch of superiority about her. For a second or two she surveyed the deck with all the manner of a great lady invited aboard. Then, aware of his eyes upon her, she dropped her pose, and turned fully towards him.

He discovered that she was much younger than he had supposed. She was slim and straight, and the skin of the throat and face was unlined. But she carried the dirt of the prisons like a barrier to whatever beauty she might have possessed. Her face and neck had the greyish tinge of long-embedded dirt; her hair, fallen from its rough knot, hung lankly upon her shoulders. She had on a tattered gown many sizes too large; it had been hacked off at the front of the hem, and at the back it trailed on the deck behind her. She wore it with an air of impoverished grandeur.

Then she raised her eyes to him. A greenish-blue they were, almost the colour of the sea, he thought. They had a calculating, questioning expression.

"It blows fresh up here, Lieutenant," she said quietly.

He glanced at her quickly, and then, remembering the guard, looked away. "That will be all, sergeant."

"Very good, sir."

He watched the man across the deck before he turned to her again. "Fresh . . . ?"

For all his trying he couldn't keep the curiosity out of his voice, and was instantly furious with himself for having answered her. It was a piece of rank impertinence that she had addressed him at all, and he should have rebuked her immediately. But with those queer green eyes fixed on him he had, for an instant, lost his head.

"Perhaps you don't notice it," she was saying. "But when one spends one's time down where I do . . . "

"Haven't I told you to be quiet!" he threw back at her. "Does nothing have any effect on you?"

He turned aside, motioning her to follow him to the passenger accommodation.

She made a little running step to catch up with him, twisting sideways to peer into his face.

"But why shouldn't I talk to you, Lieutenant? It can't harm discipline—there isn't anyone to hear us. Besides, it's a long time since I spoke to anyone like you. Down there"—she pointed to the deck—"they don't know the King's English."

He stopped short and faced her angrily.

"If you're down there with types you don't like—then it's

20

your own fault! People aren't sent to Botany Bay without good reason!''

"Oh, but . . .''

He jerked his head impatiently. "Can't you understand? I'm not on this ship to listen to you talking. Now, for the last time—*be quiet!*''

"Yes, sir.''

She made a sketchy kind of curtsy towards him, and as she bowed her head he had an instant suspicion that she smiled. But she followed meekly enough. He could hear the limp swish of her skirt as it swept the deck.

II

Sara Dane had been born in London eighteen years ago, in a top room of a lodging-house in Villiers Street, off the Strand. At least that was where her father said she was born; but he had left so many lodging-houses in a hurry, owing money to his landladies, that she often wondered how he could remember which particular one it was.

She had loved her father, Sebastian Dane, passionately and blindly. He was a tall man, shoulders stooped beneath his height, and straight, black hair falling over his forehead. She always considered that his thin, dark face, with its fatal lines of dissipation and weakness, was far handsomer than any other she had ever seen. The times when he was sober, or only slightly drunk, he had an infectious gaiety, a good humour that made people love him, and landladies forget that he hadn't paid his rent. There was a strong companionship between them. The only time Sara feared him was during the periods of real drunkenness, when he sat over his rum for days at a stretch, barely able to make the effort of rising from his chair. But this didn't happen often—for the most part he was a merry drunkard. His insidious, habitual drinking gradually drained his strength, and wore the edge off his brilliance.

He was the son of a West Country parson—though his references to the life of the rectory in that pleasantly-wooded Somerset valley meant little to his daughter, for she had never seen it. Sebastian, cynically, did not hesitate in the slightest to make capital from the fact that his father was a baronet's son— although a fourth son. He sometimes found that his name was good enough security for the money he borrowed, knowing, in

21

actual fact, that the name meant literally nothing. There wasn't even a remote hope that either his father or his grandfather might settle any of the debts he incurred. He had seen his father only once since the end of his Oxford days, when he had come down possessed of a brilliant scholastic record, and no money whatever. Since he was obviously not a candidate for Holy Orders, influence was used to find him a position as secretary to a prominent Tory politician. But he was indolent, and already drinking too much, drifting always on the fringe of gamblers and moneylenders. His employer kept him for a year, and then, weighing his touch of brilliance against his multiple failings, finally asked him to leave—not without some regret, Sebastian afterwards told Sara. He then attached himself as secretary to an ageing nobleman, who took him on a leisurely tour of the Continent for three years. The old man was charmed by him, his air of bonhomie and culture, and forgave his frequent lapses from grace. But Sebastian gambled once too often and too heavily with his lordship's money, and one day he found himself travelling back to London with nothing more than a month's wages, and an excellent knowledge of French and Italian.

A few months later he wrote to his father that he had married a woman whom he described as an actress—another proof to his family of the state of utter hopelessness into which he had drifted, for she was a type of woman they believed he would never have become involved with if he had been in his right senses. His father journeyed grimly to London, and found them in their lodgings. His ecclesiastical tongue raked Sebastian over, leaving nothing unsaid which might more minutely describe his horror and dismay over what he called "this tragic and disastrous step." The new bride did not escape his scathing comment.

"This is a scandalous affair, Sebastian!" he snapped, enraged at the prospect of having to claim such a daughter-in-law. "She is sluttish! She is a woman of . . . of . . . no refinement!"

The painful interview went on for an hour or more, and at the end of it he offered to take Sebastian back to Somerset —but the bride would have to remain where she was.

Sebastian's reply was prompt. He pointed out that his wife was already pregnant and would soon have to leave the stage. He added that to desert her in such a condition was something not even his father should ask him to do.

"In any case, sir," he finished mildly, "I find now that I have little taste for the country air."

It was the last contact he ever had with his family.

Sara remembered her mother vaguely—a tall, deep-bosomed woman, with a great deal of golden hair, and a bold, undeniable beauty. The image was not clear, and she had never quite believed Sebastian's story that his wife had died of a fever. It seemed much more likely that her mother had gone off with one or other of her acquaintances of the ale-houses or the theatres, whose back-stages she frequented, even after her marriage.

During Sara's early childhood, Sebastian passed unsuccessfully from one tutoring job to another, occasionally writing for magazines, until he was shunned completely by editors for trying to publish Parliamentary Reform pamphlets. They lived a hand-to-mouth existence, moving about from one lodging to another; for brief periods they enjoyed modest comfort with outbursts of real extravagance—at other times they hadn't the price of a meal. This state of affairs seemed natural to Sara; she had never known any other. She learned where she could buy food cheapest, and how to haggle over a penny with the shopkeepers. She was as adept as Sebastian himself in avoiding the creditors, and when they couldn't be avoided she faced them out boldly. They lived a wandering life, which always had the taste of adventure about it, so long as each experience could be shared by them both. They adored each other, and were only happy when they could be together. Sebastian treated her in every respect as if she were already a woman—she learned to read almost as soon as she could talk, and unconsciously imbibed scraps of learning from him. She and Sebastian were known in every coffee-house and tavern along Fleet Street and the Strand.

When she was eleven she took a position with one of the fashionable dressmaking establishments. Sebastian was helpless to prevent her—by this time he was accustomed to accepting her decisions about everything they did. He talked vaguely of having "other ideas," about what she should do; she took no notice of his troubled murmurs and flung herself into the business of absorbing this new phase of her experience. One of her duties was to carry messages and packages to the great houses of the city. She found herself more often employed this way because she was quick-witted, and could read and write. Sometimes she was permitted to stand by and watch a fitting, listening eagerly to the gossip which drifted through the scented rooms, the talk of balls, parties and scandals; talk of the dull court of George III. In this way she caught a glimpse of the world beyond her own; her envious fingers touched the velvet hangings and the soft carpets;

long mirrors threw back the first full-length reflection of herself she had ever seen. She saw the hustle of preparations for receptions and dinners; occasionally she even waited with the crowd outside to see the guests arrive. She became a general favourite with the ladies who patronised her mistress; she was pretty, and in their presence, made herself docile and amiable. They petted her, and would have spoiled her if she were not too shrewd to be spoiled. Even though she was still a child, they gave her discarded fineries—scarves and scraps of lace. These she either sold or put away, having more sense than to appear to imitate her superiors by wearing them. They encouraged her to chatter to them in her precocious French, which she had learned from Sebastian; altogether she had much more notice taken of her than a dressmaker's apprentice had any right to. She knew her mistress didn't approve the position into which she had manoeuvred herself. But for the moment it happened to be the whim of some of the great ladies to make a fuss over her—and so she was kept on, not without much head-shaking.

It lasted for a year. At the end of that time Sebastian escaped the debtor's prison by taking the first coach he could find out of London with Sara beside him. It happened to take them to Rye By the time they had found lodgings there, Sara had set the story going that they had made the move in search of better health for her father. He fell into an easier and more comfortable life in Rye; tutoring jobs came readily enough when he gave the names of his grandfather and the Tory politician as recommendation.

The change affected Sara strongly; she settled gratefully to the quieter tempo of life, aware that she was free of the ceaseless bustle of the capital. She became outspoken in her determination that Sebastian should alter his habits, that he should not again uproot them both. Quite suddenly, respectability seemed to her a very desirable state. She made up her mind that Sebastian, from then on, must be respectable.

"So you want me to reform, my love?" he said, playing with her hair, as it lay over her shoulders. "Well,—we'll see! We'll see!"

He made a small effort, and succeeded well enough to give Sara some hope. They gave up the lodgings and took a tiny house; living there alone she managed to keep his drinking hidden. A kind of pact existed between them to excuse his weakness, and when it overcame him, to find a way of covering it up. She invented a story of a rare, recurring fever which periodically incapacitated him. She told her story with great conviction, and it was believed; she had the satisfaction of seeing Sebastian sought after because of his undoubted merits as a tutor.

A year after their arrival in Rye, Sebastian was engaged by the Reverend Thomas Barwell, holder of the living at Bramfield, on Walland Marsh, by Romney. He became tutor to the vicar's two sons, Richard and William; each day he walked the two miles to Bramfield and back again, with Sara by his side. He had accepted the post only on the condition that she was to go with him, and that for half the day she should share the lessons with the boys. The rest of the time she would spend assisting Mrs. Barwell in light household duties. It seemed a workable arrangement—the only one whereby Sebastian would have been induced to accept the post, for he would not have left Sara alone through the whole day. Apart from that he wanted her grounded in the classics and mathematics—knowledge, most people told him, quite useless to a woman. But he had his own opinion on the matter, holding to his argument that an education was his only possession to leave with her. Mr. Barwell was aware immediately of Sebastian's determination, and he was easily persuaded to give in, anxious, from the first meeting, to have his services for his sons—the West Country scholar had an excellent reputation in Rye for the job he undertook. Besides, it was considerably cheaper than having some young man to live in.

So each day the spidery black figure walked with his daughter along the dyke roads, twisting and winding by the side of the water-courses across the flatness of the Marsh. Sara loved the windy desolation, its greenness dotted by fat Kent sheep. In the winter the winds tore in from the sea—and when the rain came with it, Sebastian would put his arm around her, drawing her into the shelter of his body. Little deserted chapels were sprinkled over the country in lonely fashion empty and ruined since the days of the Canterbury monks. By night the marsh-land was a weird, unwelcoming place, avoided, whenever possible, by those in the villages and outlying farms. There was no interference, either, with the smugglers who slipped in from the sea with the darkness, their oars muffled, creeping silently up the dykes. There were inns and farms spaced about the Three Marshes with unsavoury reputations, where honest men would whip up their horses sharply until they were far behind. So Sebastian and Sara left Bramfield with the last light of the short winter afternoons, hurrying back along the road, thankfully crossing the bridge where the Rother curved under Rye Hill. It was always with a sense of relief, of a danger passed, that they climbed the cobbled streets of the town.

Life at Bramfield was pleasant enough. Sara was two years younger than Richard, and a year older than his brother. Her life in London had never let her know the meaning of shyness, and the three worked together peacefully. But outside the schoolroom the atmosphere was less easy. The vicar's wife was disapproving of the situation which brought Sara into her household, and she discouraged the girl's contact with her sons. Sara and her father ate their midday dinner apart from the family, making light of Mrs. Barwell's coldness, and the austerity of the meals she served. They were excluded also when callers came to the house, and the two boys were summoned to the drawing-room. Sometimes they witnessed the arrival and departure, in his heavy carriage, of Sir Geoffrey Watson who held the presentation to the living at Bramfield. And when he was accompanied by his daughter, Alison, a dark, sweet-faced child, Sara would gaze at her from the schoolroom window, mildly envious of the richness of her gowns, of the fur muffs which protected her hands.

Then, sometimes, in the long twilights of the spring and summer, Richard would walk part of the way with them to Rye—these were hours when they enjoyed an intimacy not possible at Bramfield. The Marsh was green, the reeds in the dykes bending gracefully before the soft wind. Sebastian taught them the names of the Marsh birds; in spring they sought out the nests together. Sometimes they went as far as the shore itself. The shingle made hard walking, especially if the wind were against them. Pointing out across the Channel, Sebastian filled them with tales of adventure and romance in the coastal towns of Normandy and Brittany. At times like these he seemed no older than Richard himself, his laughter as young and as constant as Richard's own. When a playful mood attacked him, Sebastian would pull at the long braids of Sara's hair, loosening it, to let it fly freely. The wind caught it, whipping it madly across her face, and stinging her eyes. They laughed at this mad confusion of her hair, but there was something secret, something less open than laughter in Richard's eyes. She was gloriously happy in the company of the only two creatures she loved. And she sensed, without the need for speech between them, that Richard returned her love.

It was on Sara's sixteenth birthday, an evening of late summer just before the turn of the season, that Sebastian gave Richard his signet ring. They sat together, the three of them, on the shingle, listening to the screaming cries of the gulls wheeling and dipping above them. Sebastian was silent for a time, twisting the ring, a gold one, on his finger. On an impulse he turned to Richard.

"Here, Richard," he said, "give me your hand."

As he spoke he stretched out and took Richard's left hand, placing the ring on the little finger.

"Sir . . . ?"

Sebastian waved aside the attempted protest. "It belongs rightfully, of course, to Sara." He gave his daughter a faint, rather wistful smile. "But it's a man's ring, for all that. For her it could only have a sentimental value. I've always meant to give it myself—not have it taken from my finger when I'm dead."

He hunched his shoulders under the sombre black coat, staring out to sea.

"When you leave Bramfield to go into the Army, Richard," he said, after a few moments, "things will not be the same. We will still have our friendship, of course—the three of us —but things will not be the same. I want you to keep the ring, to remind you of us three as we are now."

Sara was thankful that Richard had grace and sense enough to protest no longer against the gift.

He sat gazing at the unfamiliar sight of Sebastian's ring upon his finger. Then he looked up, his eyes moving slowly from Sebastian to Sara. "As long as I live it will remind me of these evenings—of both of you." He looked down at the ring again, and then said to Sara:

"Since it should have been yours, may I have your permission to wear it?"

She was aware of a tone he had never before used to her—he spoke to her as if she were a woman, and no longer a classroom companion. Unaccountably, she lowered her eyes rather than look at him. Her father's shrewd gaze upon them both made her uncomfortable.

"I should be glad for you to wear it," she answered.

Then she sprang quickly to her feet. "It's getting late," she said, addressing Sebastian. "We should go." She didn't know why she added this—there was no reason to hasten the return.

They were slow, though, in parting—Richard to turn back to Bramfield, Sara and Sebastian to start the walk to Rye. Glancing behind, she had a last sight of Richard as he rapidly paced the winding dyke road.

It may have been some inexplicable premonition which caused Sebastian to present the ring to Richard at that time. for it was the last evening they were to spend together on the shore. Two nights later, when he had managed for once to escape Sara's vigilance, Sebastian was involved—perhaps blamelessly—in a brawl in a tavern frequented by the sailors who made their way in from the coast. They found him next morning lying in a side alley, dying from a terrifying head wound.

He died later in the day, and as the news filtered through the town, the phantasy-world Sara had built up crashed about her in ruins. People came with small bills and debts, tales of Sebastian's petty borrowing and lies. The evidence of his unstable life was revealed, and the stories, drifting from one mouth to another, lost nothing in the telling. From a few of those who knew them both she received pity and condolence, but from the more outraged she received contempt as the daughter of a man little better than a common thief. There was irritation also, among the townspeople, that she herself could not be branded with him.

He was given a pauper's funeral, and Sara had not even the address of the West Country rectory to inform his father of his death. Pride and loyalty to him kept her from making inquiries about the family; she let Rye and the Barwells, and anyone else concerned, keep their belief that the family and background he boasted was simply a further fabrication of lies. She herself denied any knowledge of them.

The day after Sebastian's funeral, she took stock of the situation. There was no money—the proceeds of the few possessions they had owned would have to go to meet the debts. She doubted that she could even keep back for herself enough money to pay the coach fare to London. And once in London—what then? Back to a dressmaker's workroom, or slaving under a cook in someone's kitchen? She remembered the world she had known before Rye—the grim hopelessness of trying to achieve anything without money, friends, or influence.

The memory frightened her enough to send her boldly to the one man she knew who might help her.

She put on her most becoming gown—one that Sebastian had bought her in a moment of extravagance, and probably hadn't paid for—noticing regretfully that her shabby cloak hid most of it. It was a three-mile walk to the gate-house of Sir Geoffrey

Watson's estate, and another mile beyond that to the house, but she covered the distance without being aware of it as she rehearsed what she would say to him. On her arrival she was kept waiting for an hour in the hall, and then shown into the room where the business of the estate was carried on.

Although the day was still warm the stout baronet sat before a blazing fire, a litter of papers about him. He stared at her hard for a moment, and then waved her to a low seat facing him.

"Sit down, miss! Sit down!"

She did as he told her, feeling her cheeks already scorched by the fire.

Sir Geoffrey arranged his hands expansively across his stomach. Sara knew from his gesture that he was going to manage the interview although it was she who had sought it. She waited for him to speak.

"They told me at Bramfield about your father,' he said. "I suppose there's no money for you, is there?"

She shook her head. She needn't bother to deny what the whole of Rye knew. "My father was often ill, Sir Geoffrey. It was difficult for him to accumulate money."

The baronet laughed aloud. "Drinking's the very devil for running away with money!" He thrust out a large, bandaged foot. "And when the gout gets hold of me I know the other side of it, too!"

Then, seeing her expression, his tone softened. "You mustn't take it to heart, child!' His head nodded heavily. "No doubt you were fond of your father—that's just as it should be. Always believe in children minding their parents. Now, my girl, Alison—you've seen her, haven't you?—she minds what I say smartly enough. A good girl, Alison is!"

He stirred in his chair, sending the last of the papers swirling gently to the floor. "You'll have to do something about earning a living now, miss. Can't live on air, you know."

She looked at him fully. "That's what I've come to speak to you about, sir."

"Eh? . . . Is it now? And what have you got to say?"

Sara clasped her hands tightly underneath her cloak, and plunged ahead. "I've come to ask you for a favour, Sir Geoffrey."

His eyebrows shot up. "A favour? What is it?"

"I wanted to beg you to recommend me to your sister, Lady Linton, for employment in her London house when she returns from India."

He gasped a little, looking at her more closely.

29

"How the devil do you know about Lady Linton, and her London house?"

"When I lived in London I was apprenticed to a dressmaker. I once watched her being fitted for a dress, and then I delivered it to her house."

"You did, eh? And now I suppose you think you know all about her?" When she didn't answer, he went on, "Well, damn me if I know what Lady Linton's wishes will be about staff when she returns. Her husband died in India, and she hasn't told me her plans for the future. The London house wasn't opened all the five years she's been away."

Sara pressed her point. "But surely, Sir Geoffrey, all the vacancies can't be filled already? Lady Linton has a very large house to run—her entertainments are famous." She looked at him appealingly. "I'd be very useful. I'm clever with a needle, and I can do household accounts. And I could write letters for her, and..."

He held up his hand. "A real paragon, aren't you, miss?" Then he laughed. "Well...I suppose Lady Linton would find some use for you. I'll ask her to take you on."

"Oh, thank you, sir!"

"But wait! She isn't expected until after Christmas. What will you do until then?"

"Anything," she said eagerly. "Anything...Couldn't I work for you here at the Hall, Sir Geoffrey?"

He shifted in his chair. "Well...I've never encountered such a female for knowing what she wants. No doubt you'd like to run the estate while you're about it...eh?" His tone was good-humoured, but he waved her suggestion aside. "No, no...it wouldn't do. Too many servants at the Hall already, eating their heads off in idleness."

Sara saw she had made a mistake. She remembered that she was the same age as Alison, and it might have occurred to Sir Geoffrey that their common friendship with Richard Barwell could prove a link between them. He was not the sort of man to encourage a companionship between his impressionable young daughter and someone of her own dubious standing. Clearly, she was not welcome at the Hall.

"You must go to Bramfield," Sir Geoffrey suddenly announced.

"Bramfield?" she echoed sharply. "As a servant?"

"Yes, indeed." He looked at her with mild astonishment. "Is

there something wrong with Bramfield? I always understood you were employed in domestic duties there.''

''I was *not* a servant!''

''Come, come! This is no time for false pride. You must take what offers.''

She looked at his face, and saw there was no way out. Either she must do what he said, or lose his help. So she managed to smile, while she was raging in her heart against the ill-luck that was sending her back to Bramfield as a servant. But her slanting, greenish eyes were fully upon him as she made a little speech of gratitude. He was charmed, and grew benevolent.

''You'll enjoy being with Lady Linton. She's notoriously indulgent to those who please her—and I don't doubt you'll suit her well.''

He made a gesture of dismissal. ''Be off with you, now, miss. You've had enough in favours from me for one day.''

She rose, and made a low curtsy to him.

He stopped her as she was leaving. ''I'm sorry your father's death has left you this way,'' he said kindly. ''But you'll get on all right—I can tell that. You're not the sort of girl who'll miss her chances.''

Before she left the Hall she was given a meal by Sir Geoffrey's orders, and the groom drove her back to Rye in the chaise. All the way back she hugged to herself the satisfaction of what she had achieved. She remembered Lady Linton's reputation before she had left for India with her husband—an open-handed, generous creature, affectionate and impulsive. In the dress salons they had gossiped of her brilliant receptions, of the extravagance with which she ran her household. Sara knew that in getting a place with Lady Linton she had dropped into what could only be ease and comfort. And much more might be made of it if she used her wits.

She chose to ignore, for the moment, the thought of the months that must yet be lived through at Bramfield. And as yet she could think of no way of seeing Richard Barwell once she left the Marsh. But she would see him again—she was quite determined about that.

Within a week Sebastian's possessions were sold, Sara had packed her few belongings, and was in service at Bramfield. It was now the early days of the autumn, and at the same time Richard's commission in the Army came through. Self-conscious in his new uniform he bid her a formal goodbye in the hall of the rectory. Recalling that awkward, uncomfortable parting, she thought miserably that all that seemed to remain of their idyll of a summer evening on the shore was Sebastian's ring on Richard's left hand.

Sir Geoffrey had forced her back upon Bramfield, but the interest he had displayed in her did nothing to improve her status there. She no longer had access to the schoolroom, and the books in the library were forbidden her. The servants themselves made capital of her position in the household, passing on the most menial of tasks, knowing well that she had no possible redress. She slept in an unheated attic with the cook and the one other maid kept at the rectory; she was bitterly resentful of the lack of privacy, hating their rough, country accents, and the coarseness of their conversation. Because they were uncertain what they should make of her sudden relegation from the schoolroom to the kitchen, they became tyrants, taking their cue from Mrs. Barwell's own hostility. Sara was unhappy, and bound to Bramfield as securely as if she had been imprisoned there. Only the promise of Richard's return at Christmas made the empty weeks bearable.

But when he did come he was changed. He was stiff with her, and off-handed; she saw early that he did not know how best to face the problem of her altered status—so he avoided it by avoiding her. And, strangely enough, she was able to understand this, and forgive it, too—for she found that she was herself unable to meet the situation. Richard dodged her in the house, and she astonished herself by doing the same thing with him.

She received the greatest blow to her sense of security in his friendship on Christmas Day—a day spent in the quiet and temperate fashion of a clergyman's home, a sober day, making her long for the gaiety of Christmas dinners eaten with Sebastian. In the early evening Nell, the other maid kept by the Barwells, drowsy after the large meal, roused herself reluctantly from her chair before the kitchen fire to answer the ringing of the drawing-room bell. She returned some minutes later, still grumbling and stifling her yawns.

"The parson's mightily in favour when Sir Geoffrey and Miss Alison take to calling on Christmas Day," she said, shrugging her heavy shoulders. "Tis a time for folk to be staying put at home—unless there be special reason to take them out."

The cook stirred herself to poke the fire. "There'll be a

marriage there soon, I'll be bound. Miss Alison has quite a fancy for Master Richard. And vicar'll not stand in the way—not with Sir Geoffrey's money in sight.''

Nell sniffed as she settled back into her chair once more. ''I'm thinking the lass who takes Master Richard will need all the money she can put her hands on—for she'll get nought with him but his handsome face. For all his taking ways and pretty manners, he's not the young man to push ahead for himself.''

Sara leaned far back in her seat, trusting that the dim light of the candles and the fire would not betray the flush on her cheeks. She sat very still, listening to the wind outside, and to the cook's breathing; she repeated to herself over and over again, what had been said about Richard and Alison. Her thoughts were painful to her, like the sudden opening of something secret and hidden.

She needed time and solitude to adjust herself to this new idea that Richard might indeed marry Alison. She could not squarely face it in this atmosphere of servants' gossip, in the unfriendly air of a room in which she was never welcome, Yet even with the desire to be away from them so strong, she schooled herself to sit there quietly, enduring their occasional remarks, waiting until the cook's heavy breathing had become a snore, before she rose silently and went to the door.

Outside in the passage the intense cold struck at her, and she heard a querulous voice in the kitchen raised in complaint about the draught. She closed the door, and made her way to the back stairs, mounting to the first floor, and pausing there. Above was the attic where she slept, and where she would be found if either woman in the kitchen came up. But close to this landing was the schoolroom, forbidden to her, but a secure enough retreat while the family was gathered with Sir Geoffrey and Alison in the drawing-room. Her hesitation was short, because her need for solitude had suddenly become desperate. The door was unlocked when she tried it.

Inside it was dark; the windows were squares of black slightly less dense than the blackness surrounding them. She fumbled and groped, her hands encountering objects long familiar to them, until she found the candle upon the mantel shelf. She lit it, and the single flame thrust its flickering light into the corners, revealing the bare, shabby room, no different now from the time when Sebastian had ruled in it. Her eyes rested on the clean-wiped slates, the shelves of tattered books, the huge Latin dictionary upon its stand. The uncurtained windows framed the bleak openness of the marsh, now wrapped in darkness. She moved to the desk that had been Sebastian's, and sat down, breathing in the remembered smell of ink and chalk. It was very cold. She rubbed her hands together, thinking that there had been little wisdom in her decision to come here at all. There was nothing here but memories of Sebastian, Richard, and William—William, who now, with a new tutor, held sway in this room. Draughts played tricks with the candle, and the shadows jumped in obedience. It was not difficult to fancy that she once more occupied a place on that long bench, and that presently Sebastian, Richard, and William would come to join her. The feeling was so strong that the gossip she had heard in the kitchen faded from reality—it was impossible, sitting there, to believe that Sebastian was dead, that Richard was in the Army, and already there was talk of his marriage.

Carried away by her thoughts, she heard no sound until the door opened. She turned swiftly, guiltily, to encounter Richard himself in the doorway.

"I saw the light," he said, "and I wondered..."

She half-rose, and then dropped back. The feeling of Sebastian's desk beneath her hand was security. Her spirits lifted a little, remembering her father's refusal to be subservient, and she said, with a touch of defiance, "I'm not supposed to be here, I know—but I came."

For answer, Richard stepped farther into the room and closed the door behind him.

"Do you have to talk in that fashion to me, Sara?" he asked quietly. "Have things altered so much—are we not still friends?"

She thrust her head up. "More things have altered, Richard, than the new coat you wear."

He took a few steps towards her, halted, then came the rest of the way, until he stood over her. She waited, watchful. He bent and took her chin between his fingers.

"You've grown up in these months, little Sara. You've altered also."

The touch of his fingers unnerved her. "Oh, Richard," she cried, "why do things have to change? If only we could be back here..." Her gesture indicated the empty desks, the ink-stained floor.

"Are you miserable?" he asked her, gently. "Are you unhappy?"

She could find no words to reply to him.

"I'm sorry if being at Bramfield has made you unhappy." His

34

fingers left her chin, and reached up to her hair, stroking it back from her forehead in just the way Sebastian might have done. "I hate to think of you being unhappy."

"Does it matter to you, then?" she said, too sharply.

The motion of his hand ceased. "Of course it matters!"

He straightened, dropping his hand to his side. "It won't last much longer, Sara. Not more than a few months now. Lady Linton should arrive any time—you'll be in London within three months."

She didn't look at him. "I imagine it's possible to be just as lonely in London as here on Rommey. Isn't it, Richard?"

"Lonely? Sara!" He gave a rather excited laugh. "What a silly little fool you are! Lady Linton keeps a fashionable house in London—there'll never be a dull moment! You'll forget what it was like on Romney, never seeing a new face from month's end to month's end."

His voice was so low now that it was scarcely more than a murmur. "And, Sara . . . I'll be there too!"

She raised her head, the movement so quick that the candle flame quivered thinly. "You'll be there? How . . . ?"

He smiled. "Not in London exactly. But near enough to spend some time there." His smile widened—a sudden return to the spirit of companionship they had known in this room. The smile was accompanied by a twinkle in his eyes, a sense of fun that lurked about the corners of his mouth. She looked at his handsome, smooth face, the thickness of his curling black hair, and the stiff collar holding his head in that position of faint arrogance which somehow seemed natural to him since these first months in the Army. She saw all these things and wondered if his pleasing face and elegant manners didn't bring him all he wanted too easily. He was the son of a country parson, without money or influence, but already he had won a small showing of favour with his commanding officers, and Sir Geoffrey Watson was a powerful ally for any young man to claim. The quick smile and laugh of the favourite came readily to his lips. She guessed that Richard, lacking so many other essentials, would perforce have to climb solely on his good looks and charm.

She moved her arm, as if to stretch it out to him, but then withdrew it. The candle fluttered, casting further shadows across his face. In that brief second she had a vision of him turning into an amiable, smiling lackey of those of wealth or influence.

"Why do you stare at me like that, Sara?" he asked. "Doesn't it please you to know that I shall see you in London?"

"In London...? Oh, yes, Richard!"

"Well, then, why such a long face?" He laughed, returning to his good humour. "Think of it, Sara! I mean to visit the playhouses. I'll see all the sights I've dreamed about while I've sat in this room multiplying columns of figures." He suddenly demanded of her, "What do you want to do most in London? Tell me!"

She smiled at his excitement. "London is not as new to me as you seem to imagine, Richard. Don't you remember that I was born there?"

He looked at her, and said more slowly, "Yes... Yes, I do keep forgetting that."

He put his hands behind his back, taking a half-step away from her. "I keep forgetting," he said, "that you have ever had any other life before you came here. That's selfish, I know—keeping you locked up here where you haven't always belonged." He shook his head then, slightly. "You're not like me, are you? I was born here, and I've never been away from it until this year. You've seen a much bigger world than mine, Sara, yet, to me, you belong here and to nowhere else. Away from here, when I thought about Romney, I thought about you. When I remembered the way the light was reflected back off the dykes, I couldn't help thinking of your hair. It was you all the time. I suppose I was homesick for Romney... I was homesick, and the feeling was all mixed up with you."

Abruptly his tone changed. "Do I sound stupid?"

She shook her head.

"I thought a great deal about our evenings on the shore with your father. You remember them, Sara?" He didn't wait for an answer. "Of course, you remember them. Neither of us shall ever forget, I suppose they're as perfect a thing as we'll ever have to remember."

And then he bent down and kissed her softly on the lips. "That's for all the beauty you've given me to remember."

As he started to straighten she caught his hand. "Are you sure you want to remember it, Richard?"

"Always," he murmured, and he kissed her again.

She stood up and gave him her lips fully. It was the first time she had ever been kissed in this way, and her immediate response startled her. She could feel his arms around her tightly, and her own fingers were locked behind his neck. They clung to each other, bodies pressed together, suddenly firing with passion the memories of their years of friendship. Sara knew she was casting away her childhood in that kiss, was altering for ever the relationship between herself and Richard. Yet she went on kissing him, quite aware now that this was what she had wanted him to do, what her vague longings for his return had centred upon. Plainly her reason told her that this wild feeling was her love and desire for Richard—the emotion to which, until this moment, she had never given real acknowledgment. Now every particle of her body was deeply satisfied by his kisses.

Their grip on each other slackened at last. Richard drew his lips away from hers to press them against her eyelids, her forehead. Then he put his face in her hair.

"My dear!" he said. "My sweet Sara!"

She could feel his breath against her face; he was leaning heavily on her, clinging to her. Something in his stance vaguely frightened her. It hardly seemed that he clung to her with love or possessiveness, but as if he sought help and support.

"Sara!" he said again, and now it was like a cry of entreaty.

Hearing it, she suddenly seemed to hear in her ears a rush of wind, a cold wind blowing about her like the whisperings of prudence. A touch of reality reached her at last, after the warmth of their passion.

She broke free of him, stepping back and pressing both her hands against her ears to shut out this frightening sound.

"No, Richard!" she said hoarsely. "You'll leave me and marry Alison."

His face went white. There was an expression of fear upon it—the expression of a child suddenly insecure.

"Marry Alison!" he repeated. "Marry *Alison!*" He pushed his hand distractedly through his hair. "My God, you must be mad, Sara! What makes you think that I could marry Alison?"

"They said . . ." she whispered. "I thought it was settled."

He caught her arm sharply. "*Who* said? What are you talking about?"

"Cook said it—and Nell. They said it was almost settled."

He regarded her sternly. "How you've altered when you listen now to servants' gossip! And you've accepted this as truth without having asked me about it?"

"What else could I think?" she said miserably. "How could I

37

ask you? I've never seen you alone until now. You don't make it easy to talk.''

He flushed, turning his eyes away from her. "I know. And I'm damned sorry about it. But don't think I haven't *wanted* to talk with you.''

And again he drew her to him. It was a gentle, confident movement—and when he began again to stroke her hair, more than ever it felt like Sebastian. The tenderness of his unconscious action caused the tears to prick at the back of her eyes. She wanted to lay her head against his shoulder and to sob out the misery of the last months.

"Dear Sara,'' he said, "I don't think of anyone else but you. How could I? Forget about Alison! That's all imaginative nonsense—servants' gossip! I swear to you, that I've made no suggestion of marriage to her.''

He tilted her face towards him.

"I'll marry no one but you.''

She gasped, stiffening in his arms.

"You can't marry *me*—a servant!'

He answered her with a vigorous shake. "A servant! You're the daughter of the man who was my greatest friend. Doesn't that mean anything to you? Don't you want to marry me?''

"Marry you?—of course I do. But *wanting* you, and *having* you are two different things.'' Her fingers gripped his uniform sleeves tightly.

"I mean to have you, Sara. When I get promotion I'll be able to marry you. If there's war with France I should get it quickly. Will you promise to wait?''

"Wait . . . ?'' Suddenly the knitted points of her eyebrows straightened; she smiled up at him. "Yes—I'll wait.''

Then she added quickly, "And we'll manage, Richard, somehow.''

She buried her face in his tunic, and a sense of triumph and joy swept through her. The future was before both of them, uncertain, clouded. It was there to make what they could of it—but they would do it together.

He was stroking her hair again, and murmuring close to her ear. *"You'll* think of a way, won't you, Sara? You've always been cleverer at those sort of things than I.''

She listened to him with a sense of shock. His tone seemed to appeal to her to be strong for both of them, to find a way out. She knew then that she would have to fight for her possession of Richard, or he would be taken away from her—not willingly, but inevitably. He could be taken away because he was too weak to fight the obstacles facing the marriage. But she accepted this— after all, she was stronger than Richard, tougher than he. In a sense, he was like Sebastian all over again—needing her love and strength.

"Yes. I'll find a way for us both, Richard," she said firmly. "We'll manage it."

He bent and kissed her again, his lips seeking hers with a young eagerness. They were both new to this experience. It was exciting, like the sour, sharp bite of a green apple. Neither had known anything like this before. They were flushed and shaken when at last they drew apart.

Then, for a few moments, they did not meet each other's eyes, feeling some sort of shame that their passion had broken loose, briefly, from the bonds they had learned to impose upon it. Sara, slightly irritated that something so deeply satisfying had of necessity to be regretted, raised her eyes, to find Richard's upon her. There was no apology or repentance in them. Her lips parted, and seeing her begin to smile, he laughed aloud.

Carried on the elation of the moment, he impulsively drew off the ring he wore on his left hand, the one Sebastian had given him at the end of the summer. He caught her hand, pressing the ring into it.

"Keep it, Sara," he said. "Keep it until we meet in London— I'll claim it back when we meet again."

She turned it over on her palm. "Your ring, Richard . . ."

His gaze upon her was tender and possessive. "Promise me you'll keep it until I come to claim it?"

She nodded slowly.

He smiled and kissed her, a light kiss that was there and gone before she was fully aware of it. Richard himself was gone almost as swiftly.

The draught of the closing door set the candle fluttering again, and the shadows leaping over the stained floor and the desks. Sara stood still, the ring clasped in one hand, the fingers of the other pressed against her lips where Richard had kissed them. Then she snuffed out the candle; its acrid smell mingled with that of the chalk and the old books. She made her way in the darkness to the door, groping then to the stairs leading to the attic.

She did not talk alone with Richard again before he left Bramfield. They had only momentary encounters upon the stairs and in hallways, and the secret smile that passed between them had to serve as their only communication. There was gossip, too, in the kitchen, about the amount of time he spent away from the rectory. No matter what time he returned, either the cook or Nell seemed to hear the rumble of the wheels of Sir Geoffrey's carriage when it dropped him off at the gates. But in her possession of the ring, hidden carefully in her mattress in the attic, Sara was sure of Richard. His visits to Alison's home hardly troubled her. Aware of the sluggish flow of life about her in the austere rectory, she understood how a nature like his would crave the ease and comfort of the baronet's house on the edge of the Marsh. Day after day, as the curve of the dyke road swallowed up Richard's diminishing figure, she forgave him for the characteristics she loved and feared; she let him carry all his indolence and weakness with him when he went to visit Sir Geoffrey, and she wondered again and again if the gentle Alison was completely blinded by his charm.

Spring came at last to Romney—softer winds from the sea, and a sudden showering of pale, tender greens through the grass, the reeds, and the water-plants; the new colours showed through the blackthorn hedges and the willows. Sara waited daily for her summons to London, and whenever Sir Geoffrey made a call at the rectory she hung about the hall until his departure. She began to fear he would never speak, that the plan would never come to anything, when he halted her one day as she hurried to open the front door for him. He strolled in a leisurely way from the drawing-room with Mr. Barwell, where they had been shut up for most of the afternoon.

"Well, miss!" he said, taking a firm stand upon the elegant silver-topped cane he carried, "you'll soon be off to London."

Her eyes widened eagerly. "There has been news, Sir Geoffrey?"

"Yes. Lady Linton landed at Portsmouth six days ago. She will be at her estate in Devon for three weeks, and then she plans to open the London house. She will send me word when she requires you."

Sara dropped a curtsy. "Thank you, Sir Geoffrey."

He made a move on, then paused, examining her with shrewd,

kindly eyes, almost lost in their thick pouches of flesh. "You'll be glad to go to London?"

Sara shot a glance at the ominously still figure of the rector. "Thank you, Sir Geoffrey . . . but I've not been unhappy here. The Rector and Mrs. Barwell have been most kind."

"I know. I know,' he answered. "But you'll have more excitement in Lady Linton's house, I'll be bound." He chuckled, his whole body shaking. "I'm told, Rector, that it's excitement all young girls look for. Well, there's plenty of it wherever Lady Linton is!"

He paused, looking hard at Sara. "Those clothes won't do. Lady Linton's a great dresser herself—and she likes those around her to give a mind to their appearance. Here . . ." he searched in his purse and produced three guinea pieces, " . . . take this now and buy yourself something to wear. Mrs. Barwell'll tell you what you'll need."

She reddened, and stammered her thanks, which he waved aside. Mr. Barwell's eyes, she knew, were on the money; she knew, too, that she would have to hand it over to his keeping as soon as Sir Geoffrey was gone.

"My daughter is looking forward to joining Lady Linton in London shortly," Sir Geoffrey went on. "Shopping, y'know. Nothing but the London shops will do that young miss these days. So you'll be seeing something of her."

Sara replied dutifully. "It will be a great pleasure, sir, to see a face I know among so many strange ones."

He chuckled again. "You'll not lack familiar faces, my girl. I don't doubt young Master Richard will be a frequent guest at Lady Linton's house."

Sara struggled hopelessly with the colour mounting in her cheeks at the mention of Richard being in London. But it didn't attract attention for the rector had laid a restraining hand upon Sir Geoffrey's arm. The two now faced each other.

"Surely, Sir Geoffrey, this . . . er . . . information is premature? There is nothing settled yet."

"Nonsense, Rector! Nonsense! It's all as good as settled! —will be, anyway, when Richard comes home next time. I'll talk to him myself. There can be no doubt about it. Richard is not unwilling—nor is Alison."

"That's true, Sir Geoffrey—and nothing could give me more pleasure than a union between Richard and your sweet daughter . . . But, surely . . . Gossip . . ."

41

Startled, Sara listened to them. The world seemed to wheel about her as she tried to sort out the meaning of their words. This was not what Richard had told her—this was not the truth! And yet the vicar's pale face had never seemed more serious, and Sir Geoffrey was not merely hinting at the matter. Her whole body was taut as she waited for what he would say next.

The baronet faced her again. "I'll warrant this miss is no gossip. Knows how to hold her tongue, I can tell. In any case, the news will be out soon enough. It is my wish that they should marry in the summer. However, we'll see . . . we'll see."

Without a further glance at Sara's low curtsy, he turned and went down the steps to where the rector's groom held his horse.

Sara stood and listened to their conversation.

"Looks as if we'll have rain, Rector," Sir Geoffrey said, "and I've two calls to make yet. That coachman of mine is a plaguey nuisance—been abed with a fever these last three days, and I'm without anyone to drive me. I'm getting too old now to sit in the saddle for long."

Then his speech trailed off into a series of harsh grunts while he attempted, with the aid of the rector and the groom, to mount. Sara saw that they were fully occupied, and she sped in the direction of the back stairs and the temporary refuge of the attic.

Once there she flung herself upon the mattress, letting her misery and wretchedness have charge of her body and her thoughts. She shocked herself by the fit of weeping which shook her, taking away all her strength and resistance. She was enraged as well as disappointed.

"Richard!" she whispered. "Oh, Richard, what have you done?"

She lay there while the spring afternoon faded quickly, and the light fled away down the Marsh. Richard was lost to her, she knew—he was taken beyond her reach for ever, and there was nothing she could do about it. It seemed unlikely that he was fully aware of what was being planned for him, but she felt with certainty that he would not be able to withstand the pressure Sir Geoffrey and his parents would bring on him. They would know how to play upon him, understanding that his was not the sort of strength to hold out against the blandishments of wealth and influence. He was poor and unknown, and he would be offered background and powerful family connections. His nature was not built to refuse such potent attractions. And Alison herself, with her sweet, lovely face and gentle manners, would make a wife any man might well desire. It was inevitable, she told herself. Richard's struggle with his conscience would be true enough, but it would be short. He would remind himself of the long wait, and the battle against family prejudices, before he could marry Sara, and he would say that their love could not last through such a time. He would accept what came easily to hand, not caring to fight for what, in the end, might turn out to be an empty prize. She had recognised these weaknesses in his nature long ago, and excused them. Now she called herself a fool for the excuses she had made. The images twisting and shaping themselves in her mind slowly grew more detached. She saw the future with a sharp clarity, saw Richard's visits to the London house—visits that were to Alison, not to herself. She saw the preparations for the marriage in which she would have a servant's part, the trappings of the fashionable wedding she would be expected to share. Her unhappy mind painted the scenes much too vividly. Fearfully she tried to turn away from them, feeling, even now, the agony of being forced to play her subordinate role.

As she turned restlessly on the mattress, Nell's voice on the stairs roused her.

"Sara? Sara, are you there? The mistress is looking for you this hour past!"

Sara sat up quickly, and called out, "Coming!"

Nell's rough tones were a sudden spark to her sense of injury. It was Sebastian's unsubdued pride that now flared into resentment against this indignity, and against all the others she would suffer before the summer was out, and Richard and Alison were finally married. And in that instant the thought of flight occurred to her for the first time. It chilled her for a moment; then the simplicity of the plan made her bold. Why not? she asked herself. There could be an escape from her hated position, which was also an escape from watching her lover succumb to Alison, and all the attractions Sir Geoffrey offered. There was no wind of prudence in Sara to cool her impulse, and the idea, once it occurred, was irresistible.

In a fever of indignation and hurt pride she flung herself off the mattress and groped in the stuffing until her fingers encountered Sebastian's ring. She had not held it in her hand since Richard had given it to her on Christmas Day. At the sight of it, her anger rose on a new wave, heating her face, bringing tears to her eyes. Then, with an effort, she put it out of sight, stuffing it in the folds of her handkerchief, along with the gold coins belonging to Sir Geoffrey.

Before she left the attic she changed into her heavy shoes, and threw a cloak about her shoulders. She encountered no one on the stairs; it shocked her sense of the importance of the occasion to find how easy it was to leave the rectory unnoticed. She passed the kitchen door like a quick shadow. The heavy smell of cooking food reached her, following her down the passage until the fresh air, at last, gently touched her face. She closed the door behind her, hurrying towards the low wall which separated the rectory garden and churchyard, The daylight had suddenly gone, but scents of the day were still there, drifting, unanchored. Sara was aware of this, and of a fear only half conquered, as she sped past the ghostly tombstones, and the dark, squat church, making for the dyke road, deserted and lonely in the sharp spring evening.

To keep clear of Rye, where she might easily be recognised, was her greatest concern now. She turned in the direction of Appledore. But the thought of reaching Appledore itself brought no heartening feeling of familiarity, for the walks she had taken with Sebastian and Richard had never brought them so far. Behind her, the lights of the rectory cut into the gathering dark, but only faintly. And, having looked at them once, she did not look back again. She felt no regret; her hard bitterness was softening into relief that her flight had not been intercepted, and that by morning she would be far away. She marched grimly onwards, at first unaware of the bite of the wind, and then feeling it keenly, but never once afraid of the emptiness about her—not afraid as she had been in the churchyard—the open road seemed to be her own territory, and she had a sense of rightfully belonging to the Marsh. It was the place she and Richard and Sebastian had called their own.

She had walked what she judged to be about three miles before the first rain swept her face. It came on quickly, making her gasp and twist her head away from it. And with the rain her resolution palled a little. She became more soberly aware that the lights of Bramfield lay far behind, and unknown country beyond. At the same time, the whispered tales of the Marsh stirred in her mind, the hushed stories of the wool-running to France, the inns and even the churches which secreted their share of the contraband lace, silk, and brandy. There were rumours of murder committed to safeguard the fortunes won by smuggling, and the thought struck at her now. As the rain suddenly worsened, she began to realise her utter defencelessness, and that she faced a night on the Marsh without shelter. Too late to regret that she had not bided her time at Bramfield until the morning came— and yet, in the midst of the fear that had begun to possess her, her head rebelled at the very thought of remaining at Bramfield. She began to run, trying to ignore the continual urge to glance behind; trying to forget the fact that she had not eaten since the midday meal.

She went on a further two miles. Her steps were slow again because the rising wind had tired her, and because each step and each minute brought her closer to the inn, The Angel, which marked a crossroad about a mile ahead. The reputation of The Angel, the collection of gossip and rumour which combined to give it its unsavoury character, brought fear to her head. She dreaded the approach to it, yet longed to be past and away. It represented a goal of distance to her also; once beyond, she would let herself look for some barn or outhouse to shelter until morning.

The wind dropped briefly, and in the lull the sound came to her of horse's hoofs and wheels on the road behind. She stood still, terrified. They were close, but the wind had prevented her from hearing them. She had a moment's frightened wonder, thinking that the rector, on finding her gone, had sent one of his nearer neighbours in search of her. She dismissed the idea as a more terrible one occurred. A horse and cart on the Marsh at night? She panicked at the thought, for no one cared to question the passage of a horse and cart abroad on the Marsh once nightfall came, or if seen, the incident was conveniently forgotten by morning. It was this thought which started her casting wildly about for cover. The road was treeless and bare; the night itself the only shelter. The dyke bounded the road on one side, and it was already too late to attempt to cross to the other. The swinging arc of the cart's lamp came nearer; she turned toward the edge of the dyke, flinging herself full length on the sloping bank. She dug her fingers and nails into the new spring grass, praying that the cold rain might have numbed the unseen driver's watchfulness. With her face pressed close to the earth, she fancied she felt it throb beneath her in response to the steady clopping. There were moments of agonised terror for her while the horse drew level and she sensed her prostrate body was exposed to the wavering light. She waited for a cry from the driver—but it did not come. The cart itself was level now—and then past. And the darkness covered her again. She lay still, relief breaking coldly over her; a sigh of thankfulness escaped her as the distance increased between herself and the cart.

At last she raised her head cautiously to peer at the diminishing light.

As she did, she looked directly into a second lamp, swinging only a few feet away from her eyes. She stared in horror at the hand that held it, and then her eyes lifted to take in the dim figure of a man.

She uttered one strangled sound of astonishment, and shrank back.

He advanced almost gently, then, with a quick gesture, clamped his hand on her arm, pulling her to her knees. The lamp was thrust close to her face.

"Don't touch me! Don't!" she cried, frightened, trying to twist away.

But the man's grip held her tightly.

"Well! What have we here!" he said softly. "What have we here!"

Suddenly he bellowed over his shoulder. "Daniel! Wait!"

Sara struggled to find a foothold on the sloping bank, but he jerked her forward beside him on the road. He planted the lamp on the ground, and with one effortless heave, grasped her around the waist and tossed her over his shoulder.

"Put me down! Do you hear—put me down!"

She screamed, but she knew there could be no response along the empty road. She tried pounding her closed fists fiercely into the man's back. If he felt it at all, he took no notice; he picked up the lamp again and started in a half-run to catch up with the cart.

The bouncing gait gave Sara no more breath to cry out; her terror, in any case, would have prevented it. It was useless to struggle against the giant arm holding her. The man had enormous strength. She was dizzy and shaken when he put her on her feet beside the driver of the cart.

"Daniel," he said, still in that surprisingly soft voice, "d'y see what I've found? 'Tis worth-while to tail behind with a lamp. Never can tell what you'll be lucky enough to pick up!"

Sara gave an indignant gasp as the driver leapt quickly down from his seat and caught her by the shoulder.

"Don't you touch me!"

46

She made a swing at his stomach with her fist, but he took a step out of reach and exploded into a hoarse burst of laughter. He thrust the lantern he carried level with her face.

"A lass! A right little beauty too! Seems you've picked up a rare'un tonight, Harry!" His voice dropped lower. "But what's t' do with her now we've found her?"

"I reckon," the other drawled, "that folk who hide about the dykes after dark learn more than's good for them. We'll find out more about this one later. Better be moving on."

And, without another word, he swung the petrified Sara, with the same ease as before, into the back of the waiting cart. She braced herself for the fall against the bare boards, but it was on something soft, something rolled into canvas, that she fell.

"Carry on, Daniel!"

As the order was given she sat up, and made a despairing attempt to scramble over the side of the cart.

"You can't treat me like . . . ."

She received a push that sent her on her back again. This time she hit her head against the wooden side, and the blow half-stunned her.

"If you don't be quiet I'll put a sack over your head—understand?"

The young man dropped back into his former place behind the cart, and Sara, straining her eyes against the dark, could make out nothing but the swinging light. She lay quietly on the canvas, exhausted and afraid, with no spirit left to fight. She pulled her cloak about her, turning her face away from the stinging rain. There was nothing now but submission to whatever was to follow. Her own strength was feather-weak compared to this young giant's who strode along behind. Tears of rage and fear came in a rush to her eyes; she fought them down, and lay there, cold, but unmoving, while the cart swung along on its way. At last she felt the wheels grate on rougher ground, and then they rumbled over cobblestones, and were finally still. She sat up and gazed about her.

They had entered a courtyard; stone walls formed three sides of a square which faced out into the blank darkness of the Marsh. Sara could barely discern the outline of some sort of building. The windows were shuttered; there were no lights anywhere. Harry strode past the cart, lantern held high above his head, and hammered upon the door.

"Look lively, there!" he shouted.

After a while the door opened revealing a stout woman who shielded a candle with her hand. Sara's questioning eyes moved from her to an inn sign, swinging dejectedly in the wind. She read the faded lettering before the lantern was lowered—The Angel!

The young man took a step back towards her.

"Here, Mother," he said, "I've brought you a parcel of tricks! Come and see what you think of it.

He swung Sara to the ground, giving her a light push forward. The woman eyed her suspiciously as she stumbled on the doorstep, catching hold of her arm, roughly halting her.

Sara was stung into a fury of irritation by their handling of her. She slapped the woman's hands away wildly.

"Leave me alone—both of you! I'll have the law on you for this."

The woman took no notice of her whatever.

"What's this, son?" she said. "What have you brought . . . ?" Her voice was as coarse and loud as Nell's, at Bramfield. It contrasted oddly with the voice of the man she called her son.

He laughed now. "Just what I said—a parcel I picked up along the way. Found it by a dyke." The idea seemed to appeal to him; he spoke very softly. "It seemed to me a lass oughtn't to be abroad at this time of night—so I took her along with me."

The woman stepped back from them, alarm on her fleshy face. "You brought her here—to The Angel!"

The man's voice now held a hint of impatience. "And why not? I fancied company for supper."

"You're mad!" the woman snapped. "You're drunk!"

He stepped into the inn, squeezing his large bulk past Sara and slamming his lantern down on the table.

Then he turned angrily to the woman.

"You keep your opinions to yourself, until they're asked!" He made a menacing gesture, and she shrank back against the wall, watching him warily as he let forth a stream of curses at her. She ducked before a blow he aimed halfheartedly at her head.

"Now move yourself, you lazy trollop!" he said. "Bring some supper—two suppers! Feed up this wench—she looks like a half-starved kitten."

As she edged cautiously past, he called to her, "And remember, I'm the one who says who shall come to The Angel—and who stays out!"

She vanished by a door leading into a long passage.

The young man turned to Daniel, standing alongside Sara. His tones were normal again. "See to the cart, Daniel. And if you don't rub down that horse as I showed you, I promise you you'll not have an inch of flesh on your back in the morning!"

Then he said pleasantly, "Good-night, now. See that you get your supper when you've finished."

Daniel went out and closed the door behind him.

Sara had learned by now that it was useless to try to escape, useless to pour out protests into unhearing ears, so she stood quietly while Harry attended to the fire in the stone hearth. He threw on logs from a pile beside it; then he took a candelabrum, lighting its half-dozen candles from the brightening flames. He lit several other candles in separate holders, placing them carefully about. She watched him closely. His movements were light. He was very tall, with huge shoulders bulging, threatening to burst the weathered coat he wore; his fair hair, curling above a young face, was glistening with rain. Now and again he put his hand up and rubbed the moisture which trickled on to his forehead. She was puzzled by this giant of a man, who, although so young, appeared to be the master of The Angel.

He finished his few tasks in a leisurely fashion and kicked at one of the logs on the fire with his foot. Then he swung round, and came towards Sara.

"Now we'll see what sort of maid it is who hides by a dyke on a wild night!"

He caught her, pulled her into the light of the candles and the fire, and at the same time pushed back the hood that covered her head. She felt his fingers fumbling with the clasp of her cloak; he drew it from her shoulders, letting it fall in a heap at her feet. For a moment he had nothing to say; he gazed at her silently, and she could read nothing in his face. Then suddenly he caught her shoulders, holding her at arm's length, his eyes raking slowly over her. She twisted, trying to break away, but he held her as easily as if she were a child.

Dismayed by the uselessness of her attempt, she looked wretchedly up at him, and she saw a smile beginning to break on his young-old face. He started to laugh. Sara wondered how many times she had heard that same laugh since he first pulled her from the dyke bank. The laugh and the smile came too readily after an outburst; they seemed totally unrelated to whatever he might be feeling at the moment. She began to wonder fearfully if he were in possession of all his senses.

He released her after a while, giving her a light push so that she sank down on the settle by the fire. He remained standing, saying nothing, but just gazing at her. Presently the woman he had called his mother appeared again, carrying a tray with dishes and tall jugs. These she set down on a table in front of the fire, arranged two places, and then left the room without saying a word. The man took a seat, motioning Sara to one opposite.

She hesitated, until he shouted, "Damn you! Do you want to be spoon-fed where you are? Sit down, I say!"

She obeyed him meekly enough now, her eyes fixed upon the food spread on the table. He pushed a steaming plate, bread, and a jug of ale in front of her. She took what he offered, half-afraid that this might be another of his queer ideas of jesting, and that it might be withdrawn. The food was good, and there was plenty of it; there was more on her plate than she had eaten in a single meal since Sebastian had died. She ate and drank all she wanted, her thoughts turning now and again to the poor fare served to her in the Bramfield kitchen.

Her companion's appetite was enormous, but, even busying himself eating, he kept his gaze on her.

"Eat up, girl!" he commanded, suddenly pointing the leg of chicken he was eating at her plate.

His expression softened slightly. He went on looking at her, then he said, rather gently, "You look as if you haven't eaten for days. Finish that up, and if you want more I'll give a shout for it."

Sara needed no further urging. She went on eating, turning her body sideways to the warmth from the fire. It was almost possible, if she kept her eyes away from her strange host, to forget that she was here, in one of the places most dreaded by the honest farmers of the Marsh; she was here supping royally with the man who was landlord of the establishment. But whenever her glance stole back to him, her fears returned. She recalled the whispered tales of The Angel, and, considering the place called itself an inn, was unhappily aware of the deserted room that should have been full of company, of the windows that showed no friendly light to travellers. She remembered also the careful progress of the cart along the road, and Harry's vigil behind it. Looking at his huge body and unlined face, over which the firelight moved in a kindly fashion, she shuddered to recall the alacrity with which the woman and Daniel had hastened to obey his orders.

He terminated his own meal abruptly by pushing away the dishes. He leaned back in his chair, apparently fully satisfied; he tilted the chair, lifting the two front legs off the ground, rocking himself while he considered her.

At last he spoke. "What's your name?"

She raised her brows. "And what business is it of yours?"

He wasn't at all put out by her tone. "Oh, come! I must have a name to call you by."

"It's Mary," she said slowly.

"Mary? Mary what?"

"Mary . . . Bates."

"Well, Mary Bates, we'll banter no longer. Why were you hiding by the dyke?"

She flushed at the mockery in his voice. "I didn't know who might be coming along. The Marsh is not . . . safe . . . at night."

"Ah, I see you are a prudent maid, Mary Bates! Well, that's a good thing." He nodded his head in exaggerated gravity. "But what, might I ask, is a prudent maid doing out on the Marsh after dark? Wise folk are home in their beds."

She hesitated a moment, then plunged ahead into the ill-prepared story she had devised during the meal.

"I was on my way to Appledore. I have an aunt who is ill there—she sent word for me to come."

"On your way to Appledore, Mary?" His voice was low, but his eyebrows had lifted noticeably. "So late in the evening?"

"I've come from Rye—and I took the wrong road. I've never been so far in this direction before."

"From Rye, eh? And where do you live in Rye?"

"I'm in service to Mrs. Linton."

"Mrs. Linton? Mrs. Linton? . . . Never heard of her!"

He brought the front legs of the chair down with a crash. He sprang up, hands on the table, leaning towards her.

"It's a pack of lies! And your name is *not* Mary Bates!"

Then, as quickly as his anger had come, it left him. The humourless smile spread slowly across his face.

"But I must have a name for you," he said, "until you choose to tell me your real one. I think I'll call you Liza. Yes . . . Liza . . . I like that. Does it please you to have a pretty new name?"

She said carefully, "My name is Mary."

With incredible swiftness he edged round the table, catching her arm, and pulling her to her feet.

"Don't lie to me!" he shouted.

He shook her violently, with his great hands spread on her shoulders. She pounded impotently against his chest; it affected him no more than if it were the action of a small child. She was full of terror again, and enraged.

"You beast!" she gasped. "Leave me alone!" Her teeth clamped together, and she said thinly, "I hope you hang for this!"

He roared with laughter. She gazed at him in despairing fury, her fingers arched up gradually to claw at his face, and then they halted, frozen by his next action. He bent lower and kissed her fully on the mouth, his hands drawing her closer. His giant's strength engulfed her like a torrent, the shock of his kiss numbing her for a few moments. She felt his searching hands upon her body—but, strangely, they were not rough hands. His lips on hers were determined; although she had never been kissed by any other than Richard, she knew instinctively that this was the determination of a man used to having his own way with a woman. Into the numbness of her tired brain, straining to give even an ineffectual resistance to his demands, a spark of life returned. Abruptly she relaxed her struggle, quite passively, allowing her body to be pressed against his. She tilted her head back fully to receive his kiss, and, as he bent yet farther over her, her groping fingers encountered his hair. With a gentle motion, which he might take for a caress, she slipped her fingers beneath the fair tangle of his curls. Then she gripped and pulled, bearing down with all her strength.

There was a second of astonished silence. Then he uttered a sharp exclamation of rage, and thrust her from him. The push he gave her sent her tottering backwards, until she fell against the arm of a fireside settle. She crouched there, shaken, and supporting herself with one hand, while she watched him feeling, with surprised anger, the place where her fingers had torn at his hair.

He took a step towards her. "My God, I'll teach you . . ."

His clawing hand dragged at the sleeve of her dress as he bent to pull her to her feet. It tore away, leaving her shoulder and arm bare. His nails dug cruelly into her skin. He steadied her on her feet before him, and then deliberately raised his arm. With the back of his hand he dealt her a blow across the face.

She cried out, just once, loudly, with the sudden pain and shock.

He held her quite firmly by the shoulder so that she would not fall, and he raised his arm for a second blow. Sara struggled desperately now to break from his grasp. His fingers tightened automatically, and he stepped back from her to have room to swing his arm. In that instant, while he was unguarded, she blindly seized his belt with both hands, and, using this to steady herself, she brought her knee up with a hard jerk into his stomach. He gave a short gasp, and his fingers loosened and slid from her shoulder.

He staggered back a few paces, clutching his stomach, and bending almost double. Sara's panting breath came painfully; she knew she had done herself very little good, because her blow had merely winded him, and it could not be effective for more than a few seconds. She waited for his next movement.

But he did nothing. His breathing, as he slowly straightened, was loud in the room. Sara stood there, expecting another swipe from his huge hand. But, after a minute, she was astonished to see that the familiar smile was beginning once more to crease his face. His broad, full laugh rang out.

"My God!" he laughed. "My God . . . The wench has spirit! And t'think I've given a wild-cat shelter under my roof!"

Still laughing, he collapsed into a chair behind him, motioning her to a place on the settle.

"A wild-cat with yellow hair, eh? Well, Liza, I didn't think it of you. No, by God, I didn't!"

He breathed deeply three or four times again.

"I think I like you, Liza," he said, quietly now. "Haven't any use for timid women. Fools, all of them!" He swung his chair forward, leaning closer to her. "But you're no fool, are you, my pretty?"

Sara didn't answer. She was beginning to feel the reaction from the desperate effort she had made. She despised herself for letting him see it; it was impossible now to control the fit of shivering which seized her. She pressed back farther into the corner of the settle. Whatever he chose to do, he could now do at will; she had neither the strength nor the spirit to resist. She looked with hatred at the blue, pale eyes, with the fair curls above them; she quivered with pain where he had struck her face, and knew, without even looking at it, that his nails had drawn blood from her bare shoulder. She hated him for the pain and the indignity of their raffish brawl, but all she could do was to stare at the hands that had inflicted this injury, spread elegantly across the arms of his chair.

"You were on the way to Appledore, Liza? Well . . . I'm going that way myself in a day or two. You'll come with me—I'll drive you there. And until then, you'll bide your time here at The Angel."

She jerked forward in her seat. "I won't stay here! I won't! You can't make me!"

"Can't I? Oh," he went on, grimacing as if her words had wounded him deeply. "You'll not find me dull company—I can promise you that. After all, Liza, what more could a woman of spirit like yourself want, than a man like me? You'll not be lonely—not with Harry Turner around."

She listened to him with a cold, fearful heart.

"And," he added "I've some book-learning to suit your educated tastes—in case you fancy a little of that sort of entertainment by way of a change from Harry. Upstairs there are books . . ."

Then he let out another roar of laughter, reading the expression on her face.

"Are you thinking of *that?*" He jerked his thumb in the direction of the passage leading to the kitchen. "Yes, she's my mother, all right. But," and here he winked, "my father is another story! A gentleman he is, and not too proud, either, to come and visit his son now and then."

Suddenly his face hardened; his closed fist came crashing down on the table.

"And my God, Liza. I'm more to be proud of than the sons of his lady wife! I've more book-learning, I'll warrant, and a head for business, than those fools'll ever have. Born soft, all three of 'em. They haven't done quarter the things I've done in my time—and I'll be richer yet than the lot put together. You mark my words on that!"

He lapsed into silence, sullenly chewing his lips, staring at the toe of his boot stretched out before him. He slightly raised his leg in its well-fitting, unpolished boot; the sight of it seemed to please him, for after another minute his eyes again sought Sara's, and he no longer frowned.

He said quietly, "The master of an inn is always concerned for those who pass his door by night—and for those who hide in a ditch beside it." He tapped the heel of his boot on the floor, still speaking softly. "You've been lying to me, Liza. Every word you've said is a lie. But I'll have the truth before long. Who are you? Where have you come from?"

She said nothing.

He leaned forward to the edge of his chair; his voice was no longer patient. "Answer me! Do you hear...answer me!"

Sara's back was straight and rigid against the high settle. She knew that her story, slight and clumsily concocted, would not be believed. He would keep questioning her until he got the truth— and the truth would worsen, not better, her situation. He would then know that he might, without fear, keep her here at the inn for as long as he chose. Pursuit would not seek her in a place shunned as The Angel was. This man before her, cleverer than others of his kind, in an unbalanced crazy fashion, was more than likely the organiser of the gang of smugglers reputed to use the place as a store, and a rendezvous. In the fanatical brightness of his eyes she saw no pity—she would be a thing to be used as his mother was, as Daniel was. Her mind flinched at the thought of what she faced until the time when she could escape, or he should tire of her.

"Answer me!" he shouted. He raised his hand impatiently —his own strength seemed to be a constant temptation to him.

She said slowly, "I . . ."

Abruptly his attention left her. He looked, with an attitude of wariness, towards the door. He had caught, above the wind, the sound of horses' hoofs on the cobblestones outside. He sprang to his feet, and snuffed out all but one of the candles.

Sara watched with awe and a new fear as he stood there, massive, solidly planted on his outstretched feet, gazing expectantly at the door.

They heard the thunderous hammering of fists on the panels. A man's voice cried out, "Open up, there!"

Harry did nothing. He did not speak, but there was uncertainty in his face. He took a step forward, then hesitated. His mother came silently from the passage to the kitchen, her candle a second point of light in the dimness.

The hammering sounded again, authoritative and peremptory. "Open up, there! My horse is lamed. I need shelter!" The man outside waited a moment, and then he knocked a third time. "Open up! Open up!"

Sara looked despairingly from Harry to the door. Whoever knocked was no associate of the pair here; it was someone who, innocent of the inn's character, or in desperation, had sought shelter from the night. Her mind moved quickly. Dare she risk an appeal to him for help—or at least make him aware of her presence before they hustled her out of sight? From Harry she could expect no pity, but from the stranger outside there might be a slight chance of protection. The smarting of her face, and the memory of the large hands upon her body, told her that she would fare no worse with this other man, whoever he might be.

She sprang off the settle, avoiding Harry's arm suddenly outstretched to apprehend her, and ran to the door. The latch yielded easily, and in the cold rush of wind and rain, she stumbled out against the solid form of a man.

"Good God! What's this?"

The stranger steadied her with his hands upon her shoulders. In the darkness it was impossible to see. He led her back, fumblingly, into the room.

Harry moved forward and slammed the door with a savage kick.

The wildly flickering candle-light steadied, and Sara found herself gazing into the astonished face of Sir Geoffrey Watson.

Sara was charged with stealing Sir Geoffrey's three guineas and a gold ring belonging to Richard Barwell. She was tried at the next Quarter Sessions, convicted, and sentenced to seven years' transportation.

She knew afterwards that meekness and a repentant attitude might have saved her; if she had had the sense to go on her knees to Sir Geoffrey, if she had even told him the true reason why she had run away, he might never have brought the charges against her. But she was unable to bring herself to the point of telling him of her love for Richard, and so she had to listen to him rage on about her base ingratitude, and the notion that he had once trusted her.

During the trial she listened to Harry Turner tell how he had found her, a stranger, attempting to steal food from his kitchen. By repute, Harry was far more guilty than she, but for lack of evidence, he was still entitled to be called an innocent inn-keeper, and qualified to give evidence against her. It mattered nothing to the jury that he denied all other knowledge of her; her very presence at The Angel was enough to convict her. There was no possible appeal against Sir Geoffrey's evidence; he told the court that he had given her money to outfit herself for service with his sister, and that she had run away from Bramfield with the gold and Richard Barwell's ring tied into her handkerchief.

Against one charge Sara had no logical defence; on the other charge she preferred to remain silent. She knew she could not stand before that disapproving, interested court, and tell them that Richard had given her the ring as a pledge—she couldn't bear to hear them murmur and whisper among themselves that she, a servant and the daughter of a man whose name had been dragged through the gutters of Rye, had aspired to marry the parson's son.

Sara's defence—indignant and confused—was useless. The sentence of transportation came promptly.

It is the judgment of this court that you shall be transported beyond the seas to such place as His Majesty, with the advice of his Privy Council, shall declare and appoint . . ."

The people of Rye were loud in their opinion that she was lucky to have escaped hanging.

She had plenty of time, while she waited in the stinking, fever-ridden chaos of a prison for a transport to Botany Bay, to think back to the events of the day when she had run away from the rectory. Sometimes she wondered how she could have been mad enough to have acted on the impulse of wounded pride and disappointment; she cursed her own stupidity in looking upon Sir Geoffrey's three guineas as her own, to do as she pleased with. She rejected the idea of appealing to Richard—he had not been present at the trial and certainly he could do nothing to alter her sentence. In her bewilderment and anger she felt she never wanted to lay eyes on Richard again.

Shortly after she was sentenced, she was moved from the gaol in Rye to Newgate, to wait there until the transport was ready at Woolwich. She learned the lessons of this new world quickly and brutally; weaklings and fools did not survive long, and so she learned to have no concern for any other woman but herself. In order to exist at all she had to be as cruel and feelingless as the rest of them. She meant to survive her term of imprisonment, so she bent her energies towards doing it with the least possible trouble.

When she first went to prison she had only the money from the sale of the few belongings she had been allowed to take from Bramfield. This ran out much too quickly, and soon after she arrived at Newgate she found herself relying upon the indifferent mercy of the gaoler for her food. Her hunger made her savage, but she managed to hold off the one sure way of making money still open to her—prostitution. The gaolers permitted it, and encouraged it because it was their best source of revenue. But

Sara watched the women crazy and dying from the results of it, and she decided that she could go hungry a little longer.

After a month in Newgate she managed to attach herself to a woman called Charlotte Barker, a middle-aged forger who had received a sentence of three years' imprisonment. Charlotte lived in great style, paying the gaolers liberally for the food they brought in, and receiving visitors every day. She had brought to prison with her an extensive wardrobe and dishes for her own use. Sara performed little services for her, wrote letters, washed and mended her clothes. In return this woman kept Sara in food, and made her presents, of odd sums of money. She would never allow any of the fashionably dressed men who often called on her to have anything to do with Sara—and for her part, as long as she had food in her stomach, Sara was glad to be left alone.

Five months after her trial she received Richard's letter. It had been written from his regiment in Hampshire, the day after he received news of her sentence. The letter was months out of date, addressed to the gaol at Rye, and the many greasy fingers which had handled it had almost obliterated her name. She had little idea how it had finally reached Newgate, but certainly the sum of money he mentioned enclosing was not with it. That was hardly to be expected after it had been passed round among thieves.

Richard's letter was a cry of distress at the news of her sentence—and he begged her to write and tell him in what way he could help. But his horror wasn't strong enough to cover the doubts he felt—he never mentioned the question of her innocence or guilt. Sara knew instantly that he *believed* she was guilty, and he was struggling with a wavering loyalty to make himself write the letter offering his help. It was a kind and gentle letter, the letter of a friend—but not of a lover.

She folded the greasy paper carefully, and went to Charlotte Barker to beg her to write to Richard in Hampshire telling him that Sara Dane had already left on a transport for Botany Bay.

She felt oddly calm when the letter was written and sent off. After that she tried not to think of Richard again—and she partially succeeded. The business of keeping alive, or surviving from day to day absorbed her, and the world of Richard and Bramfield seemed to fade; she dreamed less and less of the winding dyke roads, of the cries of the gulls on the shore. The crude realities of the prison were themselves effectively shutting off the past; Sara even began to doubt that she had ever known such men as her father and Richard Barwell.

She embarked with the other women in the *Georgette*, off Woolwich in mid-December, and by the time the ship finally took on her full cargo and crew, and slipped down the Thames in early February, Sara's money was exhausted. She spent the months of the voyage cramped in the perpetual dimness of the gun deck, with a daily spell of exercise on the upper deck when the weather was fair. Discipline was strict on board, which meant that the crew were prevented from mixing with the women prisoners, as happened on other transports. The food, although it was inadequate, was fairly distributed; but still the stronger ones always seemed to be in possession of more than their share. The bitter law of the prisoners remained in force here, and the weakest suffered.

III

When Andrew Maclay had appeared in the women's quarters and called her name, Sara knew at once what was going to happen. After the burial of Mrs. Ryder's servant that morning, the gun deck had buzzed with speculation about who would be selected to fill her place. They all knew Mrs. Ryder by sight, and they knew from the ship's gossip that she was frequently ill. They had seen the two lively children, and had the opinion that it would need more than a sick woman to keep them under control. The chattering prisoners had decided that one of them would be needed, and they waited hourly for the summons.

It was unfortunate, Sara decided, that the second officer had chosen just that moment to arrive. She knew she had made a bad impression on Maclay—she knew just how the scene of struggling, clawing women had appeared to him, and she, with her dirty bundle of food, must have seemed vulgar and coarse. She glanced sideways at his face as they walked almost abreast towards the quarter-deck cabins. He might give a bad report of her to Mrs. Ryder, she thought, but that wasn't the deciding factor. There was some particular reason why she had been picked from among the others, and the reason still held good. If she was being given a chance to act as Mrs. Ryder's servant she wasn't going to have it spoiled by a lack of proper humility and decorum. If Mrs. Ryder expected to see a girl with a meek, pliable manner, she was going to find her. Sara's hands went to her hair, and she furtively tucked up some of the straying ends. She looked ruefully at her filthy gown, in which the rents were almost indecent, and hoped that Mrs. Ryder was prepared to make allowances for her appearance. Whatever happened she was determined that she was going to have this chance.

They entered the quarter-deck companion-way, and she clenched her hands tightly in the first feeling of real emotion she had experienced since the arrival of Richard's letter.

Andrew Maclay paused outside one of the cabins.

"Wait here," he said, over his shoulder, as he rapped on the door.

Mrs. Ryder's voice called to him to come in. She was lying on her bunk, and she smiled when she saw Andrew. The cabin was a little darkened against the direct light from the port-hole and he could not see her very clearly. She was not much past thirty-five, still very pretty—a slight woman, dark, and rather ill-looking from the interminable voyage and the sea-sickness which kept her too often in her cabin. She was wrapped in a loose, yellow silk gown. Andrew's eyes lightened at the sight of her; he found Julia Ryder gentle and easy to talk with. She had a sweetness about her which appealed strongly to him.

"Good-afternoon, ma'am," he said, bowing. "I trust you are feeling better?"

"Indeed, yes, Mr. Maclay, thank you."

She was looking at him questioningly.

"Your husband discussed your need of another servant with the Captain at dinner, ma'am," he said. "I've brought the convict woman, Sara Dane."

"Sara Dane!" Mrs. Ryder half sat up. "But this is excellent, Mr. Maclay! I hadn't truly hoped for such good news. It seemed barely possible that she would be aboard with us."

He looked a little confused. "I trust she will fit your requirements, ma'am. She has, after all, been a prisoner for some considerable time. Perhaps she isn't . . . er . . . quite suitable."

She smiled, putting her head on one side. "Is she as bad as that, Mr. Maclay?"

He thought for a moment before he replied. "She's a convict, ma'am. I know nothing else about her."

"Ah, yes, but at least she is trained in domestic duties. I might have combed the ship and still not found..." She didn't finish her sentence; she looked at him directly. "I know what to expect from Sara Dane. She will be illiterate and coarse, and probably immoral. But I'm desperate for help with Ellen and Charles. I must take this chance when it's offered."

He wondered if he should try to tell her that Sara Dane did not fit her description very well. But he had no time, because she spoke again, rather quickly.

"Is she waiting? Please show her in, Mr. Maclay."

He opened the door and motioned his charge into the cabin. She stood in front of them, lowering her eyes before their inspection. Andrew was shocked at the contrast between the two women. He saw Mrs. Ryder's eyebrows lift, and her face contract in dismay. Her mouth opened slightly, making him immediately aware that this was the first time she had seen one of these creatures at such close quarters.

"Good-afternoon," she said feebly.

The other dropped a curtsy, but did not speak.

Mrs. Ryder glanced helplessly at Andrew.

"You are Sara Dane?" she said at last.

"Yes, ma'am."

"Mrs. Templeton, of Rye, wrote me that you might possibly be on board with us. She said you were experienced in domestic duties. Is that so?"

"Yes, ma'am."

"Have you ever taken care of children?'

"No, ma'am."

"Mmm..." Mrs. Ryder looked doubtful. "Can you sew?"

"Yes, ma'am."

"I don't suppose you can read?"

"Yes, ma'am."

"You can?" Mrs. Ryder relaxed noticeably. "Can you write?"

The question seemed to touch Sara Dane's pride. She stiffened her shoulders, and her head was raised until she looked down under the lashes.

"Of course, I can write," she said shortly.

"Oh, indeed!" Mrs. Ryder's gaze was suddenly cold as it rested on the woman before her. Andrew was half-afraid now, realising that two strong personalities had met and already there were signs of a battle for supremacy. He saw that Sara Dane was no longer demure, her eyes had grown bright and her mouth was set in a determined line.

"You interest me," the older woman said quietly. "What other accomplishments have you?

The other, apparently unafraid, answered, "I speak and read French and Latin. And Italian, too, a little." She finished up—defiantly, Andrew thought, "And I can do mathematics."

Julia Ryder's expression altered swiftly.

The little baggage! Andrew thought, aware of a growing admiration for her spirit. All Sara Dane's meekness was gone now; she wasn't, obviously, the sort to be content to hide her light under a bushel for long. She was making it evident that the Ryders had found a treasure where they hadn't expected it.

Mrs. Ryder spoke again. "How old are you, Dane?"

"Eighteen, ma'am."

"Eighteen, only? What crime were you convicted of, pray?"

The ragged figure stirred uneasily, glancing quickly from the woman lying on the bunk to the young officer who stood before her. It was an eloquent gesture, conveying to Andrew a sense of misery and wretchedness. Then she looked away.

"Come, child!" Mrs. Ryder urged. "Tell me what it was."

Sara Dane's eyes came slowly back to her.

"I was convicted of theft," she said.

Andrew recalled the conversation at the captain's dinner table— the preachers and the poachers, the petty thieves who filled the courts and prisons. He looked at the girl a trifle sadly, remembering that a short time ago he had loudly defended her and all her kind. He reflected that it was all very well to defend them when they were an anonymous mass, and didn't touch him in any way. But when they emerged sharply as individuals, such as this woman, who had education, some breeding, and still had kept her pride, spirit and a touch of humour—then the issue was suddenly confused. It was too close to him; in the space of a few minutes it had become something personal. He was bewildered and a trifle unhappy.

He addressed Mrs. Ryder abruptly. "Ma'am, if," he gestured towards Sara Dane, "this woman suits you, Captain Marshall has given instructions that she need not return to the convict quarters. May I report now to the captain?"

"Please do, Mr. Maclay. I think Dane will meet my requirements." She gave him a quiet smile. "You'll convey my thanks to Captain Marshall?"

He bowed. "Your servant, ma'am."

He turned and left the cabin.

Chapter Three

The two men in the wardroom looked up from their papers when Andrew burst in upon them. Brooks was checking a list of medical supplies in a bored fashion and welcomed the diversion. Harding, flicking over a page of the log, raised mildly astonished eyebrows at the sudden noise of Andrew's entry.

"What is it?" he said.

Andrew had only taken one step into the room. He looked from one to the other.

"Have you seen her?" he said to Brooks.

"Her?"

Andrew was impatient. "The girl. Sara Dane."

Brooks smiled slightly. "I saw her yesterday. Dirty little wretch, but I'd say she had more possibilities than any of the others."

"Yesterday!" Andrew echoed. "Then you ought to see her to-day!"

Harding had taken his cue from Brooks. He began to smile. "I suppose she's washed away the dirt of the prisons and uncovered a dazzling beauty?"

Andrew slammed the door behind him. "Well—if I'm any judge of women, she's beautiful enough to set the whole ship talking."

"The dirt is really gone, then?" Brooks's tone was still bantering.

"Yes, it's gone," Andrew replied. "She's washed her hair ..." He finished lamely, because their faces had too clearly revealed their amusement. "It's ... fair—almost white,"

Harding glanced at Brooks. "There'll be some defiance of Captain Marshall's orders now, with all this beauty let loose among us."

"Wait till Wilder sees her!" Brooks said. "She'll give him something to think about. The poor fellow is dying of boredom."

"If he gets half a chance!" Harding mused.

Andrew turned away from them. He walked to the table,

looking down at the papers scattered about. For no particular reason he scowled

"She's extremely intelligent," he said quietly. "Perhaps she's not the sort Wilder likes."

No one spoke.

He looked up, bursting out, "God in heaven, what is she doing here on a convict ship?"

After a moment Brooks shook his head, shrugging his shoulders. Harding said nothing.

Andrew left them to their papers. He picked up his own report-book and sat down at a table, resting the point of a quill before jabbing it into the inkpot. He thought unashamedly of the girl he had just seen on deck with the Ryder children, her golden head bare and soft in the sunlight. What a fool he must have seemed—gaping at her. She had worn a blue cotton dress belonging to Martha Barratt, and a bright red shawl about her shoulders. The transformation was unbelievable and, reading his expression, she had looked at him steadily for a second or two, and then smiled. He remembered her eyes, an indefinable colour, more green than blue. He was a trifle shaken by the impression she had made on him. It lingered, as the memory of her voice had lingered.

He glanced over at Brooks and Harding, but they were completely absorbed again. Sara Dane was forgotten by them. He dipped the quill in the ink, but his mind was not on the report he wrote. A girl's inquiring eyes came before him. He bent his head, and tried to concentrate.

Sara made her presence felt aboard the *Georgette* in a strange fashion, Andrew thought. Almost from that first day he had seen her in her place by the bulwark with the Ryder children, it seemed as if she had always been there.

The transition from convict to confidential servant might have been an impossible one for almost any other woman. Andrew watched her closely during the long, dull weeks of the voyage to the Cape, and found himself compelled to admire the way she managed it. Her methods were not subtle, but they were clever. She was far too shrewd to make herself a target for disapproval. Day after day, she sat on deck with the children's lesson books open on her lap, her eyes never wandering from them for more than a second. But if one of the officers stopped beside the group to talk to Ellen and Charles, Sara was willing enough to talk also, though she always waited to be addressed first.

The trouble, he thought, was that none of them knew quite how to treat her. They were all conscious that she had been, on her own admission, convicted of theft. On the other hand, she had charm and undeniable beauty and it was too much to expect that men, cut off from the society of women, would not stop to talk with her and the children; too much to expect them to keep their eyes from following her movements. After a while they stopped being self-conscious about speaking to her, they forgot that she had come up from the convict quarters in rags.

She established herself finally in her own niche when the captain paused one morning by the little group to ask how their lessons progressed. Andrew, watching the scene, saw that Sara answered quietly and with no undue meekness. Coquetry or servility would have been out of place, and she did not make the mistake of employing either. Clever minx, he thought. He knew that the captain would soon make it a daily practice to stop to listen to the lessons, commend the children's industry, and watch Sara working neatly and expertly at the needlework Mrs. Ryder had given her.

To Andrew, the most astonishing thing about Sara was her gaiety. She made Ellen and Charles laugh continually, and they plainly loved her for it; she was tireless in keeping them interested and occupied during the days that followed each other with dreadful sameness. He admired the spirit which let her throw off the effect of her imprisonment so quickly, and settle to her place naturally in the Ryders' family life. It was quite obvious that she did not expect or want pity from any of them.

He was conscious as he watched her, day after day, of growing approval of the way she set about making the best of her strange situation.

II

The tiny space of the cabin was full of the sounds of rustling silk, the scents of warm flesh and perfumed clothes, as Sara helped Julia Ryder prepare for bed. Julia was tired, and had very little to say; Sara fell in with her mood, folding garments and settling the cabin to order almost in silence. A gown of pale blue silk, which Julia had worn that evening at the captain's table, lay across the cot, and Sara gathered it up in her arms; she smoothed

65

the thin stuff between her fingers appreciatively, listening to its rustle with attentive ears. The sound and feel of the material brought back the London days, when gowns, far more elaborate than this, had been an everyday sight. With the whisper of silk she could hear again the light-hearted gossip of the dress-salon; she saw the fashionably bored faces under feather-trimmed hats, the jewelled hands slipping into soft gloves. For just a second the crumpled silk in her arms gave that world back to her.

Then she glanced across at Mrs. Ryder, seated before the small, littered, toilet-table. The other woman's dark hair was loose, and fell about her shoulders, shining under the swinging lantern. The picture she made in that gentle light satisfied Sara's sense of beauty; while Julia Ryder was here, this cramped cabin did not seem such a far cry from the London salon. She wore now her loose wrapper of primrose brocade; her nightgown was trimmed with lace that was hardly whiter than the skin of her shoulders and breast.

As Sara watched, Julia leaned forward to study her reflection in the mirror, at the same time picking up a hairbrush from the table.

"Let me do it, ma'am!" Sara said. She laid aside the gown and stretched out her hand for the brush.

She took her usual place behind Julia, pulling the brush evenly through the long hair, watching it tighten, and then slacken and curl back. She brushed in silence; and Julia's eyelids drooped. After a few moments Sara's attention wandered to the toilet-table. The mate of the silver-backed brush she held had been carelessly thrown down. The mirror, which was always propped against the bulkhead when they were not in heavy seas, reflected the scene back in a kindly fashion. The frame of the mirror was a light silver scrollwork; on a lace mat close to it lay a crystal phial of perfume. Sara's eyes went slowly from one thing to another while her hands moved mechanically.

Julia's voice broke in quietly:

"You love pretty things, don't you, Sara?"

Sara lifted her gaze from the table to the mirror; it met Julia's there.

After a pause, Sara said, "I shouldn't admit how much I like having these things about me."

"Why not?"

"You know very well, ma'am, that I was transported for theft. If I say I admire them, you may think I want to steal them."

In the mirror Sara saw Julia frown suddenly, and a look almost of sternness came across her face. Her eyes didn't leave Sara's for a second.

She said sharply, "Sara, I have only asked you one question about how you came to be on this ship. I don't intend to probe. If you wish to tell me, I'm ready to listen. But I leave the decision to yourself."

Sara had never felt for any other woman the respect which Julia had won from her. She had worked for her, had tended her when she was ill, and helped her through days when she couldn't stand upright with the rolling of the ship; she believed that in these weeks together she had come to know her completely. She decided now that she must take a risk on her judgment of Julia Ryder.

She didn't attempt to answer the question. Instead she lifted her head and stared into the mirror again.

"Are you satisfied with me, ma'am?"

"Yes, Sara—I'm very satisfied."

Sara nodded, and said slowly, "And Mr. Ryder—he's satisfied also, isn't he?"

"Yes."

"And I get on well with the children, ma'am . . . ? I mean they're fond of me, in a way?"

"You manage them better than anyone we've ever had. They obviously pay attention to you because they like you."

Sara's voice went quietly on. "And the captain, ma'am, *he* doesn't find anything to disapprove of in my behaviour? He doesn't object to the officers talking with me—why, he talks to me himself!"

Julia frowned again, puzzled. "Yes, Sara. I hear nothing but praise for you from everyone. But why . . . ?"

"Why?" Sara repeated. Then she paused to let the other have the full effect of her words. "Because I *wanted* to hear you admit those things, ma'am! I wanted to hear you say them, so that I'll be certain whenever I admire your possessions, I don't need to wonder if you think I'll steal them."

At that Julia twisted in her seat, until she was looking directly at Sara.

"I think it's time we stopped this fencing, Sara," she said. "Let us be plain with one another."

Sara's hand, holding the brush, dropped to her side.

"I've watched you very carefully," Julia said. "You're ambitious and proud—but you've also got a head full of sound sense. My servant Barratt's death was your good fortune. You seized your opportunity when it came, and I don't imagine you'd be likely to throw it away by doing something foolish.

"We're going to a new country," she went on. "The life will be difficult and strange... An impossible life, Sara—unless you're prepared to be as fair with me as I'm willing to be with you. I'm not blind. Believe me, I'm as well aware of your good qualities as you are yourself. But I beg you not to forget that in this case we both have something to offer. When we reach New South Wales, *you're* going to need my help just as much as I'll need yours."

She paused, tapping the edge of the table reflectively with her finger-nail. "As long as you're with us, Sara, I'm willing to forget that you were convicted at all—I'll forget that you have ever occupied any other position but this one. But, if I'm to trust you, then you must stop mistrusting me."

Sara was disconcerted that the other had read her motives so truly; but swiftly this feeling was replaced by satisfaction because this attitude was exactly what she had sought to bring about in Mrs. Ryder. It was the position towards which she had painstakingly worked her way for weeks. This was an assurance of her future.

She dropped her eyes. "Then I think we understand each other, don't we, ma'am?"

"I think perhaps we do, Sara," Julia said.

III

In a tiny aft cabin of the *Georgette*, reeking of cooking smells because of its closeness to the galley, Sara struggled with the weight of a studded sea-chest which had belonged to Martha Barratt. Stowed in the small space under the cot, the chest would yield only a few inches at a time to her tugging; she paused frequently to straighten her back and take a deep breath. The cabin had no port-hole; it was airless, and hardly large enough to allow her to move. She had occupied it since the day Andrew Maclay had brought her up from the convicts' quarters. It contained a cot, at the end of which, piled one on top of the other, were three wicker baskets of clothes belonging to Julia Ryder and the children. The only other furniture was a wash-table holding a metal jug and basin and Martha's few toilet articles, which Sara now used. On pegs behind the door hung a cloak and a second striped gown like the one she was wearing.

Her attempts to drag the chest into the space between the cot and the wash-table had brought the first prickle of sweat to her forehead and neck. She passed the back of her hand across her hairline, and stretched out to open the cabin door fully, so that whatever air the passage-way offered might enter the stifling little apartment. Beside the chest was another wicker basket, containing the belongings which Martha had collected during her long service with the Ryders. This basket Sara already had had full access to—the plain, neat clothes excited her very little, apart from the novel experience of having more than rags to wear. But in the chest, ponderously locked, were Martha's few treasures, seldom worn or used, kept more for the joy of possession than any other reason. Mrs. Ryder had given Sara the key that morning and told her she might have whatever she found useful. Now, in the hour of the midday meal she had time to herself to haul the chest out and look through its contents.

She dragged steadily at the handle until at last it came clear of the cot. Martha had kept the lock lovingly oiled, and the key turned without protest. Sara gently removed the folded sheets of paper which lay on top, breathing, as she did so, a wordless little apology to the dead woman whose cherished possessions were being touched by strange hands.

She lifted the lid of a white box, and fingered the pieces of neatly rolled ribbon, a few scraps of fancy lace, and lastly a soft pair of embroidered gloves. She laid these aside, turning her attention to a dark blue cloak. There was a narrow trimming of fur at the neck which gave a touch of luxury, fabulous in the clothes of a servant; Sara pressed it against her face. When her gaze fell on a pile of blue muslin; she dropped the cloak and pulled eagerly at the other garment. It was a gown, beribboned and billowing, and neither new nor fashionable. Obviously, she thought, holding it up against herself, this was Martha's best, and only brought out on the grandest occasions. It did not matter to Sara that it was out of fashion—it was still graceful and delicate. She took another look at the soft folds of the shirt and decided to try it on.

But when she tried to close the door before taking her own dress off, she found that the chest was in front of it. Unless she pushed the chest back under the cot again, the door would have to stay as it was. She felt herself flush with annoyance and irritation as she considered what she would do with the unwieldy thing.

It was unlikely at this hour that anyone would pass down the passage-way, the midday meal occupied those on board who might have used it. Sara looked thoughtfully from the dress to the open door, and decided then that she might take the risk of leaving it that way. She whipped off the cotton gown, and pulled the blue muslin over her head. Martha had been as tall as she, but of heavier build. The gown was too big; the waist-line fell below her own, and the neck, cut to fit a broader figure, hung open in the front and slipped off her shoulders She would alter it to fit and some time, she hoped, there might be occasion to wear it. Certainly, it was rather an elaborate gown for a servant, but if Martha, middle-aged and dignified, thought it suitable, then she, Sara, wasn't going to pass it by.

Searching among the more sober garments for something with which she could adorn the muslin, she came upon a long scarf of the finest black lace. It was probably Chantilly—something she was not unfamiliar with, as smuggled lengths were often seen about the shoulders of the richer women of Rye. She examined it critically—it was quite faultless and very beautiful. She draped it over her head, letting it trail across her shoulders. Quickly she turned to the wash-table for the small, handled mirror which lay there.

The only light in the cabin came from the lamp above her head, so that she saw her reflection dimly. She imagined that her mother might have looked a little as she did now. The face she saw pleased her; her pale gold hair and bare shoulders showed through the black lace. She went on gazing, reflecting that it was a comfort, sometimes, to be able to take pleasure from one's own face.

She gave a little shrug and adjusted the lace scarf to better effect. Then a sound from the doorway caused her to lower the glass and turn swiftly. She found Wilder watching her.

Their eyes met as they both strove to weigh up the situation. Sara folded her lips, waiting for him to speak. She took in his nonchalant leaning position against the doorframe, and the unpleasant smile that flickered thinly across his good-looking face.

When he spoke it seemed that his drawl was deliberately insulting. He jerked his head on one side, and his eyes moved quite openly over her body,

"Very pretty, my dear!" he said. "Very pretty!"

She managed to control her anger so that it shouldn't show in her face and give him even that small satisfaction. She kept perfectly still, pressed back against the wash-table.

But his gaze had dropped to the open chest.

"What's this, Sara? Packing? Leaving us? Shame!"

He looked at her inquiringly, and straightening from his leaning position, he stepped into the cabin. There was a touch of petulance in the way in which he banged down the lid of the chest and pushed it back under the cot. He kicked the door closed behind him.

"Mr. Wilder," she said sharply, "kindly open the door!"

He stared at her, and then laughed.

"Kindly open the door!" he mocked, imitating her tones. "Mr. Wilder has no intention of opening the door!"

Then he stepped towards her, and his hand shot out and gripped her arm. He bent his head close to hers.

"And what can you do about it?"

She thrust her hand against his chest. He was amused at her efforts to push him away.

"It does no good, Sarah. If you make a sound I'll tell whoever comes that I'm here at your invitation. It wouldn't look well, would it, if I were to say that? Not even your frozen air of innocence could stand that!"

"If you . . . " Her voice was weaker and less certain. "If you don't leave . . . "

He ended her speech abruptly by forcing his lips upon hers, pressing her body against his own until she could no longer even move in protest. Caught tightly against him, she was made strongly aware of the masculine smells he had brought into the tiny cabin, the smell and taste of wine on his lips and tongue, the faint smell of sweat from his armpits, the smell of the dressing he used upon his hair. They clung in her nostrils, and made her afraid. He had a strength and fever of desire to go on demanding with his lips a response she wouldn't give. He released her a little, and she felt him try to push her back on the chest. She closed her eyes and clung grimly to his shoulders, so that her body could not be bent back. She had only one thought as she held to him—that nothing should make her give in to Wilder, because he would use her without pity or thought. He would use her as long as he wished, and then leave her.

He began to shake her violently to break her grip, but it still held. The smell of the wine seemed overpoweringly strong, and she wondered if she were going to faint. She opened her eyes and saw the beads of sweat on his forehead and upper lip. She realised that it was on her own forehead as well.

Then he slackened his grip, and dropped his arms. She remained clinging to him, staring in a stupid, dazed fashion. It seemed foolish to have fought so grimly to prevent him coming nearer, and now, when he had drawn away, to hold him still. He put his hands up to her wrists, breaking her grip on the shoulders of his tunic with a single jerk.

Still holding her wrists he stepped back, looking her up and down. His gaze moved from her face to the limp muslin dress, hanging awry and falling off her shoulders.

"You didn't count on me coming, did you?" he said "You were preparing for someone else...for someone else, Sara! You're all dressed up for someone. Who is it?"

He put his face closer to hers. "If you don't tell me I'll break you! I'll ..." He gave her a savage shake. "Is it Roberts? Tell me! Or Maclay? Or is it one of those convict bastards you bed with whenever you get the chance?"

He shook her again, thrusting her with each movement against the hard edge of the chest

She whispered, her tone thin because of the pain in her wrists, "If you don't go..."

"Go...?" He dropped her arms. "I don't want to go." His frenzied rage seemed to have left him.

His expression softened and he put his hand upon her shoulder, one finger moving tenderly upon her flesh, stroking with exquisite gentleness the curve of the bone.

"Why do you fight me, Sara?"

The hand slipped to her throat, the same finger lingering now in the hollow at its base

"I could make things so easy for you. I'd give you money so that you should buy food when you get to Sydney. I'll get gowns for you at the Cape—and silk...Sara, do you hear me? Are you listening?"

His eyes, as they searched her face, were confident, and eager.

"Sara..." He spoke gently. "You like me, don't you?"

In reply she jerked herself free from his lightly caressing hand. Her voice came in a hoarse sort of whisper in the back of her throat.

72

"If it's a whore you want, Mr. Wilder, you'll find plenty of them below! Don't come in here looking for one!"

His hand twitched unsteadily, as if he meant to strike her.

"You blasted little fool!" he snapped. "You talk as if you were an innocent in arms. Fool . . . Fool! Don't think anyone is deceived by that . . . We all know your kind. But you won't stand out against it long after you land in Port Jackson. You'll see how quickly you change . . . it'll be a choice between your virtue and starvation then."

His angry voice dropped to a lower level. He breathed deeply, dabbing impatiently with his hand at the sweat on his forehead.

"I'll tell you, Sara, in case you've forgotten, what's going to happen when you arrive in Sydney. You'll be looked over by the military, and, because you've got a beautiful face, and a beautiful body, one of the officers will want to make you his mistress. And you won't refuse. You won't flaunt your virtue, either. You'll be much too afraid of hunger. It's a business, my dear—you'll trade your beauty for bread and salt pork."

She was looking at him with her eyes half-closed. "How wrong you are about that, Mr. Wilder!" she snapped. "I'm not up for market. My position in the colony will be as Mrs. Ryder's personal maid."

"Personal maid, eh?" he scoffed. "And what makes you think that?"

"Because she told me so herself!" she blazed back.

"Did she, indeed? How she trusts you!"

"She hasn't any reason not to trust me—and, what's more, she isn't going to get one." Her breath was so fast it hurt her to speak. Finally she flung at him, "Now, get out!"

The thin, unpleasant smile was back on his face.

"Get out? Get out, you say? Why should I?"

And, still smiling, he made a sudden lunge towards her, and caught her to him. To Sara, struggling to avoid them, his lips seemed to be everywhere, pressing into her hair and eyelids and mouth, excitedly seeking a response. Then she felt them against her throat, and on her shoulder where the gown had fallen away. His groping hands were upon her also, and she heard the sharp little sound as the wilted muslin tore. After that her restraint left her. Her anger was a hot darkness before her eyes; it exploded the frightened suggestions of caution, it mattered no longer whether the man who fumbled with such eager hands and lips was the captain or the lowest member of his crew. All she knew was that she must be rid of those hands.

She gave a quick twist, at the same time raising her right hand to his face. She dug her nails into the sweating skin and drew them sharply downwards, For a short space of time they both hesitated. Sara stared in awe at the three long scratches she had made on his cheek. The middle one, deeper than the others, had already begun to bleed.

Slowly his hand went up to touch his cheek. His fingers encountered the wetness there, and he turned them over to examine them. He cursed as he saw the blood smeared across them.

"You strumpet! Where did you learn your tricks—in a whore-house? I've a mind to break every bone in your body for that!"

He hit her twice. The second blow flung her on to the chest. She struck her head against the bulkhead and slipped down, only half-conscious.

Before her misted eyes Wilder's figure seemed to sway threateningly. He bent over her.

"I'll want nothing more of you—bitch! Stay here! It becomes you well—your chaste little room!"

He swung back on his heel and left her. The door slammed behind him with a thunderous noise which echoed in the narrow passage-way.

Chapter Four

The dead hours of the middle watch had dulled Andrew with fatigue. He had thankfully handed over to Roberts, and now, shortly after eight bells sounded, he began to make his way below. The night was fine and dark. There was a faint breeze, and the *Georgette* kept steadily to her course in a calm sea. The silence was deep as the ship slept.

The two stern lanterns cast a faint light over the poop deck and touched the helmsmen as they dragged together at the wheel. Looking away from them, as he descended the companion ladder, Andrew saw the glow of a cigar in the darkness, and made out the form of a man leaning against the bulwark. He paused, then went forward.

"Brooks?—Is that you?"

"Yes. Came up to get a breath of fresh air." Andrew could not see his face, but his tone was weary and grim. "It's a hell down there," he said. "There was a confinement—a convict woman. I've been with her all the night."

"Is she all right?" Andrew asked. He was sympathetically aware of the surgeon's ordeal among the troublesome mob of women.

"The mother is all right—the child is dead. It was born dead." Brooks turned back to the bulwark. He puffed at the cigar. "Just as well it didn't live. These babies born on transports rarely last the voyage. They're sick and starved. This one's mother has no idea who the father is."

Silence fell between them. Andrew stared out to sea, but was aware of nothing, neither his tiredness nor the blackness of the night. Presently he said, "The man who was flogged yesterday—how is he?"

"Bad. But he'll get over it, I dare say. He's strong."

The scene of the previous day's flogging had remained with Andrew. The convicts seemed to possess a fiendish talent for putting themselves in the way of trouble. God in heaven, wasn't their lot bad enough? he wondered. Yesterday's punishment was the result of a brutish attack by a Welshman on an undersized Bristol footpad. The weapon used was a single blade of a rusted pair of scissors. The set-to had been provoked by nothing more than an argument over the number of guns the *Georgette* carried. It didn't take much, he thought, to stir up a spark in the minds of men who had had no occupation for months. The Welshman was flogged before the mast in view of the assembled crew. The cat of nine tails flew until his back was too bloody a mess to continue; then it fell across the calves of his legs. The little footpad lay below, too weak from loss of blood from the scissor wounds to take his part in the punishment.

"And the other one . . . ?" Andrew asked. "Will he live?"

"Yes, he'll live. He's responding well. In any case, they'll both spend the rest of the voyage in irons."

Andrew said slowly, frowning, "I can't get used to seeing them flogged. God knows, there was enough of it in the Navy to harden me. But this is different—and when it's one of the women, it makes me sick. I pity the convicts when they're being punished in a way I'd never pity one of the hands. What else can these miserable wretches do but cause trouble?"

"You've quite a feeling for the convicts these days, Maclay," Brooks murmured.

Andrew turned to him. "What do you mean?"

"Perhaps it's not my affair. But I should hate to see you run yourself into trouble."

Andrew stiffened. "Yes...?"

"The girl, I mean. Sara Dane." Brooks said this quietly, as if he was feeling his way with care. "Good God, man, you must know how gossip spreads around on a ship! You spend a great deal of your time with her. You can't blame..."

"I love her!" Andrew returned sharply.

"You love her...!" Brooks was taken aback. "You know nothing about her—or almost nothing, how much *do* you know?"

Andrew lifted his shoulders helplessly. "What do any of us know about her except that she's beautiful, and that she has charm and spirit!"

"Beauty, yes," Brooks replied, considering. "She has that all right. Oh, and charm and spirit, too! But, God in heaven, Maclay, you don't *love* a convict for having a beautiful face!"

"But that's just it, I *do* love her!" Andrew said quickly. "She obsesses me, I tell you! I can't get her out of my mind! The thought of her torments me!'

Brooks had turned to Andrew. "You can't be serious, surely?"

"Damn you, of course I'm serious!"

"Have you told her this?"

For a moment Andrew didn't reply. Then he said, "That's the curse of it—I haven't." He went on gloomily. "You know what she's like—I never get a chance to tell her. She's just the same with all of us—Wilder, Roberts—yourself, Brooks. She's got a smile and a laugh for each of us—and that's as far as it goes."

"Oh, I'll not deny she knows what she's about. The captain can't have any reason to complain of *her* behaviour! She's a shrewd enough wench, I'll give you that!"

"Yes... yes." Andrew was impatient. "But what am I to do? I love her!"

"This is a damned awkward business, Maclay," Brooks said, at the end of a long pause between them. "I hardly know what to say. The captain won't turn a blind eye to consorting..."

"Consorting! I don't want to consort with her! I want to marry her!"

"Don't be such a blasted fool, man! How can you marry

her—it's not as simple as that. Have you forgotten you'll be parted when we reach Port Jackson?"

Andrew said calmly, "I have plans..."

"Plans! Damn' good plans you'll need to get you over a situation like this. She's a convict! You know nothing about her—where she comes from, even what crime she was transported for."

"True," Andrew said. "But I'll find out."

"Then you'll have to ask her herself. None of the convict-papers will tell you."

The surgeon had finished his cigar by this time. He threw the glowing end down into the water.

"I'm deadly serious about this, Brooks," Andrew said, "I mean to ask her about herself. I'll find out as much as there is to know—and you'll see then whether or not I'm in love with her!"

Brooks sighed deeply. "Well...I hope you're not...disillusioned. That's about all I can say."

He added, "We'd both better get below now. I'm dead for want of sleep."

Andrew followed the other to the companion ladder, and as he walked he glanced back at the stem lights standing out against the blackness of the sky. The *Georgette* rode in deep and pervading peace, as if she were an untroubled ship.

Andrew came face to face with Sara the following evening as she descended the companion-ladder from the quarterdeck. He ran up a few steps to halt her progress. She was surprised by his direct approach and gazed down on him inquiringly.

"I want to talk to you," he said.

She said nothing, but glanced about the deck below her. The passage-way from which Andrew had come led directly to the officers' quarters. Even as they stood facing each other two of the hands passed, and shot quick, curious glances at them.

"Come with me," Andrew said. He moved past her on the ladder, jerking his head to indicate that she should follow.

Sara faced him squarely when he drew her into the shadow of the lifeboat on the quarter-deck and demanded to know why she was here on the *Georgette*. He asked her outright the reason for her conviction.

She had been expecting this, and shrugged her shoulders, answering with the suggestion of a laugh.

"Oh, I ran away from a rectory—and had the misfortune to

77

forget to return to my employers three guineas, which they claimed did not belong to me.''

He let out an exasperated gasp, took her shoulder and shook her sharply.

"Don't play with me, madam! That's not the whole story!''

"Then you shall have it—the whole of it!'' she flung back at him. "And if you don't like it, remember that I didn't force it on you.''

While his hand still rested upon her shoulders, but more gently now, she told him what he had asked, going back to her life in London, in Rye, and at Bramfield. She left nothing out, not her mother's doubtful past, or Sebastian's family. He heard about Sir Geoffrey Watson and Lady Linton. The one thing she could not tell him, and never meant to tell him, was her love for Richard Barwell.

"When the time came to go to Lady Linton,'' she said, "I decided I'd had enough of living with a family in which I'd never be anything but the daughter of a drunkard and a petty borrower.'' She added a trifle ruefully: "It was the only mistake I ever made—to take Sir Geoffrey's money with me. There was no defence for me after that''

As she finished he suddenly squeezed both her shoulders tightly in his hands, and let out a shout of laughter which carried clearly across the deck.

"You little fool, Sara! Oh, you little fool!'' He laughed again. "To think you let yourself be sent to Botany Bay for the price of a gown or two! And to think I've wasted sleep over you because you called yourself a thief. A thief—of all things! You're a borrower, Sara, like your father.''

He had stopped laughing, but he still grinned broadly. "This is the best news I've had in my life.''

Without warning he bent and kissed her fully on the lips.

"Remember that until the next time, Sara.'

Then he turned and strode across the deck towards the companion-ladder; she listened to the noisy clatter he made as he descended it. He whistled softly as he went.

She stayed where she was, within the shadow of the lifeboat. Below there were many tasks waiting for her attention, but for once, she told herself, they could wait. She closed her eyes for a second, and saw again Andrew Maclay's face, gay and yet serious, as excited as a boy's. But there was bitterness in the knowledge also. What was the use of Andrew Maclay being in love with her—no more could come of it than just such another offer as Wilder's. Though Andrew's would be couched in terms of love and affection, and the inducement to yield would be all the stronger. Restlessly she turned her head, looking out towards the dark horizons. Where could such a relationship end, except in a farewell when they reached Port Jackson?—and the price she would pay was the loss of Julia Ryder's confidence. The thought tormented her. Here at hand was a man who might make her forget Richard Barwell, forget the foolishness two children had committed. Andrew had the authority about him that could easily command her love, and the tenderness to win and hold it. Before his reality, the image of Richard would fade. She acknowledged, despairingly, that it would be an easy matter now to fall in love.

But inevitably some day the *Georgette* would sail out of Port Jackson, and she would remain behind. Only fools fell in love with a prospect like that.

Four bells sounded—the signal for the end of the last dog watch. Andrew Maclay might carry the air of a man who would carve out an exciting, adventurous life for himself, he might have a swaggering charm and look at her with tenderness in his eyes, but, she decided, he was best put out of her mind before he hurt her as Richard Barwell once had done.

II

Gazing up at the sun, James Ryder breathed deeply, thankful that the seemingly interminable stretch from Rio de Janeiro to the Cape was almost over. More than two hours ago the first excited shout of "Land ho!" had come from the lookout. The echo of the cry spread abroad the ship, passing like a ripple from mouth to mouth. There was a good wind, and every passing minute brought the African coastline into sharper focus. They had made an almost perfect landfall—a fact that amazed Ryder when he remembered the immense distances of the Atlantic rolling behind them.

He planted his hands firmly on the bulwark, watching the faint shape of the land before him. Julia would be glad of this, he thought. She was weary of the cramped space, the discomforts of the pitching ship, and longing for the entry into Table Bay. Recalling this, and her patience during the long voyage, he was struck afresh by her courage. She was a damned wonderful woman, he thought, journeying halfway round the world with a husband and two children, and very little to compensate at the end of it. After many years of marriage Ryder was still deeply in love with his wife. She was a precious thing who gave him more concern than he cared to admit.

It was now over three years since their sons, twins, had been drowned when a fisherman's boat overturned in the sea off their Essex farmlands. Julia grieved for them mutely and constantly, and the shock of their deaths stayed with her. She became like a ghost, living in a world in which she had no longer any interest. Her husband had seen her apathy, tried desperately, but without success, to rouse her. Finally he begged her sanction to his giving up the farm and taking land in the West Country or the Midlands. But she refused. She would live nowhere in England except with the sound of the North Sea in her ears.

Then at last, in despair, he approached her cautiously with the suggestion of the colony in New South Wales—and, amazingly, she had welcomed it. The idea was a nebulous thing—so little was known of the settlement, it was a prison-country, its citizens felons. Yet, after their first real discussion about it, she was undaunted by the hardship it offered; its loneliness, its extremity. She was enthusiastic, leaving him no choice but to go ahead with the plan he had as yet only played with. She even insisted upon accompanying him to London for an interview with the Secretary of State, Dundas. From Dundas, they went to Sir Joseph Banks, the botanist who had sailed with Cook and landed at Botany Bay. Here, they imagined, they might expect reliable first-hand information. Banks described the new country as a land of promise, a farmer's land. On the journey back to Essex they were silent, each preoccupied with the story they had heard of the settlement.

They knew that if they settled in New South Wales they would have free land-grants and convict labour; but the drawbacks, too, were great. Reports of flood and famine offered little encouragement to emigrants, so far only a few families had ventured to go there. The sum total of the harrowing tales carried home to England was that they faced a wilderness and starvation. Ryder, contemplating this, might easily have had his enthusiasm dampened. But he was blessed with an imagination and an adventuring spirit which was an easy prey to excitement.

And yet he was not altogether blind to the dangers awaiting the free settlers, and he faced Julia fairly with them, giving her every opportunity to withdraw. But her mind was made up, and she could not be shaken. She left the Essex farm with scarcely a backward glance, meeting the challenge of New South Wales with a formidable determination.

He smiled grimly up at the sky above the billowing spread of canvas. Yes, he thought again, she was a damned wonderful woman!

He began to pace then, up and down the restricted space of the quarter-deck. After about five minutes he halted, his eyes resting reflectively on his two children. They were seated in the shelter of the bulwark, and Sara Dane was beside them. It stirred him to speculate on the possibilities the colony offered his children. If its untapped resources yielded richness, they would be the reapers. They would grow up in loneliness and isolation, estranged from their homeland; but they would grow up with the settlement now in its early infancy, and they would sit astride her promised prosperity.

But what of the ones such as Sara Dane, he wondered, looking long at her—the ones who went out in captivity to populate and work the colony? He shook his head slowly, knowing the uselessness of trying to fathom the thoughts behind those strange eyes. Not Julia—no one, he suspected, except possibly Andrew Maclay—knew why she was here on the *Georgette*. One could only accept the obvious fact that she was not of the type and class usually found in these transports. But, whatever she was, he was profoundly grateful for the qualities she possessed. She was both nurse and tutor to his children, maid and companion to his wife. It was an unexpected combination of abilities. He saw her lift her head then, and laugh at something Charles had said. The sun was fully on her face, and on her skin where her dress was open at the neck. The sight of her young beauty, highly coloured in the sun, held his thoughtful gaze for a long time.

Finally he turned and began to walk again. But he paused almost immediately. Andrew Maclay, relieved of his watch, was descending from the poop.

"Good-morning!" he hailed. "Welcome sight, isn't it?" He indicated the land with a nod of his head.

"It is, indeed, sir," Andrew replied, grinning and sniffing in the freshness of the fine morning. "I imagine Mrs. Ryder will be glad of a stretch on firm ground. She'll not find it as gay as Rio, but at least she'll have a spell from the ship."

Ryder smiled. "I hardly think it's my wife who will miss the gaiety most. I think you younger ones will be the greater sufferers.''

Andrew said nothing, but for a brief moment his eyes turned towards Sara.

Ryder's tone had been bantering, but only to cover the disturbance he suddenly felt. Maclay's attraction to Sara was obvious. It was food for ready gossip in a ship which had had little or no diversion since leaving Rio. The attachment was understandable enough, but Ryder puzzled over the fact that each of their meetings took place where a dozen pairs of eyes might witness it. To outward intent they might be conducting a gracious and leisurely courtship, with their whole lives stretching before them. And yet the circumstances mocked this façade. However unlike one she might appear, Sara Dane was a convict, and Maclay an officer in a company whose prestige was second only to the Royal Navy. The whole situation was incongruous. In most other ships he would have been permitted to take her as his mistress, and the affair would end, with Sara considerably richer, when the *Georgette* left Sydney and headed for her regular trading route. Ryder had the feeling that that was not what Maclay wanted.

The older man studied his companion gravely. In the hard light Maclay's eyes were a deep blue; the skin around them, though young, was lined, toughened and browned by the weather. He had a strong mouth and jaw; his speech, his every action, revealed a typical Scottish determination. The paradox of Maclay's character interested Ryder. He knew that night after night Maclay sat late over cards with whoever he could induce to join him— and he had fantastic luck at them. But Ryder had heard the captain praise his meticulous attention to his duties. He was one of those people who appeared not to need sleep—a seaman with the cool nerves of a gambler.

Andrew, growing restless in the silence that had fallen between them, stirred himself and asked a question.

''Will you be taking on livestock at the Cape, sir?''

Ryder, with effort, brought his thoughts back to the question.

''Yes, I hope to. I'll take on as much livestock as I can get storage for. They tell me it's beyond price in the colony.''

Andrew nodded. ''The plan all round among the officers seems to be to buy livestock at the Cape to sell to the Commissary in Sydney.''

''And will you be joining this trading venture?''

"I expect so, sir. It's reckoned to be a profitable business. And," Andrew laughed, "I'm not one to turn down that sort of thing!"

The other nodded. "I'm told that the man who has livestock does well in the colony. For my part, I don't intend sitting back and waiting on a precarious harvest. I want cows and pigs. And perhaps sheep."

Andrew considered awhile, then he said, "I've been meaning to speak to you about the colony, sir." He hesitated a further moment, beginning again diffidently. "What is your honest opinion of one's chances of settling there?"

Ryder eyed his companion gravely. "It'll be no bed of roses. And all who go willingly to New South Wales must go expecting to gamble. Everything seems to be against us—even the seasons are the other way round. We face drought and floods, and damned hard work on empty bellies." His voice was rising, his eyes had lightened in excitement. He slapped a closed fist into his other hand. "But it's a settler's kingdom, Maclay! Why, just think of it, man! It's ground cattle have never trod! It's never had seed sown into it! You cannot tell me that, rightly treated, it will not produce!"

"Yet they still starve."

"They starve, yes. But only because the colony is in the hands of naval captains and convicts. What does the Navy know about farming? I tell you, Maclay, New South Wales will only be satisfactorily settled by free men—and men who know farming. With each free settler comes that much more hope of prosperity. Put enough good farmers on the land, and then we'll see who'll starve!"

"You seem to have a great deal of faith in this country," Andrew said.

"Yes, I have faith in it. By God, I have faith in it!" Ryder leaned forward and prodded at Andrew's waistcoat. "The more settlers the greater the urge for expansion—north and south, they'll go, Maclay, and finally into the hinterland."

"Expansion behind the settlement? Surely one can't rely on that?"

Ryder sighed. He recalled Brooks's after-dinner tales of the mysteries and dangers of the unexplored continent. They were fetching stories for a man to spin out after a few glasses of wine. With his first-hand knowledge Brooks was able to roll on without fear of contradiction. He was sceptical of the idea of expansion, pointing out that close behind the coastal plains lay a long ridge of smoky-blue, impenetrable hills. Governor Phillip had tried again and again to find a way through them; the expeditions he sent out all turned back, beaten. Brooks believed that they never would be crossed, and that the settlement would stagnate where it was, without ever penetrating farther.

"Ah, you're thinking of the Blue Mountains," Ryder said patiently. "They're a barrier, I admit, but they won't stop expansion. Free men will always make room for themselves—as they do in Canada and America. Only if the settlement remains wholly penal will it stagnate.

"Free settlers will be the making of the country." Ryder's tone dared Andrew's denial. "In the beginning they'll be so few that they'll hardly count at all. They'll live in discomfort, Maclay, mind you that. They've got to settle expecting hell. They'll be isolated and their womenfolk will suffer, too. But my God, man, how they'll be rewarded!" He was smiling, his eyes glinting in the sun. "When prosperity does finally come, it's the early birds who'll be fat on it."

Ryder's smile faded slowly and his voice dropped. The conversation was ended. But as Andrew walked away he was turning over his plan—a plan he had already formed, even before he talked with Ryder, which offered a solution for himself and Sara.

III

Even in the strong sunlight Table Mountain seemed to tower rather sullenly over the neat Dutch settlement and cluster of shipping in the Bay. But Sara and Andrew, standing together by the bulwark, had no eyes for sights that had become familiar to them in the three weeks during which the *Georgette* had ridden at anchor there; there was little interest for them in the prim, yet strangely uncivilised town. Their attention was fixed on the confusion in the longboat below them, from which a noisy, clumsy cargo of pigs, cattle, and sheep was being transferred to the Indiaman. The warm air was filled with the protests of the animals, and in an accompanying boat, safely removed from the despairing struggle of the livestock, the Dutchman who had contracted to supply the *Georgette* added his shouts and curses to the uproar. The din and the smell grew; yet the determined activity of the scene held them both fascinated. Sara's eyes met

Andrew's in sudden amusement as a boatman, grappling unsuccessfully with a young pig, lost his balance and fell overboard, the pig clutched tightly in his arms. The Dutch contractor jumped to his feet with a shouted oath. Every eye turned to watch the incredible turmoil of the water, the mad threshing that followed the first splash; the contractor, after regarding the spectacle for a few seconds in fury and contempt, moved into action. Like a flash he reached the end of the longboat nearest the struggling pair. In the speed of his movement he showed his fear of losing valuable property. He leaned down between the two craft and grasped the pig by its neck. With a mighty swing of his arms he tossed it into the boat, where it lay coughing up salt water and squealing in its unexpected misery. Laconically, the contractor indicated that an oar should be extended to his servant. The wretched man was eventually hauled into the longboat by two pairs of hands thrust under his belt.

The work of loading recommenced.

"Will they complete it, do you think," Sara asked, "by nightfall?"

"I expect they'll continue by lantern, if necessary," Andrew said. "If this wind holds the captain will use it to get under way in the morning."

With his words Sara's thoughts were turned to tomorrow's departure. All day long there had been a sense of unrest aboard the ship. The officers had made their final buying and trading expeditions among the shipping in the Bay and the stores in the town; the final commissions for the captain had been executed. Most of the livestock was, by this time, consigned to the pens prepared, the water casks scoured and filled. The bustle of leave-taking had established itself in the *Georgette*. No one seemed to regret the departure—least of all, she thought, the convicts, strictly guarded during the length of the stay in port, because of the fear of an escape overside.

The ship's officers and company had no great love of the town; it lacked the mystery and heathenish splendour of the trading-posts of the East, nor did the rocky, arid scenery recall any memories of the homeland. They met here a sense of isolation which they feared; the grey-green vegetation was unfamiliar, and there persisted a lonely feeling among them that this was the last outpost of the known world. Between the Cape and the South Pole stretched the ocean, and nothing more. Among the sailors there was a superstitious dread of sailing down into those southern seas. The longest stretch of the voyage still faced them, and now, with the hour of quitting the Bay drawing near, there was an atmosphere of urgency to have it over and done with. Thinking about it she wondered if it could have been this cloud of forlornness and desolation which had swamped one of the hands, Timothy Brown, last night with a melancholic drunkenness. No one could be certain if his fall overboard was accidental or deliberate. The longboat was launched immediately, but he was already gone. He had slipped down into the dark waters of the Bay without a single cry. When the news of his drowning ran through the ship, the women in the holds became unmanageable, shrieking and shouting foul language, believing that Brown had gone overboard rather than face the horror of the voyage ahead. This morning five of the women, the worst offenders, were in irons.

Sara's thoughts were distracted by further shouts from below, and she stood on tiptoe to lean farther over the side. A furious sort of quarrel seemed to be going on between two of the boatmen, but not being able to understand what they were saying, she lost interest.

Suddenly Andrew touched her hand to draw her attention; he pointed downwards towards the livestock.

"I've bought my share in that, Sara."

She answered. "I expected that you would. You'll sell it for a good profit in Port Jackson."

He shook his head, although she wasn't looking at him, but still staring down at the loading.

"It's not for sale. I'm keeping it for myself. I'm going to apply for a grant of land in New South Wales, and farm there."

She dropped back on her heels, turned and looked at him with astonishment. "Farm . . . You? A sailor!"

"I wasn't a sailor all my life. I was brought up by a Scotsman who was the best farmer in his district—one doesn't forget the sort of things that have been preached at you like the Bible."

She shook her head "But . . . leave the sea and take up farming? Why . . . ?"

"Because," he said, "I want to stay in New South Wales and marry you."

She took a step backward, and her mouth fell open a trifle.

"Andrew," she said faintly, "have you gone mad?"

"I expect I have!" he retorted. "You've driven me crazy—

witch! I don't sleep nights thinking about you. And I keep my watches like a drunken fool. I can tell you it's been hell! Sara, will you promise to marry me, and let me have my peace back again?''

"Marry you? Oh, Andrew . . . !''

He brought his hand down with an impatient slap on the bulwark. "Don't pretend you haven't guessed that I'm in love with you! The whole ship must know it by this time.''

"In love with me . . . perhaps. But have you forgotten that I'm on this ship as a convict?''

"I haven't forgotten that—of course I haven't. But these things can be arranged. If I ask permission to marry you, I don't see any difficulty about Governor Phillip granting you a pardon. He has the power to do it, and, if he doesn't—I'll marry you just the same, and then he'll be forced to assign you to me as a housekeeper until your sentence expires.''

She turned her eyes away from him, looking across the brilliant stretch of water. She said slowly, "It can't be as simple as you make it sound.''

"It's completely simple! We have to take our chance—we have to do what hasn't been done before. I'm going to marry you, Sara. I'm going to make you free!''

She made no answer.

"Well?'' he said, finally.

She shook her head. "But I don't see how . . .''

"You don't see how!'' The words broke from him with an undertone of irritation. "I've told you how it can be managed. All we have to do is to be firm about it. Everything will fall into place. When we're married we can settle all the difficulties.''

Turning, she answered him heatedly. "But it's when we're married that the difficulties arise. Don't you see that? Just try to think of the future, Andrew—with an ex-convict wife. And your children . . .'' Her voice dropped. "My dear,'' she said patiently, "see it sensibly. It wouldn't work.''

He took a deep breath. "But this is a new country we're going to—it's a whole new world! There'll be ways of settling the conventions to suit ourselves. Forget about the rules of society that apply in England. In the colony there are none—or very few. In a new country we make the rules ourselves. It's been like that with America—why not New South Wales?''

He grew excited; his face sharpened with eagerness. "It's an adventure, Sara! It's something to fix your whole mind and heart to. If I had you with me, there's nothing I couldn't do. Nothing! Are you worried that I'd fail? I have some money invested in the East India Company—I'll withdraw it, and that will be enough to start us. It's not a fortune, certainly—but it's a beginning.

"What do you say, Sara?" he said earnestly. "Will you chance it with me? There could be wealth at the end of it— perhaps for our children. There's the excitement of a new country, and a new life for both of us.

"You'll share everything I have. It's not a great deal I offer you. I'm a plain man—a sailor, a farmer, and something of a gambler. Is that enough? Will you have me?"

She answered wildly, "If it were just a question of this year—or next year—I'd say 'yes.' But marriage is for the rest of our lives. What about the time when that adventuring blood of yours has cooled down, and you've farmed as many acres of this new land as you can count, and you've achieved everything you ever dreamed of achieving? Are you going to look at me then and tell yourself that I'm the one thing in your bright world that doesn't fit? Whatever pardon I might get from Governor Phillip, I'll always be known as an ex-convict. When you make your fortune, can you stomach my past along with it?"

Suddenly he smiled, and an expression of tenderness and joy came into his face. "My darling Sara, I'll stomach it all! Your past, and your future as well. I'll make you the most envied ex-convict in the world! You'll be so gloriously happy, so much a queen in your own home that every other woman will wish she were an ex-convict as well!"

A hot flush sprang to her cheeks. "You're laughing at me, Andrew!"

"Sweet Sara, I'm not laughing! I'm merely telling you how foolish you are. Doesn't it tempt you to consider that I could give you back all that empty respectability your heart's yearned after ever since you ran away from your blasted rectory?"

She said, in a low voice, "I'd rather stay a convict than have you look at me ten years from now, and know that you regretted marrying me."

"Sweetheart!" he said gently. "Give me the ten years, and let me show you what I'll make of them. Will you?"

"I . . . I don't know."

He frowned. "Haven't I a right to something more positive than that?"

"Andrew . . ." she said hesitantly. "Wait until we reach Botany Bay. You'll have had time to think about it more than once by then. Perhaps you'll find the idea of a convict wife isn't so attractive to you."

She swung round, making to leave him, but he reached out and caught her hand, bowing over it slightly, and pressing it to his lips.

"It's a very long voyage to Botany Bay," he murmured. "Before we're half-way there, I'll have you seeing all this as I do."

He let her go then, watching as she made her way, with her erect, even walk, across the deck to the companion-way. His face was taut with excitement and passion. The cries of the animals and the shouts of the men below seemed to swell to an unbearable tumult. He straightened himself, and turned to face the stares of the men who had witnessed the scene.

After leaving Andrew on the deck. Sara went below immediately to the Ryders' cabin. Julia turned expectantly as she entered.

"What is it, Sara?"

For the moment Sara didn't answer. She closed the door behind her, and stood with her back pressed firmly against it. She was breathing quickly and Julia couldn't tell whether it was with excitement or anger.

"Andrew Maclay has asked me to marry him," she said at last.

Julia drew in a sharp breath. So, she thought, it had finally come, this situation for which she had waited. And not altogether in the way she had expected.

"And what answer did you give him?" she asked quietly.

Sara lifted her chin higher. "I told him to consider it until we reach Botany Bay. He'll know by then if he still wants a convict as a wife."

"And if he has changed his mind?" Julia questioned.

Sara shrugged her shoulders slightly. "In that case, he'll go off to the East when the ship sails again. If he's still of the same opinion, he'll stay where he is and take up farming."

Julia regarded the other sharply. She didn't like it when Sara assumed this air of unconcern in a matter of such importance to her.

"Sara, you're not fooling me any more than you're fooling yourself!" she cried. "This is what you wanted. You've worked for this. You've no intention of letting him go—so why, in heaven's name, can't you give him a proper answer?''

Sara took a step forward. She had dropped her defiance, and now looked unsure of herself. Her face was troubled.

"I *will* let Andrew go, if he doesn't want to go through with it. I won't hold him, if I find he's changed his mind.''

"He won't try to back out," Julia said. "He's in love with you—everyone knows that. And if he has asked you to marry him, he means to go through with it.''

Sara flared into life again. "But it's an impossible marriage! I'm a *convict*—and he doesn't seem to realise what that means. He has all sorts of high-blown notions of making his own rules of convention in the colony. He thinks I'll fit in. He thinks he can make me acceptable!" She was passionate in her outburst.

Julia turned away. She sat down at the dressing-table, and let her hands rest idly in her lap. There was enough of an element of trouble in this situation to make a cautious woman draw back—but Julia was beginning to realise, with a mild feeling of astonishment, that, after all these years of placid married life, at heart she had never been a cautious woman. She considered the two young people. Andrew Maclay was nobody's fool, and Sara could match him in spirit and shrewdness, one not out-reaching the other. Supposing she encouraged this marriage? If she were openly to show her trust and respect for Sara, it could be made much easier for Governor Phillip to grant her a pardon. It might be a dangerous thing to do—interfering in the lives of two people who must make their own strange decision. Yet the idea excited her. She saw this marriage as a desperate adventure—it was bold and daring, and it appealed strongly to her. She leaned forward, tilting the mirror so that she might see Sara's reflection. They would be a good pair for a new country, she decided.

She swung around and rose to her feet.

"Sara, I think you must accept Andrew's offer. He doesn't think it's an impossible proposition, and I don't either,''

For a while neither spoke; but Julia, watching Sara's face, saw it soften, and then the excitement came back into her eyes. For the first time, also, she fancied she saw the beginning of tears there.

Chapter Five

Since rounding the tip of Van Dieman's Land, whose mountains had risen coldly out of the southern ocean, the *Georgette* had followed the eastern edge of the new continent for some six or seven hundred miles. This was the *Terra Australis* of the early navigators' maps—the coast which Cook had charted, the cliffs and inlets that were the fringe of an unknown world. At sunset on the first of October, 1792, the look-out sighted the giant headlands, a mile apart, at the entrance to Port Jackson. The *Georgette* hove to, and waited for the morning light before she attempted the passage through the channel of deep water between them.

All on board, the crew, the convicts, the four passengers, had endured an experience of utter isolation; they had survived, and were now trying to forget it. The weather, almost from the time of leaving the Cape, had been vile. They headed diectly south, nearing the Antarctic Circle, then steering a course sharply east to round the promontory of Van Dieman's Land. Few of them escaped sickness; they were all cold, suffering in this last sting of the Southern winter. Supplies of fresh food were consumed too rapidly, and they faced the deadly round of meals of salt pork, The livestock fared badly; some of it died. They had seen whales, and giant albatrosses that circled the ship steadily, dropping below the bulwark and appearing again as the *Georgette* rose and fell in the heavy seas. Their belongings had been soaked by the waves breaking inboard, and with the convicts' quarters awash there was no way of stemming the constant streams of cursing and abuse. There was a good deal of drinking among the officers, and they quarrelled frequently, bickering over petty affairs, gambling listlessly and complaining of each other. The strain grew worse as the journey lengthened, and rations of food and water grew smaller. But somehow, through all this, they managed the unvarying routine of running the ship, keeping her on a course that was always farther south and farther east, plodding on into unknown seas, constantly touched by the knowledge and dread of their isolation. Fear, as tangible and real as the foul weather itself, hung over them; no one spoke of it—it declared itself in their indulgences in drink, and their stupid, meaningless quarrels.

But there was one incident of the voyage which they would not forget. The *Georgette* was two weeks out of the Bay when the first faint rumour of mutiny among the convicts ran through her, like some soft and eerie piping. An Irishman, Patrick Reilly, transported for life, was the informer; he gave the information to Roberts when he was brought before him, threatened with punishment for insubordination. Reilly's warning was ominous; none knew, nor could guess, what desperate courage and daring the convicts might have gained from their misery and wretchedness. A thorough search for weapons revealed nothing more than a few knives, Yet the unease refused to die. Common sense told the ship's officers that these men, weakened from bad food and confinement, with disease and the threat of scurvy among them, could achieve little in the way of effective mutiny—but the fear persisted. Privately, each wondered if perhaps it might be he who would have the watch when the outbreak occurred, if it might be he who was to feel the sudden stab of the knife, hear the helmsman's warning cry. It was obvious to all that a rebellion on board must necessarily be short-lived, but even that knowledge was of little help. They each felt that he himself would be the one to die as a gesture to mark its beginning.

The sense of crisis oppressed the ship for a week before the climax. It came when the nerves of every man on the *Georgette* were taut with waiting, and even the faintest stir, which might be considered out of the ordinary, was enough to cause a mad and hot-headed panic. It occurred because one of the prisoners, sullenly fighting the pains of dysentery, was gripped in his sleep with hysterical nightmare. He screamed, and continued to scream—the piercing sounds shattered the silence of the watchful, darkened ship. The unnerved guards took this as the signal for the mutiny; they fired without aim into the blackness of the convict quarters. There was shouting and confusion and the glaring flash of shot. Four men were cut down before reason told the guards to halt.

Three of these were dead by the morning; the fourth lingered a day longer. They were dropped overside in their canvas swathing without the usual line-up of convicts to witness the ceremony, and if mutiny had ever been planned aboard the *Georgette*, its spirit died with them. The guards were punished as a token of discipline, though the feeling running through the entire company was that these two had been the unfortunate instruments of the wider, deeper fear which possessed the rest.

But other thoughts claimed them when the peaks of the mountains of Van Dieman's Land thrust themselves out of the ocean. The Georgette turned north again, and the breezes grew warmer; at times the spring sunshine was hot. They watched the coastline of the continent warily. It revealed nothing beyond long, curving beaches, and vegetation of grey and indefinite greens. Those who had not seen it before—that was everyone except Brooks—reserved judgment. The ship's company had hailed the sight with relief, reckoning among themselves how soon now they would be free of their troublesome cargo, and sailing again towards more congenial trade with India and China.

II

In the wardroom Andrew stacked the cards and leaned back in his chair. His glance flicked briefly over the other three men, Harding, Brooks, and Wilder, who sat with him.

"Well, gentlemen, I'm afraid I'll have to withdraw. I'm on watch in fifteen minutes."

They said nothing; Wilder shifted in his chair and half-stifled a yawn; Harding fidgeted with his cigar. Watching them, the ghost of a smile touched Andrew's lips.

"A lively lot, you are!" he remarked, to no one in particular. "Are none of you going to wish me well? This is the last watch I shall stand at sea in the *Georgette*—it's the end of my commission with the East India Company."

Still no one spoke, and the silence grew noticeably heavy. As Andrew looked at each in turn, their eyes avoided his.

"Well," he said, "I see you think it's wiser to say nothing, when you believe a man is about to ruin his life in one mad act of folly." He shrugged. "Perhaps you're right. A madman never listens to advice."

Then he bent over the score. The silence continued while he made his calculations.

Finally he straightened, passing the slip of paper to Harding.

The first officer noted the total with a resigned air; his lips moved visibly as he checked Andrew's figures. At last he nodded slowly, handing on the paper to Brooks, who sat on his left.

"Your run of luck never seems to come to an end, Maclay,"

he said wearily. "I'm afraid this game leaves me still considerably in your debt."

Brooks made no comment; he merely nodded and passed the paper on to Wilder. The other took it disinterestedly, then frowned and sat up abruptly as he saw the total.

"I can't owe you as much as this, Maclay!"

"It's not all from tonight's game," Andrew said. "You don't forget that you've had steady bad luck since we left the Cape? That's the total amount you owe me."

"And you expect me to pay this before we leave Port Jackson?"

"Naturally." Andrew turned from Wilder to include the other two. "I've enjoyed your company and your play, gentlemen—but this is undoubtedly the end of it. Within the next few days I'll be leaving the ship, and staying on in New South Wales. You all continue the voyage. None of us can say when, if ever, we'll meet again."

Wilder said, "But damn it—you know I can't pay as much as this immediately! I've put all the money I could spare into cargo to sell here and in the East."

Andrew's expression didn't alter as he listened to Wilder. He flicked the cards between his fingers, appearing not to take any notice of the others. He knew they were each waiting for him to answer, but he was in no hurry to come to terms with Wilder—let him have a few moments longer to consider his position, and to wonder how he was going to find the money. Andrew saw that a frown of impatience was beginning to gather on Harding's forehead. He stopped playing with the cards, and turned to Wilder.

"Part of your cargo is in livestock, isn't it? I seem to remember three cows and eight hogs."

"Yes," Wilder said.

"Then." Andrew said quietly, "I'll accept the livestock in payment for the debt."

"Oh, no!" Wilder answered quickly. "I can't agree to that. I may get a better price from the Commissary than the value of this debt."

Andrew shrugged. "That is, of course, your own risk. You may also be offered a lower price for them."

He drew a fresh sheet of paper towards him, and made some quick calculations on it. When he was finished he pushed it across the table to Wilder.

'The last record we have of prices in the colony is a year out of date. But, reckoning on those prices, the value of your livestock falls short of the debt.''

Wilder sat staring at the figures in silence. Harding was leaning forward in his chair now, watching the faces of both the younger men.

Andrew said, ''As it stands, you're the gainer on the transaction, Wilder. But when we get into Port Jackson tomorrow, you may find that the market value of the livestock has gone up—in which case you're the loser.''

Abruptly he banged the table with his closed fist. ''Will you gamble on it? I may as well warn you now that once I leave this table tonight I'll expect repayment of the debt in full—even if I have to take part of your cargo for the East as well.''

Wilder flushed angrily. ''You push this settlement as no gentleman would, Maclay.''

''I don't expect to do business in this colony like a gentleman,'' Andrew said sharply. ''Have you ever noticed how very few gentlemen make money?''

He flicked the cards with his thumb again. ''Come, now—take the offer or leave it—I must go on watch.''

Wilder glanced from Harding to Brooks, but their expressions gave him no help. He turned to Andrew. ''Very well,'' he said sullenly, ''I accept.''

''Done!'' Andrew permitted himself a faint smile, reaching for more paper. ''Now—perhaps you'll be good enough to sign a bill of transfer?'' He bent over the paper and began to write.

Wilder's lip curved contemptuously. ''I see you don't waste any time.''

''No,'' Andrew answered without looking up. ''I haven't decided to settle here in order to waste time.''

Wilder didn't reply. The scratch of the quill then was the only sound in the room until Harding, after clearing his throat carefully, spoke.

''Would you also be willing to settle for livestock for the amount I owe you, Maclay?''

Andrew raised his head only for a second. ''Certainly, sir.''

Brooks pushed back his chair, and gripping the edge of the table, swung on the two back legs. It was a rocking motion which shook the table. ''Well, it seems that I'm the only one with a debt modest enough to settle out of hand . . . I'll see that you have it before you leave the ship, Maclay.''

Andrew nodded. ''Thank you, Brooks.''

Brooks got to his feet. "Only once before," he said, "have I ever known anyone with such devilish luck at cards. *He* won himself a fortune, and drank himself to death with it." He leaned over towards Andrew. "I sincerely hope you may achieve the first, without the second."

Andrew stopped writing, and laid down the quill, staring up at Brooks. Suddenly Brooks thrust out his hand; Andrew took it readily.

"Good luck to you, Maclay! I'm an older man than you—and I couldn't do what you intend doing. But I envy you your courage."

The bill of transfer was signed, and Andrew went to take his watch. Wilder, Brooks, and Harding were left staring at each other; Brooks sat down again, and began to drum with his fingers on the table. Wilder's eyes ran over Andrew's columns of figures for the second time.

"Well," he said, "he got a bargain on that deal."

Harding stirred lazily. "I don't know that you're right. None of us can tell what price the livestock will fetch in Sydney. It's as much of a gamble for him as for you. Perhaps, after all, he'll be the loser."

Wilder said, "I still think it was a shabby thing to do. He pressed an unfair advantage."

Brooks shrugged. "It seems to me he's entitled to ask for gambling debts to be settled before he leaves the ship. After all, the livestock's worth more to him in the colony than the money."

"Oh, you can be calm—you haven't lost much to him." Suddenly Wilder screwed up the paper petulantly. "I'll wager she put him up to it."

"Who?"

"That woman—Sara Dane. I know her sort well—sharper than a monkey, and always with an eye to a bargain."

Brooks gave a chuckle. "Then they should be an excellently matched pair. It's the sort of combination which makes wealth quickly."

"Oh, she'll do that all right," Wilder said. He straightened out the paper, and was beginning to tear it gloomily into tiny fragments. "She'll always get whatever she wants—either by sheer greed, or by being suitably demure at the right time. Look how she got hold of Maclay himself! I wonder what story she told him to make him believe she wasn't a thief."

Harding spoke; his tone was heavy and thick with the amount of madeira he had taken since supper. He gestured vaguely towards the door. "I'm sorry for Maclay. I think he's ruined himself by this alliance. Supposing the farming fails, as it may very well do? Can he bring an ex-convict back to present to his family at home? And if it succeeds—can he mix with the sort of people he's used to with her in the background?"

Brooks yawned, and stood up for the second time. "I don't profess to be a prophet—but I've an idea that Maclay and the girl may surprise us all. That is," he added, "if we ever hear of them again."

Wilder said nothing. He swept the pieces of paper to the floor with a single angry gesture.

III

While Andrew sat in the wardroom bartering livestock for gambling debts, Sara remained still and wakeful upon her cot. A feeling of disquiet possessed her; it seemed to chill even the blood in her veins. The sounds of the ship came to her—the creak and strain of the timbers; wind, like a constant song up in the rigging, the patter of feet on the deck above her head. She listened awhile to the wind, knowing that this, more than anything else, was the reason for her disturbance; tonight it blew off the unknown shore that tomorrow would emerge into a land which was to confine her, possibly, for the rest of her life.

All she was certain of in the future was her marriage to Andrew. Since the day in Cape Town when he had made his proposal, he had ridden coolly over any doubts she had. He wouldn't even allow her to voice them. Everyone on board knew that they were to be married when they reached the colony. Few approved, but no one was wholly disinterested. But there was nothing she could do to alter their opinions; she had to accept the situation as it stood.

Sara had no fears that she and Andrew were not well suited. They had spent many hours discussing the life they planned, the prospects of settling and farming in the great, empty land. She realised that he had no boldness of vision that did not meet an answer in herself; there was nothing he might dare that she was not prepared to dare with him.

She stirred restlessly, suddenly impatient for the coming day. The excitement she had tried to hold down seized her; under the blankets she clenched her hands. She *would* make Andrew a good wife! She'd give him reason to be proud of her. They would have children who would grow up in importance and prestige in the new colony. He had promised her land and her own servants to fill the hungry need in her heart for respect. She knew that one day she would have dignity and graciousness in her life; she would wipe out the memory of the years of patronage.

When at last she slept, her sleep was heavy and dream-filled.

PART TWO

Chapter One

The following morning the *Georgette* sailed through the heads guarding the entrance to Port Jackson, and dropped anchor in Sydney Cove. The sun was bright and hot; points of light glanced sharply off the waters of the harbour. Those on board rested their eyes gratefully on the soft colour of the trees that stretched their grey-green fuzz far into the distance of oddly-shaped inlets and bays. There was a quiet, aloof beauty about it.

But the settlement itself offered no attraction. The convicts had built a town of mud and daub huts on the shores of Sydney Cove, with a crude, whitewashed Government House sitting atop a hill overlooking it. A few brick houses were dotted among the huts, but their harsh straight lines heightened the look of dejection about them. A barracks, a hospital, a public store-house, and a bridge over the one stream—that was the extent of this newest of His Majesty's settlements. Here and there garden patches were laid out, but they were, most of them, no more than hopeful gestures. The efforts to till and sow the land were half-hearted; the soil was poor. Drought withered the crop, then the rains washed it away. Food was the crying need, but the sunbaked earth did not yield quarter enough. The livestock were lean as they grazed on the sparse, spikey vegetation.

Andrew Maclay found the Port Jackson settlement a place of misery. He was taken aback by his first sight of it. It was squalid in its poverty, and haunted by the now-familiar figures in their filthy rags. Here the constant threat of the chain-gang and the lash ruled; there was no law but that of punishment and hunger, Frantic for food, the convicts stole one another's rations, and broke into the public stores—in the famished colony the theft of food was punishable by death. They were ill and weak—and they died easily. Some, in utter despair, broke away into the sly, unfriendly forest—and perished in the baffling green maze, or staggered back, exhausted and starved, They muttered among themselves that only the naked black man, to whom this barren country belonged, could find a living for himself among those gaunt gum-trees and the hard, straggling foliage.

The metallic clank of the chain-gangs greeted Andrew wherever he went. He hated the sight of the women—haggard wretches, with hopeful eyes that followed him about. They prostituted themselves for food, and the dusty tracks between the huts swarmed with their illegitimate children. There was a certain charm about the children, vigorous and healthier, even under the starvation rations, than their counterparts in England—but the thought of settling within sight of their squalid homes disheartened him.

A week after the *Georgette* anchored he took a boat with James Ryder up the river to the colony's second settlement at Parramatta.

He found the beginnings of a planned town there. The land was more fertile than that at Sydney; the country around had a softer, kindlier appearance, laid out rather like English parkland. His spirits rose, and a fever of planning seized him. He listened to Ryder's careful evaluation of the place—it was a ready market-centre for three tiny outlying villages, Toongabbie, Prospect, and Ponds, and it was only sixteen easy miles boat journey from Port Jackson, and the joining road improved with each year of the settlement. Together they watched the market-day barter between officer, soldier, settler, and convict of the country's few commodities—fish, grain, livestock, and clothing. It was a brisk affair while goods were available; a Government clerk registered all that was brought in for sale or barter, and chits from the Commissary served as currency. This small township had a feeling of permanency about it. Ryder wasted no time in his survey of the district. With an experienced farmer's eye he examined the rich soil of the river banks, and was impatient to return to Sydney to arrange for a grant of land.

But from the officers and settlers—the settlers were mostly emancipated convicts working small farms of their own—with whom he talked, Andrew heard tales of yet another river. This one, far greater than the Parramatta, rose in the mountains in the west, taking a sweep north-east to an outlet in Broken Bay, an anchorage eight miles above Port Jackson. Governor Phillip himself had explored it and named it after Lord Hawkesbury. Here, they said, the soil was richer than anywhere else in the colony, and Phillip had it earmarked for the free settlers he hoped would be sent from England. The vision of the great river burned like a slow fever in Andrew's veins.

He listened with not very great interest to Ryder's planning—the exact position he wanted his grant, how close to the river, how close to the road, which would take his produce either to Parramatta or Sydney. The days passed, and he made no similar plans himself. Ryder sensed that something troubled Andrew, and pressed him to talk. By this time the men had grown closer to each other, bound together by the strangeness and difficulties which surrounded them—Andrew found himself talking wildly of his dream. He wanted to make a journey to the other river, to see for himself the rich, fertile land, the lush river-flats coated with the silt that the floods brought down from the mountains. He wanted, if it were possible, to settle there.

Listening to it all at their camp by the river, Ryder shook his head doubtfully. "Perhaps you can do it, Andrew—but they say the country is rough going between here and the river. If you settled, you'd have to make some sort of track to bring up supplies." He gestured to imply all that went with such a venture.

Andrew protested quickly, "Yes—but if the soil . . ."

Ryder nodded, smiled secretly as he took out his snuff-box. It was always so with young men—the land they couldn't see was always richer, the river broader, the game better. He thought of his own choice, the gentle river, the peaceful acres which wouldn't be difficult to clear, and he was glad that the dream of the Hawkesbury hadn't smitten him also.

Andrew stayed behind at Parramatta when Ryder went back by boat to Sydney. He turned with energy to organising a party for the journey to the Hawkesbury, and he found himself unexpectedly helped by Subaltern Berry, a young man who confessed that he was dying of boredom, and had an itch for exploration that no one else would gratify. He belonged to the New South Wales Corps, a military force which had been specially raised in England for the new colony—and he had friends among official-dom who listened with sympathy to Andrew's plans, and helped outfit the expedition. They set off with a native as guide—Andrew, Berry, three convicts, and provisions for ten days. The country was wild and exotic; the warmth of spring had turned the pointed leaves of the gums red—a fiery tinge that coloured the bush with fantasy. Yellow and white flowers mingled their scents with subtle, elusive smells of the trees, adding to their feeling that they were striking into a mad, new world. They followed the guide along tracks visible only to his own keen eyes. There was no trace of softness in all this beauty, there was no trace of bounty in it for man or plant which was not its native. The tall eucalyptus trees, barks shining white in the sun, were endless and aloof. The going was hard and yet the fascination of the country compelled them to keep on.

They reached Phillip's farthest point of exploration, Richmond Hill, in a thunderstorm of sudden, tropical violence. The naked black man hunched on the ground, his face, hidden beneath a mane of matted hair and beard, was pressed into his knees while he strove to control his panic. A curtain of rain cut off the little group on the hill; long, brilliant flashes of lightning revealed for a moment the grey-brown waters of the river below. The storm did not last. It moved on abruptly, leaving them once more in sunshine. The mountain range, blocking off the west, seemed very close; the air was as sharp and clear as glass. The valleys were filled with grey mist and the rising smell of the trees and the rain-splattered dust. When the hush settled again, the guide rose and beckoned them to a descent of the hill where they would find level ground and make camp.

Andrew lingered behind under the dripping trees, his eyes wonderingly on the flat land to the south and east. This was what he would describe to Sara, he told himself—this lovely stretch of fertile, heavily-wooded country with the great river twisting down from the mountains. There were places here where he could already see his house built—places on high ground where the floods, if they came, could not reach. With the land cleared, there was pasture richer than anything he had yet seen; as he stood there he slowly raised his clenched hand, opened it, and looked at the soil that he had scooped up close to the river bank. Soil like this would give him grain so heavy it would bend with its own weight; he raised his head again and envisaged the fenced fields, with their crops ready for harvest. It was a silent, unin-habited world he gazed at, full of mystery, and perhaps unexpected dangers, and yet he knew that Sara, when he told her of it, would choose this green, unknown valley, rather than the sub-dued acres of the Parramatta district.

He arrived back in Sydney exactly three weeks after the date of landing, and found that the Ryders were on the point of moving all their belongings by boat to Parramatta; they were going to a temporary hut on a fine tract of land just outside the township. Julia, he saw immediately, had got over her first dismay at the sight of the dismal settlement at Sydney Cove. With characteristic quietness and determination she had set about making the most of what the country had to offer. She behaved now as if feeding a family on salt pork had been a lifetime's occupation.

But the greatest change was in Sara. She had gained confidence in her position as the future wife of a free settler. There was a vigorous life in her he had never seen before. She was adapting herself well, and now, for the first time, he witnessed her personality flowering without the restraint placed upon it by the confines of the *Georgette*. Her smile of welcome caused the hunger for her to flare in his heart. He kissed her with such longing that the couple of weeks' separation might easily have been years. She responded warmly, and then held him away, demanding news of the trip inland. He told her of the valley he had seen, and the deep, curving river.

She listened without interruption, and at the end she said slowly, "This is where you want to settle, Andrew?"

He answered her fervently. "Oh, my darling, yes! Wait till you see it for yourself!" He laughed in his excitement. "It's rich land there, Sara—rich and green! And it's mine! I can have the pickings before anyone else even sees it!" He demanded of her soberly, "Could you face it? You'd be there alone."

But he knew, even as he asked the question, that there was no fear in her eyes—no hint of timidity about the desolation she must know she faced. Her calmness reassured him.

"Perhaps Governor Phillip doesn't want settlers there yet," she said, a little anxiously, "Perhaps he won't give you a grant."

He drew her to him, his lips pressing away the frown on her brow. "Phillip has a whole continent to give away," he murmured. "He won't miss a slice on the Hawkesbury."

"You'll see him soon?"

'Tomorrow—if he'll see me." He had taken her in his arms. The warmth of her body excited him. "I want two things from Phillip—a grant on the Hawkesbury's banks, and a pardon for my wife. And then I'll show them what sort of living is to be made in New South Wales!"

He spoke recklessly, his emotions stimulated by the closeness of Sara, For a moment or two his desire for her mounted. He held her to him with his eyes closed. And then, as if she shared his emotion, her arms tightened about him.

"Let it be soon, Andrew," she whispered. "If Phillip should refuse . . ."

"He won't."

Suddenly she looked into his face. The frown had come back to her brow. "Andrew," she said urgently, "promise me you'll marry me as soon as possible. Don't wait for a house. I'll go with you anywhere. I'll . . ."

"Sara, darling!" he said, his lips breaking her words. "I won't even wait till tomorrow. I'll try to see the Governor this afternoon."

Andrew faced His Excellency, Governor Phillip, across a table stacked with paper, and gazed with a feeling of faint awe at the man who had pulled the colony through these first five, heart-breaking years. He was an unprepossessing figure, with beaked nose, and only of middle height; his skin had the yellowing tinge of illness. It was now common knowledge in the ragged settlements he ruled that he had been given leave of absence because of ill-health, and would probably sail for England in the *Atlantic*, at present anchored in the harbour.

From the beginning he offered no encouragement to Andrew to choose his site on the Hawkesbury.

"I know it's excellent soil, Mr. Maclay, but the help and protection of the Government cannot extend so far. You will be quite alone, without even a road to join you to Parramatta. You're in danger from floods and natives who are possibly hostile—and in the winter you may not be able to get your food and supplies overland."

"I've studied all these difficulties. Your Excellency—and I still feel I can overcome them."

Phillip looked thoughtfully at the map spread before him on the table. "Believe me, Mr. Maclay, I *want* settlers there—it's the finest land in the colony, and we could well do with its produce. But the danger lies in your settling alone . . . if there were others with you . . ."

But he argued half-heartedly, and when Andrew pressed the point, gave in. Once the decision was made, Phillip behaved as if the objection no longer existed—he was now free to encourage the settlement of land he had first explored and marked down for the free men he wanted to farm the colony. He was generous in his offers of help. The Commissary was short of even the common necessities, but Phillip's orders would give Andrew whatever was available. On paper the requisition orders were handsome—a large grant of land, convict labourers, farming implements, seed. But Andrew knew the local conditions well enough to realise that he would be lucky if one-third of the supplies could be filled from the stock of the Commissary. He pocketed the signed orders with the same feeling that he would have pocketed a counterfeit coin—wondering if it had any purchasing power left.

When the maps of the Hawkesbury were pushed aside, the Governor folded his dry, thin hands and looked at Andrew unblinkingly. He told him in a clipped voice that he had left instructions with his successor that Sara Dane was to receive her pardon on the day she was married.

There was nothing cordial in his tone as he added: "My commission from the King enables me to grant pardons, Mr. Maclay. I allow myself to use this power in view of Mr. Ryder's testimonials of this woman—and the knowledge that she will pass completely into your care."

"Thank you, sir."

Andrew wished his words could have been warmer, but there was no mistaking the Governor's tone. Clearly, he didn't approve of the marriage. But his instructions were to encourage settlement, and in this case the only way it could be done was by permitting the marriage. He was giving his consent with authority's helpless shrug of the shoulders.

Andrew brought the interview to an end without waiting for the Governor to indicate that it was finished. On the veranda of the whitewashed Government House he paused, wondering if he would go back and argue Sara's case more forcefully. But his quick judgment of Phillip's character told him that the gesture would be futile. He slapped his hat on to his head, and stepped out into the sunshine, hot and resentful.

II

Andrew reached the site allotted him on the Hawkesbury after a long, tortuous journey. He made an encampment on the river bank—a small group of tents to house the twenty assigned convicts, two overseers, and four ex-convicts whose sentences had been remitted, and who had agreed to come with him for a wage, their food, and a daily ration of rum. From this beginning, he set about to clear the surrounding forest for the fields where he planned to sow his crops and the spot he had marked for his house. The axes swung and the trees fell rapidly, but still not quickly enough for him. His impatience was never satisfied.

In Parramatta they had shaken their heads over this impatience; they advised him to wait until there were other settlers to accompany him to the Hawkesbury. But he took no heed; he went ahead with his task of collecting the few available supplies, choosing his overseers, and finding extra labourers, He waited to help the Ryders and Sara with their move up-river from Sydney Cove to the new land at Parramatta, and he saw his own livestock penned along with James's, close to the hut where they would live until their house was ready. Then he made plans for moving of his own equipment to the Hawkesbury. He worked long hours—it was slow, exasperating work that met with endless frustrations and setbacks. The colony was short of every single item he needed—shoes and clothing for the convicts, cooking utensils, carpenter's tools, firearms for hunting, spades and axes for clearing the land. He endured tedious sessions of bargaining and bartering, fuming over each new delay and hold-up.

Following a hint from his friend, Berry, he sought out an ex-convict settled on a grant of land at Toongabbie, who exchanged him three axes for two gallons of rum, and another at Prospect who let him have two more for only one gallon. He didn't know where the axes came from, and didn't ask.

Berry expended himself in his willingness to help; he produced a carpenter of sorts, a man whose sentence had been remitted, and who was prepared to work on the Hawkesbury property for a guaranteed daily rum ration. Andrew realised that a carpenter, even a poor one, was a priceless find in this place which seemed to be without trained workmen of any kind. He guarded his prize greedily, already visualising the house this sullen, toothless man would build for Sara to live in. Fear that someone else might claim first rights on this emancipist galvanised him into action; he swore the man to secrecy and commenced the rum ration immediately.

He found that this high-pressure speed was necessary to get all he wanted. He had to be quick and ruthless. The constant sight of Sara was driving him on, urging him to decisions which, three months ago, would have seemed impossible. It seemed as if, overnight, his gambler's instincts had turned towards trade and barter—he sometimes smiled at the idea of himself so swiftly becoming a man of affairs.

When his provisions and gear were assembled at last, and the nerve-racking weeks of planning and scheming were over, he paid his final visit to the Ryders. He said goodbye to Sara, unwilling to leave her behind, and making no attempt to hide the impatience evident in all his actions these days.

He set out for the Hawkesbury on the first of December.

Through the long, hot days he worked as if he were driven by a demon—he was up at dawn with the convicts, and at night by the fire he was wakeful, planning after the rest of the camp slept. The clearing of the land was slow, yielding to them grudgingly, reluctantly giving up each acre that had never known movement other than the soundless tread of its own dark people. Occasionally he shot kangaroo and wild duck to vary the diet of salt pork. He made the most of the game while it was available, knowing that soon—as had already happened at the other settlements—it would retreat from the advance of the white man.

The days of unvarying routine spun out—his dreams were of the grey gums crashing down, and the astonished faces of the natives he sometimes saw standing stock-still and rigid on the edge of the new clearing. They were not hostile, but they never came nearer the camp than the sheltering outskirts of the forest. Neither the white man nor the black interfered with one another—Andrew's orders were that the blacks were never to be unduly noticed, and never molested.

He was not completely alone with his thoughts in his nightly watches by the fire. He found a companion in one of his overseers, Jeremy Hogan, an Irishman, transported for organising, with a minimum of discretion, new recruits for Wolf Tone's United Irishmen. He was young, twenty-six, and built like a giant. He had still a touch of laughter about his deep blue eyes that the convict transport had not stamped out. Andrew found it difficult to take Jeremy's politics seriously—he humoured him, delighted by the strange quirk of chance which brought this type of man to share his fire. They talked softly together in the dark, their eye on the bright, unfamiliar stars of the South. The sound of the river came continuously, like a patter of voices. Of the other's background, Andrew could learn almost nothing; there was, though, the obvious fact of education and breeding. He thanked his good fortune in having been assigned Jeremy Hogan, talking to him easily in the silence of their nightly camps, telling him without awkwardness of his cherished dreams, for the land over which they both toiled.

Each day a small portion of rum was allotted to the convict labourers. As long as they were assured of this, these men were prepared to work until they dropped; no threat of flogging or any other punishment meant as much to them as a suspension of the rum ration. With reluctant fascination he watched them lining up for the spirit, which was their only hope of forgetfulness. Their eyes and hands were greedy for the sight and feel of it, It was the spirits, he knew, which he had brought off the *Georgette,* that had done far more to bring him to his present position than any of the privileges ordinarily given to settlers. Rum was needed to make his men work; rum would bring the small comforts to make this sort of life possible for Sara. He calculated his store and found that it was dwindling fast. It was obvious that he must find some means to supplement it.

At first he felt his way cautiously, but as soon as the opportunity opened to give him not only rum, but other vital supplies, he took it without hesitation. He risked the money he had invested, the slice of land by the Hawkesbury River, even the hope of soon being able to marry Sara—everything he had he risked on the turn of a card. He played coolly, fully aware of the weight of his gamble. Sometimes he lost, but more often he won.

The officers of the New South Wales Corps were his mark. Since Governor Phillip's departure, the Corps had become supreme. Francis Grose, the Lieutenant-Governor, was steeped in militarism; he was strangely pliable in the hands of his officers, who, each in his turn, was given the position and authority to behave as a small despot. The civil courts had been closed in both Sydney and Parramatta, and a jury of six military officers and a judge-advocate now dispensed a rough justice to their own soldiers, the convicts, and the few private citizens. It was a world suddenly ruled by a select military elite, and Andrew found his way into its heart with a pack of cards.

He was accepted in the first place because he had held a commission with the East India Company. Although most of them were contemptuous of his plan to marry an ex-convict, they faced him readily enough over a table set with glasses and cards. He found the little bored groups willing to gamble on anything from five gallons of rum to a chit on the public stores for a frying-pan. As soon as he was quite certain of his place among them, he made frequent trips to Sydney and Parramatta almost with the sole motive of drifting into an evening's play at the barracks.

"He has the devil's luck!" they grumbled, disheartened, but playing on in the hope that his run of luck might turn. Whenever he was beaten he paid up calmly, and came back again the following night.

He played to a purpose which took him some time to achieve. He was impatient, but waited until the debts began to mount up heavily against his partners, and then he suggested that they should be cancelled by concessions for him in the trading-ring they had formed. Their monopoly methods were simple—they had permission from the Lieutenant-Governor to pool their credits in England and to buy the entire cargo of the occasional American ships which were beginning to appear in Port Jackson; they were allowed to charter ships to run to the Cape and the East for the purpose of their own trade. There was no single transaction in the colony from which one or another member of the redcoated ring didn't make his profit. The bartering power of rum was higher than anything else, and it flowed into New South Wales in an increasing stream. Andrew bought his right to share in the rum monopoly with his skill over a cardtable. He gained more and more ground with his friends in the Corps, until even the arrogant, black-haired John Macarthur, the leader of the trading-ring and the most ambitious, energetic man the colony possessed, no longer questioned his right to share the prized cargoes. Like the rest, Andrew bartered rum for convict labour, rum for food, rum for boots and loads of timber. His supplies were taken inland over the rough track to the Hawkesbury; he went with them light-heartedly, and worked, for a few weeks, as hard as two men on the clearing of his land. And then, when his stocks began to run out, he started back again for the barracks at Sydney and Parramatta.

The walls of his house rose slowly during the months of the autumn and early winter; the forest reluctantly yielded space to sow his crops and run his livestock. The progress was hardly measurable week by week, but at the end of May, Andrew judged that the house would be ready to live in before June was over. It was small—only four rooms, with a lean-to kitchen, whitewashed, half-furnished, and uncurtained, patterned exactly on the Ryder's new house. Sara, demanding to hear every detail, begged to be allowed to return with him to the Hawkesbury when he made the next trip. Remembering the loneliness and silence awaiting him by the great river, he was seized with impatience. He looked at her eager face, and suddenly knew that he could not wait any longer to have her there with him.

Chapter Two

The wedding took place in the Ryders' house on a bright, cold morning in June. There had been a frost the previous night, and the sun had scarcely broken it up by the time Sara entered the sitting-room for the ceremony. The sharp smell of the eucalyptus-leaves, which Julia had used for decoration, came instantly to her. James held the door open wide; his gloved hand reached out for hers. She took it, but stood still, aware of the stir her entrance had caused, pleased and reassured by the expressions she saw on the faces of the group waiting for her. She was wearing a gown of white silk brought from China, and paid for in rum; on her feet was a pair of embroidered slippers from Calcutta. She held herself erectly, outwardly calm, yet she sought Andrew's eyes with a sense of relief. Then, after that one brief pause, she went slowly forward to make her curtsy to the Lieutenant-Governor.

Julia was the only other woman present to listen to the words of the marriage service, read in the Reverend Richard Johnston's prim tones. The New South Wales Corps was well represented that morning, their red coats brightening the pale sunlight in the room. The guests, with the exception of the Ryders and Johnston, were mostly gambling partners of Andrew's. John Berry was there, and three other officers from the barracks. John Macarthur, whom Grose had put in charge of all public works in Parramatta, had surprisingly accepted the invitation; Grose himself, up from Sydney on a visit of inspection, had accompanied him.

But the colony's three women of note were absent. The clergyman's wife and Mrs. Macarthur had been invited, but both had declined on the flimsiest excuse. Mrs. Patterson, wife of the Corps' second-in-command, had also declined. Sara had not expected more or less than this. She had known how she would be regarded by that narrow clique of female society; she was not abashed by the snubs, and she carried her head stiffly and proudly among the circle of red coats.

The ceremony was short. Johnston had no great liking for either Sara or Andrew, and he wasted no undue sentiment over the duty he was called upon to perform. They were married just before noon, and left—Sara, Andrew, the overseer, Jeremy Hogan, and another convict overseer, Trigg, brought along to help with the baggage on the return journey to the Hawkesbury—after a gay meal of wild duck and roasted kangaroo meat. The wine, shipped from the Cape, was plentiful enough to loosen tongues, and as she changed from the silk dress into a new riding-habit, Sara could hear bursts of laughter from the narrow, simply-furnished livingroom. She imagined, with a smile which was half-bitter, half-amused, how these men would recount the tale of the ceremony they had just witnessed.

The Lieutenant-Governor led the group which streamed out on to the veranda to see the party mount, and most of them, in the heat of wine and good humour, seemed to have forgotten that this was no ordinary wedding. Sara made her last curtsy to Grose with a sharp feeling of thankfulness in her heart that, whatever his reason, he had chosen to come this morning. His presence had given the marriage the envied seal of official approval. She disliked the weak, indefinite character of Francis Grose, but for what he had done for her today, she knew she would never cease being grateful.

Sara had said her private farewell to Julia before they moved outside, and Julia kissed her softly. "Do write to me, Sara. I shall expect a letter each time Andrew comes to Parramatta—now you will write?"

Sara nodded, and her lips formed words which seemed stuck firmly in her throat. Impossible to thank Julia for the past months together—even for the strenuous efforts which had produced the wedding breakfast. From that first day on the *Georgette* they had grown steadily closer, Sara taking Julia's uncommon good sense to leaven her own impetuous nature, learning from her, copying her in certain ways. Their relationship was complete—still undemonstrative, it had gone deeply into each of them, and there was a comfortable assurance that it would always remain.

Suddenly Sara put her arms about Julia, hugging her fiercely. "I can't thank you—there isn't any use trying. Nor for all that I've had from you. But I've never loved another woman before if that counts for anything with you."

Then she drew back. "Well...that's enough," she said briskly, dabbing at the faint moisture that had appeared on her lashes. "I'm not going to make a fool of myself, and a show of you, Julia, for this handful of red-coats."

Then she stepped lightly out on to the veranda. Julia followed, smiling a little as she thought of Sara's words. Of course she hadn't loved a woman before—and she was nervous and rather reluctant to admit it. Men had been her whole world, and very skilfully she had made use of them. So mature she had appeared as she stood beside Andrew during the service, but she was still like a child in learning some things. Perhaps the last months had taught her more than she knew.

The watching group stayed together on the veranda until the little party disappeared from sight along the Parramatta Road. As she turned to go indoors again, Julia caught the tones of a familiar voice among Andrew's guests.

"...I didn't believe he'd have the nerve to marry her in the end. Still, it's done now. An admirable gesture, I'm sure. Let us hope the fellow won't find time to regret it."

II

When the dusk came they were still seven miles from the Hawkesbury. Andrew ordered the men to make camp beside the rough track which was their only road. He dismounted himself, and turned to lift Sara down. She fell stiffly into his arms; the long hours in the saddle, to which she was still unused, had wearied her almost beyond speech. Jeremy Hogan had spread a blanket for her on the ground; she staggered to it and sat down without a word.

The winter's night dropped down quickly after a short dusk. In that latitude the light never lingered in the sky. A bitter little wind blew in the tops of the trees, and touched Sara's cheeks sharply. The first stars came out, the big, overbright stars of the southern hemisphere. She shivered, moving closer to the fire which Jeremy was banking up. She sat still, gazing eagerly into the flames, and listening to the muted sounds of the men's voices.

They ate a meal of cold pork and bread by the firelight. Andrew uncorked the wine which James Ryder had given him. It was a strange wedding feast, the wine slowly warming in their hands, and the cold silence of the bush all around them. The starlight grew stronger, and the tree-barks were white and ghostly. There was a mournful, eerie feeling about the bush at night, aged and remote. By night it had no passion; it was secretive and sly.

Soon after the meal Trigg withdrew to his roll of blankets on the other side of the fire; it was arranged that Jeremy should wake him at two o'clock to take his turn at watching. When the overseer had moved off into the shadows of the spot where he had chosen to sleep, the other three drew into a new intimacy; it was the same sort of intimacy that Andrew and Jeremy had shared by the camp-fire on the Hawkesbury's banks.

Sara's fatigue had lessened. The wine and the cold wind had sharpened her senses, so that when the two men fell into talk, she watched Jeremy closely, seeking in his manner a clue to what her own relationship to him might be in the future. Her mind was already half made up about what she might expect—the smooth-tongued and barely disguised insolence of a gently-born man confronted with his master's wife, who had received her pardon only yesterday. She felt that he had done his own summing-up where she was concerned. He was no fool, and, for the present anyway, seemed prepared to serve her willingly enough. In that first hour, as she sat listening to them talk, Sara sensed that his intelligence and strength had won a kind of ascendancy over Andrew; she had a feeling of being shut out of their comradeship. She was hurt and a little piqued, yet she knew already Jeremy's worth to Andrew. She didn't want their intimacy broken; rather she wanted desperately to share it.

She looked at Jeremy, deciding that he must be made to serve her for her own sake—not because it was an order from Andrew.

And then, as if he guessed her thoughts, he raised his eyes and addressed her directly.

"Is it decided yet what you'll call the property, Mrs. Maclay?" He seemed amused as he gave her the title.

"My husband," she said, slyly emphasising the words, "wants to call it 'Kintyre.' It's a Scottish name."

"Kintyre . . ." He rolled the two syllables softly on his tongue. "Not so lovely as the name the natives give it. Still . . ." He shrugged and said lightly, "At least it can be spelled. These picturesque native names are impossible."

He stared at the fire. "Well . . . you're the first on the Hawkesbury—but they'll follow you. Within a year . . . a few months even, they'll be settling on your doorstep. A man is

113

never left alone for very long when he farms land like you've got. I doubt, though, if ever any of them will make up the start you've had."

Suddenly he laughed. "Thanks to rum you've got it!'

Andrew joined him in the laughter, not in the least embarrassed. "Thanks to rum, as you say—and the fact that his officers lead Grose round by the nose. Why shouldn't I also have what they're all getting? The man who doesn't belong in that circle might as well not be alive as far as advancement in the colony is concerned. As friends their tempers aren't always reliable—but I've no notion to become their enemy."

Jeremy glanced sideways at him. "There speaks a canny Scot—you'll prosper in the land, my friend."

He held up his glass. "A toast!" he announced. "A toast to the name of Maclay..." Then quickly he added, as if he had just recalled Sara's presence. "And to the mistress of Kintyre..."

They drank it solemnly beneath the full, bright stars.

Sara woke in the half-hour before dawn when the stars were fading. The tent-flap had been flung back, and she could see the sky, now more grey than black. The bush about the camp was very quiet; the wind seemed to have died. She stirred in Andrew's arms. He felt her move, and, without opening his eyes, he turned on his side and drew her closer. They lay under rugs of wallaby skins, the warmth of their bodies and their sense of relaxation defying the cold day breaking outside.

In the dim light she saw that his eyes had opened. His voice was drowsy.

"Too early yet for you to wake."

She smiled at him. "But I wanted to wake—do you understand that I just wanted to lie here, and be awake?"

"Little fool!" he murmured, "You'll learn differently."

Her head rested on his arm. He felt for her hand and drew it out from under the furs. He kissed each of her finger-tips in turn—and then he began to bite gently at them,

"Oh, woman..." he said softly. "You've tormented me! You've driven me mad for a whole year! I don't believe yet that I have you at last—sharing my *"mia-mia."*

"Mia-mia?" The words belonged to the liquid native tongue. She repeated them again, half-afraid, because Andrew had spoken them with such spell-binding tenderness. *"Mia-mia?"*

"It's the name the natives have for their bark huts. They

spread the earth floor of their *mia-mia* with kangaroo skins, and that is their marriage-bed—no more or less than ours.''

She sought his lips. "We have the most sumptuous marriage-bed in all the world, my love. We'll keep it just like this.''

They were quiet for a time, and then he said, "At the moment I possess all I ever dreamed of . . . I can see the stars dying, and I lie here on furs and listen for the wind . . . And in my arms I hold a woman like you—not submissive, Sara, but acquiescent . . . sharing my love as if you had always known it would be like this.''

"I have always known it, Andrew,'' she whispered, her mouth close to his. "Always.''

For a moment she was silent, then, "I'll be a trying wife for you. I'll need so much of your mind and your heart.'' Her words were suddenly fierce. "I'll make demands on you. You'll have to be everything to me—husband and lover, brother and father . . . everything!''

He put his lips close to her ear. "I'll be everything you want, Sara—so long as this doesn't alter. I want nothing more of you than to be able always to lie with you like this—and hold you like this.''

Then he kissed her, and his tones drifted towards passion. "Sara . . . Oh, Sara!''

The campfire was dead, and the daylight had not properly broken when Jeremy woke. He opened his eyes and lay quietly beneath the soft warmth of his kangaroo skins. Sleep still dulled his mind, and full consciousness came slowly. He remembered where he was, and the reason—and remembering, he turned to gaze at the tent where Andrew and his wife lay. He saw the open flap, and wondered if they were awake, murmuring in the intimacy of lovers—their words tender, for themselves alone. For the moment he knew completely the world they held within their arms, and he felt his flesh creep with longing to have a woman once more beside him, a woman whose lips would seek his willingly. Desperately he wanted again to bury his face in a woman's scented hair, and to lie and listen to her gentle breathing as she slept.

Without attempting to check his thoughts, Jeremy let them wander to scenes of the past . . . Irish skies, and mist, and lakes that spattered the country in silver and shadowed purple . . . Fine horses, beautiful women, and politics had been his playthings. He had used all of them dangerously; often merely for the delight of the danger. To this blackhaired man, lying still and wakeful in the early-morning cold, the names of his beloved beauties came flowing back to him. Horses and women mixed in his thoughts like a lovely dream ... Larry ... Black Fern ... Geraldine ... Rosalie ... He whispered them, moaning softly in his longing.

Then, with the advance of the daylight, the shrill, maddening laugh of the kookaburra rang out. *Gourgourgahgah*, the natives called it. It perched, its head and beak sharply outlined against the sky, on one of the highest branches of a tree above him. The mockery of its laugh scattered Jeremy's dreams. He was not in Ireland, and he had twelve years of his sentence still to serve. He was an assigned servant, he reminded himself—merely that, to the man who had been given charge over him, body and well-nigh soul. Dreams of beautiful women were not for him—instead he must endure this sense of desolation here in the camp in the bush, with the strong scent of the gum-leaves, and the wood-fire that had burned all through the night. He must lie and endure the knowledge of complete intimacy within the tent, and the thought of the golden-haired girl who had yesterday married Andrew Maclay, lying now in his arms, warm under the wallaby skins—the girl who only two days ago had been a convict like himself.

III

The house stood upon a gentle rise facing the river. Sara first saw it at noon, with the winter sun dazzling on its new white-wash, and its uncurtained windows turned blankly towards the mountains, A few trees had been left around it, and on the cleared ground of the slopes was the beginning of an orchard. It was a stark, raw-looking building, whose bricks had been carted up from the brick-fields at Sydney. There was no touch of vine or shrub to soften its outlines; its whiteness was harsh against the grey-green of the trees.

The sight touched Sara's heart strangely. She looked at it for a long time without speaking It was no more or less than Andrew had led her to expect—low, and one-storied, ugly and crude in its unfinished state, a wide veranda round it, with three or four unornamented steps. But this was the first house that had ever stood upon the Hawkesbury; only the frail bark of the natives' *mia-mia* had stood here before, The simplicity of the house was in a sense not unworthy of its setting.

She gazed up the slope with a mixed feeling of possession and pride. The first moment her eyes had fallen on this house, it had become her own—something to be loved and defended with every ounce of her will and power.

Without saying anything, and still without taking her eyes off the house, she gestured to Andrew beside her. He interpreted the vague movement swiftly, motioning to Jeremy behind.

"Go on ahead, Hogan. Tell Annie we've arrived. Mrs. Maclay will want hot water to wash in immediately."

Jeremy nodded and urged his horse into a trot, Trigg followed closely. The sounds of the horses were sharp in the noon hush of the bush.

Andrew dismounted and turned to lift Sara down. She stood stiffly on the uneven ground, letting her gaze move in wonder across the scene before her. It took in the great sweep of the cleared land, reaching down to the river; she saw the convicts' huts at the back of the house, and the railed-in enclosures for the livestock. The scars upon the virgin woods were raw and fresh, great, jagged holes torn in the blackman's territory to make way for the usurper's crops and cattle. She was keenly aware of the intrusion here in this wilderness; with not even a decent road to link it to the proper settlement, it was an undeniable fact. But she saw it as Andrew had seen it—land waiting to be taken, fertile land lying idle, disturbed only by the natives' hunting parties, skilful, hardy young men, moving soundlessly through the bush in the trail of the kangaroos. Every instinct bred in her tough childhood among the London lodging-houses revolted against the waste of good land. She had learned something of the thrift and hard-headedness of the Romney Marsh farmers when it came to assessing the value of land. She had seen their prosperity based on rich grazing for their sheep, and supplemented by smuggling. The sight of the broad river, and the wild acres still waiting beyond the clearings, touched off a fire of ambition in her. She clenched her hands in excitement, and under her gloves she could feel a prickle of sweat. The pulse in her throat leapt with a swift passion. In England, land had meant wealth. And here in this country land was given for the asking. There was wealth before her eyes in these miles of winter evergreens stretching as far as she could see—providing the gods were kind . . . providing the rain came in the right season, not too little, not too much . . . providing the river did not rise to sweep the crops away, and the fires did not race through the bush to destroy them.

The gamble for such colossal stakes exalted her. She turned and clutched at Andrew's arm, demanding a reassurance in his eyes.

She found it there, and pride and eagerness as well.

"Don't see it finally as it is now, Sara," he said tremulously. "In a few years I'll build you a beautiful house. I've planned it all—it'll be large and white, with a terrace and columns facing the river. I can see it . . ."

She cut him short.

"I don't want a Greek temple in the woods, Andrew. Whatever money there is must go into the land. The house can stay as it is. I'm well content."

He gave a soft laugh, reaching to her and taking her shoulders between his two hands. His lean, roughened face reflected her own excitement and passion, as if her emotions had spilled over and affected him as strongly. In that moment they both knew that they were one in mind; the union of their marriage was complete. His expression hardened, and his grip tightened.

"You're as greedy as I am—you damned woman!" he said, his lips dry, the skin stretched. "You ought to have been a man, Sara. It excites you too, doesn't it, all this? You see, as well as I do, what's waiting for a man with the brain and the heart to work?" His hands were feeling their way slowly down her arms. "But it's just as well you're not a man—you couldn't restrain yourself as I do. You couldn't hold yourself off the rum traffic, could you? Or keep yourself out of every shady transaction this corrupt hole hatches out? You'd be the biggest rum-peddler of them all, my sweet."

"Probably," she admitted. "But I'll find plenty of ways of helping you, all the same, Andrew. As soon as I can mount this wretched horse without fear of falling off, you'll find me as good as three overseers. I'll know every inch of your land—and every ear of corn that grows on it."

"Be as you are now—I don't ask for any more, Sara," he said thickly.

Jeremy and Trigg rode into the yard at the back of the house. A mongrel dog, which Andrew had brought home from his last visit to Sydney, started up his barking at the sounds of their approach; he raced round them in a frenzy of welcome. The ceaseless clucking of fowls reached them from the pens in the shade of the big mimosa tree.

As Jeremy dismounted a woman came out of the lean-to kitchen, which was joined to the main building by a short covered passage. She was small and wrinkled, and wearing the graceless garments of a convict. Her face was red from the heat of the kitchen fire.

She approached the two men, wiping her hands in a cloth. This wiping of her hands was a habitual gesture; Jeremy was used to it. She did it now with greater emphasis than usual. As he began to unstrap the saddle-bags. Jeremy glanced back over his shoulder at Annie Stoke's round, bright eyes and button nose, at the low brow furrowed in an expression of acute anxiety.

"They're coming," he announced briefly. "Is everything ready?"

The small eyes flashed with a touch of spirit. "O' course it is. Haven't I slaved myself half to death these past weeks putting things to rights? There's duck for dinner, and if they don't look sharp, it'll be on the table before they're ready!"

Jeremy nodded. "And see you don't shake the wine more than you can help."

Annie's thin little frame stiffened. "Me!" The word was an indignant gasp. "Me, what's served in taverns all me life! What's dished dinners to the gentry! Worked for Lord Delham, I did! 'Tisn't likely I wouldn't know what to do with a bottle of wine!"

Trigg gave a low laugh. "Y'know what to do with it all right. Dead drunk, I've seen you, Annie—and you praying to the Lord, what you've never prayed to before, to deliver you from this cursed country."

Annie gave a toss to her head. She took a hesitant step towards Jeremy, beginning again to wipe her hands in the cloth.

"What's she like?" she said.

"She?"

"The mistress."

Jeremy straightened and looked at her. Under his direct stare she wilted, and retreated a little. He snapped a reply. "You're here to see that Mrs. Maclay is served in every way possible—not to ask questions!"

Annie turned on her heel and slipped away towards the kitchen like a scuttling, grey rabbit. Jeremy watched her go, but wasn't in time to check Trigg's coarse shout.

"She's a rare beauty, is the mistress! And looks as if she has a mind of her own. I'll lay she won't stand no nonsense. You'll have to mind yourself now, Annie!"

Trigg's loud, deep laughter boomed across the yard.

Listening to it, Jeremy felt slightly sick. And later, locking the storehouse, where they had laid the provisions brought up from Parramatta, Trigg touched back on the subject of Andrew's wife. He stood with his hands on his hips, surveying the row of eucalyptus that marked the line of the cleared land.

"She'll have no easy time of it, I'll be bound," he said in a low voice, half to himself. "Pardoned or not. I don't envy her trying to show she's any better than the rest of us. Who'll believe it, anyway?"

Jeremy was at a loss to answer him. He knew well enough that Trigg had merely put into words what every convict labourer at Kintyre must be thinking—what was being said in every house and humpy in the colony, and over every barrack-room table. Andrew Maclay was going to suffer for his wife's reputation, he thought. He gestured impatiently to silence Trigg.

"Listen, they're coming! I'll go round to the front and take the horses."

He hurried round the side of the house and, as he watched the Maclays approach, he saw that Andrew was carrying Sara's hat; he saw the sun on her hair and in that moment he felt that he almost hated her, hated the splendour of the body that the dark habit revealed, hated her faint arrogance and superiority. Even one short day of marriage had seemed to alter her. She was more confident and at ease, sure of Andrew, like a child triumphant over a prize. He looked at the two faces as they came close, seeing in them something which had not been present when he saw them last. They were alive now, he thought, both of them; they were united with a kind of passion that he felt was not wholly the outcome of their physical bond. They had a sort of ruthless eagerness, as if they were both reaching out for something which had just come into sight. Whatever emotion they shared, it was for themselves alone.

He took her horse's head. He had an opportunity then to look at her closely, and he wished that she might have been vulgar and coarse, and then he could have despised her—and ignored her. But he was all too keenly aware that she was not the type of woman to be overlooked. Intelligence and quick-wittedness were there, and she would not allow herself to be ignored. He reflected on Andrew's camp-fire conversations about this un-known girl, and he knew now why it was that Andrew loved her. There was intoxication in those greenish eyes if one looked into them long enough, and charm and power in that smile. She appealed strongly to the gambler in Andrew, the part of him that wanted nothing that was tame, or too easily won. He knew from their talks that Sara had not been swiftly wooed, nor would she ever submit meekly to any man's authority. He was angry with her because she had kept herself aloof, and he was ready to believe that she had schemed for all she had now, and was triumphant because she had won.

It suddenly occurred to him that he might possibly be jealous of her.

As he waited for Andrew to dismount and come round to lift her down, he realised that her eyes were on him.

"Welcome home, ma'am," he said.

"Thank you," she replied, meeting his gaze steadily.

He felt himself flushing, realising that she held a position from which she might patronise him if she so chose. But her eyes left his. She turned to smile at Andrew, and Jeremy knew he was forgotten.

Chapter Three

In the two years following her marriage, Sara watched the Hawkesbury Valleys slowly filling with settlers. Each ship now arriving in the colony brought its family of free settlers, and the terms of some of the convicts expired, or were remitted, and they, also, moved out to take land. By 1795, there were four hundred people living along the river, and their farms extended for thirty miles on either bank. A passable road had been made to link the Hawkesbury with Parramatta.

During this time Kintyre had become the most prosperous farm in the district. This was mainly due to the fact that Andrew was now firmly established in the trading-ring, enjoying to the full the privileges of the military—but he had also chosen his land in the place least likely to be touched by the seasonal floods which damaged and swept away the crops of those on the low-lying river-flats. Labour was cheap; many of the ex-convict settlers, having no money and no knowledge of farming, after their first few months gave up any attempt to cultivate their own land, and were glad to hire themselves out. As the acres were cleared, there was more pasture, and Andrew began to make regular trips to Parramatta for the market-day livestock sales. In a little more than a year Kintyre's herds and flocks couldn't any longer be reckoned in a quick glance. The rich river-flats gave a heavy yield of grain—so long as it could be harvested before the level of the water rose with the autumn rains. It wasn't much more than a modest kind of prosperity that the farm enjoyed— the outhouses and stables were still rough, the fencing incomplete— but with prices in the colony always favouring the trading-ring, Andrew's profits mounted steadily. When the first two years were over he had moved beyond the stage where he was haunted by the fear of failure.

To the house itself he added three rooms, setting them at right angles to the main building, so that the whole long veranda faced a complete curve of the river, giving a view in two directions. A dull-green vine climbed the walls, and trailed along the veranda-rails, softening and warming the stark outlines of the house. A small garden was laid out in front, and slender fruit-trees covered the slope at the side—when the trees broke into bloom for a brief time, there was the frail, transient beauty of an English spring to contrast with the evergreens. The house itself was losing its look of impermanence and rawness; its height commanded a fine stretch of the new road, and to those who travelled along it, it proclaimed the Maclays' stature and position in the colony.

Sara felt the great peace of these two years; they were the happiest in her whole life, and it took her some time to accustom herself to her sense of freedom and security, and to the knowledge that there was no longer any need to scheme and contrive for what she wanted. Only gradually could she learn the fact that she was the mistress of a farmhouse, and of Annie Stokes and the two other women who had been assigned to help her; the workers at Kintyre, free and convict, touched their caps to her as they passed, and she had to school herself not to show her satisfaction and delight in that small gesture. Curtains appeared at the windows of the house, and rugs on the floors—there were even a few pieces of indifferent silver exhibited about, which Andrew had bought from a newly arrived settler. Sara was enchanted with them. Each time she passed she gave them a few furtive rubs with the corner of her apron. The plain wood floors gleamed with wax-polish, and the soft light from the lanterns lent some beauty even to the simply-fashioned furniture.

Right from the first month of her arrival at Kintyre, she flung herself into learning the management of the farm. She kept the accounts herself, making them up from the rough notes that Andrew gave her. She learned quickly; after a time she did them with ease and speed, and Andrew, responding to her interest, left more and more of the book-keeping to her. But she was not content to confine her knowledge of the farm to notations on paper. She took to riding every day, accompanying Andrew on his rounds, inspecting the work on the fences, and the deep ditches which the torrential rains made necessary; she began to know something about the condition of the livestock, and the diseases which could attack them—all matters to which she had paid scant attention when she had heard them discussed among the farms on the Romney Marsh. As time passed the farming of Kintyre's lands became almost as much her concern as the running of the household, and she listened to the conversations between Andrew and Jeremy on the subject of stock and crops. Along the Hawkesbury they began to say that Andrew Maclay had married a woman as shrewd and businesslike as himself.

The world of the colony beyond the Hawkesbury she knew only from the gossip Andrew brought back from his trips to Sydney and Parramatta, and from the frequent letters that passed between herself and Julia Ryder. James was settling well to his farming, and enjoying it, Julia wrote—her house was gradually being furnished, and a garden made. In short, James Ryder was prospering like every other hardworking farmer who had started either with money of his own. or who had some place in the trading circle. It was a time when money was to be made quickly from the fantastic privileges which the New South Wales Corps, in the absence of a Governor to restrain them, granted to themselves. So long as a man was accepted by the officers of the Corps, nothing could go wrong for him—land was free, rum was cheap, convicts were assigned without question, and with all this went the right of buying the cargoes offered for sale from every ship entering Port Jackson.

Sara found little to tempt her to Sydney or Parramatta. There was hardly more to be seen now than the tired-looking huts and the few houses that had been there when she first arrived, and there was no one to visit except Julia Ryder. A few wives of the Corps' officers had come out from England to join their husbands, but there was no possibility that she would be admitted into their tight little circle. Over this, she could do nothing but shrug her shoulders; Kintyre and the work there suited her, and there wasn't much else she wanted. In the Hawkesbury district itself the women were mostly the wives of small settlers, many of them ex-convicts, married to ex-convicts. She knew they envied the prosperity and ease of life at Kintyre, and her appearances on the Hawkesbury road, mounted on the horse which had been set aside for her own use, did nothing to endear her to them. Resentful eyes under faded bonnets peered at her as she went by. There was no place yet for her in the colony—nothing between these hard-working women who envied her, and the officers' wives who would not receive her. She had to content herself with her rather solitary and aloof place at Kintyre.

So when she knew that she was pregnant, almost her first thoughts were for Julia—whether or not she could be spared from her own farm to make the journey to the Hawkesbury at the time the child was expected. Memories of their former relationship as mistress and servant still remained with her vividly, making her reluctant to write her request to Julia. But before she had finally settled to writing the letter, Andrew carried the news back with him from his next visit to Parramatta that Julia had asked if she might come two weeks before the baby would be born. But when the time came, she was delayed for a week with Charles, who had some sort of slight fever, and when she at last reached Kintyre she was greeted with the news that Sara's son had been born the day before, after only four hours' labour. The surgeon, D'Arcy Wentworth, who had travelled up from Parramatta with Julia, was seriously out of humour over the long journey made to no purpose. He seemed to be of the opinion that no gentlewoman would have produced her first child with so little difficulty.

The baby was christened David. To the scandalised women along the river, the short time which had elapsed between the child's birth and Sara's first appearance on her horse was barely decent. They were not to know what impetus the sight of their first child had given to the ambitions of Andrew and Sara. After David was born they were close in a way they had never been before; work at Kintyre took on a new aspect seen in the light of a son to inherit it. They had no visitors, and lived with a simplicity which, in Sydney, would have caused slighting comment; but they themselves were satisfied, and each season more ground was broken by the ox-drawn hoe, and better farming equipment arrived out from England. Kintyre took on the trim, whitewashed look of a typical Scottish farm.

It was Jeremy Hogan who caused the only unhappiness Sara knew in those two years. Between them ran an undercurrent of hostility, begun on the day Andrew had brought her to the Hawkesbury as his bride. Plainly, Jeremy considered her not half good enough for Andrew, a common little piece whom, by some misfortune, he had found attractive. They never openly quarrelled, both realising that Andrew would not have stood for it. But, at best, their politeness to each other was chilly; at worst—when Andrew was not present—they stopped short only of outright rudeness. In every matter their ideas seemed to conflict. Jeremy was an excellent farmer himself; he made no secret of the fact that he, Andrew, and Trigg, were capable of running the farm without help from Sara. She said nothing on this score to Andrew, but simply settled to learning as much as possible from him, without troubling Jeremy.

She knew well enough why Jeremy took this attitude towards her. His memories were all of lovely Irish women—gentle, soft-voiced creatures who bent to their husbands' will, whose minds never strayed beyond their favourite horse, their children, the style of their dress, and who would not have admitted to being able to add a column of figures. This was the sort of woman Jeremy understood—not one who bargained like a gipsy for what she wanted, who trailed her petticoats in the mud to see the progress of the work in the fields and garden, and who still called herself mistress of a farm, and wife to a man whom he respected. She knew there was no trace of the dependent helplessness in her which Jeremy wanted to find.

His resentment was never put into words. It remained just below the surface, and the only way he could give vent to it was by ignoring her when he discussed the farm with Andrew. Clearly, his object was to show her her place, and make her keep it. She had no power against him; he was necessary to Kintyre, he worked on it as if it were his own, and she would have suffered even direct insults from him in order to keep him there. She often thought of the wonderful relief if she could have raised her crop and hit Jeremy just once, as he turned his half-insolent gaze upwards towards her when she rode to inspect the work he was supervising in the fields.

Sometimes she indulged in a fanciful day-dream of finding

some way of convincing him that a practical, unsentimental woman was a better wife to Andrew, in his present position, than any of his own notions of soft-eyed beauties. Then she pulled up short, and laughed at herself for such indulgence. Jeremy's opinion of her would have to be worn down by the slow method of proving him wrong in small ways; but it was a method that was little suited to her mood.

II

These years, without proper government control, the officers of the Corps used to form the nucleus of their estates—mostly on the profits from rum. Sara, watching from Kintyre, could trace the pattern these men were making—they were uncovering their own ambitions to establish themselves as the gentry of the new country, and they were doing it by the classic method of grabbing, in as short a time as possible, all the land available to them, leaving the refinements and niceties of their unique position until later. Andrew, except for the fact that he wore no red coat and drew no pay from His Majesty's Government, was hardly different.

The news reached them, almost a year old, of the execution of Louis XVI of France. They also learned that England had joined Prussia, Austria, Spain, and Piedmont in declaring war against the French Republic. To the people of New South Wales the events of the world they had left behind were remote and far-off, like a tune heard tinkling faintly in the distance. They were absorbed in their own affairs, and the troubles of Europe hardly touched them.

Chapter Four

After a week of rain in the early spring of 1795 the Hawkesbury rose suddenly. The lands belonging to several farmers who had settled close to the banks were under water; one man was drowned. For three days the swirling brown flood held its place twenty-five feet above the usual level, and then gradually receded. It left behind a generous layer of silt, and scores of dead livestock, bloated, and beginning to smell vilely. The farmers returned to their ruined fields of Indian corn, the mud-caked wrecks of their homes, and they ruefully counted the numbers of cattle either drowned or strayed. They reckoned their losses against the possible return of the floods each spring and autunm. They discussed the prospect among themselves and whatever way they viewed it, it looked gloomy. Some determined to hang on—counting that the yield of one good season here would compensate for two bad ones; others decided to cut their losses and sell.

Kintyre was practically untouched by the disaster that had come to the valley. At the first sign of a rise in the river, Andrew had moved his livestock to higher ground close to the house. When the water went down he had no losses to count, except one field of corn destroyed. He made capital out of the flood. He watched the panic spread among the other settlers, and when the trek began he was able to buy up the small farm adjoining his own, and a further ninety acres a mile or so down-river. More ex-convict labourers were hired, and an overseer found to master them; Jeremy began his task of bringing the productivity of Kintyre's new lands into line with the old.

The spring also brought the *Reliance,* bearing the awaited Governor, John Hunter, into Sydney Cove. Rumours circulated among the New South Wales Corps that his commission held a paragraph charging him to suppress the rum traffic. On September 11th, the Corps paraded with full military pomp, and with an obvious tongue in the cheek, to hear the commission read, quite fully determined that nothing a King or Parliament on the other side of the world could do was going to stem their profiteering in the rum traffic.

II

"Jeremy, do you think these accounts are . . . ?"

Sara broke off and laid down her pen, as the sounds of a galloping horse broke into the afternoon stillness. Jeremy lifted his eyes from the account-books spread on the table between them. From the bottom of the slope they could hear the heavy beat of a horse being ridden at full speed. For an instant they exchanged a questioning glance. Then Jeremy was on his feet.

"It's news of some sort!" he rapped, flinging open the door of the room Andrew used as an office. "No one rides like that for the pleasure of it."

"Wait!" Sara sprang up. "I'll come with you!"

She swept out, and as she hurried down the passage to the front door, standing open in the spring sunshine, she was possessed of a strange fear. Never before had a horse been ridden to her very veranda steps at such a speed—not even when a long-awaited ship arrived, bringing letters from England. Her thoughts flew instantly to Andrew, who had left two days before to attend the reading of the new Governor's commission in Sydney. Her mind envisaged him ill or injured, and the hoofbeats had a desperate, urgent sound. The horseman was almost at the top of the slope now. She gathered up her skirts and ran the last few yards to the doorway.

Here Jeremy sprang past her, racing down the steps to take the bridle of the horse; a scatter of small stones flew up as it was brought too sharply to a halt. Sara recognised it immediately as the dark chestnut which their nearest neighbour, Charles Denver, had brought out with him from England. The man riding it was his overseer, Evans.

At the top of the steps she paused. "What is it?"

Evans was dishevelled and breathless. He gazed up at Sara for a few seconds while Jeremy tried to quieten the horse. At last he leaned forward and called out hoarsely, unbelief in his voice, "It's the convicts, Mrs. Maclay! They've broken out!"

Sara's own voice was strained, like Evans's. "What's that? Whose convicts?"

"Ours! They've murdered Mr. Denver!"

She clutched the veranda post. She felt an appalling sickness suddenly swamp her, and for a moment she could think of nothing but the closeness of Kintyre to the neighbouring farm. An outbreak! Her hands clenched. This was worse than the flood, worse than the skirmishes with the natives. It was worse than anything the bush could offer in terror and violence. Through her fear she knew her desperate need of Andrew now. Charles Denver had been murdered, and perhaps their own lives were threatened by this outbreak; she and Jeremy faced it alone.

She thought of this a moment longer, and then forced herself to walk calmly down the steps until she was standing beside Jeremy at the horse's head.

"Tell me what happened," she said.

He breathed deeply, and she could see the sweat matting the lank hair on his forehead. His shirt was soaked, and with a fresh stab of fear she saw bloodstains on his hands. The blood was dry and caked around his nails.

"I was driving six head of cattle back from Sam Murphy's," he said, panting, and trying to get his breath. "As soon as I got in sight of the house, I knew something was amiss. Didn't look right, somehow—but I couldn't exactly put my mind to what was wrong. I didn't have time to think much about it because someone started shooting at me from the house. I rode down to the river, out of their range—and that was where I found him."

"Him?" Jeremy said tersely. "Mr. Denver?"

Evans nodded. "Aye, Mr. Denver. His skull smashed in with a pickaxe—the back of his head."

"Good God!" Jeremy said.

Sara's eyes moved again to the bloody hands. She stared at them, fascinated and repulsed.

"He was dead, of course?" was all she said.

"Dead, aye! When I left this morning he was supervising the building-up of the bank, in case the river rose again. He must have turned his back on them. There was the other supervisor, O'Brien, with him. God knows what happened to O'Brien. More than likely he's joined the outbreak. They'd loot the house for food and firearms, and then, probably, take the boats to cross the river."

"What about the women on the place?" Jeremy put in quickly.

"There were two convict women," Evans answered. "Can't say what became of them. Probably with the men."

"How many men?" Sara asked.

"Ten, ma'am—and O'Brien, if he's alive."

She ran her tongue over dry lips. "How many guns?"

"Mr. Denver had four."

"Four..." she repeated. Her eyes searched his tired, taut face. "You came here immediately?"

"Yes, ma'am. As soon as I found him, I came."

"Did they see you come this way?"

"Don't see that they could help it, ma'am. And they'd probably guess that I'd make for the camp to get the troops."

"That's true," she said. "Yes, of course they would."

Jeremy burst out. "Hell! They've picked their time well for this. I'll swear there's no more than two or three men of the detachment still on the Hawkesbury. They've all been sent to Sydney or Parramatta to make good muster for the Governor's parade."

The truth of his words struck Sara. She clung to the bridle for a moment in silence, afraid to let go for fear she would stumble and fall. The cunning of Denver's convict labourers enraged her—they had known to wait until the troops stationed in the district to keep down the natives had departed before they rose to their murder and looting. She looked at Jeremy, knowing well that his face must be a mirror of her own expression, grave and fearful, as they each made a swift reckoning of the extent of the danger.

She turned again to Evans. "You'll ride immediately to Parramatta for help. They can't have sent all the troops on to Sidney. Tell them they'll have to muster horses from somewhere—if they wait to send a detachment on foot, it will take anything up to two days to reach here."

Evans looked doubtful. "It's twenty miles, ma'am, and I must stop by each farm on the way to warn them. Unless the moon's clear, I'll not get speed out of this horse. There's no telling what time I'll reach the town."

Sara said sharply, stamping her foot in impatience, "Oh, damn you, can't you understand that you must get help here quickly. Whatever time it is they must make up a force and send it immediately. Three soldiers with a musket apiece won't hold down a gang of murderers. Tell them they've got to send all the firearms they can spare. We'll need them.'

She let go of the bridle abruptly.

"Now, go as quickly as you can."

But Jeremy's hand still held it. "You'll go as well, Mrs. Maclay."

She regarded him fiercely. "Go? Why should I go? I'm staying here!"

"You'll go at least as far as the Murphys' house. They'll not reach there too quickly."

Her voice choked with anger. "I'm staying here—where I belong! No convicts are going to take my house while I run off and leave it to them. I can fire a gun, and I suppose I can shoot a man as well as most if I'm forced to."

Jeremy's chest heaved. "The baby?" he said levelly.

"David will stay here," she replied swiftly. "At the moment he's as safe here as anywhere else on the Hawkesbury. How can we tell which way they'll go? They may pass by Kintyre altogether, to put the troops off their trail. They may cross the river right away, and if they do, that's the last we'll hear of them.

If I take David in the cart, I may meet them on the road. Staying or going—it's a chance.''

Jeremy wouldn't let it go at that. He said loudly, "But I'm responsible . . ."

"Since when have you been responsible?" Sara demanded hotly.

"In your husband's absence . . ."

"This is one time when I give the orders," she retorted. "And that applies to you too, Evans. Now, go—at once!"

With that, she stepped back from the horse. But Jeremy waited a few moments longer, obstinately clinging to the bridle, looking for some sign that she was weakening. She returned his gaze coldly, daring him to make any further show of defiance. Then he glanced up at the grim, white face of the man above him, and with a gesture of hopeless anger, he relaxed his hold. Evans touched the horse with his heels; it wheeled quickly, raising a shower of broken earth, and started down the slope again.

Sara and Jeremy had no time to watch it out of sight; instead they turned to each other immediately. Anger still flared in each face, but it faded in the swift realisation they both had of their aloneness in a danger which had come upon them too suddenly. The sounds of the galloping horse were dying fast; with them, it seemed that their link with the world of security and peace was gone. Their eyes met in a moment of full comprehension of their plight. Then Sara jerked her head, motioning him back towards the house.

On the steps she glanced over her shoulder. What she saw made her clutch Jeremy's arm in alarm.

"Look! They've fired Charles Denver's house!"

He swung round. Together they looked in the direction of the neighbouring farm; a faint column of smoke drifted above the trees. It seemed no more than a wisp, but it came from a distance of almost two miles. On any other day it would have passed for the burning of timber on a newly-cleared space; it would have gone unnoticed. But they knew, both of them, that to-day the smoke meant that either Charles Denver's house or his stores were burning.

She uttered only a single word.

"Hurry!"

For a second or two Sara stood to see Jeremy stride down the slope to where the main body of convicts were working under Trigg. The only hope of stopping the outbreak from spreading was to lock their own convicts in their huts before they had a chance to realise what was in the air. The devil of it was, she thought, that they were never all in the one place at the same time. Two were working at the moment in the vegetable garden, one in the orchard, and probably one in the stables. Jeremy was alone against them, and with the nagging doubt whether or not Trigg would stick by him if the men broke. She watched him hurrying purposefully across the field, the gun he had taken from a locked cupboard in Andrew's office held as inconspicuously as possible by his side. Her half-closed eyes followed him a moment, and she prayed desperately that he might be able to fight the odds against him.

Then she cocked the loaded pistol that he had thrust into her hand, balancing its weight as evenly as she could before turning and going back into the house again. She made straight for the kitchen; the door was ajar and she flung it open, standing squarely in front of the three women. They all raised their eyes at the sudden entry. Their expressions altered from inquiry to amazement and fright as their eyes fell on the pistol.

The youngest uttered a sharp exclamation in a rough Irish brogue.

"Glory be to God, what's this?"

She dropped the potato she was peeling and jumped to her feet.

Annie drew her hands slowly out of a basin of dough and wiped them in her apron.

The third, a heavy creature with the dull eyes of a halfwit, gave an unintelligent grunt.

Sara stood well back from them, holding the pistol with a steady hand. She was afraid, but was, more than anything else, terrified that they would detect her fear.

"Not a word from any of you—do you understand?"

No one spoke or moved. Sara tensed herself, half-expecting that the young Irishwoman might rush forward in a mad attempt to take the pistol. Her only hope of keeping them under control lay in shutting them up before the shock of the situation wore off and gave them time to think or to plan any action.

She waved the pistol slightly towards a small storeroom leading off the kitchen; it was no more than a large cupboard, with a shuttered window high in the wall.

"In there, all of you!" she rapped.

Immediately the gaze of each of them shifted to the storeroom, then back again. No one moved.

Sara looked angrily from one to the other. "Didn't you hear what I said? In there with you!"

Annie wrung her hands, and set up a faint whining. Sara took not the slightest notice, but she was afraid of the Irishwoman. She watched her anxiously, seeing a brief show of emotion on the thin, white face, the shrewd eyes narrowed down, as if she were rapidly calculating the connection between the horseman's hurried arrival and departure, and now her mistress's unexpected appearance with a pistol in her hand. Sara realised that this woman was intelligent enough to put two and two together and suspect that trouble concerning the convicts was afoot. Again she gestured purposefully with the heavy pistol. But the other woman, defiant, and playing for time, stood her ground.

"Why?" she demanded.

Furious, now, Sara shouted at her. "Don't ask me questions! Do as I say!"

"But I likes to know . . ."

"Silence! You'll do as I say! Now, hurry on with you !"

The Irishwoman didn't move; she glanced from the cringing Annie to her other companion, standing solidly and open-mouthed. Sara knew beyond doubt that she was reckoning how much support she could count on if she attempted an attack; she knew too that she daren't lose another second considering the chances.

"You wouldn't like a bullet through your leg, would you, Mary?" she said calmly, staring straight into that rebellious face. "Because that's what you'll certainly get if you don't move before I count three." She raised the pistol a trifle. "I haven't learned to handle this for nothing!"

The Irishwoman stirred in an agony of indecision.

"One . . . Two . . ."

Annie let out a despairing wail, and the sound seemed to unnerve the other woman. With a final, defiant shrug she submitted, leading the others into the storeroom.

Sara followed them, the pulse in her throat fluttering with relief, and her wrist suddenly feeling as if its bones had turned to water.

Grimly fingering her bunch of keys, she faced her three captives as they lined against the wall. Her eyes moved from one to the other—Mary's expression of sullen fury, Annie's frightened, cowering stance, the third's look of dumb wonder. She met their stares coolly, knowing well enough how potentially dangerous they were; an unguarded second or one sign of weakness would bring them down on her like a pack of wolves. Give them only a chance of freedom with survival in the bush, and they would strip the house of food and firearms and be gone within a few minutes.

"Remember this," she said, sliding a key into the lock, "if any of you try to escape, I'll see to it myself that the magistrate sentences you to a flogging that won't leave an inch of skin on your back. Remember it well—because I mean it."

With that she slammed the door and turned the key.

As she picked up her skirts and sped back along the passage to David's nursery, Sara's thoughts were anxiously upon the inadequacy of the storeroom as a prison. Any three women with will and strength could break out of it; she relied, without conviction, on her threats forcing them into docility. It was never safe to rely on the docility of a convict.

David woke up. He made a good-humoured, crowing noise, thumping his fists together energetically. She snatched up a shawl, bundling it around him, fighting down his hands, eager to play with the ends of her hair.

"Be good, David!" she said softly, her mouth close to his ear. "Be good, now! I'm not leaving you behind to that gang of rogues."

He gave a crow of excitement, and his hand closed firmly over a lock of her hair. As she hurried from the room with him he began to pull at it; he pulled harder, delighted with this new distraction; tears came to her eyes; David's pulling was painful, and she felt sick with fright and anxiety. But there was no time to stop and quieten his restless hands. Clutching the pistol, and balancing the heavy child against her hip, she ran back through the kitchen. Crossing it, she could hear muffled thuds coming from the storeroom. It was useless, encumbered as she was with David, to investigate. And in any case, she told herself, if she were to catch them trying to escape, she could not stand with a gun levelled at them until Jeremy arrived back to help her. So she hardly paused on her way through the kitchen; she went out by the back door, and crossed to the stables.

Once inside them she drew a deeper breath. It was quiet and dim; the smell of horses and hay came to her strongly, a peaceful, homey smell on that spring afternoon, a smell that seemed to have no relation at all to the world so abruptly turned upside down. The effect was demoralising; it urged her to rest, to desist from her fantastic scheme. Above, the hay-loft lured her with its security, its promise of a hiding-place. She shifted David in her arms and gazed about.

At the same moment Andrew's Arab stallion, Fury, only lately bought from the owner of a trading vessel, stirred and whinnied softly, half-turning his head to look at her. The movement broke Sara's mood of hesitation. The horses were valuable; the three standing there so quietly, and the one he himself had ridden to Sydney, represented Andrew's gains of the three years in the colony, his position among its leaders. Not for lack of effort on her part was she going to see them ridden away into the bush by a pack of desperate men, to be most likely killed and eaten when the looted food ran short. She was filled with a sense of great pride in these animals, and sudden terror in case they should be snatched from her possession.

"Oh, not you, my beauties!" she murmured to them. "They'll not have you if I can help it."

She turned away quickly, dragging down some hay from a wall box, and put David lying on top of it. He mistrusted this strange sensation of being deposited so firmly among the rustling softness. He gave a cry of protest, and his face began to wrinkle uncertainly.

Sara looked at him in dismay.

"Don't cry. Davie-boy! Oh, don't cry now!"

She glanced around in desperation, and then, selecting two long stalks of hay, thrust them into his open hand. For a moment he regarded them in wonder, tentatively placing one in his mouth. The taste seemed to please him; he settled contentedly to chewing on it.

She left him without another word, turning her attention to fixing bridles on each of the horses. The stallion was always docile in her hands; he allowed her to handle him without stirring. The second horse was her own. It hindered her by nuzzling her face and neck, and thrusting its nose along the folds of her skirt, searching for the carrot she always brought. She talked gently as she worked, striving to keep her hands calm and patient while her mind raced ahead to what might be happening about her ... the possible advance of the convicts from Charles Denver's farm, the women breaking down the door of the storeroom, Jeremy, without help, setting out to round up their own labourers.

Her hands were stiff and clumsy as she fumbled with the straps. The third horse, a young bay gelding, catching her mood of unease, pulled restlessly away from her. It took her a long time to get the bridle secure.

"Well, *you*, my lad," she said sharply, "may be more trouble than you're worth!"

She had to decide quickly about David. She took away his shawl, ignoring the cries of protest he let out, finding the hay against his skin no longer soft. Folding it and knotting it at two corners, she hung it over her shoulder like a sling. She picked him up and settled him into it, supporting his weight with her left hand, leaving the right free for the bridles. He didn't like the new arrangement and set up a persistent, lusty howl.

She looked at him grimly. "There's nothing I can do about it—you'll just have to get used to it."

His puckered, exasperated face stared back resentfully at her.

Sara frowned down at him. "I only ask you to lie there. Davie," she said despairingly. "If only you'd be quiet!"

His angry cries split the afternoon air, and Sara, with a shrug of her shoulders, decided there was nothing to be done to pacify him.

The stallion and Goldie, her own horse, came forward eagerly as soon as she laid her hand on the bridles. The bay was, by this time, thoroughly unnerved by the child's cries. He stood still and frightened in his box, refusing to come forward. She breathed hard, wondering what to do now. Holding the bridles of the two first horses, and supporting David as she did, she was unable to go into his box and bring him out. Nor could she afford to wait any longer. The only thing was to leave the box door open, and trust that he would follow the other two.

She settled David as securely as possible against her hip, and pulled at the bridles with her tensed, sweating hand. It would take ten minutes, she calculated, to reach the edge of the cleared land. The screen of the surrounding bush was thick and comforting; once they were within the fringe of it, the horses would not be seen by anyone who did not actually stumble on them. Tethered there, they would be safe and unseen. Safe . . . Her mind echoed the word doubtfully. There were still the hours of the night to live through before she could be certain of safety—for her child, the house and stores, and herself. The thin column of smoke above the trees was there to remind her of what she might yet expect.

As she crossed the yard, tugging at the bridles to force the horses to a better pace, she heard a clatter at the stable door. Looking back she saw the bay gelding; he paused a moment, hesitant and nervous. Then, seeing the other two horses, he trotted over to join them, falling in meekly at the rear of the procession.

Sara's mouth relaxed in a faint smile of relief before she turned her face once more towards the edge of the cleared land.

Sara stood in the kitchen doorway and gazed warily about her. Everything was exactly as she had left it to go for the horses, Annie's cooking-spoon lay on the floor in a pool of congealed fat. The last of the afternoon sunshine threw her shadow before her, long and thin. Her wrist ached with weariness as she raised the pistol level with her waist. Then she stepped inside.

Finding himself once again in the warm familiarity of the house seemed to bring to David a renewed sense of his grievances. He struggled wildly in his improvised sling, setting up a lusty howling that was part hunger and part anger. Sara clamped him firmly to her side with her left hand, and tried to stifle his cries against her breast. The sling, which had taken his full weight during her tramp across the fields with the horses, was cutting into her neck like wire. His waving arms beat at her, and with every fresh attempt he made to escape, the hard knot of the shawl bit deeper into her flesh.

She held back her tears of fatigue and vexation, and paused to listen to the wild hammering on the storeroom door that had greeted David's first cries. The hammering went on, and his screams became piercing. Sara held him tighter, fixing her gaze on the door, pistol held level.

Through the confusion and noise Annie's voice reached her. "Open up, ma'am! Oh, open up, for God's sake! The others have gone!"

Sara did not reply. Her eyes narrowed in suspicion; she edged closer to the large kitchen table, resting David's weight on it, giving herself better control of the pistol.

"Oh, ma'am . . . ma'am! Let me out, for the love of God!"

The words carried in them a sob of despair and fear; they were cries from a woman, terrified and alone. Two years had taught Sara to know Annie Stokes thoroughly—she was a rogue and an intriguer, but she was no actress. Sara felt that for once she was

137

speaking the truth. She placed the pistol on the table, and fumbled for the key of the storeroom.

She opened the door, and Annie stumbled forward stiffly.

"They've gone!" she gasped, her Cockney's whine rising shrill and unnerving. "Through the window!" she added unnecessarily.

Without speaking a word, Sara stood looking into the storeroom. The young Irishwoman's shrewd brain had seized upon the situation, and had taken the chance of a breakout. Without being at all sure of what was taking place, she had gambled literally with the skin of her back, on the chance that she might follow the protection of the firearms and food of the men convicts in their escape into the bush. The second woman, slavish in her attitude to Mary, and too stupid to properly grasp what was happening about her, had, as a matter of course, gone also.

Together they had rolled a row of molasses kegs to form a platform beneath the shutter, and then, using their combined strength, they had battered away at the wood with an empty keg. Reflecting on the terrifying power in the arms of that clumsy, slow-witted creature, Sara could well understand that it had taken them only a short time to make their escape.

The wall beneath the shutter was badly scarred, and there were splinters of wood lying thickly on the floor. She turned away dumbly, her shoulders drooping.

Annie had begun wringing her hands. "I didn't go, ma'am!" she wailed. "They said I was a fool . . . But I wouldn't go with them, Mrs. Maclay, ma'am! I wouldn't leave you . . . now."

Sara nodded mechanically. "Yes, Annie. Yes . . . I know."

Annie had much more to say, a stream of information, comments, and emphatic protestations of loyalty. Sara listened with half her mind, picking out of the flow of words only the bits that were important. Gradually the story was pieced together. Annie gabbled on, telling her how they had known of the hasty arrival of Charles Denver's overseer, and had guessed by his agitated manner and the column of smoke above the trees most of what had happened. Being locked in the storeroom at gun-point had confirmed their guesses. Standing on a keg, with her eye pressed to a crack in the shutter, Mary had seen three convicts, whom she did not recognise, armed with a gun, a roughly fashioned pike, and a pickaxe, slip quietly past the house. They had not attempted to enter, but made towards the outhouses. It was then,

Annie said, that the Irishwoman had ordered her companion to help her batter down the shutter.

Sara cut her short. "Three strange convicts, you say? And armed?"

"Yes, ma'am."

Sara feverishly hoisted the sling around her neck, pulling it over her head.

"Here," she panted, thrusting the angry, screaming child into Annie's arms, "take him, and give him something to eat. See if you can make him quiet."

Cut short in her recital, Annie looked at David with an expression of astonishment, and then gave a gasp as Sara turned and fled from the kitchen.

In Andrew's office Sara unlocked the cupboard again, taking out the second gun of the three he kept there. She loaded it as he had taught her, thankfully remembering the hours of practice he had insisted upon in preparation for just such an hour as the one which faced her now. She loaded and checked the ammunition meticulously, and then turned to go back to the kitchen.

But beside Andrew's desk she hesitated and halted. She thought a moment before sliding open the top drawer. Her hand fumbled among the quills and extra candles, closing over a small, carved dagger, of Italian workmanship, which they sometimes used for cutting paper. It was a delicate, evil-looking thing with a slim blade, and as she picked it up her mind was grimly moving forward to what might happen if the convicts overran Kintyre, recalling too clearly Evans's blood-stained hands and his story of finding Denver's battered body.

As she stood there, she heard the first shots fired—four of them.

She laid the gun down on the desk for just a few seconds she needed to push the dagger into the bodice of her dress, so that the carved handle didn't show. The coldness of the pointed steel between her breasts was a faint comfort to her.

Then she picked up the gun again and started towards the kitchen.

At the sound of the shots Annie had commenced a peculiar, monotonous shriek—something between a howl and a scream. Sara clenched her teeth. She was going to put a stop to that unearthly noise if it was the last thing she did. If she was going to die, it wasn't going to be to the sounds of Annie's shrieking.

As she reached the kitchen she heard the crack of another shot being fired.

The single shot had silenced Annie abruptly. She turned to Sara with a desperate look of appeal.

"It's all up with us now, ma'am! We're finished!" With a half-sob she pointed to the window. "There's Trigg, now—wounded, by the looks of it. And no sign of Hogan."

Sara sprang past her to the open shutters, the sickness of fear deep in her stomach. She was suddenly too much aware of the dependence of Annie and David upon her, and her own hopeless inadequacy in defending them if the convicts attacked the house. It was mainly for reassurance that she raised the gun and steadied it against the window frame. If the convicts came, two guns wouldn't hold them off for very long. She hoped that Annie wouldn't realise this too soon.

The principal outhouses were about three hundred yards from the house itself. They formed a square, facing inwards—two huts were allotted to the convicts for sleeping quarters, with a smaller one for Jeremy and Trigg. There were two store-houses for the convicts' provisions and farm equipment, and the long hut which Andrew used to house the extra labourers he hired for seasonal work—harvesting and sowing, and the quick clearing of new land. He had built the outhouses at this distance because he had not wanted the presence of the convicts to weigh too heavily upon his own life. They were necessary to the workings of Kintyre, but, beyond that, he baulked at giving them recognition. At this moment, Sara wished that the distance were twice as much.

In the fading light she strained her eyes to see across the kitchen yard. In the space between the stable and the barn, she recognised the figure of Trigg. He leant, as if he were breathless and weak, against the wall of the barn; he was hugging his right arm close, and his head was thrust back as he sucked in great gulps of air. He rested for only a few seconds in the shelter of the wall. Then he lowered his head and ran, with just one backward glance, across the yard to the kitchen. Sara tensed herself, waiting for some sign of pursuit, but there was none. Wounded, and unarmed, Trigg was of no importance to the convicts for the time being.

She lowered the gun, but still kept her place by the window as

Trigg stumbled up the two steps to the kitchen, and stood there, leaning heavily against the door-frame.

He was very white; his whole right arm, from shoulder to wrist, was covered in blood. He wore no coat, and the blood was already running in a thin stream from the tip of one of his fingers. He tilted his head back, gasping for breath, looking spent and exhausted, as if that last dash from the convicts' huts to the house had entirely drained his strength.

Annie let out a horrified squawk, and at a nod from Sara, laid David, quiet now, down on the table, and rushed to help him.

Sara, unmoving, looked at them both. Annie's loyalty had proved itself now, but Trigg . . . She was still suspicious of Trigg. His dash to the house might have been a gallant effort to protect the women and the baby; it might have been a determination to crawl into shelter to nurse his wounded arm. She was prepared not to place overmuch trust in him, but he pushed Annie aside and turned to her.

"Hogan and me, we had our men rounded up and almost in the huts when those other devils arrived, ma'am," he gasped weakly. "Not a chance they gave us, but came up behind, round by the stable, and fired. There's about ten of them, ma-am . . . and four have guns. There was no holding our lot, once they got the gist of what was happening. I got it in the arm, and then had to run for it . . . or stay and be murdered."

His voice had died a little more. He said falteringly, "Mary and Bessie have gone with them. I heard them yelling. I knew you and Annie and Master David were here alone." He made an effort to straighten, but it was feeble. "I'm not much use now. But I reckon I could still fire a gun."

Sara nodded, running her tongue across her dry lips. How wrong she'd been about Trigg; she found it difficult now to look at him without shame.

"And Hogan?" she asked faintly.

"He got it in the back . . . twice. 'Tain't much chance he's alive now."

III

There was nothing to do then but wait. During the next hour Sara didn't stir from her post at the window, the gun propped beside her. In enraged helplessness she watched the plunder of the storehouses, and then, finally, what she had been dreading—and

141

waiting for as well. The first pale flame shot above the roofs of the storehouses. At dusk a stiff breeze had sprung up; it fed the fire which raced from building to building with a swiftness that struck terror into her heart. Soon the outhouses were a blazing fiery square in the early darkness The wind came in her direction, and brought the wild voices of the escaped men. The rum they had plundered from the stores added frenzy to their success. It had given them a new boldness—a boldness which the certain knowledge that they faced the lonely bush and the river, and the solid, unknown mountains beyond it, had not yet chilled. They shouted and yelled to each other in their flush of victory. Sara could soon see their figures outlined against the flaming huts; she watched their staggering progress, their determined shouldering of the bags of food they had looted.

They made no attempt to come near the house. She imagined this was because they had found the empty stable and thought the Maclays had ridden off and left Kintyre to whatever fate threatened it; and because they were already loaded with as much food as they could carry. For a while she waited, terrified that the possibility of firearms and more ammunition might lure them to the house. And then it occurred to her that they wouldn't bother with the house—they were working against time, and once they had their food collected together they would be off. If, as Evans had feared, they had seen him ride in the direction of Kintyre, then they wouldn't linger, every minute they expected the arrival of troops. The trek to the river and the two boats moored at the small landing-stage began soon after the outhouses were fairly ablaze.

Sara clenched her hands tightly in an effort to keep her rage in check; she felt sick, and there were tears in her eyes as she watched the roof of the nearest hut cave in with a crash that sent sparks flying in all directions. She knew—none knew better— why they wasted precious minutes firing the outhouses. They were making their only effective protest against their masters and gaolers. Their memories of the holds of the prison ships, the lash, and the chain-gang came up to urge them on in their destruction. They called to each other in their drunken courage before setting out to beat the trackless forest, certain that they would find a way across those baffling blue hills and that somehow they would survive where no white man had lived before. They each of them must have known that the chance of survival was slender; and the knowledge seemed to have made them even more desperate. Sara knew it all, she knew the feeling running strongly among them, one to the other—the anger, the bitter resentment, needing only one spark falling from a hot head to set their fury alight.

When the last of the escaped convicts appeared to have made his way to the boats, and the fires were beginning to die down, Sara roused Trigg and Annie. David was asleep in a basket under the table, so she left him undisturbed. Trigg's arm was bandaged and in a sling made of torn sheeting; he was still in great pain. He followed Sara out of the kitchen and across the silent yard, stumbling several times on the path down to the huts. Sara handed the lamp she carried to Annie, and supported him herself on his uninjured side. In her right hand she carried the gun. The wind blew towards them from the dying fires, bringing a warm breath against their faces, smuts and hot ashes, and the smell of roasting salt meat.

They found Jeremy lying face down in the middle of the square. Annie helped Sara turn him on his back. He was quite still, making no sound as his body rolled over. There was blood on the shoulder of his coat, and it had clotted in his hair and on the side of his face. Sara wasted no time searching his face, in which there was no sign of life; she tore down his shirt, and bent to listen for his heart

In a few moments she raised her eyes to the two heads that bent anxiously over her.

"He's alive!" she said.

Then she looked at Trigg. "Can you manage to carry the lamp and the gun?"

He nodded.

To Annie she tossed a sharp order.

"Give me your apron. We'll have to tie up his head before we try to get him back to the house. Somehow we've got to keep him alive."

IV

Sara gave a final glance at the sleeping figures around her in the sitting-room, before she reached out to take up the lantern from the table. She rose with no more noise than the rustle of her skirts.

Annie was sitting on the floor, as far as possible from the

window, her back gently sagging against the wall, her mouth hanging open in sleep; every now and then her breath made little hissing noises through the gaps in her teeth. David was beside her, in the basket brought out of the kitchen. Jeremy and Trigg lay against the opposite wall; Trigg in the quiet, motionless sleep of weakness and exhaustion; Jeremy was conscious only for brief periods, the rest of the time he twisted and turned in a kind of fever. Throughout the night he had occasionally woken to ask her for water, his eyes flickering over her face in a few moments of clarity before he slipped back into semi-consciousness. Sara paused before him now, holding the lamp directly above his head. He was not as badly hurt as she had first feared—a bullet had grazed his temple, and there was another still lodged in his shoulder. He had lost a good deal of blood.

He turned his head away painfully, and she lowered the lamp. Jeremy wasn't going to die, she told herself firmly—not if a surgeon arrived in time to remove the bullet. Her tongue flicked nervously over her lips as she calculated the chances of a surgeon being among the first of the troops to reach the Hawkesbury. It seemed a very slight chance.

She lifted the latch of the door softly, and moved out into the passage. This would be her last patrol of the night. In a little more than an hour the bush would be grey in the first light, and then she would rouse Annie and Trigg to watch in her place. Her eyes were blurred with fatigue as she started the rounds of all the window-shutters. First, the dining-room . . . She halted in the doorway, the lamp casting long shadows before her. She had nothing to do but to try the three windows in a row on one wall, yet it seemed to require a lot of time and effort to do it. She went to the kitchen next.

Nothing had disturbed the silence of the house during the long night. She had sat, the gun across her knees, too frightened to drop into even a doze while she listened for the sound of anyone trying to break into the house. As the hours dragged quietly out, she became calmer, and felt safer. But the silence was wearing; sleep dragged at her body, and yet her nerves, taut as wire, would not let her relax. It was a relief whenever Jeremy called to her for water, or when Trigg woke because the dressing had slipped on his arm, and needed changing.

She walked along the passage to the kitchen, and opened the door softly. She held the lamp down low, looking towards the heavily shuttered windows, hoping that the first streak of light might have appeared against the chinks. It was as black as when she made her last round, an hour earlier. She stood still, her thoughts on the escaped convicts on the other side of the river, wondering what sort of camp they had made to sleep off their drunken stupor. In the daylight they might raid farms on the opposite bank—or they might make their way as quickly as possible beyond the range of the settled areas. She didn't know what their choice would be, and for the hundredth time that night she pondered the question, and tried to answer it for herself. She sighed, and rested her tired body against the door-frame.

"If only it were light..." she whispered, her voice coming back softly to her out of the darkness. "If only the troops would come..."

And as she spoke she felt the breeze of the cold spring morning on her right cheek. It was sharp, coming down off the mountains, with a hint of frost in it. The thought froze in her mind... a sharp breeze in a room that was shuttered!

She straightened then, leaning forward into the room and trying to fight off the fatigue that dulled her brain. She raised the lamp, peering into the gloom towards the storeroom. Its door was open. The shutter that the two women had torn down was letting in the wind in cold gusts.

Her eyes narrowed in fear and bewilderment as she struggled to remember if she herself had opened the door, and left it open. Had she done that in her last round? Her memory fought for recollection. But her mind remained blank—apprehension as well as suspicion crowding into it.

She was certain now that something was wrong, and it seemed to her more dangerous to go back and rouse Trigg than to stand her ground. She put the lamp carefully down on the floor. Then she levelled the gun, and moved towards the storeroom. The weight of the gun made her well aware of how clumsy and cumbersome it felt in her hands; she thought longingly of the pistol, left lying beside her chair in the sitting-room. Fool! she told herself, a little whistling breath of dismay escaping through her teeth.

She couldn't see into the storeroom; the half-open door blocked her view. The boards beneath her feet creaked so loudly that she bit her lips to check the cry that rose in her throat. The lamp threw her shadow in a long line before her, and, seeing it, she stopped still. She stood as if she were frozen, listening. Then, after a few moments of reassuring silence, she took a step nearer.

Before she could move again, a man's figure suddenly thrust itself round the edge of the open door. She raised the gun instantly, and stepped backwards. But he was tall, and moved with the swiftness of a hawk. His hand shot out, knocking the barrel aside before she realised fully what was happening. She fired automatically, but the gun resounded with nothing more than the dull click of a jammed chamber.

The man was huge and bulky, towering over her; he bent to look into her face. She tried to take another backward step, but he gripped her wrist; he twisted it backwards, and she moaned faintly with the pain. One by one her fingers slipped off the trigger. He might have knocked it out of her hand in the first place, but he seemed to prefer to wait until she let it go herself. It fell on the ground between them. She opened her mouth to call Trigg, but his rough hand, smelling of sweat and rum, was clamped over her face. She clawed at it madly, until he reached round her body and, with one arm, pinned both hers to her side.

"Not a sound out of you, or I'll break your neck! Do you hear?"

The huge hand slipped down and circled her throat.

Terrified, Sara stared up at him. The hoarse, whispered voice had the tones of a countryman with a London accent overlaid. He was drunk. The reek of his breath as he leant over her made her stomach heave. His face was shining with sweat, his eyes red-rimmed. He swayed as he held her.

"How many men here?" he said. "Two?"

She didn't answer.

His hand tightened threateningly on her throat. "Don't try to trick me—I saw them! Both wounded—dead by now probably." He touched the gun with his foot. "The ammunition for this—where is it?"

She made no answer, except to jerk her head backwards in the direction of the door and the passage leading to the rest of the house.

"Any food?"

"Over there." She nodded towards the shelves lining one side of the kitchen.

He gave a satisfied grunt.

"They left me behind, curse them!" he said. "I fell and knocked myself out, I did, and the bastards took my gun and left me lying there by the river bank." He gave a low, expressionless laugh, shaking her a little. "But I'm not one to be easily beaten—and now I've got more than any of them. I've got a gun and food—and no one to go shares with me. And I have you as well!''

Her eyes widened slowly.

A smile spread itself over his sweating face. "You don't remember me, do you? You've been playing the fine lady too long now to remember your pals of the *Georgette.*"

She stiffened, and tried to break away.

"Ha! You didn't like that, did you?" He rocked back on his heels. "Oh, I've watched you—a year it is now since I first came here. I don't forget how it used to be. You, with rags on your back, and not a shoe on your foot. And now you'll turn your nose away from the bad smell of us—from the likes of us who slave on this farm to put silk on your body, and gold in your husband's purse. Well . . . you made the most of it on the *Georgette,* didn't you? You found your way into that fool's bed while the rest of us rotted under the hatches. D'y think I don't remember? I remember every time I clap eyes on you—and I've ached to get my hand round this white neck of yours and choke the life out of it . . . you scheming whore!"

"Who are you?" The words were nothing more than a whisper, because of the pressure of his hand on her throat.

"You'd have no cause to remember me, Mrs. Maclay. Except you might happen to remember that they flogged the skin off my back twice on that voyage. Johnny's the name. Johnny the Penman, they used to call me in London. A pretty well-known citizen I was before they hung a sentence of fourteen years round my neck. Time was when I could have forged the Governor's signature so as he wouldn't know it himself. But not any more. Not since I lost two fingers cutting wood for your bloody fires! I nearly lost the whole hand, but did Mrs. Maclay know about it, or come to bind it up? Not a chance! The great lady doesn't put her foot inside a convict's hut!

"But let me tell you," he said, his face sickeningly close to Sara's, "you'll never escape it. No matter how long you're in this colony, or how far behind you leave the *Georgette,* you'll never be allowed to forget it. Every convict has you marked— and every fresh arrival hears your story. There'll always be someone to reach up and drag you down, like I'm doing now. Do you understand? You'll never be allowed to forget it!

"Well . . ." He shook her roughly. "I won't have to care about it any more. I'm free, and I don't have to look at you any longer, or hear you giving orders, or see you lift your skirt out of the way, in case it might touch one of us. No more of it, d'y hear? I'm getting away, across the river where they won't find me. And I don't care if I never lay eyes on another white woman again. The native women will do for my purposes."

Then he spat out of the corner of his mouth.

"The horses," he muttered, "where are they?"

"I don't know."

"Don't lie, you whore! There should be three horses. They were gone from the stables even before we raided the stores. Where have you hidden them?"

"I don't know anything about the horses."

He struck her then across the face. "Whore! Tell me!"

"I don't know!" she gasped.

He shook her again, his eyes suddenly crazy. "I'll make you tell me, gutterbrat!" He struck her a second time in anger. She reeled back, almost out of his grasp.

Abruptly, his expression altered. His sweating face became alive with a new emotion, a vicious, drunken lust that hitting her had awakened. He rode his sensation with deliberate abandon, laughing wildly. He took one of his hands away from her, and looked down at it, as if surprised at the power there.

"We'll see now who can touch you, and who can't. You're not too good for a convict to have, Sara Dane, when he has his mind to it. Whore . . ." He breathed this softly. "You were glad to take what you could get when you were on the *Georgette*. Now I'm not asking!"

His hand jerked out and ripped open the bodice of her gown down to the waist. He was half-smiling.

He loosened his grasp a moment to kiss her, and Sara suddenly tore his hand away, and clutched fumbling at her breast. But she wasn't quick enough to catch the tiny Italian dagger. It fell to the floor between them, tinkling, with a sharp little sound against the gun.

The man looked down, and his slight hesitation gave her time to stoop quickly and snatch at it before he did. She crouched, with the dagger in her right hand, facing him. Maddened, he lunged at her, hitting her again across the face. The blow knocked her to the ground; she lay there sideways on her elbow. For a few seconds he stood looking down at her, and then he dropped to one knee, balancing drunkenly with his hand on the floor. From that position he began inching forward.

She let him come as close as she dared, then, like a flash, she twisted and rolled on her left side, thrusting the pointed dagger upwards with all her strength. His mouth fell open the instant he realised what she was doing. He made a clumsy stab to push her away, but as he bent forward, the blade punctured the skin of his throat.

A glazed, startled look sprang to his eyes, an expression both of terror and disbelief. He grasped frantically at his throat, his fingers encountering the dagger. He dragged at Sara's hand, trying to loosen her hold, but the movement sent the point farther home. Blood began to gush out. A bubble of blood appeared at the side of his mouth, and his hand slipped away nervelessly. Slowly he fell forward, the dagger sinking into his throat up to the hilt.

He fell across her grotesquely, with arms outstretched. He was already dead when his body struck her, and the blood came in a bright red stream from his mouth. She pushed at his shoulders until at last he slid off, rolling to one side. He lay face upwards, his eyes open, and the dagger slanting downwards at an angle from his throat. The delicate silver handle gleamed in the faint light.

Sara twisted away from him and began to get stiffly to her knees. But she paused and shuddered. The man's blood was still warm on her gown, and on her bare breasts and throat. Her face twitched with pain from the blows he had given her. She looked down at her hands, and then over at the dead man. Her stomach heaved; she wanted to be sick.

And while she knelt there, the sounds of stumbling footsteps reached her from the passage. She lifted her head, too weary to care now who it was. She waited, and at last Jeremy's figure appeared in the shadowy doorway. Her breath came in a little gasp of relief. In the lantern-light she could see the sweat standing out on his forehead and his upper-lip, but his eyes no longer had the mad brightness of fever. He swayed unsteadily, clutching at the door-frame.

"Sara . . ." he said, using her name for the first time.

"Jeremy!"

She began to crawl across the floor towards him.

V

Jeremy watched her closely across the office table. They sat there alone. She poured a second brandy for them both; her hands were unsteady, and some of it slopped over and ran down the edge of the glass. The lamp stood on the floor; it threw the shadow of the table upwards to the ceiling. Sara's features were darkened and distorted by the shadow, Her hair hung down her back in a wild tangle; the blood had dried on her torn bodice, on her breast and hands.

She put the glass to her lips, biting on it to stop their trembling. Then she gripped it with both her hands and set it carefully down.

"There's nothing more to tell you," she said dully, looking away. "Now you know the whole of the story that will be ringing through the colony in a few days' time." She cupped her forehead in her hand. "I can just hear it . . . 'Mrs. Maclay, with an ex-convict's special gifts with a knife, kills one of her own labourers' or what's worse still, 'one of her old associates of the *Georgette*.'" Her head sank down farther, and she gave a low groan. "Oh, Jeremy, what meat the gossips will make of it! I have at last fulfilled all their ideas of a tavern-room slut. That's what he called me—a whore!"

"Sara!" Jeremy leaned forward, the movement making his head spin with pain.

She lifted her eyes to his. "What do you care about that? You've never expected any different from me. If you dared, you'd call me a whore as well."

He gripped the edge of the table with both hands and made a slow attempt to rise.

"If I were capable of it, Sara," he said faintly, "I'd go round and shake you for that."

She raised her eyebrows. "Do you deny that you've thought that of me . . . ever since the day of my marriage? Deny that you've thought Andrew no more than a madman to have married me."

After a long silence, he said slowly, "I don't deny that I thought it, once. But my views have changed."

Jeremy focused his eyes on the damp rings the glasses had made on the surface of the table.

"It's not what happened in the last few hours that's changed it," he said. "Though, God knows, I owe my life to you—neither of the other two would have gone to bring me in." He smudged one of the rings with his finger. "No . . . the change isn't as recent as that. No man in his right senses could have done anything but admire you right along."

She made a sound that might have meant anything.

He looked at her quickly. "I was jealous of you, Sara—because Andrew loved you. A man who's cut off from the normal society of women is apt to either hate or love the one woman within his reach—and at the same time out of his reach. I desired you, but wouldn't acknowledge it—even to myself. God knows, that's understandable. You're lovely enough for any man to want to possess.

"Andrew and I were friends before you came. And then you confounded me because you *were* all the things he had boasted you would be . . . efficient, calm, intelligent . . . You never complain about the sort of life you have here at Kintyre. You never mention the loneliness. I've seen you bear your child away from the company of other women without showing the fear you must have felt. I've watched you grow to meet every fresh demand Andrew made. And I've watched you become more and more vital to his being every month you've been together. He wasn't much more than a small gambler when he came off the *Georgette*. What he is now you've made him."

She did not move; she watched him closely.

After a pause he said, "And even in face of all this I was half-disappointed because you hadn't turned out to be the slut I'd hoped. If you want the truth, Sara, I was disappointed that you didn't fall into my open arms."

He leaned back and took his hands off the table.

"My jealousy was finished when I saw you in there." He nodded in the direction of the kitchen. "That made me finally realise that since yesterday afternoon you had done what I didn't believe any woman would do. Whatever you care to do in the future will seem all right to me."

He lay back in the chair with his eyes closed, his hand gingerly going to the place where the blood had clotted on his shoulder bandage.

"From now on, Sara . . ." He paused and opened his eyes. "From now on I'll slave for you. You can take that just whatever way you like. But you can take it from me straight what my motives will be. They'll be love and desire—because I doubt if Andrew ever loved or desired you any more than I do now." His voice had become hard, and his lips too dry. "I'll have to forget this talk—act as if it had never happened—because you belong to Andrew. You're his . . . but I shall serve you whatever way I can as long as I live."

She did not reply, merely nodded. Then her head sank down

on her arms folded on the table. As Jeremy watched, her shoulders seemed to shake; she might have been weeping, but he wasn't sure. The soft glow of the lamp shone on her skin where the gown had been torn away. The mad disarray of her hair gave her a look of troubled youth. He watched her, and longed to reach across the table and lay his hand reassuringly on her arm. But she gave no sign that she wanted him—or was even conscious of him any more.

They sat in silence for a long time while the daylight grew stronger at the chinks in the shutters. For half an hour Sara did not move; she lay with her head on her arms, like a piece of warm-coloured stone. Finally, the same sound roused them both. Sara stirred and lifted her head to listen. Then she rose and walked with dragging steps to the window.

"The soldiers," she said. She opened back the shutters and the sounds of the horses came clearly to Jeremy.

"Six of them—and Lieutenant Grey."

She turned slowly and faced him. Her face was tired and old.

"Do you realise that Andrew will hear this story—everyone else's version of it—long before I have a chance to tell it to him myself?"

She dashed a hand frantically across her eyes.

"And what a story they'll make of it, Jeremy! A dead man lying in the kitchen, and Mrs. Maclay hasn't even troubled to wash off his blood!"

Then she laughed, the sound was hysterical and false.

VI

Andrew reached Kintyre at dawn the following morning. Sara, lying awake in the shadowed bedroom, heard the hoofbeats distinctly break into the silence. She sat up and listened—she listened also to the footsteps of the soldier who was posted on guard on the veranda.

The horse came up the slope at speed; Andrew's voice impatiently answered the sentry's challenge. His heavy boots clattered over the wooden boards. Sara lit a candle beside the bed, and waited.

He opened the bedroom door, and for a few seconds stood there looking at her. Then he pushed the door closed with his foot. She felt his arms go about her shoulders, and he thrust his face against her breasts.

"Sara! Sara!" His tone was muffled, but she was aware of his relief. His body trembled, and his clothes carried the smell of the horse's sweat.

He raised his face to hers. "I came as soon as I heard. I've ridden all the way from Sydney without a break. Sara—you're not hurt?"

She shook her head. "Just tired out—and not able to sleep."

"The swine!" he said. "If they've as much as put a finger on you . . ."

"They didn't, Andrew. They fired the outhouses—and looted. . . . That's all."

"David?"

She gave a little smile. "David is all right. He slept through most of it." Then her eyes grew suddenly afraid. "Andrew, it was terrible. There's so much to tell you. I . . ."

His hands moved and gripped her arms. "Don't try to tell me about it now, Sara. Everyone has the story—in one form or another. I'll hear it from you when you're fit to tell me."

She closed her eyes, and he gently pressed his lips to them.

"Dearest," he said, "when the news first came they said you were hurt—and then that you were dead. I didn't know you were safe until I got to Parramatta." He thrust his head once more against her breast, gripping her in an agony of possessiveness. "God in heaven, Sara . . . If they had killed you . . ."

He looked up at her. "If you had been dead, I couldn't have lived."

She lifted her hand and stroked back the matted hair from his forehead. It was stuck with sweat and dirt.

"I'll not let it happen again," he said. "By God, I won't! They'll never be trusted again, as I've been fool enough to trust them in the past. It won't worry me if I'm the most hated man in the colony—no convict is going to get the better of me. From now on I'll make every use I can of their bodies for labour, and I'll forget about their souls. If any of them have souls, they're too insignificant to be troubled with."

He relaxed his grip on her, and she fell back against the pillows. His lips were thin and determined as he spoke; he had the angry, passionate look of a man thwarted. Sara knew that whatever past leniency he had shown the convicts was finished. Andrew had never been a patient man, and he would not make an effort now to be either patient or forgiving.

At last he straightened and took a backward step away from

the bed. He said reluctantly, "You need rest, my darling. I must leave you . . ."

He hesitated, poised on one foot.

She held out her hand to him, "But I think there's something else you want to talk about. There's something beside the convicts . . . ?"

He shrugged. "Nothing. Well . . . it must wait until you've rested."

She smiled. "I'm not so tired that my curiosity wouldn't keep me from resting." She leaned her head a little to one side. "Andrew, come and tell me."

He smiled broadly at her; it was a grin that wiped the fatigue from his face. With a single movement he was beside the bed again and had flung himself down full length on it. He lay close to her; he was on his back and he stared up at the ceiling.

"What a girl you are, my Sara! I'd be lost without you!" He reached out and caught her hand. Their fingers laced together, and locked. He closed his eyes.

"I want to start building in Sydney," he said.

She sat up at that and bent over him, her fingers gripping his tightly.

"Andrew! You mean to give up Kintyre?"

He opened his eyes. "No, keep Kintyre—and go on expanding as we've always planned. In spite of what those swine did to the stores, Kintyre will still be the richest farm on the Hawkesbury."

The grin spread over his face again, and made it, even with its toughened, weathered skin, seem like a boy's face. He drew her down until her lips were almost touching his own.

"Kintyre is only a part of what I want," he said eagerly. "Sara, things are stirring in Sydney. The world is beginning to know of its existence—and the possibilities of trade are bringing ships in. More than ever I'm convinced that the colony is going to command great prosperity—and Sydney is the port. As it opens up there'll be need for stores and warehouses and wharves— and I must be there and have land to keep up with the growth. I might even be able to get my hands on some sort of ship, and make voyages to the East for cargoes. It would be a gamble, of course . . . But with you to help me . . ."

She drew a little away from him, and she could see the flame of ambition and a young man's excitement lighting his face. The silence of Kintyre that she loved so much was all about them, and in her mind she saw it replaced by the clatter and confusion of the ugly little town sprawling over Port Jackson's bays. Andrew was asking her to go back to face the world of women and prejudice from which she had broken free. Because of his streak of trader's blood she realised that she was being asked to endure the loneliness of long voyages. Kintyre would become a refuge only to be visited occasionally, a place to be longed for in the midst of Sydney's discouraged-looking dwellings. For a moment her eyes turned to the window. The peace of the Hawkesbury Valley was real and very precious in the early spring dawn. She found it hard to believe that he wanted her to leave it.

But she looked again at Andrew; her fingers moved slowly over his cheek and forehead, and then they curled about the lock of matted hair.

"Dearest," she said softly, "tell me what it is you plan to do."

PART THREE

Chapter One

The house that Andrew Maclay finished building for himself at the end of February, 1800, was something as close to a mansion as Sydney was likely to see for some time to come. If it lacked quite the touch of grandeur he would have liked, its proportions were spacious and graceful enough, with wide, cool verandas facing out over the harbour. He built it on a site above Woolloomooloo Bay, removed from the noise of the township's dusty streets, from the sounds of horses and oxen teams, and from the stream of raw, undisciplined life that was part of the tiny port.

In the five years since Andrew had made his decision to leave the Hawkesbury, the colony had altered subtly. Twelve years since its foundation, it was acquiring now an air of permanence, although the Colonial Office was tardy about admitting it to the status of something more than a penal settlement. It grew steadily—free settlers dribbled in, and small exploration parties, most of them organised and driven on by the personal need of land, were opening up the hinterland, pushing always farther along the rivers. The mountain barrier still defeated them, but Governor Hunter was encouraging exploration of the coast. Young Lieutenant Matthew Flinders, with his friend, naval surgeon George Bass, had made a voyage through the strait Bass had discovered earlier, sailed round Van Dieman's Land, proving that it was not connected with the mainland They were hardly more than boys, both of them, but the southern ocean was giving up its mysteries to their eager adventuring.

But the administrative framework of the colony was very little

156

altered since the hey-day of Lieutenant-Governor Grose. The ruling few of the New South Wales Corps still lined their pockets with the profits from rum and trade, while the rest struggled for their very existence. The military dictatorship had supposedly ended with the arrival of Governor Hunter—its activities had not ended, but were carried on only slightly less blatantly, with a mock deference and a raised eyebrow towards the unhappy, powerless Governor. They retained the monopoly on the sale of the cargoes of ships trading with the port, they distilled and distributed rum illegally—and since very little agriculture was undertaken on the Government's behalf, the military still demanded and got their fantastic prices for the grain, without which the colony could not surive. Hunter was hopelessly caught up in the bonds forged during the three years when there had been no responsible Government. He had not the cunning to match wits sharpened by greed, nor did he have control of the troops. The troops obeyed only their officers, and it was to the advantage of the officers to forestall, frustrate, and even ignore every order the Governor issued. It had never at any time been an equal match, and Hunter knew that he was fast reaching a stage where he would be forced to admit his defeat. Beyond that point there was nothing but his recall to England, and the hope of a pension.

Andrew Maclay had had his generous share in the pickings of these fruitful years. He had made his profits, with the rest of the buying-ring. Kintyre's acres had increased, and it was still the most prosperous farm on the Hawkesbury. He had fulfilled his dream of the store in Sydney; it had not been done easily, but it stood now, like a banner for his triumph, and a warehouse was building up beside it. He was the registered owner of a sloop, the *Thistle*, which traded regularly in the East. And he was still talked of as the luckiest man with a pack of cards in his hands that the colony yet knew of.

But these alone had not built and furnished the house overlooking Woolloomooloo Bay. To do this he had had to go beyond the colony—to the East, and back to London itself.

The eyes of the colony had fastened with keen, and, for the most part, rather malicious, interest on Andrew when he announced in 1795 that he intended to trade in Sydney. He was given his grant of land at a noisy, busy intersection of streets close to the public wharf—hardly the place, the curious whispered, that a gentleman would want to settle his wife and family. But, after all, when that wife was a former convict . . . The colony still shrugged its shoulders in amusement and scorn at the very idea of Sara.

After seven months the Maclay store, with living-rooms above it, was finished, and Sara arrived from Kintyre, household belongings and bundles piled high on a wagon. The upstairs windows looked out on to the shipping in the harbour, and to Government House on the rise above it; close at hand were the uncobbled streets, either dust choked or pools of mud, according to the weather, and never free, day or night, from the clamour of Sydney's rowdy, often quarrelsome inhabitants. On the day of her arrival, Sara, strained by the upheaval of the move, gave one backward, regretful thought to the peace she had left behind at Kintyre, then turned briskly to making a home out of the bare rooms.

Her appearance at the opening of the store was brief, and after that she was seldom seen. Two months later her second son, Duncan, was born. It seemed to the colony that the confinement was barely over when Mrs. Maclay gave a sharp impetus to scandalised gossip by leaving David and the new baby in Annie Stokes's hands, and appearing daily in the store to attend to customers. And it was noted, almost immediately, that the store was always crowded with men—many of whom went by the name of gentlemen—at the times when she was known to be there. Seated behind a small desk she took orders, discussed the possibility of securing certain goods in short supply, smiling and talking pleasantly and keeping a wary eye on the young clerks, fresh out from England, who rushed about and perspired freely in their efforts to please her. The women of the colony said that Andrew Maclay must be short of money when he needed to have his wife to attend to the business. The menfolk said nothing, and continued to take their custom to the Maclay's store.

The sloop, the *Thistle*, was Andrew's biggest business venture yet. He bought her after she had limped into the harbour at the end of a nightmare voyage from the Cape, her timbers rotten and taking in water at every seam. Her owner-master was not a coward, but he could not face another voyage in a vessel that was literally going to pieces under his feet. He sold cheaply to Andrew, glad to be rid of his burden. Andrew, trusting to fortune for a good harvest at Kintyre, borrowed money to refit. From amongst the motley host of men that Sydney, as a seaport, was beginning to collect, he found two who claimed once to have been shipwrights. He put them in charge of his hired labourers, and the rebuilding of the *Thistle* began. Material was short, labour was short—and Andrew himself spent many days squeezed into the narrow space of the carpenter's walk, working on the hull.

The harvest was a good one; there was more money, and the *Thistle* was ready for sea at last. With a sense of aching relief, Andrew paid back his loan, and got together an oddly-assorted crew from the seamen who had drifted into the port and had been left behind. He engaged a short, wiry Yankee skipper, who was idling about without a ship, to take command. Everything was ready for her to sail for Calcutta when the first mate fell ill. After an hour's earnest talk with Sara, Andrew took his place. The *Thistle* left with the tide, and Sydney sat back to enjoy the spectacle of watching a woman trying to run both town store and Hawkesbury farm. It was an engaging item of gossip and speculation, and the store was always crowded with men anxious to see what she would make of it.

Sara made a better job of it than even Andrew believed possible. With Jeremy Hogan beside her, she became a familiar sight on the road between Sydney and the Hawkesbury. Work went on in the usual way at Kintyre, as if Andrew himself were there, and she even took his place in the buying-ring when a ship entered harbour with a cargo for sale. At first she was an object for curiosity and slight amusement; later Sydney learned that she had a business head as hard as her husband's, and that she was never to be outwitted in striking a bargain.

"No gentlewoman could have done it," was the general opinion in the colony.

But Sara appeared to care very little for general opinion. As long as trade came to her door, as long as the herds of livestock increased each year at Kintyre, and the acres under cultivation grew, she seemed content to bear the loneliness, and the dust which drifted into her upstairs rooms during the scorching summer months.

Both she and Jeremy knew that scandal was waiting to link their names at the first opportunity. The friendship they shared since the night of the convict outbreak on the Hawkesbury was now so strong that they dare not display it. Jeremy never stayed with her longer than was necessary, and kept rigidly to his role of Andrew Maclay's overseer. He spent all of his time at the farm, except when he received her request to accompany her to a sale, or to come to town to bring her back to Kintyre for a brief visit. The hopes of the gossip-mongers were dampened, but never quite died.

Winds were favourable, and Andrew was back in the leaking *Thistle* months before anyone expected him. He unloaded a cargo that ranged from frying-pans and silks, to sandalwood and cashmere shawls. His cargo carried the look and feel of the East with it, and people starved for colour and excitement flocked to inspect—and those who could afford it, to buy. The store had never been so crowded before, or the shelves so crammed with goods. Jeremy rode down from Kintyre to help them, and when he returned, Andrew, Sara, and the two children were with him.

Andrew basked in the peace of Kintyre for a two weeks' spell, counted his herds, went through the accounts with Jeremy, and with thoughtful, careful eyes appraised the startling different quality of the wool of the tiny flock—three ewes and a ram of merino sheep, which Sara had persuaded John Macarthur to sell her. It was well known that Macarthur was experimenting with wool—he was the best farmer in the colony, and he had an unshakable belief in the future of his merinos. Andrew considered him worth following.

The short period of rest at Kintyre seemed to renew Andrew's energies. He had now seen what an entire cargo of his own could realise in clear profit, and he couldn't for long resist the temptation to repeat his venture. As soon as he returned to Sydney he started once more on the job of patching up the *Thistle*. Two months later he sailed in her again, bound for the East. From an upstairs window Sara watched her sails breaking slowly; she watched her out of sight down the harbour.

The colony never learned the full details of Andrew Maclay's second voyage. The captain of an American vessel brought Sara letters from Calcutta. She told no one what news they contained, except that her husband intended going on to London. But the captain himself had a tale to tell, a story he claimed had gone the rounds of Calcutta—a story of the sort of chance of which a man sometimes idly dreams. After a storm off the coast of Bengal, he said, the *Thistle* had come upon a Bristol merchantman, piled with a valuable cargo, and drifting helplessly towards the rocks. It was a feat of splendid seamanship to make contact and bring the vessel into port, and it was the opinion in Calcutta that Andrew Maclay had truly earned every penny of the salvage money.

That was the story as it was given to the colonists—no one knew if it was the true story. Then, nineteen months after she had sailed from Port Jackson, a sloop bearing the name of *Thistle*, but in no other way resembling her battered predecessor, dropped anchor in Sydney Cove, within sight of Sara's windows. In less than an hour the news had spread through the whole town that Andrew Maclay was back.

Many curious and speculative eyes watched him come ashore, watched him stride along the dusty street towards the store. But there was no one to witness his meeting with Sara, or to hear what they said to each other in that first hour. Not even Annie Stokes, ear against keyhole, heard that.

The result of the trip was a cargo for sale that kept Sydney talking for a month, and buying for much longer; Andrew said he bought the new *Thistle* in London—and no further talk of his voyage would loosen any information about the Bristol merchantman, or of salvage money. But it was noted he applied immediately for a grant of land, and began building himself a house on Woolloomooloo Bay—a private residence far grander than anything Sydney had yet seen. Within another month the *Thistle* sailed again for the East, still under the command of the Yankee captain; this time Andrew remained behind. Sydney already knew that Sara was expecting her third child.

The child, another son, Sebastian, was born above the store a few weeks before the house was completed. By then, from the evidence of the improvements to the Hawkesbury property, a smaller farm at Toongabbie which Andrew had just bought, and from the furnishings and silk hangings he had brought out from England for the new house, most people were convinced that the story of the salvage deal was true. Andrew Maclay was spending far more money than any small ship-owner and trader could be expected to lay his hands on readily. Sara moved her belongings and the three children from the store to the new house—finally given its name of Glenbarr by Andrew—on one of the last summer days of 1800, when the street into which she looked for more than four years was choked with dust. The townspeople watched, smiling broadly at the future prospect of a convict attempting to set up house in the manner of a lady of fashion.

The late summer of 1800 also brought the first ship into the harbour with the news that Napoleon was back in France, having slipped out of Egypt, leaving his army where Nelson's victory at the Nile had bottled it up. He was back in Paris to overthrow the Directorate, and assumed the position of First Consul. Paris had welcomed him in a frenzy of joy.

Sydney discussed the news, digesting it warily, remembering that five years earlier they had not even heard of Napoleon's name. They could recall too that those five years had also seen the rise of Nelson, and the triumph of the Navy at Cape St. Vincent and Camperdown. There had, also with this, been the blow to British security and pride dealt by the naval mutiny at the Nore; and in 1798, Ireland had broken again into open rebellion.

On the colony itself the war in Europe had three direct effects—the Colonial Secretary had neither time nor supplies to meet its growing demands, the backwash of the Irish Rebellion had already hit it in a wave of political prisoners, whose Jacobite views and murderous humour made them singularly unwelcome; and almost the worst effect, from the Governor's point of view, was that, with a war to fight in Europe, there was no chance of fresh Army officers, uncontaminated by rum and power, being attracted by the idea of service with the New South Wales Corps.

The Governor cursed Napoleon for more than the obvious reasons.

II

Jeremy's brows were drawn together thoughtfully. He held his wine-glass loosely as he surveyed the room. After a few days it would take shape as the drawing-room of the Maclays' new house—at the moment it wore the ugliness of bare boards, uncurtained windows, and the litter of half-emptied packing-cases. In the centre, at the table covered with oddments of china, Sara and Andrew stood together, close to the single lamp, concentrating on carving a cold roast duck. There was an eager, restless look about their faces, and neither betrayed fatigue, although the household had been stirring at dawn that morning. The lamplight, seeking out the lines in Andrew's weather-toughened skin, and the warm colour of Sara's hair, also caught the glitter in their eyes, and the swift half-smile which kept appearing on each face. Sara wore a limp cotton gown, faded by the sun of three summers, and Andrew's coat was the one in which he had worked with the carpenters on the old *Thistle*. Their movements were confident, and full of a sense of youth and excitement.

Jeremy listened to their odd snatches of talk.

"... and the garden must be laid out properly this time, Sara."

"Yes—" Sara paused to lay some of the meat on a plate. "But not too much. Formal gardens don't suit the landscape here. In any case," she added, "it could never be half as lovely as the garden at Kintyre."

Andrew glanced quickly over his shoulder. "Do you hear that, Jeremy? I've built my wife the finest house in the colony, and on her first night in it she can think of nothing else but that miserable hut on the Hawkesbury."

Sara came towards Jeremy with the plate. "If this house is as happy as Kintyre, then I'll be happy too."

Jeremy smiled at her. "A woman's first love is like no other, is it, Sara?"

Her lips pursed a little. "No, like no other."

They sat down on packing-cases drawn into a rough circle to eat their food. The lamp stood on the floor between them. One long window looking out on the bay was open to the soft wind of this night at the end of summer. Outside the trees stirred gently; in the house there was no sound to disturb the silence. The working-party had left at dusk, and the three children already slept, with Annie snoring beside them, in makeshift beds in a room above the wide entrance hall. There was a full orange moon above the harbour, and beyond the rays of the lamp Jeremy could see the pale, white light on the floorboards in front of each of the long windows.

Suddenly raising her head and looking about, Sara caught Jeremy's gaze.

"It's so quiet here," she said. "And no lights anywhere. We might almost be back at Kintyre."

Andrew laid down his knife with a clatter. "Must you talk of Kintyre that way? One would think it was ours no longer. You know it's waiting there whenever you want it."

His voice was touched with impatience, but the sharp-edged tone disappeared when Sara turned towards him and smiled. The look that passed between them was meant for themselves alone, and Jeremy cursed silently and wished they would remember that they were *not* alone. They were too prone, he thought, to count him as being part of their own happiness, and not to remember that he was a man, someone to be driven half-crazy with an unnamed longing whenever Sara smiled in that fashion. In the years since the convict raid on Kintyre, the relationship between the three of them had deepened into a trust and comradeship that was not definable in words. As far as the rest of the colony was concerned he was merely Andrew Maclay's overseer, and when anyone else was present that was the role he assumed; but alone with them he was close-knit in a unity of three people who had worked and struggled for the same end. Nevertheless, it was still torture for him to witness the intimacies of their married life, like the expressions written clearly on their faces now. Looking at them, it would have been easy to forget the years since their marriage, and the three children sleeping in the room above the hall.

Impatiently, he bent and caught up his glass from the floor. He spoke before he could check himself, and the words he uttered were the very last he wished to recall to the Maclays—they betrayed his frustration, and the years of being without women of his own kind.

"Do you remember . . . ?" he burst out. And then he halted.

They turned to look at him inquiringly. He pressed his lips together, and swallowed hard.

"Yes?" Andrew said.

"Do you remember," Jeremy went on slowly, "we drunk a toast at the camp on your wedding night . . . to the mistress of Kintyre?"

Andrew caught his mood at once. His face warmed with an expression of recollection, of tenderness. Watching him, Jeremy suffered an agony of envy. For a minute they sat there, remembering, all three of them, the cold wind which blew that night and the stars, too bright and close.

"Do I remember . . . ?" Andrew murmured. "It's almost seven years ago." He turned to his wife. "Full years, Sara, for both of us. Who could have known . . . ?" Then he shrugged. "But these seven years are only the beginning There's still so much yet to do."

Sara said gently, almost as an aside. "Will you never be satisfied, Andrew?"

"Satisfied?" He laughed. "Why should I be? Only fools are satisfied. Why should I sit in a chair and let the world spin about me?"

He stood up. All around his eyes Jeremy could see the lines, too deep, and too many for his years. The eyes themselves were a strained, faded blue, as if the sun of the long voyages had taken the colour out of them.

"I shall be a rich man yet," Andrew declared. "But not in the way this narrow corner calls wealth. I want wealth as the rest of the world knows it—wealth that even London would acknowledge!"

Andrew rose and took a couple of paces across the room, hands behind his back. The lamplight revealed the stained coat, the frill of torn linen at the wrist, the unpowdered hair. But how much more impressive now, Jeremy thought, than when he appeared in the magnificence of lace, silver-buckled shoes, and the brocaded coats he had brought back with him from London. He stood with his legs wide apart, as if he were on the deck of a ship.

He turned round and looked down at his wife.

"Some day I'll take you back to London, Sara. You'll have everything you ever wanted then. Some day . . ."

His lips parted in a smile. "In the meantime, we'll live here—removed from the noise and muck." He gestured to indicate the township built above the adjoining bay. "I'll have land—more land and more ships. And I'll make the house here beautiful before I'm finished. Like this . . . I'll show you!"

His enthusiasm flamed suddenly and he stooped to pick up a fisherman's knife they had used to cut the rope around the packing-cases. Then he squatted before the case he had been sitting on, reaching out at the same time to draw the lamp nearer. With unhesitant strokes he began sketching lines in the rough wood with the point of the knife. The hard surface resisted him, and he swore softly with annoyance. The other two watched while the plan of the house as it now was, became recognisable.

"Now . . ." Andrew said stabbing with the knife, and turning towards them.

He broke off, and raised his head. The door-knob rattled softly; then silence followed. Sara and Jeremy twisted their heads to look behind. Andrew straightened slowly, the knife still in his hand. He moved quietly towards the door.

He opened it with a jerk, and stopped. His eldest son stood there, startled, barefooted, with his nightshirt almost reaching the floor, and his hand outstretched, as if he were still grasping the knob.

"Papa . . ."

"David!" Andrew stared at the child. "Laddie, what is it?"

David took a step into the room. He looked at his mother. "I woke up—and I heard you."

Sara was beside him in an instant, and had swept him up into

165

her arms. He settled contentedly there, his head against her shoulder, his inquiring eyes roaming round the unfamiliar room. He glanced from his father to Jeremy, and then gave an excited wriggle.

"May I stay, Mama?"

Sara smiled over the top of his head at Andrew. "Let him stay a little. After a few nights they'll be used to this house—and the quiet—and then they'll settle down."

Andrew nodded, reaching out to tousle the boy's flaxen, curling hair. "Why not? You've never been up as late as this, have you, my son?"

He walked back to the packing-case, and Sara sat down again, with David in her arms. She stretched the nightshirt Annie had made for him to cover his feet; he promptly thrust one foot from underneath and wriggled his toes expressively. Sara's left arm was round him, pressing him close to her. Her free hand rested in his lap. He clutched it tightly, staring in wonder at the knife his father held.

Andrew squatted once more before the rough carving. He added a few lines. "I want another wing here . . ." The plan cut into the wood was now L-shaped. "It will face north-west, to get the afternoon sun."

"A new wing?" Sara said. "What for?"

"That's going to be the new drawing-room—and whatever other rooms we want above it. And we'll have a conservatory along this side."

"A conservatory?" Sara echoed faintly, glancing at Jeremy.

"Yes—why not? The native plants are certainly worth more attention than the people here give them. Think of the orchids we could grow! We'll have a gardener out from England. And, later on, we'll terrace the lawns down to the water's edge."

Sara laid her cheek against David's hair. "This all sounds very grand—for a little place like Sydney."

Andrew winked at her, grinning. "Sydney won't always be a little place. When I build my new wing, I'll bring the carpets from Persia, and the chandeliers from Venice."

Sara's eyes sparkled suddenly. "When will this be?"

He shrugged. "When trade opens up enough to allow me to carry my plans through—when the population has expanded, and can support more trade. I will want two ships—even three ships."

Then he shrugged again. "All that is for the future—for the

present we'll manage well enough." His hands opened expressively, taking in the spacious proportions of the room. He said, "The new wing would be merely a showplace—something that represents land on the Hawkesbury, ships in the harbour, and a store to sell their cargoes. Give me ten—fifteen—years like the last seven, and there's nothing I won't be able to do."

As he spoke he looked directly at his wife and son.

Jeremy sipped his wine thoughtfully. He felt the conviction in Andrew's words, he felt that these dreams would materialise; he had now come to believe that, so long as Andrew lived, this fabulous luck would hold, and his preposterous fantasy of conservatories and laid-out gardens in a country still unable to feed itself would, in time, be realised. He would have his new wing, and the display of magnificence his heart craved. But he was an adventurer, a trader, and a gambler; he understood the hard facts of his business too well to become immersed in the mere trappings of wealth. It would, as he said, merely represent the solid assets of land, ships, store, and warehouse. It would be no more than his recreation, while he gave his life to attending to the things which made it possible.

Jeremy spoke suddenly, the trace of a smile on his lips.

"Another toast." he said. "This time to the house of Maclay!"

He raised his glass to the three of them.

Chapter Two

Under the low beams of the main room in the Maclay store there was always the mingled odour of sandalwood, spices, new candles, and coffee-beans. Andrew claimed he could supply every need of the settlers; the store's wide rooms, crammed to the ceilings with the cargoes the *Thistle* brought back, almost justified his claim. Ranged about the walls were the deep, fat kegs of molasses, the bins of flour, sugar, and rice; huge cheeses stood swathed in white cloth. The shelves were piled high with calico and muslin, and an occasional odd roll of silk; there were carefully stacked boxes for shoes and beaver hats. Beside the door was a long rack holding a selection of walking-canes and riding-crops. At the end of a row of bacon sides hanging from the ceiling, the light from the open door caught the satiny gleam of the wood of a guitar. Sara had secured it to a hook by a bunch of coloured ribbons. It swung there gaily—an incongruous support to Andrew's claim.

On a morning in the middle of April, two months after the family had moved to Glenbarr, Sara sat working over the accounts at the desk in one of the store's curved front windows. The autumn sun fell across her shoulder on to the open books, above her head a green parrot clutched the bars of his cage, and muttered vaguely in French. A year ago he had made his first appearance in the store on the arm of a dark-skinned sailor; David, beside his mother's desk, had seen him at once, and played with him delightedly; Sara gave the sailor an unreasonably large amount of tobacco in exchange for him, and, since that day, he had looked down on the life of the store from his cage, obviously revelling in its atmosphere of orderly bustle. He was given a name at the time, but the children had so persistently called him "Old Boney" that no one could now remember the original name.

Sara was deaf to his muttering attempts to distract her. She finished re-checking a column of figures, then she looked up, motioning to one of the three young men who ran the store under her supervision.

"Mr. Clapmore!"

"Ma'am?"

"If the native, Charlie, comes here this afternoon with fish, send him up to the house with them immediately. And mind you only give him half the tobacco he asks for. He's been getting far too much lately in exchange for his fish."

"Very well, Mrs. Maclay."

Sara returned to her figures, basking in the gentle warmth of the sun on her back. This was one of the long succession of perfect autumn days which, every year, the country seemed to throw back as a compensation for the fierce heat of the summer. The air had a softness more mellowing than spring; when a wind stirred it brought a smell of the bush and salt water with it. Her lips moved soundlessly as she worked, but her thoughts kept turning to the memory of how Kintyre looked in the autumn— the noon hush of the bush, and the flow of the great river.

The quill halted above the paper, then she sighed, and, with an effort, began the column again. At the moment there was only one customer in the store—she knew by sight this farmer from Castle Hill who was making a careful selection of printed calico for his wife. A midday quiet was beginning to fall on the streets outside. In a far, dark corner a clock ticked loudly; Boney picked at his seed in a bored fashion.

She glanced up as a shadow darkened the doorway. She smiled, rising at once to greet Major Foveaux, of the New South Wales Corps.

"Good-morning, Major!"

He bowed. "Good-morning, Mrs. Maclay!" He waited until Boney's scream of welcome had died down. "I hoped I'd find you here as usual at this time . . ."

"Can I be of any help to you, Major?"

"Indeed you can, dear lady. I'm looking for a gift . . ."

He shifted his weight uneasily. "I thought perhaps a shawl . . . Yes, a shawl would do nicely, I think."

"Why, certainly." Sara moved past him, towards the shelves. "I have one here from China—a lovely thing." She selected a box, and turned to him again "I'm so glad that you have asked to see it, Major. I always hoped that someone with taste and discrimination would buy it."

"Er . . . quite!"

She carried the box back to the desk, opening it and spreading the embroidered silk before him, letting the sun play on it, letting him take his time feeling and examining it. It was like spreading out the East under his hands, and for a time they were both silent.

Then, as Foveaux considered it, Sara said quietly, "What news of the *Speedy,* Major?"

She spoke of the vessel which had dropped anchor in the harbour the previous morning. As always, the interest of the whole colony had centred upon the ship's arrival—the passengers and cargo, letters from home, and news of the war. In Sydney, with the mail and dispatches still on board, twenty-four hours was still not too short a time to start the ball of gossip rolling.

"The news, Mrs. Maclay?" Foveaux turned to her with the trace of a smile that might well have been malicious. "There's no news that we haven't all been expecting for some time past. But the manner of its arrival is—well—abrupt. The *Speedy* brought out, among her passengers, Phillip Gidley King, whom, you probably remember, was Governor Phillip's lieutenant, and commander at Norfolk Island. It's now definitely known that the dispatches Mr. King presented at Government House this morning carried the Duke of Portland's appointment of him as the next Governor!''

Sara's brows lifted, she did not speak.

"Hunter has been ordered to return to England in the first possible ship," Foveaux said.

Sara glanced warningly across her shoulder. A small group of men were sauntering in from the street.

She said, in a low voice, "Then they're well aware at home of what has been going on here? The Colonial Secretary knows that Hunter has failed to carry out his instructions?''

"Obviously." Foveaux's voice also was low. They were both quite certain of their own part in the machine that had wrecked Hunter—they represented the money-making circle he had not been able to break.

"It's an attempt, then, to tighten control." This, from Sara, was a softly emphatic statement.

"It may be—but they'll soon find out that it will take more than a new Governor to do that. No Governor on earth will stop us trading as we wish to. After all, it's *we* who bear the risks—we produce almost all the food of the colony—it's our money that brings in the few commodities to make life supportable. Things like this . . .' He flicked the shawl, and the silk rose gracefully in the air. "What is the price, might I ask, Mrs. Maclay?''

Sara told him gently.

His eyebrows shot up. He let the silken fringe slip from his fingers, "That's a great deal of money, ma'am.''

She gave him a provoking smile. "It cost my husband a great deal also, Major Foveaux. And then, look . . ." She ran the length of the shawl through her hands. "There's not a trace of sea-water on it. So few of these beautiful things arrive here unstained''—she looked at him fully—"that the price of those that survive is necessarily high.''

Suddenly, with a flash of exotic colours, she flung it about her shoulders. "You see, Major, it's quite perfect.''

"I *do* indeed see, ma'am. But the wearer enhances it beyond all that's fair.''

Sara accepted the compliment smilingly, but unmoved. After four years of such compliments, she was able to judge their commercial value to within a hairbreadth. She reluctantly let the shawl slip from her shoulders.

"In a way, I hate to let it go. Any woman would lose her heart to it.'' She gave a faintly audible sigh. ''Shall I have it wrapped for you, Major?''

''Er . . .'' He capitulated before her inquiring gaze. ''Er . . . yes, if you please.''

''I'm sure that it will . . .'' Sara paused here. Major Foveaux had not mentioned the lady for whom the shawl was intended, and she had long ago learned that, in business, the customer's private affairs were best left to himself. ''I'm sure you won't regret it,'' she finished.

''I hope not, Mrs. Maclay,'' he answered, a little unhappily, watching anxiously as she handed it over to Clapmore for wrapping. It *had* cost a good deal more than he had expected.

She turned to him again. ''Is there anything else I could show you, Major? I have some ribbons . . . And I've quite exquisite lace . . .''

''No,'' he replied hastily. ''Nothing more in that line. But I've a list of provisions.'' He fumbled in his pocket and drew out a slip of paper. ''My housekeeper tells me that my stocks of provisions are low—which is nonsense. I bought enough of the last cargo to feed an army, but it's quite unaccountably used up. These convict house-women, they have the run of everything—they've stolen my stocks, of course, and probably traded them for rum. But there's little I can do about it. I can't stand to see a woman flogged . . . I suppose I could send them packing and try others—but, then, they'd more than likely be twice as bad.''

While he talked, Sara had taken the list from his hand, noting with surprise the quantities he had marked.

''This is a large order, Major—with tea at six shillings a pound, and sugar at four shillings.''

He frowned. ''As much as that?''

She regarded him calmly. ''Surely you are not unaware of the prices, Major? After all, you buy your own share of the cargoes, and then help to fix the prices at which they will be re-sold. You also know that my husband is not permitted to under-cut.''

''Well . . .'' Foveaux shrugged. ''I'm in the unhappy position of being unable to do without these things, whatever the cost. I can't give my guests too bad an impression of the colony in the beginning. They'll know it all soon enough, won't they, Mrs. Maclay?'' He gave a low, quiet laugh, as if this were a joke only they themselves shared.

She smiled demurely, seating herself at the desk. ''Then you have friends among the new arrivals in the *Speedy*, Major?''

"Hardly friends, yet, dear lady. Captain Barwell and I met only briefly in London some years ago. He wrote that he was coming here—and of course I was delighted to offer him and his wife hospitality until they can make their own arrangements. Barwell was wounded in the fighting in Holland and seems to be unfit for further active service. He exchanged his last commission for one with the Corps."

Sara sat still, looking up at him. A chilled sense of wonder had fallen on her; the sun still lay across her shoulders, yet she was cold. At the sound of the name on Foveaux's dry lips, a sense of fear, close to panic, possessed her. She put the hand that held the list firmly on the desk to control its trembling.

"Barwell?" she repeated weakly. "Did you say Barwell?"

"Why, yes—Richard Barwell. Is it possible you know him?"

She groped wildly in her mind for some of the caution the past years had taught her. But it was suddenly gone, In an instant she was like two women—the one rigidly schooled in discipline and discretion, guarding her tongue and her actions from the gossip-hungry colony, keeping the name of Richard Barwell for ever shut away in the secret places of her heart; the other was the girl she once had been, the impetuous girl who ran away from the Bramfield Rectory because of her love for Richard. Now she must sit and listen to herself wrecking the discretion and the long silence, spilling out a claim to having once known Richard. She knew she could not stop herself; it was not possible for her to let Foveaux go without finding out the truth.

"Barwell—from Kent?" she asked.

"Yes. I believe he and his wife are both from Kent. She is the daughter of Sir Geoffrey Watson. Perhaps you know . . . ?"

"I once knew . . . of both families," was all she would say.

"Oh—I see."

The Major made no further comment. There was an unwritten law in the colony—gaining strength each year with the increasing number of convicts whose term of sentence had ended, and who were then entitled to call themselves free men—that the past was never to be spoken of, never to be questioned. A man's past might be guessed at, and spoken of behind his back—but never to his face. This rule was applied to Mrs. Maclay in a special degree; she was the wife of the most prosperous of the free settlers, and still, as an ex-convict, she was not received by the women of her own standing. It created a delicate problem when her past returned to her in such a tangible fashion. It was implied, in the pause that fell between them, that he was not welcome to inquire into the circumstances in which she had known Richard Barwell and his wife.

Her eyes moved, first to the paper in her hand, then back to Foveaux's face.

"I would be obliged if you would not mention this discussion to Captain Barwell, Major." She knew she threw this sop of discretion to her own outraged sense of propriety; this was the gesture of the foolish girl to the wiser woman.

"Of course, ma'am—just as you wish."

Sara acknowledged his half-bow with a slight nod. Until this moment she had always regarded Foveaux as a rather tiresome, amiable fool. Now, as she looked at him, she saw that his eyes were kindly, and that he was perplexed. Perhaps, she thought, he would keep his knowledge of her acquaintance wtth Richard Barwell to himself. She wished that, instead of standing there with his air of helpless wonder, he would go.

"Could you have the provisions sent as soon as possible, Mrs. Maclay?" he asked.

"Immediately, Major."

He saluted her, and left. He walked with the quick, eager step of a man glad to be on his way.

Sara sat there for a long time, the list lying unattended beside her. Her mind did not yet play with the reason for Richard's coming—why he was here, how long he would stay. All that would come to her later, in the hours of wondering and thinking. The only thing that she could clearly grasp was the fact of him coming, unwished and unbidden. He had come back where she did not want him. Sitting so still in the warm sun, with the everyday noises of the store about her, with Boney clawing at the cage practically above her head, she began to question herself about her feelings for Richard since the day she had married Andrew. Her questioning laid open the fact that Richard had been in her thoughts often in the early days of her marriage, and always there with a sense of soreness and grieving; and then he was with her less frequently as Andrew had learned to match all the desires of her heart and body, and as her children had taken her thoughts for themselves. But the picture she had held of Richard was a distinct one, remote from her own life, and therefore never possibly a part of it. He could never seriously interfere with it, dragging the past behind him like a trail of dust. She had loved him once, and she had believed that her love was finished and done with; it destroyed the confidence she had imagined was hers to consider that when he stood before her again she might find her love not so easily put aside a second time. She was shaken and bewildered to realise that, where Richard was concerned, she could not trust herself.

At last her cold fingers took up the list for attention.

"Mr. Clapmore!"

He came hurrying forward "Yes, ma'am?" Then he paused. "Why . . . Mrs. Maclay, are you ill? You look . . ."

"I'm perfectly well" she said sharply. "Please have this order filled out and sent to Major Foveaux immediately."

He took the list from her hand, and made to turn away.

"And, Mr. Clapmore . . ." She spoke more gently, regretting her sharpness.

"Ma'am?"

"Please send for the chaise. I'm . . . going home now."

II

Bennett placed the decanter beside Andrew's hand, hovered noiselessly for a few minutes, and then withdrew. Charles Bennett was Andrew's latest acquisition—a luxury in which it pleased him to revel to the full. He knew, as the whole of Sydney seemed to know, that Bennett had once been in the service of a duke, and that he was dismissed for insidious tippling, But that could not be counted beside the fact that he waited on table without a clatter which halted all conversation. Andrew guessed that he had probably been nothing more elevated than an under-footman in His Grace's household, but he had learned to preside over a meal with great aplomb; his services had been highly bid for in the colony.

To-night, however, Andrew hardly noticed the merits of his manservant. As soon as the door closed he rose from his chair, carrying glass and decanter, and moved to where Sara sat at the opposite end of the table. He filled both their glasses, and then he drew a chair up close to hers.

"What is it, my darling?" As he spoke he took her hand in his own, gazing anxiously into her face. "You've looked whiter than a ghost ever since I came home."

She smiled at him with her eyes, half-relieved, yet half-fearful of his sure knowledge of her. "Dear Andrew—you are never deceived, are you? I've been waiting all day to talk to you."

She sensed him stiffen apprehensively.

"Yes?" he said. "What about?"

"About . . ." She hesitated, her gaze dropping to the glass.

"Sara . . . ?"

She gathered her resolution about her, and looked at him again.

"Andrew . . . Do you remember me telling you about the Barwells—the family my father was tutor to when he died? Do you remember there was a son with whom I used to have lessons—Richard Barwell?"

His hand tightened over hers. "Of course, I remember. What of him?"

Sara tried to raise her glass to her lips, and was forced to put it down again, because suddenly her fingers had grown stiff and clumsy,

She said slowly, "I heard to-day that Richard Barwell has arrived in Sydney with his wife."

Andrew leaned towards her. "Good God! He's here . . . Why?"

"I don't know. Oh, Andrew . . ." she said wretchedly. "I don't know anything except what Major Foveaux told me—that he arrived with the new Governor in the *Speedy*. And that he had exchanged his commission for one in the Corps."

"And his wife?"

Her mouth hardened. "It's as I expected. He married Sir Geoffrey Watson's daughter, Alison."

"Watson? The man who . . . ?"

"The man who charged me with stealing his money," she finished for him. "The one who found me that night at The Angel, on the Marsh."

She put her free hand on top of his, conscious immediately of the warmth. "What shall I do now?" she whispered. "What shall I do?"

He sat, his unpowdered head bent over her hand; with the tip of his finger he absently traced a vein. She had a moment of dread that he would chide her for being melodramatic over Richard's sudden appearance. How to tell Andrew that she had once been in love with Richard, and that she was afraid of her own emotions when she saw him again? Andrew, she thought, you wouldn't understand. Not even you would have understanding enough for this. This was the hidden Sara Dane who had given her passionate young love to Sebastian and to Richard Barwell, of Romney. In honesty to herself, and in fairness to Andrew, she did not expect his tolerance to extend to the girlish caprices of a Sara he did not know.

He raised his head, and she watched his face closely for his expression to change; it came slowly, the strange, preoccupied look that was habitual when his mind was working too swiftly for her to follow its processes. He had the wary and suspicious gaze of a man whose possessions are threatened. It is my happiness he is concerned about, she thought. He will try to stop Richard spreading any knowledge he has of my past. The look on Andrew's face chilled her a little, and still comforted her; it meant that Andrew was not defeated in the way that she was, without a plan of combat, without even a hope of retreat. He had not climbed to his present position on the backs of other men without having nourished his own streak of ruthlessness. His eyes grew bright, until they glittered; the lines about his mouth deepened by the merest fraction, while he continued to stroke her hand with the tip of his finger.

"Are you afraid, my darling?" he said.

"Yes . . ." Her voice was not more than a whisper. "Afraid in a way I've never been before. They can harm me so much. They can harm you and the children. Everything you have built up here, they can tear down with a little talk."

"Then, by God, they *won't* talk!" Andrew snatched his hand away from hers and smacked it down on the surface of the table, "*I* have some say in how matters are run in this colony. Mister Barwell must needs learn quickly that you are neither a servant at Bramfield Rector, nor any longer a convict!"

"Andrew . . ." she breathed. "What will you do?"

"I don't know what I'll do until I can find out more about him—why he's here to begin with. He must be vulnerable in some way—and I must find that way."

She nodded slowly.

"Every man has his vulnerable point," Andrew said, after a pause. "So I imagine the best way of finding Mister Barwell's is to go straight to the source of the information. Is he staying at Foveaux's house?"

"Yes."

"Then . . ." He rose, pushing his chair away regardlessly. "I think I must concoct some immediate business with Major Foveaux."

"Andrew . . ." She stretched out and touched his sleeve. "I *am* afraid. The Barwells can tell the whole story if they choose to—they can give the colony what it's been waiting to hear for years."

He bent and kissed her fully on the lips. "No one will hurt you while I have any power left to fight them. So don't be afraid, my Sara."

He went then and left her sitting at the table, staring straight ahead, the untouched glass close to her hand. He had taken some of her fear with him; but the real fear, the fear of her old love for Richard, sat like a spectre beside her, a companion for the hours until Andrew returned.

Above the constant patter of rain against the window, Sara heard Andrew's careful footsteps on the stairs. She sat up in bed, and waited for the door to open; the knob turned softly, and he came in. The candle by the bedside fluttered wildly in the sudden draught.

He closed the door, and walked towards her. "I hoped you'd try to sleep, Sara. You shouldn't have waited . . . It's very late."

She leaned forward from the pillows to take hold of his hand. "There was no possibility of sleep," she said. "Tell me . . . what is the news?"

He hoisted himself up to sit on the bed beside her. There were drops of moisture on his head, as if he had stood bareheaded in the rain for some time; in the candlelight his face seemed very sun-tanned and weathered in contrast to the immaculate white frills of his shirt.

"More news than I hoped for," he said. "I let Foveaux have slightly the better of me in a deal over some cattle. We shared a bottle of madeira, and he grew—talkative. He knows a great deal more about the Barwells than he was prepared to tell you this morning."

He burrowed his hand down into the quilt in the hollow between their two bodies. After a few moments he looked at her again, and he said, "Among the mail that arrived with the Speedy was a letter from a friend of Foveaux, who was in Barwell's regiment—the man who had first introduced them to each other. It appears that the Barwells have had money troubles of one kind and another for some time now. They were all right so long as Sir Geoffrey lived, and while he had the money to keep them generously supplied. But it seems that Mister Barwell and his wife have extravagant tastes, and it wasn't easy for them to cut down their scale of living when the old man lost most of his negotiable fortune.''

"Lost it?" Sara said. "How?"

"He had money in ships. Two were captured by the French in the Channel. And another was lost in the Caribbean. The estate, of course, is entailed, and when he died there wasn't much of his money left for Alison.''

"And so . . . ?" Sara urged quickly.

"And so Captain and Mrs. Barwell lived merrily on what was left until it ran out." Andrew was talking slowly, as if he were enjoying the story he told. "Barwell found that an officer's pay won't keep a lady of fashion for long—nor does it stretch to the sort of tastes he himself had acquired. At the time Foveaux's correspondent wrote, they had been living with Alison's aunt, Lady Linton, for a year. Apparently this good lady was very attached to Barwell—from all accounts she made quite a pet of him. But being a woman of sound sense, as well as fashion, she soon realised that Barwell would do nothing for himself while he relied on her for support. Foveaux says she's an extremely shrewd business woman. It set her thinking hard when she heard tales of this fabulous New South Wales—how it's possible to receive pay from the army, and still build up quite a sizeable fortune in other ways. It's Foveaux's private opinion that she sent them out to learn the proper uses of money, before she dies and leaves her own fortune to them."

"Then they'll stay here indefinitely? They'll take up land?"

Andrew nodded. "It seems so."

"Are there children?" Sara was quite unable to keep the edge of sharpness out of her voice as she questioned him.

"None—so far. Foveaux says Mrs. Barwell is delicate. Perhaps this climate will make an improvement . . .''

"Hothouse plants are likely to shrivel in such heat!" she retorted.

Andrew smiled at her wryly. "I had the impression from Foveaux that she was a creature of considerable vivacity and spirit—rather the sort who uses up more energy and strength than she can afford."

"Then she has changed," Sara replied shortly. "Or else Richard has changed her. However . . ." She shrugged, and the corners of her mouth drooped. "We have more information than we hoped for. Now we must wait and see what develops."

Andrew leaned towards her; his grip on her hand tightened, urgently.

"This is no time for waiting, Sara!" he said. "I've already taken steps in the matter."

She caught her breath. "What do you mean?"

"Quite simple, my dear. I asked Foveaux to present me to Barwell."

"Andrew!"

His eyes darkened with a touch of sudden anger. "I've told you before, Sara, that I don't intend to be intimidated by men such as Richard Barwell. Nor have I the time or patience to wait and see which way he will jump. I *had* to know what his attitude towards you would be."

"Well?" Sara uttered the word through tight lips.

'Foveaux went to bring him from the drawing-room—his wife had already retired. He came—it seemed to me—very readily. We talked of you—he told me he had already asked Foveaux if he knew what had become of you."

"What had become of me!" she repeated. "He said it just like that?'

Andrew gave her hand an impatient shake. "How else could he have said it? For all he knew you might have died in Newgate."

"Exactly! I might have died in Newgate!" She choked angrily. "But go on . . . I must hear the rest of this."

"The rest of it is that I've asked him to bring his wife here to dine with us on Wednesday evening. He accepted—gladly, I thought.'

She fell back against the pillows, staring at him unbelievingly.

"You asked them here! Andrew, you didn't!"

He let go of her hand and caught her firmly by the shoulders. "And why not? Don't you see how important it is for him to be willing to bring his wife with him here? He means to be friendly—if you will let him."

"Oh, but Andrew . . ." she protested "Richard and Alison here so soon! I don't think I can face it—not yet."

"You *must* face it some time," he answered sharply. "Far better to do the facing here, in your own house, where you can control the situation. Remember that by now they know the new Governor very well—they travelled out from England with him. They could be powerful friends, Sara."

"But Alison will soon know—she probably knows already—

that none of the officers' wives visit me, or invite me to visit them. She'll come once, and that will be the end.''

"I shouldn't think that our friend, Foveaux, would leave the Barwells long without that bit of news. But, nevertheless, my invitation was still accepted.

"And what's more, Sara," he added, "before long I'll find some way of making certain that the Barwells want to go on claiming our friendship."

She half-closed her eyes, lying quite still, and thinking over what he had said. His invitation was for Wednesday—and this was Monday. Two days in which to school herself to the idea of meeting and talking to Richard, to discipline her emotion so that Andrew's discerning eyes would not detect it. And there was the dread of facing Alison, the slight, darkhaired girl whom she had now and then glimpsed in the hall at Bramfield. Was two days long enough?—or would she ever be ready to face Richard? In her mind she sought about wildly for an excuse to delay this meeting—and she could find none.

She opened her eyes fully, and found that Andrew was looking at her unblinkingly. She was grateful for the pressure of his hands on her shoulders.

"I shall send a message to Julia Ryder in the morning," she said. "If she and James could be here on Wednesday evening . . ." Her words trailed off as she considered the idea.

III

Julia spread herself comfortably in the easy-chair in the main guest room at Glenbarr, and unfastened her cloak. She looked about her carefully; her scrutiny was critical, but finally she nodded in approval.

"It's a fine house, Sara," she said. "You have made it very beautiful. And Andrew . . . Well, Andrew is an incredible man. This place should suit him well. Are you quite settled now? Are you happy here?"

Sara gestured towards the windows, where the gardens were already lost in the dusk. She gave a soft laugh, and reached to take the other's bonnet.

"You've spent too much time with us in our rooms over the store, Julia, not to know how grateful we are for the space and quietness here."

"I shouldn't regret that time spent in the store, if I were you, my dear," Julia replied briskly, stretching her feet towards a low stool. "Young people shouldn't have all the comfort they want immediately—it leaves nothing to work for, and that isn't good. You've made a handsome profit from the store—and running it has taught you some valuable lessons." Suddenly she looked inquiringly at Sarah. "And so far as I can see you've come to no harm by it, have you?"

"Oh, I don't regret it," Sara said, perching on the edge of the bed. "But I do find that experiences that are good for one are always much better when they're over. I still go to the store every morning, and I'm glad to do it. But it *is* a comfort to have this peaceful, quiet house waiting for me when I return to the midday meal."

As she talked she was taking in the changes in Julia's appearance since she had last seen her at Christmas time. At Christmas, Sara and Andrew had taken the three children to the Ryder's at Parramatta for four days. This had been in the nature of a farewell visit to Ellen and Charles, who were both leaving for England in the next ship. Ellen had been enrolled in a young ladies' seminary at Bath, and Charles, showing little of his father's aptitude for farming, but a passionate worship for Admiral Nelson, was to join the Navy. Since Christmas, Sara thought, Julia's face had become worn and thin; it showed the signs of exhaustion and pallor which were the legacy of the long, hot summer. Her movements, too, seemed slower, although the calm tones of her voice were unchanged. There was much grey in her hair now.

Julia broke in on her thoughts.

"Come, now, Sara! You haven't brought me all this way just to be philosophical. What is it? Your note told me nothing of any importance. So I packed and came—all on faith!"

Then she gestured impatiently. "I hope your request that I bring a dinner gown means that you're having some grand entertainment. I'm starving for some diversion."

"Dear Julia!" Sara said warmly. "You're always the same. I wonder how many times I've come to you to have my problems sorted out. Do you remember the first time—when we were coming out in the *Georgette?*"

"Yes—and very sound advice I gave you on that occasion, madam." Julia's brows drew together. "So it's a problem again, is it? Well?"

Sara took a deep breath. "This is going to take quite a time,

Julia, because I mean to tell you what no one but myself and Richard Barwell knows.''

''Barwell . . . Barwell? Didn't I hear that someone of that name arrived with the new Governor in the *Speedy?* He's married to a baronet's daughter—is that right?''

''How fast news travels!'' Sara gave a little laugh. ''Yes. Alison Barwell is a baronet's daughter. Think of it, Julia—a real lady for the colony to fuss over, now. The niece of a countess! What a scramble there'll be to entertain her! Her dress and manners will all be faithfully copied—because, despite all the sudden riches, New South Wales is rather short of genuine ladies, isn't it?''

Julia ignored the tone of the remark. She said with quick annoyance, ''Enough of this, Sara! Come to the point!''

''Well, then . . .''

Sara edged back on the chest and began to talk. The dusk grew deeper in the unlighted room, and a faint swirling sea-mist rolled up from the harbour. She kept her eyes fixed on Julia's face, on which the glow from the fire in the grate played gently. She found it surprisingly easy to speak truthfully to the other woman, older and wiser, and someone to be trusted with the story of her life with drunken Sebastian Dane, in Rye, and at Bramfield Rectory. She told the true reason for her flight across the Marsh on that cold spring night.

''We *did* love each other! I'm sure of that, even though we were hardly more than children. But all the circumstances against us were too much for Richard. I blamed him, and perhaps I shouldn't. After all, I had nothing to lose—he might have lost everything.''

''Andrew knows nothing of this?'' Julia asked. ''About your feelings for Richard Barwell?''

''He knows that I worked for a time at the Rectory. But I have never told him that I was in love with Richard. Why should I tell him that? When I married Andrew I had no thought of ever seeing Richard again. It was as if he were dead!''

After a moment Julia said dryly, ''But now he's here. And Andrew has forced a meeting.''

''Yes,'' Sara answered wretchedly. ''You know what Andrew is—he believes in taking the initiative. I knew myself that the meeting must come some time—but this has come too soon. I have only until tomorrow night. Julia . . . I may do anything— disgrace myself, or let Andrew see . . .''

"Nonsense!" Julia retorted. "You of all people, can't be telling me that you don't know how to take a grip on yourself. You've made it your business, ever since you came to the colony, to see that no one should ever have cause for gossip about you. Surely Richard Barwell can't shake your composure after all this time?"

Sara looked unhappily away. "How can I tell what he'll do? Once before I made a fool of myself over Richard—who's to say I won't do it again? Even knowing all his faults and weaknesses as well as I did, I still loved him. What if it should be the same way now?"

"Sara! Sara! It won't be the same way—unless you let it."

"But Richard . . ."

"You must forget that Richard was ever anything but your father's pupil. Stop eating your heart out for something you never could have. And, Sara," Julia's voice was sharp, "try to remember that your husband is one whom many women in the colony envy you."

Sara rose stiffly, and bent close to the fire to light a taper. She put it carefully to the two candles on the mantelshelf, watching them as the wicks sprang into life. Then she blew softly on the burning taper; the smell of the smoke was pungent in her nostrils.

And suddenly, as if she were too weary to do anything else, she rested her forehead against her two hands clamped before her on the shelf.

"If only he hadn't come, Julia!" she whispered, staring down into the fire. "Oh, why did he have to come?"

IV

The crunching of the carriage wheels on the short drive outside brought Andrew to his feet. Sara, glancing at him, also rose, though more slowly. The tension communicated itself to Julia and her husband. James fiddled with his watch, compared it with the little French clock, and shut it again with a click.

They could hear Bennett's hurrying footsteps in the hall; then a low murmur of voices, and again the sound of footsteps approaching the drawing-room. The door was thrown open with a flourish more suited to London than to this raw, colonial town.

"Captain and Mrs. Barwell!"

Sara advanced only a step. In spite of having schooled herself,

183

her glance went immediately to Richard. He stood there, in the new uniform of the New South Wales Corps, a smile on his lips, and his eyes wearing a questioning look. The last time she had seen him, he had been standing unhappily in the hall at Bramfield, at the end of his Christmas leave; this evening there was a loose, careless elegance about him that was wholly lacking then. His face was thinner and more handsome than she remembered it; a white scar, no thicker than a strand of cotton, ran across his forehead, and his hair was streaked with grey where it furrowed into the scalp. She saw at once that he held that indefinable air of confidence and ease of a man who is accustomed to a considerable success with women. She guessed that he had, by this stage in his career, penetrated far into the gay, fashionable world of which he had dreamed naively during his dull boyhood on the Romney Marsh. Even with the new coating of veneer, she didn't find it difficult to recognise the Richard Barwell she had once known—he was standing there with a smile for her like a small boy's, his eyes pleading for her forgiveness, and begging to be admitted to her favour again. And at the same time, she felt, he was quite certain that she would not resist him.

She looked then at Alison. Alison was also smiling—a faint, prepared smile. She wore a fabulous gown of kingfisher blue satin, which offset her white skin and dark hair. Beside Richard's height, she seemed incredibly tiny; her small hand rested possessively on his arm. Sara was struck by her appearance—not beautiful, she thought—but Alison had fine eyes, and black eyebrows that were drawn on her forehead like wings. She was slim and erect, and she, like Richard, carried the air of a fashionable world about her.

Sara halted her speculation about these two. She realised now that she had hesitated too long, and she hurried forward with a smile she hoped was welcoming.

"Good-evening, Mrs. Barwell," she said extending her hand.

Alison responded in a calm, level voice. Sara turned to give her hand to Richard.

He took it, bowing over it, and seemed quite unconscious that he held it too tightly.

"My dear Sara—what a pleasure it is to see you again!"

He watched the faint flush mount in her cheeks. He had not intentionally set about to make her angry, but his memory of her told him that in such a situation her pride would be ready to be pricked by almost any remark. He studied her carefully. The years in this southern climate had left their mark; her skin had a darker shade than he remembered, and the sun seemed to have bleached her hair to a colour that was near white in the candle-light. But the promise of great beauty he had seen at Bramfield had been fulfilled beyond his expectations. He had forgotten how tall she was, and the way she had of looking unwaveringly into one's eyes when she spoke. Her gown was the colour of pale jade, and the crusted, gold embroidery on the tight bodice and sleeves told him that it had come from the East. He was anxious to take in every detail of her appearance—to form his own opinion of this woman whose story was now part and parcel of the colony's history. Ready gossip gave her as being ambitious, hard, and grasping; but he had not heard it said that she was anything other than an excellent wife and mother, and that her children openly adored her. He knew, by now, that she had profitably run a farm as well as the store during her husband's absences in the *Thistle*, and he was well familiar with the tale of her having fought off a gang of convicts during an outbreak on the Hawkesbury—of her killing, with a dagger, one of them who had molested her. A smile of admiration spread over his face. He recalled momentarily the young, emotional Sara he had known— and here she was now, the mistress of the best the colony could boast of. All achieved, so gossip said, by a husband even harder and more ambitious than herself. It made curious hearing, this story of the girl who had once joyfully walked and idled away a summer's evening with him along the dykes of the Romney Marsh. She was strange and beautiful. In the years, since his marriage, Richard had made his way into many of the great houses of London, and he had found favour in the eyes of many beautiful and distinguished women; yet he was conscious that in all that time no woman had ever looked at him like this, and no other woman had ever managed to disconcert him as Sara did now.

She twisted her hand in his, and broke away from his clasp. "Indeed, Richard, I'm very glad to see you also."

Then she turned to present her husband to Alison.

To sit working at the square of tapestry clamped in its frame had always brought Sara calm and relaxation, but now, as she threaded her needle in and out of the canvas, she noticed that her hand still trembled. The interminable meal was finished, and a glance at the French clock told her that Andrew was holding the men an unusually long time over the port. Sitting opposite her, Julia and Alison kept up a conversation—mostly they talked of the items of news that had been fresh when the Barwells left London. Sara was aware that she herself made an occasional contribution, but she gave them little heed. Her mind was back with Richard.

The hour just past had been dreadful beyond anything for which she had prepared herself. It was a slow nightmare, a struggle to hold herself together in the face of an emotion as strong as any she had ever known before. Throughout the meal Richard had laughed and talked, entertaining and amusing them with his quips and his stories, told with a light, skilful touch. And for every minute he had sat there, fingering the excellent wine, drawing the threads of conversation always into his own hands, she felt her resolution ebbing. It was as if he had stretched out his hands and taken her bodily to him. She felt that she might go on endlessly telling herself that Richard was weak, Richard merely played at life while he waited for its best things to fall into his lap, Richard had not one jot of the worth of Andrew—and yet, for all that, he could command her attention as easily now as he had done in the Bramfield days. She was still, she confessed, the girl who had explored the Marsh dykes with him, pale-coloured with the new green of spring; she was the girl who was utterly fascinated by him, obedient to his will, eager to give in to his wishes. An insect drawn by a brilliant light—she knew she was that. Never mind that the light might be transitory and false; it was there, in front of her,   ⁓

It had been madness to have believed all these years that Richard could be forgotten at will. Andrew had taken part of her love, and all of her devotion and loyalty, but the core of her had always been Richard's. And he had returned now to lay claim to it, just as if there had been no separation. She was ashamed and fearful, angry with him that he had revealed her own weakness to her. *He* knew it, she told herself—under the lightness and the laughter. Richard knew well that she was again his willing fool, the eager Sara who had smiled for him when she was bidden, and had been sad when he was sad.

"Curse you, Richard!" she whispered, under her breath. "I still love you."

She stitched away at the tapestry, half-hearing the conversation. Thank God for Julia, she thought, feeling truly grateful for the presence of the elder woman who held the situation as steady as a rock, covering her own silence, making bearable this awful time until Andrew should return to support her. Sudden tears pricked the back of her eyes; she would gladly have cried tears of rage and dismay at the turn affairs had taken. It sickened her to recall that four days ago she had imagined Richard Barwell was safely back in the past.

Even bound up as she was in her own turmoil, she was conscious that Alison had risen and was coming towards her. She knew the piece of tapestry was going to be inspected and she offered it reluctantly.

Alison looked at it, head tilted to the side.

"Oh, but this is quite beautiful, Mrs. Maclay!" she said at last. "And how swiftly you work!"

Sara's temper swelled at the platitude, but she managed a stiff smile.

"Oh, yes," she said. "I've always worked at speed. Perhaps you don't remember that I was once employed in a London dressmaking establishment?"

Alison turned away, with a sharp swish of her satin, and Sara imagined she caught a flicker of annoyance cross her face; she paced the length of the room, pausing before the open keyboard of the piano. Behind her back, Sara looked over at Julia and deliberately winked. Julia's eyebrows shot up, and then she frowned, shaking her head.

Sara addressed Alison gently. "Perhaps we can persuade you to play for us, Mrs. Barwell? Have you anything of Beethoven's? People arriving in the colony speak of him—but it's a matter of great regret to me that we never hear his work performed."

"Beethoven is known to be a great admirer of Bonaparte," Alison returned rigidly. "I hardly consider it patriotic to encourage the work of such people."

"Just as you wish, of course," Sara said determined to remain umsnubbed.

Alison sat down at the piano. She chose to play Mozart, confidently, and with unmistakable enjoyment. Watching her, Sara wondered what she would do to pass the time in this place, where there were never enough books, and no music at all, where people were mostly too busy making money to have time for the niceties of the cultivated mind. She would want a piano, of course, and Richard would find that shipping a piano from England was an expensive and doubtful business. It would, more than likely, be smashed to splinters during the voyage. But Sara, watching the other's determined little face, felt that before very long there would be a piano on the way.

Alison was determined, certainly, Sara decided, watching the slightly swaying figure. She was determined and intelligent—but away from her husband's presence she had changed visibly. During dinner she had been rather gay, amusing at times, and self-possessed, but here she made it plain that she was not at ease in the completely strange company in which she found herself. She was aloof and a little critical; she was more noticeably fragile now—like a painting in her exotic blue gown, a slight child-like figure without physical strength of any kind. Andrew had reported that Alison had suffered terribly from sea-sickness during the voyage, and Sara wondered how this slender, white-skinned woman would live through the long months of the summer.

The music finished, and Alison withdrew her hands from the keyboard.

"Charming!" Sara said. "Thank you, indeed, Mrs. Barwell! Mozart is delightful—though I myself have always preferred Bach."

Alison nodded absently, and began to pick out the airnotes of a Bach fugue. The sounds scarcely reached the other end of the room. "You," she said, looking up, "play, of course, Mrs. Maclay?"

"Unfortunately, no," Sara replied lightly, turning the tapestry-frame to examine the back of her work. "I often think it's just as well my children are all boys—I, alas, have no accomplishments to pass on to a daughter.

She carefully selected another length of silk from her sewing-basket. "I understand you and Richard have no children yet, Mrs. Barwell?"

Alison's lips tightened as she shook her head. The kingfisher satin stirred, and seemed to quiver. She rose stiffly from the piano. But when she began to walk slowly down the length of the room, she was, in every inch of her small figure, Sir Geoffrey's daughter, poised, and sure of herself, sure that she was above the vulgar taunts of a woman who had once been a servant and a convict. She smiled charmingly at Sara, graciously ignoring the vulgarity, and seated herself on the sofa beside her. Sara recalled her remark to Julia that the colony suffered from the lack of real ladies; here, she thought, was one who would be a match for every situation.

Julia, desperately uncomfortable, was speaking, saying the first thing that came into her head.

"I'm afraid you'll find it very dull here, after London, Mrs. Barwell. There are so few people . . . and so little to do."

Alison's eyebrows lifted at that. "On the contrary, Mrs. Ryder. I don't imagine that I shall find it dull. My husband intends to farm, and I know I'll be most interested in that."

Sara paused at her work, laying it aside. She glanced at Alison; against her will she was moved to a kind of pity over what she had heard. In all her life, this gentle creature had probably never done anything more arduous than make herself pretty for a party; she had come straight from a world of ease and gaiety, and she was as ignorant as a child of what lay ahead of her. Could she possibly have any notion, Sara wondered, what sort the country beyond Sydney was, what it was like to handle sullen, reluctant convict women, or see the envy and hatred in a man's eyes, as he raised them from the garden-patch where he was digging? Did she know that the natives sometimes murdered and robbed, and the floods carried away the crops, and fires swept through the dry bush, which was in itself a sly enemy? She talked of farming as if this were Kent or Sussex, and that Rye were close by, comforting and familiar. She faced her new life with the confident, innocent air of one who had only a four-day knowledge of the colony's hardships. Her talk had implied that she hoped desperately that farming would not bore her; clearly, she had never thought of it as being dangerous.

Sara said tentatively—not to Alison as Richard's wife, but to a woman who was wholly ignorant of the difficulties she faced, "I sincerely hope that when you are ready to begin farming you will allow me to help you a little. Andrew and I have farmed all the time since we were married. We were the first settlers in the Hawkesbury—and I think I know as well as most men in this colony what is likely to be needed."

Alison's expression changed, hardening a little; she opened her mouth to reply, and then broke off, looking towards the door, which Andrew threw open noisily. She half-rose at the sight of her husband.

Instantly Sara knew that something more than social pleasantries had detained the men over their port. On Andrew's face she recognised an expression he wore whenever something happened to put him in a high good humour. James Ryder was grave and non-committal. As for Richard . . . Sara couldn't read Richard's face at all. He was flushed; his eyes were bright, and moved nervously round the room. He looked like a man who has attempted something of which he is a little afraid.

The little French clock chimed off five more quarter-hours, and still the Maclays' guests stayed on. Sara had the impression that Alison would gladly have left, but she waited patiently on her husband's whim. A coldish sea-fog pressed against the windows, but the fire was banked high, and the curtains of gold silk made a false sunshine within the room.

Richard and Alison went to the piano together, and, to her accompaniment, he sang some of the light, sentimental ballads which were going the round of the London drawing-rooms. He seemed to have shed his air of disquiet, he was elegant now, and casual. He had a charming, light, baritone, which he had obviously used many times to considerable effect. Watching him, listening to him, Sara could well imagine how he had suited the extravagant, spirited personality which gossip ascribed to Lady Linton. He would have blended with the London of Lady Linton perfectly—Richard, with his jagged scar, worn like a medal for courage; his reputation as an expert with the rapier, and a matchless horseman; his ability to charm a woman—any woman— when it pleased him. This was the kind of man London hostesses always drew about them.

She recovered her sense of humour enough to smile wryly over the picture he made against the gold curtains, and to reflect that gifts of Richard's order would be sadly wasted in such a place as this.

In the last hour since the return of the men to the drawingroom, Sara had calmed herself considerably She was better able now to sum up the situation, and she was pretty certain, by this time, what sort of relationship existed between Alison and Richard. At her husband's entrance, a mood of gaiety had come upon Alison. She was never still, stirring, twisting, and laughing in an endeavour to hold his attention. She was so easily satisfied—a smile, a nod from Richard was all she required. It angered Sara to see how absently, how nonchalantly he bestowed these light caresses upon his wife, as if she were a child whose desires were never complex or difficult to gratify.

Sara recalled the face of that young girl who had visited Bramfield so eagerly all those years ago—the same pale, determined face now laughingly turned to Richard's, as he came to the end of a rather risqué song. Alison had loved him then with a child's unsubtle passion, and her father had bought him for her, with the lure of a world of which he dreamed. She still clutched her prize as uncertainly as if it had been in her hands no more than an hour.

But when Richard's gaze left his wife, her face dropped back into lines that Sara was beginning to note were habitual. The kingfisher satin became only the bright plumage of a nervous, fluttering bird. Alison is ill, Sara thought—and weary! Her talk of interesting herself in farming was merely to cover her bewilderment over this new life to which Richard had brought her. She didn't dare to stop talking or laughing, in case it gave him a chance to notice that her fine, baby skin was beginning to stretch tightly over her face, and that there were lines about her mouth. Sara was appalled by the thought that suddenly struck her. Alison was afraid! She was afraid that Richard might tire of her!

She watched as Alison ran a finger swiftly along the keyboard, and she said, laughingly, "Now, Richard—*my* song."

He glanced at her, an absent, indulgent gaze that did not even see her. "Certainly, my love."

He turned and looked directly at Sara as he waited for Alison's introduction.

"Drink to me only with thine eyes . . ."

Sara felt herself tense, and then grew cold. Only Richard could do this, she thought, angrily. Only he could sing for another woman a song that belonged to his wife—sing it and not care what he was doing.

It seemed that every eye in the room must have followed his. Her cheeks burned with shame and rage, and the guilt of her unwilling love.

Sara laid down her hairbrush and listened to the last words between her husband and James Ryder on the landing

Andrew came noisily into the candle-lit bedroom; his hair was awry, and there hung about him an air of triumph and elation which he so often had at the end of a successful business deal.

He came directly to her, making a place on the littered dressing-table for the candlestick he carried. And then he stooped to kiss her forehead. She sensed his excitement in the roughness of his hands against her shoulders.

He laughed down at her. "A successful evening, my darling."

She avoided his eyes. "A successful evening . . . ? I . . . Do you truly believe it *was* successful?"

"Well, they *came*, didn't they? No last-minute, lady-like indisposition from Alison—which is what I honestly expected. And the dinner was not to be sneered at. They won't get food to better it at any other table in the colony. And the wines . . . Not many people in London itself could offer them wines as good as they drank here tonight."

He gestured flamboyantly. "But even had the food been foul, and the wine undrinkable, I think it would hardly have mattered."

Looking up at him, she said slowly, "Andrew . . . what do you mean?"

He smiled. His smile was too rakish and too mischievous for Sara's peace.

"We've routed them, Sara! Or better, we've captured them! Richard Barwell has committed himself into my hands just about as neatly as he could possibly have done. I'm lending him enough money to buy the Hydes's farm that's up for sale, and to build a house here in Sydney."

She sprang to her feet.

"You're *what*!"

She waved away his attempt to answer, pacing to the foot of the bed, and back again. For a few seconds the only sound in the room was the swish of her loose robe and the soft crackle of the fire.

Then she turned to face him. Her voice was low, with the tight control of anger.

"Have you gone suddenly mad, Andrew? *Lend him money*! My God! Why do you think they were forced to come out here? I'll tell you why—*because the pair of them have never been able to save a penny piece in their lives!* Lady Linton is tired of keeping them on velvet cushions. They've been living fabulously. What do you think that gown Alison wore cost? And did Richard look as if he were turned out with an eye to economy?" She flung her hands wide, in a gesture of contempt. "I tell you lending money to them is simply throwing it away!"

She began to pace again. "What sort of farmer will Richard make, do you suppose?" Her back was towards him, and her long hair hung about her shoulders. "Hopeless! He may be a pretty horseman, and a brave soldier, but I'll wager my soul he doesn't know a hoe from a spade!"

"There'll be an overseer to manage the farm."

"An overseer!" Sara swung round fiercely. "Good God! And will that fashionable pair disport themselves in Sydney on the money a farm is presumed to bring in? Do they *know* what it's like to begin farming? Do they know how we started at Kintyre? • Well . . . you may bid goodbye to your money. Once it's in Richard's free and generous hand, that's the last you'll see of it!"

There was a silence after her outburst. Then Andrew said, "Come here, Sara!"

She was unwilling, but she came because he spoke quietly and purposefully. He looked down into her flushed and angry face; he saw the tight arrogance of her mouth, and her heaving breasts under her nightgown.

"Listen to me, my Sara,' he said.

She raised her eyes, and he thought, for a moment, there was the trembling brightness of tears in them.

"Have you thought what the money we lend to Richard Barwell will bring back to us?"

"I know well enough what it will bring," she retorted. "When Richard finally realises that he can't make a farm pay, you'll discover you've thrown away good money for an unimproved piece of land. And don't imagine for one second that once the Sydney house is built you'll ever get them out of it. People of their sort can sleep happily in their beds with a howling multitude of creditors outside their windows. Shame won't drive them out—and they won't leave until they have somewhere better to go. *I* know their sort uncommonly well—do you forget that my father escaped the debtors' prison by only a few hours?"

"All this is true enough, Sara," he said patiently. "But aren't you calculating only the face value of the money?"

"What other value has it?" she demanded.

He laughed. "Woman, where is your heart! No wonder they tell me you managed the business with the coolness of an iceberg while I was away!"

"Andrew, stop playing with me! Tell me what you've done!"

"I've bought you Alison Barwell's friendship. I've bought you a past, and a well-born friend." He was speaking to her as gently as he would have spoken to one of his children if they needed an explanation of a difficult situation. "You see what this means, don't you? It only needs Alison Barwell to call you

'Sara,' once in public—and you'll have every wretched female in the place fawning over you.''

Her hands dropped down limply by her sides. He saw the flame of colour leave her cheeks, and they became pinched and ashen; he looked at her pale, still lips, and for a moment he was afraid.

"Have I done wrong, my darling? Is it wrong to want to see you in a place you should have had all these years? A woman shouldn't live as you have done—shut off from other women.''

"I haven't *needed* other women!'' she declared miserably. "I don't want them!''

'That may be so. But our children will grow up, and *they'll* feel the absence of the women you ought to have about you, Sara.''

She lowered her head for a few moments, and when at last she raised it, the tears were rolling unchecked down her face.

"But Alison . . .'' she whispered. ''She'll never do it. She won't want me . . .''

He brushed her protest aside. "Alison will do as her husband says—she'll do anything at all for the sake of pleasing him. And they need money—they need it badly if they're ever going to live at anything approaching the style to which they're accustomed. Alison is no different to any other woman in love with a man she's not sure of. She'd rather die than let Richard see her in a gown that didn't dazzle him. When a woman is as much in love as all that—and frightened—there's very little she won't do.''

"You saw that—in Alison?''

"Only a fool could have missed it,' he answered shortly. "When I recognised it, I knew I had my greatest chance of success. Richard himself would have been easy enough, because for all his airs of worldly knowledge, he's gullible—and greedy. Alison was a different matter. There are some things that just can't be bought, and I feared her co-operation might be one of them. But a woman in love is vulnerable to an extraordinary degree. She's vain. She couldn't bear the thought of living and dressing in any other way than as the soft, precious creature that Richard married. She needs servants around her—and all her accustomed comforts. Do you imagine she'll let the sun touch that lily-white skin? Or will she go outdoors when the hot winds come? Not Alison! Not if she can find a way to avoid it!

"Believe me, Sara,'' he said, placing his finger gently under her chin, "Alison loves her husband desperately. And in face of that, she has no pride, no defence—nothing. She'll do as Richard says. I'm certain of that.''

He folded his arms about her, rocking her quietly, feeling the sobs shaking her body. With his lips pressed lightly against her forehead, he murmured, ''And I don't give a damn who suffers if in some way you can be made happier, my darling.''

Chapter Three

The full light of the autumn afternoon was dying on the harbour. The wooded shores of the distant promontories seemed to glide farther back, merging into the darker green of the high ground behind. On the west side of the bay the shadows crept gradually out from the brown rocks, making the water appear thick and oily. Beyond the shelter of the Maclays' own bay, they could see the catspaws of wind darkening the surface. Out there the colour was the particular cold, hard blue of the Pacific in autumn. Sara identified two specks a long way off as native skiffs heading in the direction of the settlement. She watched them for a long time, her fingers tightly hooked in Duncan's belt to prevent him standing up and rocking the boat. Her dreaming gaze saw the two black figures grow larger and more distinct, until an exclamation of triumph from David brought her attention back.

''Mama, look! Another one!''

He held aloft on the end of his line a small fish, and when he was sure his mother had carefully noted and admired it, he pulled out the hook, with a gesture that was meant to appear as nonchalant as those of Ted, the boatman. He tossed it alongside his afternoon's catch, three others, lying in the bottom of the boat.

Sara smiled gaily at him. ''You'll be able to have them for breakfast, darling—you and Duncan.''

Duncan twisted his face round to look at her. He had impudent blue eyes, bolder even than Andrew's, and young as he was, he had a supreme sureness about life.

''Won't Sebastian have some also, Mama?''

She shook her head. ''Not Sebastian—he's too little yet.''

Duncan considered that, Then he said, ''How long will it take Sebastian to grow up?'

"Oh . . . I suppose as long as it's taken you," Sara answered cautiously.

He ran a hand that smelled strongly of fish through his fair hair, and turned away, apparently satisfied.

"Ted!"

The boatman looked over his shoulder at his mistress.

"Ma'am?"

"I think we must put in. It's growing cold. The wind has changed—it's coming off that point now."

Ted touched the shapeless cap he wore, and quickly drew in his line. He drew in David's also, keeping the child's four fish separate from his own pile, and complimenting him, in his rough, good-natured voice, on his catch. Ted O'Malley had arrived in the colony after the 1798 rebellion in Ireland. He was a Cork fisherman, and a man of such mild serenity that Sara often wondered what attraction rebellion could possibly have had for him. He had once mentioned to her that he had two young sons of his own; sometimes it saddened her to see his gentle devotion to David and Duncan.

With swift strokes he began to pull towards the Maclays' small beach, lying below the sharp drop of the wood. Farther along the bay, through the trees, they could see the roof of Glenbarr. It had a solid comfort about it, that roof; it had the look of permanency which was beginning to appear in Sydney's new buildings. The land on this side of the bay was steep and rocky, useless for farming, and, Sara thought privately, useless for the landscaped terraces Andrew talked of. It was thickly wooded, and the beach itself was merely a narrow shelf of pale sand breaking the irregular line of rocks.

David, from his seat in the stern, suddenly pointed.

"Look, Mama, there's someone on the beach! A gentleman!"

Still holding Duncan, Sara twisted to look towards the little beach. At first she could see nothing—only the whitish trunks of the eucalypts, and the rocks. And then, close to the path leading to the house, she picked him out, a tall, languid figure, sitting, knees drawn up to his chin, on a flat-topped boulder. As she watched, he raised his arm and waved. Slowly she put up her hand in a faint-hearted response.

"Who is it, Mama?"

"I think . . . it's Captain Barwell, David."

David examined the distant figure with interest. "The one

who came to dinner last night? The one who was wounded in the war?''

Sara nodded absently.

''Will he tell us about the fighting, do you think, Mama?''

''I expect so, David . . . some time . . . if you ask him politely. But not now. He's only been in the colony a few days, and perhaps he's rather tired of people asking him about the fighting,''

''Did he fight against Napoleon, Mama?''

''No—at the time Captain Barwell was wounded Napoleon wasn't in charge of the fighting. Not many people had even heard of him then.''

''Oh . . .'' David's interest faded. He looked down at the fish at his feet, and began then to compare the size of his catch to Ted's pile lying beside it. By the time the boat scraped the sand, he had decided that he had done quite a good afternoon's work.

Richard was waiting at the water's edge. He grinned cheerfully at Sara and the boys, as he bent his back to help Ted drag the boat clear of the tide-mark.

''I came for a leisurely afternoon call,'' he said, lifting Duncan out of his seat and placing him down on the dry sand. ''They told me you were all out fishing, so I made my way down here. I've been sitting over on that rock for the past hour. It reminded me of us two as children to see you in a boat again, Sara.''

''I find myself in a boat frequently these days,'' she answered lamely. ''The boys . . .''

He looked at her two sons, smiling, and holding out his hand. ''I'm indeed happy to make your acquaintance, David—and yours, Duncan. I used to know your mama a long time ago, before she came here to New South Wales.''

Over David's head he looked at Sara. ''Yes . . . a long time ago.''

''We have a baby brother,'' Duncan announced firmly. ''He sleeps all the time. And he can't talk yet.''

''Sebastian,'' Sara murmured, in explanation. ''He is so dark in contrast to these two. My father's kind of darkness. It seemed right, somehow, that I should call him Sebastian.''

''Your father would be very happy about that, Sara. Especially if he grows up as these two have. Do you remember how your father . . .'' Richard broke off, shrugging. 'Oh, well that's all in the past.''

He glanced down at the two children, and then at Sara. "I expect you'll want to go back to the house now."

She hesitated. Richard was offering her an escape from him, but she knew he didn't want her to accept it.

She touched David's shoulder. "Take Duncan, and go with Ted. Ask him to clean the fish for your breakfast. You can stay and watch how he does it."

David smiled his farewell to her, and less certainly to Richard. He took his brother by the hand, and they walked to where Ted stood waiting, loaded with the sack of fish, his coiled lines, and a tin of bait. He motioned them to precede him; he touched his cap to Sara and Richard, and turned towards the path.

They watched them go, Ted's stocky, bent figure hovering protectively above the children.

"Well now, Master David," they heard him say, "the very next foine mornin'..."

As the three made their way along the winding, sloping path between the trees, the children's clear voices echoed back sharply, Duncan's shrill and dominating his brother's. Ted's deep, soft brogue was lost beneath it.

They vanished from sight among the trees, and finally went beyond earshot. The little bay was abruptly silent; it was a sombre place now that all sound had left it. The sun was almost gone; there were long shadows on the water. The wind that touched Sara's cheek was cool.

Richard turned to her slowly.

"Perhaps I was wrong to come to you like this. But I couldn't stay away any longer."

She looked, not at him, but across the bay, to the dark colours of the opposite rocky shore. "You *were* wrong to come. It was...unwise." She faced him reluctantly. "You have a great deal to learn of our life here. The town is like a village—and gossip is scarce and eagerly sought. Ted will say nothing, because he is devoted to me...but the servants in the house..."

He checked her with a touch on the arm. "Can this be Sara I hear talking? How much you've changed! All this caution and prudence! Ah, my dear, the way you used to mock my mother's primness, and shame me into some defiance of it myself! Your father would be astonished to hear you now."

"Defiance of convention is only for those who can afford it!" she answered shortly. "*I* can't!"

He shrugged. "That may be—but even gossip can't make anything much of the meeting between two old friends."

He took her arm, edging her towards the rock where he had been sitting.

"You'll sit awhile, surely? I'll only keep you a few minutes. And then we'll go back to the house—and cheat Sydney gossip of a tit-bit!"

He was smiling slightly as he spoke, and Sara was disarmed. She sat down on the rock beside him, spreading the skirt of the plain, salt-water stained gown which she wore, and patting into some order her wind-tossed hair.

The silence in the bay was so deep that almost unconsciously they had lowered their voices; they were aware of the slap of the small waves against the wet sand, and the occasional rustle of the trees behind them. Yet they were engulfed in a silence of waiting and expectancy.

Quietly, without fuss, Richard placed his hand over hers, lying still on the rock. "I had to see you, Sara." he said simply.

When she didn't answer, he went on:

"Last night was unbearable. You were so close, and yet I couldn't talk with you. You wouldn't look at me either. You sat at the head of a table—as beautiful as any woman I've ever seen—but cold."

His hand tightened on hers. "And now you look like a girl again—the Sara Dane I remember!" Suddenly his hands were on her shoulders, and he swung her round to face him. "I nearly went crazy with joy to see you in that boat." His eyes went to her untidy curls. "I longed to rush to you and do as Sebastian always did... Do you remember how he used to pull your hair free. It blew in the wind, and then you pretended to be angry. *That* was what I wanted to see. I wanted the Sara who was dead to come back to life again."

He was searching her face in a bewildered way.

"But your children made it all unreal," he said quietly. "they spoiled my fantasy—they reminded me too much that you have gone far beyond the girl I remember."

She twisted her body abruptly, jerking free of his hold, and covered her face with her hands.

"Richard... I beg you! Please don't talk of this any more, You *shouldn't* have come! And I haven't the strength to send you away."

"Send me away? Why *should* you send me away? Surely after

199

all these years we have the right to talk with each other—to talk as freely as we please, not as convention dictates.''

She stiffened, and when she spoke there was an edge to her voice. "Don't talk of 'all these years' as if they really meant something to you, Richard. You can't pretend that you've spared me much thought since I left Bramfield.''

"Sara! I deny that—*completely!* You couldn't know how much you've been in my thoughts. All these years, believe me, you have meant a very great deal to me.''

There was a silence between them, and then he said, "You're thinking I didn't care about your conviction. But, damn you, I did! I wrote you immediately I had news of the trial, and months later a letter came back from Newgate, from a woman called Charlotte Barker. She said you had already sailed for Botany Bay. Well . . . what could I do? You were lost to me then. I was young and ignorant, and I married Alison in the firm belief that I would forget you." His voice changed, hardening. "But I didn't forget you. You rose like a ghost between me and every single thing in life that could have given me joy and satisfaction. I couldn't cast you off . . . you were a torment to me! If I had been free I would have gone willingly to search for you; but it was too late for that. I went to fight in Holland with the thought that if I were killed I should be gladly released from the torture of self-accusation. I believed that I had no soul above the material things in life that attracted me—but I found that you were my soul.''

In the fading light he leaned nearer to her, until their faces were close together.

"I wrote you letters that I never sent," he said, "I sought news of you wherever I could find it. When ships, returning from New South Wales, berthed in the Thames, I used to hang about the docks, in the hopes of picking up scraps of information about you. And finally I had the good fortune to meet Admiral Phillip—he told me that you were to be married to an East India Company officer, and that he himself had given an order for your pardon. After that I insinuated myself with Sir Joseph Banks. I couldn't count the number of Royal Society dinners I sat through so that later I might talk with any of the guests who had recently come back from the colony. It didn't always bring results . . . but gradually I was building up the picture of your life. I knew about your farm on the Hawkesbury, and your two eldest sons. I knew what sort of man your husband was. And then, when he visited

London, I almost made myself known to him. He came to a reception in Sir Joseph Banks's house—all the colonists eventually found their way there. Andrew Maclay was pointed out as a man reputed to have made a fortune from salvage, and who was, at the moment, fitting out a new vessel for trading. I was about to ask to be presented . . . I wanted to meet him, and to ask about you. But I couldn't . . . I couldn't make myself go forward. I was jealous, Sara . . . jealous of everything that man possessed. It was a relief when the *Thistle* finally sailed from Greenwich, and took him out of my reach.

"My married life, all this time, was going to pieces. I had begun it in the belief that I would forget you—but I was wrong. I was not happy with Alison—although I knew she loved me and I was fond of her. You, Sara, had spoiled every other woman for me. But Alison and I had enough distractions to cover whatever dissatisfaction we felt with one another. It changed, though, when Sir Geoffrey lost his money. He was broken after that—he didn't live long. The estate was entailed; it went to Alison's brother. Lady Linton knew the state of our finances—she offered us a home, and we accepted gladly. She adored Alison, and she tried to make a son out of me—although she used always to laugh and say I was not promising material. She spent money lavishly on us, and we both knew that Alison would inherit her fortune. But, with all that, she was nobody's fool. No, by God, she wasn't! I found that she was watching me. She knew every move I made, and practically every thought in my head. It didn't take her long to sense that something was wrong—something that drove me to gamble much more than I could afford, and to ride a horse as if I cared less than nothing for my own neck. I often stayed out the whole night—and it wasn't always with women. I would sometimes find myself at dawn, stupid with drink, babbling about Botany Bay, in some sailor's tavern around the docks.

"All this time my love for you was the fatal malaise that I had heard others talk of and had never believed in myself. You possessed me—you never left me any rest. Lady Linton suspected something, though of course she never could reach anything near the truth. It was I who first suggested New South Wales to her—and I made her believe it was her own idea. She talked to Alison about this, and convinced her that I should do well in the colony. I was to farm—to work out my own salvation. Once the idea was planted, Lady Linton was adamant. She bought my commission in the Corps, settled my debts—which were by no means trifling—and packed us off with barely enough money to cover the expenses of the voyage. Obviously the cure was to be drastic. 'Training for your inheritance,' she called it. Poor soul, she didn't in the least want us to go,''

Sara shivered, and involuntarily she leaned forward and pressed her face against his shoulder. "Oh, Richard, what could you hope to gain by coming here?"

'The sight of you—that was what I hoped for. I wanted to live where I could occasionally see you, where your name could be spoken aloud. Nothing has been right for me since you went,'' he said. "But I hoped to make something of my life if I could be where you would see my efforts. My achievements will be for you, Sara. I've taken the offer of money from your husband because I want the tie with you, and because it gives me the chance to do more than fret my life away on a captain's pay.''

He put his hand to her hair, smoothing it back from her temple, touching the soft skin of her forehead. "You have all the witchery of the devil. Sara! I've fought you for ten years, but I won't fight you any longer. I've tried to forget you in other women—I've flirted with many, made love to some, and always with the image of you before me. When I took a mistress, I felt I was unfaithful to you. God how people would laugh to know of it—that is, if they could believe it!''

Slowly she raised her face to him. "They won't believe it, Richard, because they'll never hear it. I'm as dead to you, as lost, as ever I was.''

"Not lost, my love," he murmured. "I can see you, and talk with you. I'll find peace, perhaps, because I've stopped searching for you.''

"But Andrew . . ." she began.

"Andrew! Do you think I care about Andrew?" he said roughly. "I can adore the very ground you walk on, and he won't know it. He'll never find out. I promise you that.''

She shook her head wildly. "But I love Andrew!''

"You loved me once.''

"Once—yes! But I was a child then. Surely even you, Richard, can see what Andrew and I have built up here for one another. We have knitted our lives so closely that nothing can separate us. We are necessary to each other.''

"Yes," he said. "But you only love Andrew because he is a copy of yourself. All your ambitions and dreams, are his also.

Only a man like Andrew Maclay could match your spirit and energy. Only he could have achieved for you what he has.'' He leaned towards her again. "I am not Andrew. I couldn't build a world in the clouds for you. But I am the first man you ever loved. My claim on you is an old one, and it's strong. I need you!"

"No, Richard!" she breathed, afraid and tense. "You have no claim on me. I owe you nothing. I love Andrew, I tell you! He . . ."

"I need you," he said again.

"Andrew also needs me."

'You can love us both, Sara. It's not as a mistress I want you, and there's nothing Andrew has that I could possibly take from him. You can go on being all the things to him that you have been through these years—but for myself, I want what you were at Bramfield. *That's* the Sara he's never seen or known."

"I can't let you come here to destroy what I have built up," she whispered. "You will destroy my peace of mind—my whole life. I love Andrew—and he won't be fooled."

He caught her up in his arms, holding her close to him, talking wildly. "Sara . . . Oh, Sara! Can you deny that you love me also? Say that you do . . . just say it! If I could only be sure of that. I would leave you in peace if I knew."

Her arms slipped upwards about his neck.

"God forgive me . . ." she whispered. "I still love you."

He stood up and pulled her with him, drawing her into his arms and bending over her upturned face. The last time he had kissed her was in the schoolroom at Bramfield. Now he kissed her in this silent, deserted bay with all the passion and longing of the years in between. Her lips, the warm, sweet lips of a woman, in the place of the child she had been then, moved under his. He was vaguely aware that she was mouthing some protest, and yet giving herself to him at the same time. As he kissed her, the sense of desolation and loneliness seemed to slip from him; the years did not count now, only the mad joy and exhilaration in his heart.

"Sara! Sara! I've found you again!"

II

In an upstairs room of the store—a room once used as a sitting-room when the Maclays had lived there—Sara squatted on her knees before a low shelf packed with rolls of cloth. She murmured to herself as she worked, writing swiftly in a notebook balanced on her knees.

"Calico—dark blue—eight rolls. Calico—flowered—five rolls." And then she frowned, adding to the last item, "—slightly water-stained. Broadcloth . . ."

As she wrote, she listened absently to footsteps coming up the stairs, pausing when she realised that they did not belong to any of the light-footed clerks who attended the store. List in hand, she looked expectantly towards the door.

It was Jeremy Hogan who tapped and opened it. He did not smile his usual greeting. He came in, and she saw immediately that he was wet. The shoulders of his greatcoat were sodden; raindrops dripped off the brim of the hat he held in his hand. His boots were splattered with mud.

"Jeremy!"

Sara jumped to her feet, smiling, warmed with the pleasure of this unexpected visit, "I'm glad to see you, Jeremy! Have you just come from Kintyre? What brings you?"

"I had a note from Andrew," he explained briefly. "Stock sales at Parramatta. For some reason or other, he's going to flatter my vanity by deferring to my judgment—though in the end he'll buy what he himself fancies, as he always does."

She put out her hand and touched his shoulder. "You're wet right through—and hungry, I imagine. Did you call at the house?"

"I did, of course," he said, shrugging. "But I was told the master was from home—doubtless drinking the afternoon away and pretending to do business—and the mistress was stocktaking at the store. Annie Stokes's tone rather suggested that it was permissible for you to be here in the mornings, but any real lady would be sitting pretty in her own drawing-room at this time of the day."

Sara laughed. "I still haven't learned to be the real lady that Annie longs to wait upon. Perhaps if I live long enough I'll succeed."

Jeremy cut in, throwing his hat on a packing-case, and turning to look at her with eyes that she suddenly realised were angry.

"You'll live long enough, Sara . . . if gossip doesn't soon have your blood."

She took a step backwards, frowning. "Jeremy! What do you mean? What are you talking about?"

He thrust his hands into his pockets, awkwardly. "I sometimes encourage gossip, Sara. It's a habit of the Irish. Besides, I've been on the Hawkesbury for months now, and news is stale there. So as soon as I got to town . . ."

"Oh, Jeremy, go on!" she snapped.

"I made two calls after leaving Glenbarr. One to leave my horse at Joe Maguire's stable, and then to Costello's for a bite of cheese and some ale. It was the same story at each place."

"*What story?* For pity's sake, *tell me!*"

He was looking at her fully. "Oh, it was couched in casual enough terms, but the meaning was unmistakable. Had I heard that great friends of Andrew Maclay's wife had arrived with the new Governor in the *Speedy*? And wasn't it fine now for Mrs. Maclay to be having her friends with her again, especially as they were the quality, no less?" Jeremy's accent was a good imitation of Pat Costello's, as he concentrated on the drawing of a tankard, and the spinning of a story. "And here, my dear Sara, was a digression while the histories of Sir Geoffrey Watson and his countess sister were related to me. Captain Barwell's history, it seems, is rather more obscure. But the story-tellers returned at last to the original theme. Wasn't it grand, now, they said, that Mrs. Maclay had such good friends from the old days to be spending her time with? And wouldn't you all be having fine old yarns about them together? Though, to be sure, *Mrs.* Barwell had only once been to dinner at Glenbarr. But the Captain, now well, *he's* a different matter, entirely. Hasn't he a track worn to the front door, with the number of times he's called? Now, let me see . . . was it four times last week, and twice so far this week? Of course, they quite understand that Mrs. Barwell isn't very strong, and couldn't so often make the tiring journey to Glenbarr."

He broke off, and his voice lost the half-whine of Pat Costello. "I tell you, Sara, it made me sick in my guts to hear it."

With huge, angry steps he paced the length of the room, and back again, coming to a halt in front of her.

"And it made me more sick still to realise that the tall, handsome officer I passed almost on your doorstep was the same Captain Barwell!"

Sara was deadly white, her eyes like hard green stones, brightened by the rage that suddenly filled her. She was standing close enough to him to raise her hand and strike him fully across the face. He did not move, but stared back at her with a slight look of disbelief. The mark of her hand stood out plainly on his cheek.

"Lies!" she said. "Gossip! Stable talk that you're not above listening to, Jeremy Hogan!"

"One can hardly help it," he answered testily. "All Sydney is listening to it."

"It isn't true!" she said, backing away from him. "You know they gossip about me. They'd pin anything they could on me."

"Yes, I know it—only too well, Sara. And this is the first time you've given them anything real to pin on you."

"There isn't a word of truth in this!" she said hotly. "All these gossipers are making a fool out of me!"

His mouth twisted a little. "No, Sara, not the gossipers. It's Richard Barwell who's making the fool out of you."

"Jeremy!" She swung away from him, turning her back.

For a long time she didn't speak. He watched her shoulders rise and fall in time to her hard breathing, and then he said, very quietly, "I'm telling you straight, my dear Mrs. Maclay, that I wouldn't have the slightest hesitation in wringing your mercenary little neck if you let this nonsense go on. For it is nonsense, isn't it?" His straight black brows lifted in question "It's just gossip? There's no truth at all in it?"

At the soft insinuation in his tone, she turned to him again.

For a few moments she stood looking at him. Finally she said, "Richard Barwell comes to the house because he wants advice about what he's going to do in the colony." Her voice rose a little. "It's advice I have in plenty, Jeremy! There's nothing else to his visits. Nothing, I tell you! If the gossips want to make something else out of them what can I do?"

"*Do*!" he rapped. "Tell him to go to hell! Or if you won't, I'll do it for you!"

She looked as shocked then as if she too had been struck across the face. She ran a hand distractedly over her forehead.

"Am I asking you to do the impossible?" he said.

She shook her head slowly.

"Then what are you waiting for? He's up at the house now."

She didn't move. Her expression was half-defiant, half-afraid.

"Sara, listen to me." Jeremy's voice had dropped, and softened, but his eyes, looking into hers, were flinty. They commanded what his words merely suggested. "Everyone is talking about these visits of Barwell's. Andrew can't remain deaf, or blind, much longer."

Her lips trembled, and she pressed her hands together to still their agitation.

"Jeremy," she said, "Will you come back to the house with me. I'll go now and get my cloak."

"What are you going to do, Sarah?"

"Do? Why . . ." she paused, and ran her tongue over her lips. "If he has waited, then I'll say to him . . . I'll say exactly what you told me to say."

Sara entered her drawing-room to find Richard standing before the fire, one foot, in elegant riding-boot, resting casually on a low stool. He turned to her, and straightened.

She closed the door, and stood with her back pressed against it. Outside the rain poured down steadily. It made a hollowed, drumming noise against the roof of the veranda; the unfinished lawn beyond the windows was a dark sea of mud, with the raindrops cutting the surface. At the end of the planned garden, where it began to slope towards the trees, dozens of little rivulets had forged their own channels. Under the heavy sky the eucalypts had lost their colour, and were a drab, blackish green.

All this Sara saw as she stood with her back to the door, and she realised that in some inexplicable way it all matched the loose, indifferent fashion of Richard's stance, the look of unusual gravity in his face. He came towards her, holding out his hand. She accepted it, and allowed herself to be led forward. With gentle fingers he undid the clasp of her cloak drawing it from her shoulders, and throwing it across a chair. He was still clasping her fingers loosely, and then he reached for her other hand and held them both pressed between his own.

"You're cold, Sara. And your hair is wet. You look like a young girl. Do you remember how . . . ?

She shook her head. "Hush, Richard—no more! This isn't the time for remembering what we used to do, or how we did it."

Firmly she withdrew her hands from his. "Or for holding my hands, and dreaming of a time when it was possible to do it. All that is long over."

"Sara . . ." He frowned uncertainly. "Just for the little time we're together we could pretend . . ."

"Pretend? What's the good, when we both know the pretending must come to an end?'

"Must it?" he asked quietly.

Without hesitation, she said, "It *has* come to an end, Richard.

Pretence never lasts. I ought to have remembered that—only this time they have taken it away almost before it began."

"They?"

She nodded. "The sharp eyes, the busy tongues. I warned you that Sydney was no more than a village. One is watched ...daily ... ceaselessly. It's so easy to count the number of times you visit here—and to exaggerate the number. There's gossip about us already. Soon Andrew will hear—and Alison,"

His eyes narrowed suspiciously. "To whom have you been talking, Sara? Who has put this into your head?"

It was not easy for her to follow Jeremy's advice—to tell Richard he must go, and why. She shrugged her shoulders, as if all this was simple to explain. "Does it matter? The gossip is something I would have noticed myself, if I had not been blinded temporarily."

"Sara, tell me!" he said sharply. "Who was it?"

"It was Jeremy Hogan, if you must know," she said. "I have just seen him."

"Jeremy Hogan? And who is Jeremy Hogan, that he is privileged to say such things to you?"

She raised her hand to caution him. "Quietly, Richard! You must be quiet! I am not Alison, to be shouted at—or to be affected when you choose to sulk."

He folded his lips. "I want to know about this Jeremy Hogan. Who is he?"

"Well," she said patiently, "Jeremy Hogan is a political prisoner . . ."

"A convict!"

"You might call him a convict. To Andrew and myself he is brother, friend—and our overseer at Kintyre. Before now, I have trusted him with my life. When he comes to me and says there is talk about us, Richard, then I trust him in that also."

He looked at her, scowling like an angry child. "What fools you and Andrew are at times. This Hogan is some damned convict that you both pamper and flatter until he fancies himself a little god. And it's *his* advice that you listen to, is it? You tell me everything must end between us because an impudent upstart like that bids you."

Sara ached to smooth away his scowl then, to kiss him and tell him that she had not meant a word of what she said. But she thought of Jeremy, and she knew that she was afraid of the scene

Jeremy might make with Richard if she had to tell him she had not done as he ordered.

She drew away a little, *"Everything must end between us!"* she repeated coldly. "Nothing has happened to make an ending of. I kissed you once—that was madness, and I freely admit it. And in the last three weeks you have visited me more times than was prudent. Nothing exists between us that can't be stopped just like *that!*" She snapped her fingers decisively. *"Nothing,* Richard!"

His brows drew together in an expression of disbelief and disappointment. "Sara, you said you loved me! That day on the beach—you *said* it!"

Her face flamed. "I said I loved Andrew also.'

"But you loved me first!"

"But I loved Andrew when I was old enough to know what love meant!"

He said triumphantly, "But I was first! And you can't deny that you love me still!"

She gazed long at him, at the handsome dark face enflamed with self-will and passion. Suddenly she was angry with Richard as she had never been before. He had changed so little, she thought, crossly, in all these years—never really learning that there were some things in life that a display of rage and temperament would not give him. Alison and Lady Linton had between them ruined whatever chance he might have had to change this. Together, they had spoiled and indulged him, and he stood here now, anger distorting his features because she dared oppose him.

"No, I don't deny it, Richard," she said steadily. "It would be useless. But I want you to understand that what Andrew and I have made together is going to stand as it is. You aren't going to be the one to destroy it." She threw her head back. "I am telling you now, and I don't mean it lightly. You must not come here again unless Alison is with you."

She held herself rigidly, afraid of softening to him.

"One kiss, Richard," she said. "There wasn't anything else— and don't try to make it so."

He put his hands into his pockets, and looked at her half-sneeringly. "Is it too much to ask that I should merely come to visit you? I don't expect anything so precious as your kisses, as you're so chary of giving them. Like a well-behaved spaniel, all I ask is permission for a space in your drawing-room. I should also like sometimes to talk with you alone. But no—you prefer to take the word of a low-minded convict that there is gossip about us, and then to turn me out with the high-handedness of a duchess."

Sara whitened, but she was no longer afraid of softening. She drew herself up fully, her eyes almost level with his, when she spoke.

"I must ask you to remember two things, Richard. Firstly, in my presence, no one may call Jeremy Hogan a low-minded convict. And secondly, that although I am not a duchess, I still am mistress of this house. And now I want you to leave it immediately. And I'll have your promise that you will not come here to see me alone again."

Richard stiffened, but in his face anger fought with dismay. His eyes held the appeal of a child's.

After staring at her for a few moments, he said quietly, "I am not Andrew, Sara—and never could be anything like him. I couldn't make a fortune for you, or conquer a world to lay at your feet. But I have need of you—more need, I think, than even he has." He paused, his voice rising again. "And what's more, I believe you need me too! However, you've made your very noble choice, my dear. May you be well content with it!"

He turned slowly and walked to one of the long windows. He opened it wide, and the damp air stirred in the room. For a few moments he stood staring out into the garden, his hand thrust upwards against a heavy fold of the curtain. The rain came down ceaselessly; it was driven by a light wind across the width of the veranda, and splattered against the windows. The view of the harbour was lost in fine mist. Richard took a step forward, and then stood still, with the slanting rain hitting him. Sara shivered— the misty air, and Richard's unmoving figure seemed almost to cast a spell on the room. It was as if they were locked together in a brief enchantment. He possessed a strange power, just by standing there, to make her feel despair and pain.

"Richard! Richard!" she whispered to herself. No sound came from her lips, and he did not stir.

The wind rustled in the tops of the trees; the garden was desolate and lonely. At last he turned to her again.

"This isn't the finish, Sara. We will see much more of each other—Andrew has ensured that by his generous offer. And I hope that you will suffer as I have done in the past. I hope that you will know even a small part of my torment." He gave her a slight bow. "We have much time before us—you and I."

Then he strode across the veranda, and vaulted over the rail.

A few minutes later, at the sound of a horse cantering down the drive, Jeremy Hogan rose from his seat in the dining-room, where he was finishing the meal Annie Stokes had brought him. He opened the long windows, and stepped out on to the veranda. As he did so, he caught a glimpse of Sara moving back quickly into the drawing-room.

He leaned over the veranda rail to catch the last sight of the rider, the flash of the bright uniform against the sombre trees. His horse was black, of thoroughbred stock, and shining in the rain.

"Well . . ." Jeremy muttered aloud. "Well, you might ride as if you and the horse were born together—but I wouldn't weep, Captain Barwell, if I heard you'd fallen and broken your bloody neck!"

III

On an evening three weeks after the Barwells' arrival, Andrew stood by one of the long windows in Major Foveaux's drawing-room critically surveying the crowd about him.

As yet, only eight or so couples had made their appearance, but outside he could distinctly hear the rumble of carriages, and the bad-tempered tones of their drivers, forced to hold restless horses in line, waiting for their turn to draw up before the open doorway. They would all come, he thought—every one of them; even from as far as Parramatta they would come, because the pull of curiosity was strong. There was not a woman in the colony who, given the opportunity, would excuse herself from meeting Alison Barwell. And not a few of them knew that King, the Governor-elect had promised to attend this reception in Foveaux's house.

Across the room Andrew bowed to John Macarthur's wife, standing before the fireplace, but his attention wandered to the group just inside the door. Alison was there, fabulously gowned, and beside her, Richard. A handsome devil, Andrew reflected— a good match for Alison's air of distinction. Foveaux hovered about them, occasionally signalling to the servants, who moved with their trays among the sprinkling of early guests. On Alison's right hand, just a little behind her, stood Sara. Andrew watched his wife with pride—tall, in her gown of rose silk, and only the heightened colour of her cheeks and the slightly restless movement of the fan in her gloved hand betrayed, even to his familiar eyes, that she was nervous.

There was a buzz of conversation in the hall. Foveaux moved forward to greet his guests. They came, a group of about six people, through the door. Alison was introduced, then Richard. As each guest was about to move away, Alison turned, and with her charming smile, presented Sara.

Earlier, with the first arrivals, Andrew had caught Alison's gentle words.

"Of course, you know my friend, Mrs. Maclay..."

From some of the women there had been a marked reaction of hostility, a raising of eyebrows, a stiff bow. The more uncertain among them gave shy, rather frightened smiles, and then noticeably drifted off to discuss this unexpected development with friends in far corners of the room. On the faces of the men, almost without exception, Andrew could read admiration, and in some cases, pleasure in the knowledge that at last they were meeting and talking to Sara Maclay elsewhere than across the desk in the store.

James and Julia Ryder came in. The room filled rapidly then, and soon it was too crowded for Andrew to see clearly the little ceremony which was being repeated over and over again by the doorway. He moved among the guests, bowing here and there to acquaintances, but not pausing to become involved in conversation, lest he should lose anything of the general trend of talk. The voice of a woman, whose reputation for gossip he knew well, reached him.

"...and I'd like to know how that creature, Sara Maclay, happens to be Mrs. Barwell's friend. It's a perfect scandal that she's invited here to meet decent people..."

Then a man's voice, gently, "But *both* the Barwells say they knew her when they were children."

With a faint smile, Andrew moved off again.

He stopped to catch the words of a young bride, a recent arrival from England.

"Do you think Mrs. Maclay will be *received* after this?" She gave a slightly nervous laugh. "I think...I should like to know her, though she rather frightens me. Well, we'll see first how Mr. King receives her..."

And a young lieutenant said admiringly to a fellow-officer, "They tell me she killed an escaping convict. Jove!"

Andrew made his way towards the group by the door, but he

still did not join them. Alison was a consummate actress, he thought; or else she had been rigorously schooled by Richard. Every other minute she turned to consult Sara, tapping her arm lightly with her fan, laughing, leaning forward to listen to the other's replies. It was the perfect picture of old friends, familiar and at ease with one another. She kept Sara close, forcing any guest who approached to include her in the conversation. It was all managed with loving attention to the niceties of social behaviour; never once did Alison's manner imply her awareness that the women who spoke now with such tightened lips had never before acknowledged Andrew Maclay's ex-convict wife. To Andrew, Alison Barwell made an unforgettable picture that evening—her charming vivacity never slackened, never faltered. Her poise was equal to every demand made upon it. He smiled to himself. She was a lady, and a lady that could always be trusted to behave as her breeding dictated—even if the world turned upside down, as Alison must now be feeling hers had done.

An abrupt, intuitive hush fell upon the crowd. No one had announced the arrival of the new Governor and his lady, but the whisper of it had run through the company like a wave. Heads turned and craned; any talk that continued was abstracted while the owner's eyes were fixed on the doorway.

Philip Gidley King and Josepha Ann, his dark-haired wife, swept in. It was not yet proper to give them the welcome reserved for the true Governor. Nevertheless, they commanded the attention of the whole room. Behind them were Captain Abbott, and his wife, at whose house they were staying.

Andrew watched with keen interest the little ceremony of greetings and curtsies. Alison was known to be a favourite with Josepha Ann, and King himself smiled upon her warmly. She acknowledged her introductions to the Abbotts, and then she gracefully stretched her hand towards Sara

The silence deepened in the room. One woman among the crowd, who could not see above the heads of the men, stood on tiptoe, and almost overbalanced. Her stifled gasp was plainly audible.

Alison's clear tones reached them all.

"Sir, may I present my dear friend, Mrs. Maclay? We have known each other a very long time—almost since we were small children."

King bowed. "I am indeed happy to make your acquaintance, madam. Any friend of our charming Mrs. Barwell is, of course..."

Andrew's eyes were half-closed as he watched the shimmer of Sara's rose silk as she sank in a low curtsy. He knew beyond doubt that King would have been fully informed of Sara's history. The colony was too small to allow a new Governor to live here four full weeks without pressing on him the domestic and financial details of all his prominent citizens. Andrew was aware that King would know, equally well, that this ex-convict's husband was not without power of his own, the power of his reputed wealth, and the weight he carried in the trading-ring. King's main purpose was to smash the monopoly of this ring, either by peaceful persuasion or open warfare. Whichever way events turned, it would do him no harm to win friends among the men he sought to subjugate.

So the Governor-elect of New South Wales smiled upon Andrew Maclay's tall young wife, now being presented to him by a woman of unimpeachable reputation. Always loyal, Josepha Ann hastened to follow his example.

IV

For more than two months after the reception at Foveaux's house, Richard did not appear at Glenbarr alone. He came formally with Alison, and sometimes he and Andrew sat late discussing details of the Hyde farm—which by then had passed into Richard's hands. During these visits he was distant to Sara; his detachment lay coldly in his eyes, and she believed that he would never again come alone—until the afternoon Annie came bustling into the nursery to announce that Captain Barwell was waiting in the drawing-room.

Sara went downstairs immediately, to find him leaning nonchalantly against the mantelpiece, his fingers idly toying with the fringe of the bell-cord. He smiled at her, and when his smile met with no response, he frowned and tossed the cord aside.

"It's no use looking like that, Sara," he said. "I intend to come whenever I feel like it. No—not whenever I feel like it—whenever I know that I must see you for a few minutes, or do something crazy."

He tapped the heel of his polished boot against the fender. "But don't worry, my dear. It won't be often enough to ruin your honour or your reputation."

She was standing at the back of a big tapestry-covered chair. Her fingers gripped the scroll-work of the frame.

"I could refuse to see you," she said quietly.

He looked at her, shaking his head. "No, you won't do that. It would look bad, wouldn't it, if you refused to see me? After all, how could Alison continue to visit here, if her husband is not received? Think of it, Sara."

She thought of it, and saw what he meant her to see—Andrew's attitude if there was an open break between herself and Richard, Alison's suspicions, and the gossip of the Glenbarr servants sweeping through the town.

Richard, with no small show of triumph, won his point, and throughout the winter appeared in Sara's drawing-room for an afternoon's call, once in every two or three weeks. At first they were uneasy visits—Sara, furious and sullen that he had forced his way in on her, Richard because he knew he was not welcomed. They talked together in clipped, isolated sentences. But familiarity wore down their sense of strain. Sara soon learnt that it was impossible to quarrel politely in a drawn-out fashion. She gave in, and then they ceased throwing words about like a pair of petulant children. Richard relaxed enough to tell her his plans for the Hyde farm—he spent a part of each week there, returning eagerly to report the progress. The house was now in order; he was building hog-pens, and bringing up some oxen from Sydney. Sara shook her head doubtfully over the accounts. Richard was no farmer. He threw himself into the project with the recklessness of inexperience. There was no advice she could give him that he would heed. The farm was his, he pointed out, whenever she tried to dissuade him from some scheme or other—his alone. Andrew might have lent him the money to buy it, but that fact gave no one the right to tell him how to work it. Sara found, when this sort of mood took him, that she kept peace between them by shrugging her shoulders and having nothing further to say.

During those months there were unmistakable signs that the women of the colony were beginning to take Alison Barwell's lead. They did not immediately call at Glenbarr, but in the streets Sara was greeted with a discreet bow, and in the store their former attitude of ignoring her was abandoned. But as the winter passed, she was more and more certain that Alison had a suspicion of some relationship between her husband and the woman he told her she must call her friend. She came often enough to Glenbarr; she invited Sara back to the house on the Parramatta road, which they had bought from an officer returning to England. but she acted as if she obeyed an order; as if Sara herself mattered less than nothing in comparison with the fact that Richard must be pleased. They never advanced towards intimacy—but then, Alison was the sort to be intimate with no one. Richard was her entire world, and other people existed only in relation to him. She seemed to see Sara Maclay's husband as the provider of the luxuries of life that Richard demanded, the horses, the good wine, the gowns which were essential if she was still to have him look at her with admiration. Andrew Maclay had also provided the money for the farm, which, one day, she believed, was going to allow them to live on luxuries which were not borrowed. She had implicit faith in Richard's ability to both farm his land, with the help of an overseer, and carry out his duties at the barracks. New South Wales had many men now who were doing the same thing—and were succeeding in building up small fortunes. What neither saw was that Richard was no farmer, and that his chances were slight of ever catching up with the shrewdness, ruthlessness, and frank ambition of the others. He and his wife lived in a dream of the future, when the Hyde farm had made them at least moderately prosperous—and to Alison, prosperity also carried the idea that she would not have to visit so regularly at Glenbarr, since they would no longer be in debt to Glenbarr's owners. In the meantime, it was convenient— more than that, it was a God-send—to draw money as it was needed from the steady stream that Andrew Maclay showed no signs of checking. Luxuries were costly, Alison noted with regret, and they owed a shocking debt already to the Maclays. But, she told herself, if they were ever to succeed, they must make their start now—and in the only way open to them.

So, through the winter months, Sara and Alison clung determinedly to their facade of friendship; the wives of the colony's officials began to bow and nod to Mrs. Maclay when their carriages chanced to pass in Sydney's muddy streets. Gradually a phrase passed among them—"Of course, Sara Maclay's case is rather different from that of the other convicts." One or two of the husbands suggested that their wives might try inviting Sara Maclay to their tea-parties. It was well known that she possessed a great deal of influence with her husband—and there were many people in the colony who, for one reason or another, wished to retain Andrew Maclay's goodwill.

And while this went on, while winter gave place to a pale, warm spring, Richard continued to visit occasionally at Glenbarr, to tell Sara his plans, to listen to her encouragement, to disregard her advice. If Andrew were there, he stayed only a short time; if they were alone, he sat on before the drawing-room fire, talking on and on, until the intimacy of the walks on the Romney Marsh was once again established. And always he rode away from Glenbarr at a mad pace, with a look on his face of a man who has had a great weight lifted from him. Sometimes he didn't go directly home, or to the barracks, but turned aside to the road heading to the South Head.

Once Ted O'Malley, the Maclays' boatman, had reported meeting him on this road, after a visit to Glenbarr. He told Annie—who promptly repeated it to Sara—that Captain Barwell had cantered along, singing a soldier's song at the top of his voice, and with a strange, wild look on his face.

Chapter Four

Sara gave an audible sigh of relief as the straggling hamlet of Castle Hill appeared at the end of the stretch of road. There was not much farther to go now, she consoled herself. Three miles on the other side of the rough little settlement ahead, a track led off to the left, curving for a couple of hundred yards to a ragged farm-building, known locally as Priest's. Joseph Priest had died four months ago, and for the past six weeks the Maclays had been the owners of the worked-out, neglected property. Sara reflected happily enough on the prospect. Within two years, if Andrew was right, this piece of land would wear the same prosperous, fertile look that characterised their Toongabbie and Hawkesbury farms. Andrew's ambition was a restless, growing thing.

He and Jeremy were both together at Priest's, living in the comfortless, leaking shack, alone except for the one sickly ex-convict labourer who was the sole remnant of the labour-force of a dozen men once needed to run the property. The stacks of rum-kegs piled in the yard at the back were sufficient testimony of the reason why the farm had failed. But the place had promise. After a few weeks of combined hard work, Jeremy was to stay on, while Andrew returned to Sydney. It was Jeremy who would guide Priest's through the difficult years of re-birth, while Andrew's impatient nature sought a dozen different occupations.

All of this Andrew had written in two hasty letters to Sara.

She pictured the farm as he described it—even its hideous decay softened and beautified by the burst of spring wild flowers, and the single, exquisite white gum-tree, bending towards the creek. She had thrown the second letter aside, and, on an impulse, had packed a box with a few of her oldest clothes, and ordered the carriage to be stocked with extra food and cooking utensils. She left the store in the charge of young Clapmore, Glenbarr to Bennett, and the children to Annie.

She promised herself in this visit to Priest's a complete return to the early days on the Hawkesbury. There would be just herself, Andrew, and Jeremy working and discussing together the problems of over-worked land, diseased. neglected stock, the shortage of labour. She would cook for them and for two weeks share the unbroken companionship of the two men who had built her world. She knew she was attempting a flight into the past, and she recognised the possibility that it might be a dismal failure. But, along with Andrew's letters, she had also experienced that odd restlessness and dissatisfaction that comes with the spring; this flight was a brief indulgence of that mood. It was an acknowledgment of her vague desires for a return to the simplicity of those first years, a simplicity which, at most times, she was sensible enough to recognise as having gone for ever. The success of this impulse depended upon Andrew and Jeremy. If they accepted her presence at Priest's as naturally as she had come, then she would know that the spirit of adventure and comradeship had survived Andrew's growing wealth—and she would be satisfied and happy.

At Glenbarr, David and Duncan were still engaged in a struggle, now a month old, to win supremacy over their new tutor, a huge, untidy young Irishman of great learning and shy charm, whom Sara had engaged by letter eighteen months ago; Sebastian, in the nursery, was beginning to haul himself up to stand totteringly on his lanky, strong legs. Under Bennett, Glenbarr ran itself, and, short of the unexpected arrival of a ship with fresh cargo, there was nothing at the store to need her attention for the next two weeks.

Her carriage suddenly jolted into a rut and she braced herself against the back of the seat, the dispirited, whitewashed buildings came closer. By the side of the nearest house a solitary mimosa tree had burst into bloom—outrageously yellow against the harsh blue sky.

Sara shook the dust absently from her skirt, and straightened her bonnet, acknowledging, in the privacy of her own thoughts, that she had done perhaps the wisest thing by not remaining too long in Sydney while Andrew was staying at Priest's. Richard was due to return after a two-week period of duty at Parramatta, and she recalled past occasions when Andrew's absence seemed to give him licence, which he didn't hesitate to accept, to visit Glenbarr whenever he chose. Sara sighed, and ran her hand across her eyes. From the doorway of the cottage, in whose withered, brown garden the mimosa flowered, a woman paused to watch the carriage. At her skirts a small child waved shyly. Sara leaned forward smiling. As she waved back to the little girl, she knew suddenly that she was impatient with the problem of Richard. She wanted to be with Andrew and Jeremy again, in an atmosphere where the greatest problem would be coping with an evil-tempered stove, or deciding how many head of stock the neglected pastures at Priest's would carry in the first year.

They were now among the haphazard buildings which formed the Castle Hill settlement. The heavy spring rains had turned the road between the thatched and whitewashed houses into mud, and the constant passage of horses and carts had cut it into deep ruts. The ruts had dried in the past week of hot sunshine, and there was already a film of dry dust over everything. A flock of geese crossed serenely in front of the carriage, moving on in the direction of the shallow stream at the side of the road. Three men, and two soldiers off-duty, lounged around the door of Nell Finnigan's cottage. Nell was a large, handsome woman, an ex-convict who ran her husband's house as a kind of inn—though it was widely known that she made her obvious profits from the sale of rum. Glancing at the shining neatness of the cottage as she passed, Sara idly wondered which of the gentlemen, living off the fat of the land in Sydney, was responsible for her supply.

The carriage jolted to a halt before the blacksmith's forge. Sara immediately thrust her head out of the window, waiting for Edwards, Andrew's ugly, grizzled coachman to climb down.

"Why are we stopping?" she said to him.

He pushed his hat back inelegantly. "Lor, ma'am! I thought you'd'a spotted it miles back. Goldie,'ere,'as gone lame on me. I reckon the master'll not be too pleased if I take her farther than I have to while she's like this. Carson, the smithy 'ere, can probably let us have another horse, and we could leave Goldie 'ere."

She nodded. "Ask him—but be as quick as you can."

"Yes'm." He touched his hat, and started, with his bowlegged gait, towards the forge. He vanished into the dark interior, and then reappeared with a small grey-haired man, wearing a leather apron. For a few minutes they talked together; Carson finally called over his shoulder to a young man who came out of the forge and followed him round to the side of it. They headed towards a rough stable at the back.

Edwards approached Sara with a grin lighting up his cracked face. " 'Tis all settled, ma'am. Carson has another that'll take Goldie's place. We'll be harnessed up and away in no time."

He cleared his throat a little, looking at her with concern. She had noticed in the past that whenever he drove her alone he always displayed a solemn interest in her comfort, which he was wont to express with unpolished bluntness. "Now, ma'am," he said clearly. "I was wonderin' if maybe this sun might be too fierce on you—with you just sitting here waiting. Carson sends his respects, and says you're welcome to sit awhile in the forge—if you'll not think it too dirty,"

Sara had already made up her mind not to stay in the stuffy carriage during the change-over. She stepped down on to the road, looking up and down the row of cottages. "If I go across to Nell Finnigan's, perhaps she'll give me some cold water. I'm thirsty."

His face wrinkled in dismay. "Oh, ma'am! Nell Finnigan's . . ." His tone left her no doubt as to what he thought of Mistress Finnigan.

She turned, picking up her skirts to cross the dusty road.

"Go and help Carson," she said. "I think I'll hardly come to harm with Mrs. Finnigan in the space of ten minutes."

She heard him muttering doubtfully as she made her way towards the flower-bordered cottage near the end of the row. Outside the soldier's guard-house a dog rose up from his sprawling position close to the steps, and came over hopefully to her; a soldier, tacking a notice to the board on the veranda post, eyed her up and down, grinning impudently. The sun seemed to grow hotter as she walked, and the scraggy settlement looked as if not even the spring could shake it from its apathy. When she reached Nell Finnigan's, the small crowd who had stood drinking ale outside her open door had drifted, glasses still in hand, down the lane running between the cottage and the guard-house. She watched them a moment. They were joined by perhaps a half-dozen others, and on the outskirts of the group three or four children shuffled their bare feet in the dust.

Sara was filled with curiosity. But she had only to take a few steps down the lane before she knew the reason for the crowd. The yard at the back of the guard-house was in full view now, and the people too sparse to screen what was happening there.

She came upon it suddenly; there were no cries to warn her. The man who hung at the post was unconscious, and the only sound was the whirr of the cat, as it swung backwards and around in the hand of the flogger, and then the crack as it hit the naked flesh. After each stroke a soldier standing near the post recorded it in a sing-song voice.

"Forty-seven . . ."

Another whirr, and the crack.

"Forty-eight . . ."

She had seen it before—too often. It was stamped in her memory from the days of the *Georgette*, and even before that. It was part of the discipline that ruled the colony—as common a thing as, in England, the gibbet, and the swinging corpse at the cross-roads. This was always a public spectacle—as the magistrates wanted it, because its grim warning struck home at even the hardened sensibilities of the ex-convict watchers.

The bright, flowing blood glistened in the sunlight. The ragged trousers hanging on the hips of the man at the post had absorbed all they could hold. It trickled down his calves, and lay in the dust about his feet. The sounds ceased abruptly, and a second man stepped up to the flogger and took the cat from his hand, shaking the knotted things, twisting it in his hands to get the proper balance. Then he swung his arm backwards, and then again came the whirr and the sickening crack.

"Fifty-one . . ."

Sara clapped her hands over her ears, turned, and fled back towards Nell Finnigan's door. In the dim, cool passage she saw no one. She leaned against the wall for a moment, pressing her hand against her mouth, and breathing heavily. At last she straightened, groping her way clumsily in the half-dark. She tripped on the hem of her gown, and stumbled up against a door. Her outstretched hand touched the latch, and it opened with her weight. The door swung back with a crash; she clutched wildly at the frame to save herself falling.

She had a confused impression that a man, seated at a bench beside the window, sprang to his feet. Both her arms were gripped steadily, and a pair of dark, shrewd eyes were fixed on her face.

"Are you ill?"

Confused now, Sara shook her head. "No..."

She felt herself being led firmly to the seat the man had just left. It was almost impossible for her to believe, as she looked at the sunlight pouring through Nell Finnigan's fresh muslin curtains, that an unconscious man hung at a flogging-post not more than a few yards away. She rested her elbows on the scrubbed boards of the table in front of her, and put her face into her hands. The sun was fully on her back, but she could not hold back the fit of shivering which gripped her.

Gently the stranger's hand came to her shoulder, giving her a little shake.

"Drink some of this," he said. "It is wine, bad enough to take the lining off your throat—but it is better than nothing."

He held a glass close to her lips. She had not yet looked at him fully—just his eyes, in that first instant, and now, the thin, brown fingers curling about the glass. She hesitantly stretched out her own hand to take it, but he wouldn't yield it to her completely. She was forced to drink with her fingers touching his around the base of the glass.

The wine was raw and harsh, and made her cough a little. But the relentless hand held it to her mouth until it was gone. Then a fine linen handkerchief dabbed at her moistened lips. She crushed the handkerchief into a ball in her hand and leaned back against the window-sill.

"Are you feeling better now?"

For the first time she looked at him fully. He was lean, and very tall, with unconscious grace in his stance. The shrewd, questioning eyes fixed on her were almost black; his unpowdered hair was black also. She wondered if she considered him handsome, and studied the narrow, well-formed face, dark olive skin stretched above high cheekbones. Brows cut thick and savagely across his forehead. His mouth was too thin, a trifle cruel, she decided—in a sense, it didn't match his eyes, which regarded her now with obvious concern.

He repeated his question quietly. "Are you feeling better?"

She nodded. "Thank you—much better." She hesitated. "I think perhaps the sun..."

"Or the flogging?" he suggested.

"You saw it also?"

222

"That was hardly to be avoided." He lifted his shoulders expressively. "I offer my sympathies, madam. It was not a sight for a lady."

As he spoke, Sara's mind was busily storing the details of his speech and dress, and puzzling over his identity. The colony was still much too small to allow a stranger, and especially one who looked as this one did, to arrive without causing a great flutter of comment and speculation. Her eyes swiftly flicked over him, taking in the cut of his coat, the fit of his long boot, and the perfection of the emerald he wore on the little finger of the left hand. His English was perfect, but he spoke it with the slightest of accents. He was dressed, and he behaved, as any prosperous man in the colony might, and still in each detail he was somehow a little more than life-size. He brought a touch of the exotic, a breath of the civilised and cultivated world into the scrubbed room. Even the way he spoke of the flogging carried a trace of worldly cynicism with it. But he was not indifferent to the flogging, she felt—he merely suggested that such things were painfully necessary and unpleasant.

Then her mind reached back to some vague, unconnected gossip she had heard between two clerks at the store the day before. This was undoubtedly the man of whom they had spoken—a Frenchman, who arrived in the American sloop which was riding at anchor in the harbour these past two days, Apparently he had made the voyage from Ile de France, intending, no one knew why, to remain for a while in New South Wales. Even the idle conversation between Clapmore and the junior clerk had managed to convey the air of mystery which presumably surrounded this French stranger. Sara realised that he must have been able to convince the port officials that he was genuinely an emigré, and entertained no Bonaparte sympathies, otherwise, when the American sloop prepared to sail again, he would be firmly aboard her. According to Clapmore's gossip, the Frenchman was taking his time about disembarking—his boxes had not even come ashore yet. Later in the day she had heard the story over again from two different customers. And yet, here he was, these many miles beyond Sydney already, and it was hardly past noon. The Frenchman, she thought, obviously moved quickly, once he decided to move at all.

She saw that his straight, heavy brows were raised in a look of inquiry, and she realised that she had been staring at him like any clumsy country girl. It occurred to her that it was possible that he was bored by the obligation to affect concern over a dull, stupid woman.

He bowed slightly. "Madame, might I be permitted to offer you a little more wine? I grant you that it is abominable—but they do assure me that it is the best they have."

Sara flushed, feeling absurdly ill at ease under his steady scrutiny. Then she straightened, answering him with a trace of hauteur.

"You are very kind, sir. I should be glad of it."

"It is indeed a great pleasure," he said quietly. "I will send for a bottle."

He turned to the door, and then stopped and looked back at her. He came again to the table, facing her across its width. The concern was gone from his eyes. They held a friendly, faintly amused air.

"Before we share a glass of wine," he said, "perhaps it is better if I introduce myself."

He sketched another small, graceful bow.

"Madame—Louis de Bourget."

He raised his head again, and when his eyes met hers they were bright and questioning; the corners of his mouth puckered.

"I see by your expression, Madame, that you wish me still to give an account of myself. Is that not so?" He smiled indulgently. "Perhaps it will satisfy you if I tell you that I disembarked this morning from the American ship, the *Jane Henry*—I am now on my way to Mr. William Cooper's house. He and I became acquainted during the few weeks our ships were in port together in Cape Town. And now I go to avail myself of his offer of hospitality. I assure you . . .'

Laughingly, Sara waved him to silence.

"Forgive me, Monsieur! I must appear very boorish . . . A complete stranger is such a rarity to us here! And I must warn you, you'll have to expect a great deal of curiosity."

Then she held out her hand.

"You're very welcome to the colony, Monsieur de Bourget! My name is Sara Maclay."

A slow, warm smile broke on his face, and it lost its quizzical look. He took her hand firmly, bowing over it. Then for the first of many times, he kissed it.

Nell Finnigan had a plump, shapely figure, and, as she stood in the doorway watching Louis de Bourget, she jerked her sprigged cotton gown into position in order to define it better. She had just seen him hand Sara Maclay into her carriage outside the door. Her curiosity was ablaze about this good-looking stranger—and the reason why Mrs. Maclay had arrived unannounced in the back parlour. She tossed back her head, letting her black curls swing coquettishly under the dainty white cap she wore.

She leaned against the door-frame, and addressed de Bourget.

"More wine, sir?" She ignored the fact that the bottle was still two-thirds full.

He rested back against the sill, as Sara had done earlier, and looked at Nell carefully. He liked the cleanliness of her, the shining hair, the soft white skin that this murderous climate appeared not to have affected. With a touch of amusement, he noted that deliberately provocative stance she had adopted; she was more than skilled in displaying her quite considerable attractions. De Bourget had his own ideas about the type of woman he admired, and this one was too full-blown, too obvious in type to suit his taste. But the room was strangely empty now that the golden-haired Mrs. Maclay was gone, and he knew the woman standing before him would while away the next hour in effortless coquetry. Women who smiled in just that fashion, who thrust their bodies towards a man, as this one did, were never hard to entertain.

He gestured towards the bottle. "As you see, it is hardly opened yet. Perhaps you'll share it with me, Mistress Finnigan?"

She made no show of reluctance. "Always glad to share a bottle." This was said with a particularly sweet smile.

She seated herself on the opposite side of the table and, without waiting, poured herself a full glass. She tossed half of it back with a swiftness that made him wince. Then she seemed to remember what she had come for in the first place, and turned directly to her subject.

"Mrs. Maclay is probably on her way to join her husband," she began.

Louis raised his eyebrows encouragingly. "So . . . ? I'm afraid I don't know . . ."

"Her husband is Andrew Maclay—he's just bought the old Priest place three miles farther on," she volunteered easily, "Clever as a monkey with money, he is. He's made himself a rich man in the eight or so years he's been here—with a bit of gambling on the side, to help things along. And there was talk of him getting salvage money—a lot of it—for a ship in India, or

China, or one of those foreign places." She laughed a little. She was a pretty woman, with beautiful eyes. "But there's not so much gambling for Mr. Maclay now, believe me!"

"No?"

"No, he's getting too important these days, too respectable. And as for that wife of his . . . Well, look at the way she's dressed, for one thing, You'd never think she'd landed here as a convict, now, would you?"

He leaned nearer to her. Her wide, bold eyes were fixed on him unblinkingly. He could smell her faint, clean smell, that seemed to come from the generous expanse of bosom her gown revealed.

"So Mrs. Maclay was a convict, was she?"

Nell Finnigan shrugged her plump shoulders. "Oh . . . It's an old story. Everyone knows it . . . how she had Andrew Maclay all tied in knots before he ever stepped ashore in this place. It was this way . . ."

As she talked, Louis refilled her empty glass.

II

Ten years ago, when Joseph Priest first cleared and fenced his land, he had had dreams of how his property might be in the future. With reckless disregard of both time and labour, he had found and transplanted forty young mimosa trees, spacing them at regular intervals among the eucalypts, twenty each side, along the avenue leading to the house. He was one of the first who came to the colony to find beauty in this harsh, austere landscape, and with the impractical soul of a poet, he had made his gesture to it. Priest drank heavily. Year by year he and the farm deteriorated with equal speed; he dismissed more labourers, and the very promising property gradually slipped into ruin. But every spring the mimosa trees were a little taller, the avenue turned bright gold in the midst of the green, and Joseph Priest smiled whenever he looked at it. He found contentment in the fact that, although he was counted a failure, he had created here a thing of lasting beauty—created it out of an untouched wilderness. Crazed with drink, and overwhelmed by hopeless debt, in the end he could not wait until the trees bloomed again. He hung himself from the tallest and strongest of them before the winter was over.

The mimosa were in their golden bloom when Sara drove

along the avenue for the first time. Something of the spirit of Joseph Priest touched her, she had a sudden understanding of his practical notion to fashion a thing of ordered loveliness out of the resources at hand. This was the sort of thing she longed to do for Kintyre—but at Kintyre, prosperous as it was, and well-run, time and labour could never be spared, as this madman had spared them. She breathed a prayer of thankfulness to him for all his wild folly.

The house itself was an unpainted ruin. It had a badly thatched roof, and sagging, rotten verandas around three sides of it. Once there had been some attempt at a garden, and a straggling orchard beside it. The garden was choked and overgrown, and Sara's experienced eyes knew that the trees had not borne fruit for some years, although now they made a show of heartbreaking beauty, with sparse, frail blossoms on every bough.

She saw Jeremy appearing round the side of the house before the carriage stopped. Her bonnet, which she had taken off when they left Castle Hill, lay on the seat beside her. She picked it up and waved it excitedly. He hesitated, and then came forward at a half-run. The carriage lurched and halted, and Jeremy flung open the door.

"Sara! What brings you here? Oh, but this is wonderful! Wait until Andrew . . ."

She laughed a little, accepting his hand as she stepped down. "Am I welcome, do you think, Jeremy? Or is this a time when no woman should intrude?"

For a moment his fingers tightened round her hand. "What a tease you are, Sara! You know that Andrew will be delighted. We never thought, either of us . . ."

He paused, aware that her smile had grown broader, and that she was looking beyond him. He turned, and saw Andrew come running along the veranda and jump down the three steps. Sara dropped Jeremy's hand as if it had never been there, and he watched her outstretched arms go about her husband's neck. They clung together tightly, quite unmindful of either his own gaze, or Edward's sardonic grin from the driver's seat.

At last Andrew loosened his grip; his hands slipped forward a little until they rested on Sara's shoulders. He held her back a little, looking at her with a beam of pleasure on his face.

"How good to have you here!" he said.

She laughed delightedly. "How could I stay away? Your letters

227

made me so envious. Both of you here—and I kept out of all this!''

With a slight gesture she indicated the tumble-down house, the ruin of the orchard and garden.

Andrew patted her shoulder. ''We've needed you here, haven't we, Jeremy? We're killing ourselves with our own cooking!''

Sara's eyebrows shot up. She said, with mock severity, ''If a cook was all you needed, I'm quite sure that there's more than one to be found in Castle Hill.''

Over her head Andrew winked at Jeremy. ''Oh, of course! And more than one who'd be willing to share the house with a handsome bachelor like Jeremy, I've no doubt.''

They all laughed together, and Andrew began to lead Sara towards the steps, his arm loosely about her shoulders. Jeremy walked on the other side, holding her discarded bonnet, and listening to their talk.

''Come and see the house first,'' Andrew said. ''It needs a great deal done to it, of course—but it should be pleasant enough when it's finished. The farm . . .'' He shrugged. ''Priest hasn't done a stroke of work, or spent a penny-piece on it for years. But we'll soon have it in shape. I think in a few weeks we can bring the first stock here.''

Andrew and Sara went on into the house. Jeremy stayed on the veranda, walking back to the three rickety steps. He could hear their voices as they planned together. They were excited, he thought—not bitterly, but a little sadly. He felt the ribbons of Sara's bonnet between his fingers, pulling them tight, and then loosening them. He thought of them tied beneath her chin, and his blood quickened. He wondered when it was that he had first begun to love her—perhaps the night in the bush as Andrew's bride, perhaps the night the convicts broke out at Kintyre. Perhaps he had always known and loved Sara—might she not have been the myth of every love-dream he had ever had? He didn't know.

He leant back against the veranda post, and his eyes were on the golden bloom of the mimosas.

III

Andrew stood at the foot of Glenbarr's wide staircase, staring up at the landing above him. He looked at his watch for the second time in five minutes, brushed unnecessarily at the sleeve of his coat, listening all the time to the murmur of voices coming from the main bedroom. Suddenly, madly impatient, he leapt up three steps. "Sara!" he called, "Are you ready?"

The voices ceased. A rustle of stiff brocade answered him, and the sound of Sara's footsteps. When she reached the head of the stairs, his quick glance took in the gown of palest blue and silver—extravagant material he remembered having brought her from India. She was smoothing her gloves as she came down; a trace of a smile lingered on her face, as if she had just heard something that pleased her. Behind her, rigid and thin in a starched apron, came Annie Stokes. She carried her mistress's wrap on her arm and her wrinkled features wore a look of fierce pride and satisfaction.

Bennett opened the door as Sara came forward. She stood on the doorstep, while Annie adjusted the wrap, sniffing at the scent of the early dew. The night was dark, though later there would be a moon. The lanterns of the waiting carriage glowed warmly; one of the horses pawed gently at the gravel.

Bennett remained by the carriage door until Sara and Andrew were seated, then he signalled to Edwards perched up on the box.

Edwards gathered the reins in his hands. Ahead of him was Sydney's huddle of lighted houses. He squared his shoulders, and, for the pure pleasure of hearing it, announced in a loud voice:

"Government House, sir! Right!"

The Maclays' names echoed through the long drawing-room at Government House, and many heads turned in puzzled fashion to look at the latest arrivals. They watched Andrew's bow, and Sara's curtsy, noting, with eyes accustomed to discerning the degree of vice-regal favour, that the Governor was affable, and that Mrs. King had a welcoming and gracious smile. Eyes turned away rather hastily, in case the inquisitive stares might be discovered, and the buzz of conversation rose louder than before.

The two new-comers advanced farther into the room, to join the Ryders; they were instantly aware that most of the talk was centred on them. Sara's position in Sydney's tiny society was still irregular—although, since Alison Barwell's claims of friendship, she had been more or less accepted and treated in the way that Andrew's position demanded. But society had not let itself go with any noticeable generosity, until the seal of official approval and acknowledgment was offered her. And this evening it was bestowed for the first time in an invitation to Government House.

But the Kings were very new to their position of governing the colony, and more caution had been expected from them at the beginning. A question was asked and repeated among the little groups in the crowded drawing-room. Why was Sara Maclay received, when no other ex-convict had ever been given this privilege? One man in the gathering had the explanation on undeniable authority, and he saw no reason for holding back his knowledge. He leaned forward and whispered in his companion's ear; then, from behind open fans, the tale was spread until no one had cause to wonder any longer.

Mrs. King, on acquainting herself with Sydney, had had the idea of starting a girls' orphanage for the illegitimate offspring of hundreds of casual matings—children who roamed the streets, and had already learned how to beg a living, and evade authority. These were to be rounded up and suitably housed; for this purpose Mrs. King needed money. The story travelled around the drawing-room that Sara Maclay's invitation to Government House, a graceful gesture on Mrs. King's part, had come after she received a donation of a thousand pounds from Andrew, and a firm promise of further help.

Interested eyes turned to look at the man who was a thousand pounds poorer for his evening's entertainment.

Voices grew harsh in their effort to be heard above one another; the steady stream of talk continued, almost succeeding in drowning the announcement of each guest's arrival. The soft lap of the water against the rocks below Government House was lost; groups had spilled out through the open french windows on to the veranda, but, so far, only a few had paused to notice that the rising moon had cast a brilliant track of light across the harbour. There were plenty of other nights, Sara thought, for them to watch the moon, and, sensibly, most of them were concentrating on the business in hand.

Half a dozen times Andrew was checked by men anxious to have a word with him, as he made his way, Sara at his side, towards the corner where they saw that Julia Ryder had found herself a comfortable sofa. Macarthur stopped them, his dark face bland and smiling—smiling more broadly, with a bow to Sara, at Andrew's invitation to call up at Glenbarr the following morning. Robert Campbell also made a bid for Andrew's attention, desisting when he saw that the other was not to be side-tracked. Normally these men were Andrew's business associates, the colony's men of affairs, the men whose word was power. At any other time he would have been wrapped in conversation half the night with them. But, under the curious stares all around, he seemed bent on proving that, when his wife was at his side, he had eyes for no one else.

"My dear Sara—how lovely you look this evening!" In full view of the room Julia offered her cheek to be kissed.

James Ryder smiled upon her with real pleasure. It touched his sense of humour to think of the effect on the present gathering if he were to suddenly recall—as he most certainly could—the picture Sara had made the first time Andrew had brought her up from the Georgette's filthy hold. She was a beauty, even then, he reflected—but those rags! He coughed into the crisp ruffles at his wrist, to hide the chuckle that rose in his throat. Julia twisted and glanced at him suspiciously. Then her face relaxed, as if she guessed his thoughts.

"Sara does us great credit, do you not think so, James?"

"Indeed, yes!" he replied, letting his grin out of control, his eyes on Sara's face. "There's more satisfaction in watching Sara than there'll ever be in that prim daughter of ours." He gave an exaggerated sigh. "Ellen's a good girl—but a prude. It doesn't seem possible that any daughter of Julia's brought up in a place like this, should turn out such a simpering little madam. But Ellen has somehow managed it."

"England will change her," Sara said reassuringly.

"In that select Ladies' Academy in Bath?" James gave a hopeless shrug. "She's doomed to prudery, I'm afraid—and my only son gone off to pin his heart to Lord Nelson's sleeve!"

A shade of fear touched Julia's face, but she spoke quite firmly. "Charles will be back when he's had enough of the sea. He'll come back because he loves this place more than he cares to admit. As for Ellen . . ."

Sara didn't listen any longer. At the other end of the room she heard Captain and Mrs. Barwell announced, and she stepped behind James to get a better view of the doorway. Alison was rising from her curtsy. She wore a white gown that made her look like an exquisitely turned-out doll. In an instant its simplicity caused every other woman in the room to look overdressed, though no feminine eye was deceived about its cost. On Richard's arm she began to move through the crowd. Sara quickly turned her head, because Richard was looking about him in a way she had come to recognise. His gaze would find her soon enough, she knew, but she was not anxious to appear conspicuous, and she drew back again behind James.

"Mr. William Cooper!"

"Monsieur Louis de Bourget!"

Again Sara's head turned. The volume of talk swelled perceptibly after the announcement of this last name, and there was shifting and craning to get a better view.

"... de Bourget ... de Bourget?"

She could hear the running whisper of it, as he made his bow to the Governor and his wife, and she felt that for the rest of the evening the gathering had found a far more absorbing topic of conversation than herself. She moved her fan gently, watching with narrowed eyes. He and Cooper were detained in talk by King, and she thought that now, with a cluster of English faces about him, his Gallic look was far more pronounced than when Nell Finnigan's parlour had been his background. The magnificence of his dress was yet another feature to distinguish him. The dark red coat and gold-buckled shoes were too grand for this dull little vice-regal entertainment; but Mrs. King's face wore a look of pleasure which told Sara that this Frenchman was well enough versed in the art of subtle flattery.

She flicked her fan again, and turned to Andrew.

"This is the man," she said, "whom I told you about. He is the Frenchman I talked with at Nell Finnigan's."

Julia looked at her with raised eyebrows. "You've actually *met* him? Then that's a great deal more than any one else besides William Cooper has done."

Sara shrugged. "I called in at Finnigan's on my way to Priest's—de Bourget was there, on *his* way to Cooper's house. It seems they became acquainted when their ships were waiting together in Cape Town some time ago."

James gave another chuckle. "Then I had no need to waste all my afternoon gathering information about this fellow. All I need have done was to ask Sara."

Sara shut her fan briskly. "Indeed, I could hardly have helped you then. We only arrived back from Priest's this morning, and I know nothing of the man beyond his name. He's a Frenchman, but as to what he's doing here ..." She shrugged. "His nationality seems to be the only remarkable thing about him."

Andrew laughed. "Don't pretend, my dear, that you're the only woman in the room who doesn't find the cloth of his coat remarkable—and the number of rings he wears! For myself, I'm utterly fascinated by his look of prosperity. I find this unknown gentleman extremely attractive."

James cleared his throat. "Then do give me the pleasure of relating the gossip I've so carefully patched together from snippets I've picked up all over the town. No woman could have done it with greater skill. I assure you. Though, I must warn you, the source is none too reliable. The tales of this man, de Bourget, were begun by the captain of the *Jane Henry*, who brought him here from Ile de France. And *he* claims to have heard the story all over the island."

His wife reached up and tapped his hand with her fan. "For pity's sake, James, *do* tell us! I'm dying with curiosity!"

"Well, in that case ... The rumour has it that Monsieur de Bourget is a kinsman of the Marquis de L ... The name is only whispered, my dear Julia, in case it should prove to be wrong. De Bourget was a member of his household—assisted him with some of his estates, or some such thing. Our young Frenchman has no money of his own, but he possessed considerable influence with the Marquis. But he was also, it's said, very well known in other quarters of Paris. In fact, he exercised his full right to mix with people less well born than his noble cousin. He belonged, in a sense, to both worlds, as a young gentleman of no fortune is often obliged to do. He would have been a fool if his influence with the Marquis hadn't occasionally been sold at a price."

James was enjoying his audience. He continued, "The family tarried too long after the Revolution. The September massacres came upon them, and the Marquis realised that he would never escape from Paris. He had often suspected that his penniless cousin had Jacobin friends, and he begged him to take his only child, a girl, to London. De Bourget managed to get her away from France—and with them both went the family jewels."

Julie caught her breath. "The child ... what has become of her?"

"The child was ill, even before she left Paris. She died in London a year later. Apparently de Bourget had nursed her devotedly."

"And the jewels ... ?" Andrew was concerned, and frowning.

James's shoulders lifted a little. "The jewels? What do you

imagine? The whole family was wiped out in the massacres—even the nephews and cousins. The girl was the only survivor—the girl and de Bourget.''

Andrew looked doubtful now. ''And how much of this do you believe?''

The other man spread his hands in a gesture of uncertainty.

''That's the point, exactly,'' he said. ''The story has travelled half-way round the world, distorted, no doubt, with each telling. And it's said that de Bourget himself is not to be questioned about it. He neither confirms nor denies it; he expresses neither royalist nor Jacobin sympathies. All that is certain is that he seems to possess a great deal of money, and that he has travelled continuously for the past five years. France was in utter chaos when the Marquis sent his child away. So who can be certain that de Bourget was anything more than a trusted secretary? He might not have been a blood relation at all.''

''Is that possible?'' Andrew asked dubiously. ''Surely there were some among the emigrés in London who would have recognised a kinsman of the Marquis? An impostor could hardly expect to live amongst them, and remain unexposed.''

''That, of course, occurred to me,'' James acknowledged. ''In the emigré circles in London the story must be well known. Perhaps such a story will only bear repeating on this side of the world, where we're so far removed from the source. Whatever the truth is, the child's death put de Bourget in possession of a fortune, and no one else has come forward to lay claim to it.''

''Has he a wife?'' Julia asked.

James nodded. ''That fortune wouldn't escape a woman's hands for very long. He married the daughter of a small Gloucestershire squire. They were together only about a year. She went on a visit to her family, and never returned to de Bourget. There's a child, I believe . . . a daughter.''

''I see you've had a busy afternoon, James,'' his wife said mildly. ''The information you've collected in these few hours would do credit to the powers of any six women put together.''

''Oh . . . it wasn't all from the captain of the *Jane Henry*. I fancy William Cooper has been talking also.''

''A fortune in jewels . . . and still his wife can't bear him for longer than a year . . .'' Sara pondered the information. ''It makes very little sense. Perhaps he stays away from England because of her . . . Or because someone else may come forward to claim a part of the fortune.''

234

Andrew touched her arm. "If you dare to, my dear, you can question the Frenchman all you please. Macarthur is bringing him and Cooper directly across to us."

With burning of cheeks, Sara swung round. John Macarthur was almost beside them now, and de Bourget, with William Cooper, a pace or so behind.

"Mrs. Maclay..." Smiling, Macarthur gestured towards the Frenchman. "Monsieur de Bourget claims to be already acquainted with you. Surely he dreams...?"

Sara tossed her head back. "No, Monsieur de Bourget doesn't dream."

Louis de Bourget stepped up beside Macarthur. He took Sara's hand, and bowed low over it.

"Madame," he said, "I am surrounded by strangers. I trust you and your husband will forgive me for flinging myself upon your society in this fashion?"

He raised her hand to kiss it, and Sara knew that every eye in the room was on them in that instant.

Chapter Five

Some quality in Louis de Bourget answered a need in Andrew, of which, until that time, he had hardly been aware. At first his feeling for the Frenchman was scarcely more than curiosity; then he admitted being amused by the other's cynicism, his air of having weighed up all that life offered a man, his manner of poking sly fun at the manoeuvrings of the colonials in their race for wealth, and hiding all of this under his mask of polite concern. Andrew talked to Louis, and found what he had long lacked—a confidant who was far removed from the struggle which waged unceasingly for profits, for concessions, for gain. De Bourget returned to Sydney, to stay in William Cooper's new house; in the two months following the Government House reception, Andrew began to look forward to sharing a bottle of wine with him, relating the latest rumours and speculations and then listening to Louis' dry, often scathing comments on the whole of the colonial scene.

"I despise them all!" Andrew would declare roundly. "Profiteers! Land-grabbers!"

"Naturally, you despise them," Louis answered, with a calculating smile. "Most of them are not nearly as practised in the art of profiteering as yourself—and I'm beginning to understand that you have very little time for the second-rate."

Andrew was accustomed to laugh at such a remark. There was about this Gallic temperament a freshness which both fascinated and irritated him.

"Damn me, if I can think why you stay here at all!" Andrew said. "We appear such bores to you—so bourgeois."

Louis shrugged. "The bourgeois are prolific breeders—and their children inherit the earth." He yawned elaborately, and then finished, "Though I must confess that the good William Cooper is a rather overpowering example of the species."

"I can't imagine why anyone suffers your rudeness—unless it's because your politeness is so much worse." Andrew said this dryly, but he was smiling. "If Cooper wearies you, come with us to Kintyre for a few weeks. We're going to spend Christmas there. We could have some shooting."

A look of animation crossed the other's face. "That, my friend, is something I should like very much."

II

For a time Sara sat quite still, studying Louis carefully. He was perched on the rail of Kintyre's wide veranda; he was booted and spurred, and wore a coat that only a London tailor could have fashioned. Occasionally he swished his riding whip at the midsummer mosquitoes that buzzed about his head. He was turned side-faced to Sara, staring down the reach of the river that Kintyre, from its height on the hill, commanded. He was unusually thoughtful, as if he had forgotten that his role rarely permitted him such moments. There was almost a look of moodiness about him, a brooding air, as he gazed at the twilight stretch of water. Over the bush there was that same withdrawn appearance it had worn for Sara from the first time she had seen it. Clouds were gathering, a dusky purple; off in the mountains she heard thunder, and saw a sudden flash of chain-lightning dancing along a gaunt, mile-long escarpment. A low bar of red above a ridge was all that was left of the day. Down on the river some stray sound disturbed the wild duck. They rose with swift grace, silhouetted, for a moment, against the sky, and then were lost out of sight.

Louis turned his head towards her, and she realised that she could no longer distinguish his features clearly.

"In a week or so, Sara," he said, "I intend to go and stay on the Nepean for a while."

Folding the nightshirt she was making for Sebastian, she answered his remark lightly. "And who, pray, is next to have the honour of your company?"

He flicked his hand sharply at what might have been a mosquito. "Sara, you're impossible! You imply that I have not enjoyed my stay at Kintyre. You know, surely . . ."

"I know," she said soothingly, smiling. "I *am* impossible. Put it down to feminine pique. I merely wished to know who was to steal you away from us."

"No one," he said, shaking his head. "At least, no one but the river."

"The river! You can't mean you're going all that way just to look at the river?"

"And why not? I intend to travel along the Nepean as far as settlement has gone."

"Why?" Sara's tone was no longer light; she leaned forward to try to see his face better.

"I thought that if I liked what I saw, I might apply for a grant of land."

Sara gave a faint gasp, and leaned back rather limply in her chair.

Louis swished at the mosquitoes as before, and seemed quite unperturbed. He glanced over his shoulder as the thunder in the mountains grew louder.

"I've talked it over with Andrew," he said. "It seems there could be no objection to my settling."

At this, Sara came to life again. She sat up straight. "No objection, of course—but, Louis, why? What can there be here for you? This is not your country, your background. These are not your people, your customs. Why, hardly anyone even speaks your language."

He laughed softly. "You're right—hardly anyone speaks it. *You* do, but you won't give me the pleasure of it, because you say your accent is bad. Sara, shame on you, you're cruel!"

And then, abruptly, the jesting tone left his voice.

"You're right about the other things as well. But they no longer matter to me. I have no care now who my neighbours are, or what they think of me. England, I have never liked—and I am

237

weary of travelling. So why should I not stay here for a while? If I dislike it more than other places, then I shall leave. I have learned enough to know that it makes very little difference to oneself where one lives—or with whom, providing it is not with enemies.''

Sara was frowning. "But land cannot be taken up for you to play with, Louis," she said sternly. "You must be prepared to farm it—and I think I'm right in assuming that you're no farmer."

He chuckled faintly in the growing darkness "No more or no less a farmer than your friend, Richard Barwell. If he can take land, so can I."

"It's not the same thing!" Sara replied hotly. She knew she betrayed herself in the sharpness of her tone. She knew also that she was rather afraid of Louis de Bourget, for the depth of his cynicism, for his ability to view a situation, and weigh it up for exactly what it was. She hoped desperately that he would let the subject of Richard alone.

"Sara," he said. "you're so feudal in your fashion. Land is your god—you want to see your estates grow, to count your wealth in acres. You would be a small despot if you could."

Suddenly he flung his arms wide. "But look at it here—this great, empty land! There are miles—hundreds of miles—untouched. And yet it shocks you that someone like myself might be given a minute piece to play with. If I choose to farm it, or make a garden of it, who is to care? Or who should say that I oughtn't? What if I give myself the pleasure of building a house high above the river, as you have done here at Kintyre? A white house, Sara—yes, I should like to build a white house, if only for the joy of seeing it among these dull green trees of yours. And if I tire of my toy when it is completed, why should I not sell it, and be as free to go as I am now? True, the life about me would not be one to which I am accustomed, or one I admire much—but where is one to find the customs of France, except in France?''

"I am told," Sara said slyly, "that emigré society has made a miniature Versailles in England. Could you not be happy with them? Or why not in France itself? Many have gone back and accepted the new order of things, or are, perhaps, waiting for a Restoration."

Louis let out an exclamation of contempt. "Those who expect the monarchy to return on the old terms are fools. And the emigrés are a stupid lot of fools bleating together, and taking nostalgic trips to Dover. Besides, I don't like England."

"Then that leaves France," Sara murmured quietly. "If you are so contemptuous of the forlorn hope of a Restoration, why do you not return to make your peace with the new order?"

His body was clearly outlined against the reddened sky as she spoke; she watched his head tilt backwards, and heard his slight, mocking laugh.

"Sara, you have been listening to tales."

"Tales of what?"

"Tales of the dark past of Louis de Bourget." He waved her to silence as she began a half-hearted attempt to protest. "Oh, don't bother with denials—I know quite well what they say. It's said that I was once a penniless kinsman of the Marquis de L . . . Isn't that so? And it's pointed out that I spend my life travelling, and that I appear not to lack money. All of which is true."

He went on talking quietly; the distant rumble of thunder was fairly constant now, his voice low against it.

"And don't they also say that I dare not remain in England for fear an heir to the Marquis should suddenly turn up? And that I'm not well received in emigré circles, and so take care to keep out of reach of their power. Isn't that what they say?"

She answered him levelly enough. "Well, you seem to know it all, Louis."

"Of course I know it all. Only a fool would not know it. But they who speak without knowledge of Paris in those days are also fools. It was a nightmare of chaos and fear. There was no time for second thoughts about anything. Decisions had to be made swiftly, and within the very shadow of death. They were very brave, those people, and rather stupid. Courage was about the only thing their tradition and breeding had given to them. It seems to me an incredibly proud and foolish thing to allow oneself to be taken without first dispatching a few Jacobins. But courage was the only virtue of my noble cousin, the Marquis. He had no resources, no imagination. Where better could he turn than to me—who had lived out all my precarious life learning to be indispensable to the rich, and knowing from bitter experience the ways of the poor? Could any one of the Marquis's brothers, or nephews, have got himself out of Paris and to the coast in those September days? There wasn't one among them who knew the value of a sou, and who would not have betrayed himself in travelling the first half-mile. Those who have scattered gold about all their lives cannot assume frugal habits in a single day. No—the Marquis chose rightly when he asked me, the humblest of them all, to take his daughter. I knew the ways of the peasants—I understood their minds, and how they could be expected to act. It took us twelve days to reach the coast—a further two weeks to find a boat to take us across. As soon as I arrived in England, I heard that the Marquis was dead."

"And the child?" Sara asked quietly.

"Jeanne lived only a year," he said. "Three sons and another daughter of my cousin had also died of consumption."

"And there was no one else?"

"Ah—there!" He shrugged elaborately. "That is a question which has interested many people. Who can be sure that somewhere in France there doesn't still exist a man with a closer claim than mine? Might there not be a surviving relation who lives in ignorance of the wealth the Marquis placed in my hands? But he also placed a delicate daughter in my hands—and I am owed at least a debt of gratitude. Jeanne died in a soft bed of her own, not at the guillotine. The lawyers may fret over the situation, but I was in possession of the jewels my cousin entrusted to me, alone with Jeanne. His houses were destroyed, his estates parcelled out to a thousand eager hands—but the jewels he gave to me."

Sara remained silent, thinking back over his words, seeking a flaw in his story, a point on which she might question him further. But there seemed to be none. She thought that perhaps he spoke the truth. It was evident to her that Louis de Bourget was at ease in the ways of fashionable life—she was well competent to judge that quality after her years in London as a dressmaker's apprentice. If he were a lowborn impostor, and no kinsman at all of the Marquis, then his manners never betrayed him in the slightest. What man without breeding could dare to be rude and bored, as he often was? Who could wear such clothes as he, and never appear to notice them? His thin, olive-tinted face would have been completely in place among the aristocratic ones that faced the Paris mob from the scaffold.

"And my marriage," he continued, his voice low, but still distinct, even against the background of thunder. "That is another subject for idle speculation. I have done no worse in that than many men before me—except that my mistake is more evident. She was so lovely she overrode any feeling of prudence

I had that warned me we were not suited. She was so young I believed she would mould herself to my own wishes but I was utterly mistaken. She had the will and spirit of a woman twice her age. Until she came to London that season she had never known anything but what passed for life in that huge, uncomfortable country house. The only conversation was hunting—in the summer they languished. This was her only world, and I hadn't got the wit or sense to see that she wanted no other. After our daughter was born she went to visit her family. It was then she wrote to tell me that she never meant to return.''

"And you were content to accept that?''

"The truth is, Sara, that I no longer cared enough about her to try to sway that unimaginative soul. Once her lovely face was out of my sight, I found I was not very much affected by her. She was not to be wooed with any gifts but horses, and a woman who cares only for horses can be a tiresome creature to live with. I imagine it's considered an everlasting shame by her family to have had her quarrel with me made so public. But she refused to return to me—not unless I found her a house close by and settled to the hunting routine. The proposition didn't interest me at all. So she lives with her parents still, and we exchange an occasional letter—mostly over money matters.''

"The child—your daughter?'' Sara prompted.

"I know almost nothing of her. Her mother has singularly little talent for letter-writing. I imagine, though, that she will learn to ride a horse long before she can spell with any certainty.''

"It's sad,'' Sara murmured. "So wasted . . .''

"Wasted . . . exactly! Both our lives are wasted. She was cold as a splinter of ice. Her greed and selfishness I could have forgiven her readily—but not her lack of warmth. I could not live with a woman to whom a husband was something merely to be suffered . . .''

Sudden pity for him touched Sara. She had never imagined that she could pity Louis—the assured and cynical; from that moment her feeling towards him was changed. She could sense the frustration and bitterness where before she had only seen his light, charming manners—his amusing conversation—only those and his bored acceptance of whatever came his way. In a few seconds she knew he would revert to them, but at least he had shown her a glimpse of something else beyond them.

Abruptly she rose and came across to him. A flash of lightning played above the trees on the opposite bank of the river. It lit up Kintyre's well-laid acres, and every detail of Louis' appearance, every feature. He was waiting, a detached smile about his lips, for her to speak.

She held out her hand.

"Thank you for telling me this," she said. "My curiosity didn't deserve such rewards."

He took her hand, not holding it upwards as he had always done previously, but gripping it as if she were a man.

"Reward?" he said. "Ah, no, Sara! I *cared* what you and Andrew believed of me. The rest . . ." He shrugged. "Well, let them have their little gossip, if it makes them happy. But if I am to remain in this country, then I must have you both for my friends. You and Andrew—you are the spirit of this place . . ."

He broke off as the thunder crashed about their heads. On a sudden rush of cool wind the rain came down off the mountains. It hit them with a tropical violence and density, slashing against their faces and bodies before they could move back from the rail.

Louis reached quickly to gather up Sara's sewing-bag from the chair, and followed her at a run along the veranda to the door. The noise of the rain was heavy as it hit the sunbaked earth; the lightning lit up the garden brilliantly. They both paused for a few moments to watch it, looking backwards with wonder, as to something they had been lucky to escape. Then Sara turned, trying to smooth down her damp hair with her hand, and stepped into the hall. Louis held the door for her, then followed. As he passed behind her, his eyes held a rare look of softness and pleasure.

III

It had rained all night, the sound drumming and monotonous against Kintyre's roof. But by noon the next day, when Sara took her daily ride along the road in the direction of Parramatta, the rough storm-water ditches by the side of the road were already drying out. The smell of the rain lingered in the scrub, in the eucalypt trees, giving the bush almost the freshness of a spring morning. As she rode along she noticed the curved, prominent heads of a dozen or more kookaburras perched on a high bough of a ragged gum on her left. They remained motionless until she drew level; then their heads went back, beaks opened, and the bush for a mile around was abruptly regaled with their mad, wild laughter. Not in all the years that she had been familiar with the sound had Sarah been able to accept it as natural, nor had she schooled herself not to laugh with them. Her mouth curved delightedly; she threw her head back as they did, and laughed inelegantly, and without restraint. The noise they made followed her down the road, infectious, mocking; as strange and different as the country that had bred it.

The next bend would bring her just over two miles from Kintyre. Peering up at the sun, she judged that it was more than time she returned. But at the bend itself she halted, wrinkling her forehead and staring down the road, where the heat conjured up a mirage like water, and the midday haze was thickening. Two horsemen, no more yet than specks, held her attention. She stared at them, shielding her eyes against the glare; then, in a few moments, she raised her crop to wave excitedly.

Both men answered her wave immediately, and urged their horses into a canter. She drew into the shade of a big blue gum to wait for them.

"Richard! Jeremy!" she called, as they came close enough to hear.

And while she sat her horse with an easy smile on her lips, she was pondering the reason for them being on this journey together. There was no feeling of friendship between Richard and Jeremy; their antagonism towards each other was too obvious for them to willingly ride side by side up from Parramatta. As far as she knew, Jeremy had had no intention of leaving Priest's; he was busy there and had even refused Sara's request that he should come to Kintyre for Christmas. The two men must have met on the road, and a desire for company had prompted Richard to stay by Jeremy's side. It would have been more in keeping with Richard's feelings about the Maclay overseer if he had given a brief nod and ridden on.

In the last few yards Richard moved ahead of Jeremy; he was the first to come to her side. His clothes were covered in fine dust, and there were rivulets of sweat on his face.

He smiled his pleasure at seeing her, leaning over in the saddle and taking her outstretched hand.

"Sara! How are you?"

"I'm well, Richard, thank you." Her answer was smooth, and cool. "And yourself—and Alison?"

"Well enough," he said impatiently, staring into her face with a look of disappointment. Then he swung round, only half-stifling an exclamation of annoyance, as Jeremy's horse jostled his own. "Can't you mind . . . ?"

Richard didn't say any more. He sullenly watched Sara's hand go out to grip Jeremy's.

"We'll be glad to see you at Kintyre, Jeremy," she said. "But what brings you? Something important, surely—I was beginning to think nothing would ever shift you from Priest's, when you wouldn't even come back at Christmas."

"In ordinary circumstances nothing would move me from Priest's yet," Jeremy said. "But this happens to concern the great John Macarthur." He tilted his hat back a little, and went on. "It seems that Andrew did him some service a short while ago—and now he's pleased to inform me that he's changed his mind about selling some of the ewes and a ram from the merino flock. That is, he says, if Mr. Maclay still has a mind to have them. I can't help thinking that Macarthur may want yet another favour from Andrew—his merino flock are almost as precious to him as his own children."

Sara's eyes opened wide. "The merino flock! Andrew will be delighted! Macarthur's sheep are beginning to produce wool that he believes will better the Spanish merino. We've been hoping to get a few more . . ."

Richard broke in. "*Must* you talk wool and sheep the very moment one sees you, Sara?" His tone was light as he said it; obviously he repented the impatience he had let her see. But his horse moved sideways, and he made little attempt to hold it. The movement, and his words, effectively ended the conversation between the other two, and turned their attention back to him.

Sara laughed, though she could feel a flush of annoyance mounting in her cheeks. "Why, Richard! I imagined such a farmer as you would be more than interested in the prospects for wool!"

His lips folded slightly, and he shrugged. "Oh, I leave the experiments in wool to the Macarthurs and the Maclays—to the really important people of the colony. Hyde Farm occupies quite enough of my time in its own humble fashion. I'll be content to follow in ten years' time where the pioneers of today lead."

He intercepted the glance that passed between Sara and Jeremy, and it seemed to infuriate him.

"Well, are we going to loiter about here in the sun all afternoon? Let's get on, shall we?"

Without waiting for them, he wheeled his horse, and started at a trot down the road.

They followed, and as they drew level, he addressed Sara again.

"I hear that you have the Frenchman staying at Kintyre?"

"Yes, he spent Christmas with us."

He nodded vaguely. "He's trying out the colony, I suppose. What do you think of him?"

"Andrew and I both like him. So will you, I'm sure, when you know him better." Sara glanced sideways at him. "He never discusses wool and sheep."

"Obviously not," Richard said shortly. "He has enough money to hold himself aloof from matters of mere commerce. But I wonder was he so disinterested in making a little money at any time prior to the Revolution? From what I hear, he suffered an embarrassing lack of the commodity until then."

"People, no doubt tell a great many tales of Louis de Bourget," Sara returned coldly. "The pity is that they don't tell the full story. What is left out in his history is quite as important as the few facts already brought forward. If one has the inclination to learn it—that is, if prejudice hasn't blinded one—there's a great deal more to Louis than the smooth fit of his coat."

They rounded a bend and were now within sight of the fork leading to Hyde Farm. Looking at Richard, Sara saw his face twist, and then his hands, usually so confident and relaxed on the reins, grew taut. Richard was contemptuous of nervous hands on a horse, but he seemed quite unaware of his own at the moment.

"I don't find this Frenchman's story plausible at all," he said, looking straight ahead. "What brings him to a place like this—without introductions, and without any stated purpose? He left a wife and child behind him, too, I believe. It's suspicious—I tell you, no honest man behaves in that way. And if he has all the wealth rumour gives him, why didn't he remain in London where he could enjoy it?"

"It's just possible that he may not regard London as the paradise you found it to be, Richard." She spoke savagely, and then was furious with herself for letting him see her disturbance.

"I imagine you'll be at Hyde Farm for a few days?" she continued quickly. "Doubtless you'll come to Kintyre to see Andrew. I advise you to talk to Louis then and judge him for yourself. You'll be in danger of becoming as narrow-minded as the rest of us colonials, Richard, if you continue to place such a trust in gossip.''

He swerved in his saddle so suddenly that Sara's horse halted without warning, nearly unseating her.

"If your husband wishes to see me on business matters,'' Richard said, "I'll be found at Hyde Farm for the next two days. But I'll be damned if I'll come to Kintyre to quarrel with you over that bloody upstart. You and Andrew make me sick with your grovelling to a turncoat Frenchman, who was more than likely a Jacobin before his money forced him to be a royalist. You can find your friends in any doubtful place you choose, Sara—but don't expect them to be my friends as well!''

"You've said enough, Barwell!'' Jeremy's voice was thick with anger. He leant across and caught the other man's bridle.

Richard turned on him furiously, unbelievingly.

"What the devil do you mean?''

"I mean that Mrs. Maclay expects an apology!''

"Jeremy . . . !'' In alarm Sara cried out. "You . . .''

"An apology is just what Mrs. Maclay is not going to get!'' Richard snapped. "I meant every word I said—and, by God, I'll thank you to keep your nose out of my affairs! I'd like to know what right any damned convict has to dictate to me! Take care that I don't have you before a magistrate for this piece of work.''

Jeremy's eyes were glazed with anger. "Threaten me with what you like, Captain Barwell. But when you insult Mrs. Maclay, you insult her husband—and you'll find neither he, nor myself, afraid of you, or a magistrate's court, or anything else you care to threaten.''

"Why you . . .''

With a muffled oath, Richard raised his crop high, and brought it down with his full weight on Jeremy's hand, which still held his bridle. The other winced, and his horse pulled away, almost dragging him from the saddle. But he clung, managing to bring the animal under control again. Richard struck his hand once again, and when the fingers didn't slacken, he swung his crop sideways, slashing it across Jeremy's face. At the same time he dug his heels in hard, and his horse sprang forward. Jeremy was forced to let the bridle go.

Richard galloped away, making for the fork that led to Hyde Farm.

"Curse him!'' Jeremy muttered, enraged. "I'll beat that . . .''

His face was white with fury, and blood was already trickling from the corner of his mouth. His hat had been knocked to the back of his head, giving him a wild, half-crazy appearance that terrified Sara. She saw him dig in his spurs to go after Richard, and at the same moment she hit her own horse smartly. It shot forward in a sudden lurch directly in Jeremy's path. They cannoned together, both almost unseating. Sara managed to pull up before she reached the ditch; Jeremy's horse reared, and he had to fight with it for control. By the time it was quietened, Richard was far down the road.

"For God's sake, Jeremy, don't be such a fool!"

In her anxiety, Sara snapped at him. The fear of the moment had shaken her violently; she was angry now to think of what passion the two men had unleashed in the matter of a few seconds, and over a Frenchman neither of them knew. She was panting, and her fear made her sharp and scathing.

"Don't you know that if you touched him you'd be flogged and sent to a chain gang? In heaven's name, why do you lose your head like that? You're not a child—and you've had more than enough practice in schooling your temper!"

Jeremy brought his horse beside hers. He said tersely, "There's some things that no amount of schooling will rid one of, Sara—and nothing will ever let one forgive. If I were free, I'd call him out and kill him for that."

"But you're not free!" she reminded him tartly. "And you're not in a position to make a fool of yourself by challenging him."

"But all the same . . ."

"A nice figure you'd make, Jeremy Hogan," she cut in, "swinging from the gallows. Now, let's have no more of this mad talk. There's been enough heroics for one morning to defend the Maclay honour. We'll get back to Kintyre, and do something to your face before Andrew sees it."

Very slowly he ran the reins through his hands. "You're a woman without a heart, Sara," he said. "I doubt that you've a natural feeling in your whole body. What a general England has missed because you're not a man! Rashness would never have outplayed strategy in your cool head. Even Nelson has his human side in Emma Hamilton, but there would have been no such indulgence for you. I wish that you could see yourself just once . . ."

Jeremy's words trailed off; he stopped and looked at her in amazement.

"Why, Sara . . . You're crying!"

She dashed a hand furiously across her eyes. "Yes—and I can't help it! I'm crying because..." Her voice rose in an aggrieved tone. "Because Richard made such a fool of himself—and because you frightened me to death by putting yourself in danger over him. Oh, Jeremy, can't you see—he just isn't worth it! Men are supposed to be able to keep their wits about them pretty well, but no sensible woman would dream of behaving as you've just done!"

She began searching in one of the pockets of her habit for a handkerchief. Taking it out, she dabbed her eyes, and then said sharply, "Well... don't just sit there like that! We'd better go down to the river and do something about washing that cut. It's bleeding worse now. It would be a nice thing, wouldn't it, if someone rode along and found me snivelling like a five-year-old brat, and Master Jeremy with the blood running down into his collar! A pretty pair we make, I've no doubt!"

A ghost of a smile played on his lips, as he followed her off the road and into the scrub. A Sara who was frightened and shaken was a rare spectacle; he looked at her gently heaving shoulders ahead of him, and was not displeased that he himself was half the cause of her upset—even if he had to share it with that arrogant upstart, Barwell. His hot anger against Barwell was fading—shocked almost out of existence by Sara's tearful reaction to it. He wished he could again see her face, with the tears sliding down it, and the look, half of tenderness, half contempt for her own weakness, that it had worn.

She was following a vaguely defined path down to the river, refusing to allow him to go ahead to pick the way through the undergrowth, clinging to the lead, as if she felt the need to assert her own authority. The sound of the river reached them clearly; the banks here were low, but the trees screened it completely, until almost the very moment when they broke through, and it lay, broad and deep, with the sun on it casting a dazzle that, for a minute, hurt their eyes. On the opposite bank the land had been partly cleared, and a small herd of cattle grazed quietly. Beyond, on a slight rise, was a whitewashed house that Jeremy recognised as belonging to Michael Macarthy, who had come out with Governor Phillip as a marine, and had stayed to take up land. The scene before them was peaceful, and all signs of the rain of the night were gone.

Jeremy dismounted and tethered both horses to the low bush. Then he lifted Sara down.

"Give me your handkerchief," she said stiffly. "Mine's useless."

He offered it, and she took it without a word, scrambling down the sandy incline of the river bank with it rolled up in her hand. He watched her bend and wring it out in the water, and then come back to him.

"Let me look at that cut." Her voice was gentler now; it was a little hoarse and rasping in her throat, as if, perhaps, she still held back tears. She dabbed at the congealing blood at the corner of his mouth, making clicking sounds with her tongue, and shaking her head.

"You won't mention this to Andrew, will you, Jeremy?"

She stood on tiptoe as she pressed the handkerchief against his mouth, murmuring absently, as to a child.

He drew back abruptly. "Mention it to Andrew? You take me for a greater fool than ever! I . . ."

She followed his withdrawal, and began to dab again with the handkerchief. "Oh, hush, Jeremy!" she said. "You know I didn't mean that. I was merely trying to reassure myself. Richard behaved like a madman—and the sooner forgotten, the better."

He caught at her wrist and held it, forcing her to halt her attention to the cut, and look at him directly.

"Richard Barwell *is* mad where you're concerned, Sara. He's mad with love and rage and frustration. He's jealous of Andrew—not only because of Andrew's possession of you, but of his position in the colony, and what he can do. Barwell may have been all that London desired in the way of an amusing drawing-room attraction, a horseman, and a swordsman. But *here*, beside Andrew, he doesn't cut such a fine figure. Envy can drive a man to many things—to drink, for one thing. And to spending far more money than he can afford."

Suddenly his grip tightened almost brutally on her wrist.

"For how much longer is Andrew going to give this fool money to throw away? Surely, after six months, he can see that Hyde Farm isn't going to pay—at least not while it's run by Richard Barwell."

She broke her wrist free of his hold. "Andrew will go on lending Richard money just as long as Richard continues to be useful to him—which, it seems to me, will be as long as he remains in the colony." She was speaking harshly again, and the bright colour had come into her cheeks. "Of the two, Andrew is by far the cleverer. He'll profit from Richard and his wife, even if he never gets back a penny piece of the money."

"Profit? What sort of profit?"

"You're not blind, Jeremy!" she said tartly. "You can see all of this—you know it without me telling you. You don't have to ask why Andrew throws his money down a bottomless well. He does it because of *me*—and don't pretend you don't know, because I wouldn't believe you."

"All right, I won't pretend—I *do* know it. But I didn't think even Andrew would continue..."

She cut him short, impatiently. "Andrew is more ambitious, more tenacious—more ruthless, in a way—than any other man I've ever known. He'll have what he wants, and the cost be damned! In this case, all he asks is Alison Barwell's friendship for me—and he pays for it."

Her face twitched as she spoke, and then it softened. She looked at him fixedly, and raised her hand to the cut on his mouth. But this time she didn't touch it with the handkerchief. Gently, with the tip of her finger, she traced the thin line running out towards his jaw.

"I will never forgive him for this," she said. "He is more dangerous than I thought. He loses control of himself, and then he's like a child in a rage—a weak, vicious, brutish child. In these last months he's dangled me on a string—but I swear to you now, Jeremy, that he'll dangle me no longer. For the future, I'll use him as Andrew has done. I'll use him for what he's worth to me, and beyond that I don't care a rap what becomes of him."

She shrugged her shoulders faintly. "So don't mock my cold heart again, Jeremy. Be glad of it, because it will need to be wrapped in ice to resist the memory of what Richard once meant to me."

She turned aside and said no more. She put her foot in the stirrup, and then Jeremy lifted her into the saddle. He held the bridle while she settled herself, and held it long, because some new expression in her eyes seemed to root him there helplessly.

"Come nearer, Jeremy," she said.

He stepped in closer to the horse, without thinking what she meant to do. Clinging to the pommel, she leaned down suddenly, and kissed him on the cheek.

As if she had struck him, he sprang back.

"Damn you! Don't do that!"

She flushed scarlet at his tone. "I didn't think you'd object quite so strongly," she said stiffly.

His eyes were dark and angry, staring up at her. "You know

250

right well that I don't want kisses like that, not from you, Sara. Don't think you can settle debts by giving me a sisterly peck on the cheek. I'll have from you the sort of kisses I want—or none at all!''

Then he went and untied his horse, mounting without a word.

This time it was Jeremy who led the way back to the road; Sara followed closely behind.

There was silence between them for more than a mile. The heat increased; the road was shadeless, and the sun beat down on their backs. The flies followed them, buzzing about their faces, and settling on their horses' flanks. They met no one; they did not speak to each other, nor did they even turn their heads as they passed the fork leading to Hyde Farm. For all the signs either betrayed, the incident with Richard might never have taken place. The hot, noon hush of the bush was complete.

Then they finally came to the last bend in the road, the spot from which Sara had had her first sight of Kintyre. The same memory returned to them both, like a sudden renewal of that distant day—the day they had discovered their jealousy over Andrew, the day they had found each other's strength, and had been determined to master it. Without a word they checked their horses.

Each could remember, with no trace of sentimental wistfulness, what Kintyre had been then. They remembered the scarred hill, where the trees had been torn out to make way for the house in its crude whiteness, its bare, blank face turned to the river and the mountains. In both their eyes, the vines were, for the moment, stripped from the walls, and the orchard was a few, slender young trees. It was again raw and new, like every other mark the white man had set upon this unused land.

The situation of the house upon the hill was still a challenge, a landmark thrown up boldly to meet the gaze of everyone who used the road. But both Sara and Jeremy admitted to themselves that they couldn't for long hold their first vision of it. It was gently mellowed now, and the years had brought the trees back on to the hill, and soft, English grass grew in the spaces in the orchard. It was the old Kintyre still, but changed. It no longer represented Andrew's struggle to hold his own against the bush and the natives, even against the climate, and the threat of the floods. This was permanent, secure—the most loved of all his possessions, because it had been the hardest to win.

Sara took her eyes away from the house and looked at Jeremy. It did not occur to her to inquire his thoughts. She was certain that they were on Kintyre, on the part he himself had played in making it.

"It isn't any use thinking we can quarrel in this way, Jeremy," she said at last. "We all of us—you, Andrew, and myself—need one another too badly."

He nodded, accepting her statement as natural—in the same way he accepted the frustration of having loved both of them though the years that had gone into the creation of Kintyre, and every other part of Andrew's scattered possessions.

"Yes," was all he answered, but his meaning was well enough understood by them both.

With a slight nudge of his heels he urged his horse forward. He and Sara started up the hill together.

PART FOUR

Chapter One

During the next two years Louis de Bourget startled the colony by doing what he had said he intended to do—he travelled on foot as far as exploration of the Nepean River had gone, selecting his land with more care for the site on which the house would stand than for the quality of the soil, and then announced his decision to settle permanently and farm in New South Wales. Comment, as he had expected, was at first sceptical, then mildly annoyed when it became clear that he would spare no expense to run his farm successfully. Where good livestock was to be bought, he was able to bid a higher price than anyone else; two of the best and most experienced overseers were enticed away from their employers to come to him.

But it was the plans for the house itself that roused most interest. He had travelled in America, and was taken by the mansions the cotton-planters of the Southern states were building for themselves; he decided that his own new house should follow them in pattern. But he had a French love of an ordered garden, and so the gentle slope on which the house stood was to be cut and terraced. There were many raised eyebrows when the news of this went around. So far, no one else in the colony had either labour or money to spare on such a thing. Andrew Maclay had had a like scheme for Glenbarr, but the job was never wholly completed because materials were short and too expensive.

Louis paid little heed to the raised eyebrows; he went on with no more than a shrug to indicate that he had heard what gossip had to say of him. Every ship arriving in Sydney Cove carried goods bought for him by his agent in England—books, marble fireplaces, silk to curtain the long windows, Louis Quinze chairs—the stream of his possessions that travelled the road to the Nepean seemed endless. He tried planting foreign trees, and saw most of them die; he built an aviary and filled it with exotic native birds, and birds from the Indian jungles and the East Indies. He even toyed, for a short time, with the idea of an ornamental lake—but he realised that seasonal drought would defeat him; also his sense of fitness told him that the great river running at his doorstep, and the unsymmetrical blue mountains behind it, were too strong and individual to mate happily with a stretch of smooth water. So he dropped the idea—not without a lingering regret for the future consternation such a plan would have caused among his neighbours.

The house was finished in the spring of 1803. At the time it was completed there were very few people who had yet seen it; the Nepean farms were remote, and the state of the roads didn't invite travel. So the house remained something of a legend while it was being built. By this time, Louis had many friends among the leading families, and each of them knew that, in due course, they would visit at his invitation. But it was Andrew Maclay, with his wife and family, whose carriage was the first to begin the ascent from the road by the river to Louis' front steps.

II

From the bottom of the hill Sara, at the carriage window, had leaned forward to see the house. It stood boldly on the rise, its white walls glistening in the sunlight. The sight of it took her breath for an instant. This was not the cotton-planter's house Louis had talked of; this had the look of what Andrew had once rashly promised to build for her at Kintyre. It was fronted by a portico of ten white columns, severe and unornamented; the building itself was wide and low, and the crest of the hill behind it was visible, crowned with a ridge of eucalypts. At one end of the portico, a short flight of steps led down to the level of the drive. Beyond the drive was the first of three unfinished terraces, cut into the hillside.

Sara was silent, not even listening to Andrew's comments, or to what the children's excited chattering was all about. As the carriage came to a halt, Louis ran down the steps and flung the door open. He welcomed them to his home, and then, smiling, he handed her out. He turned to lift Sebastian, still too young to negotiate the high step.

In the midst of the bustle, with two servants strenuously carrying out Louis' orders about unstrapping the boxes, the high babble of the children, and remarks passing between Andrew and his host, Sara found nothing to say. Taking Sebastian's hand, she mounted the stone steps very slowly. When at last she reached the level of the broad portico, she stood still. The Nepean plains, the river and the mountains, wrapped in their blue haze, were spread before her in one huge sweep. In front of the house, and at its sides, the timber had been cleared, so that the view was uninterrupted. Down on the fringe of the river, stretching away from the opposite bank, the gums had turned the reddish tinge of spring, and through the valley, an occasional wild, flowering tree, scarlet, yellow, white, thrust itself into prominence. Sara held Sebastian's hand tightly, feeling that, until this moment, she had not known the true beauty of this harsh, familiar landscape.

Louis mounted the steps behind her. She did not turn, but she sensed him standing there behind her, his gaze following hers. For a few moments longer she looked at the scene, while the boxes were being carried past her, and Andrew talked quietly with Edwards, below.

At last she said, in a low voice, "This is genius, Louis! You have done what no one else would dare to do."

He came to her side then. "Why shouldn't one do what this place pleads for? Here is sun, and space, and a view! Why build a house with narrow windows and shut it all out? The skies are not soft enough, nor the hills gentle enough to allow me to build something like the sort of house that belongs in an ordered park. The country here is a challenge—I have done my best to meet it."

"You have succeeded—admirably," she said gently.

As she spoke she was thinking how strange to have to acknowledge that it needed a Frenchman, a stranger among an English colony, to show them how to blend a house to this uncompromising background. It lay back against the hill, rested against it almost, and the ten white columns, of classic simplicity, its only adornment. It faced its outlook superbly, its lines solid and dignified.

"I have called it Banon," Louis said.

She looked at him. "Banon?"

He nodded. "Banon is the name of a town in the south of

France. I went there once on business for the Marquis. I stayed in an inn outside the town, in the season when the mimosa bloomed. All the time I have been building this house, I have been able to call it by no other name.''

Sara smiled, her eyes bright. ''Your house is the loveliest I have ever seen.''

He bowed slightly. ''If you approve it, then I am more than rewarded.''

His words were formal enough, and yet she realised his very deep satisfaction. His thin, sunburnt face was darker now than ever, but some of the strain was gone from it. He was smiling a little, his eyes crinkled against the sun. She glanced down swiftly, and saw that he no longer wore the massive rings, and by the state of his hands she judged that, perhaps, he himself had taken a spade when the terraces were being dug away. She was surprised; the suave Frenchman who had arrived in the colony three years ago could hardly be imagined with a spade in his hand.

His gaze returned to her, and he said quickly, ''Forgive me, Sara! I keep you standing here in the sun, when you must be fatigued from your journey.''

He reached down and took Sebastian's other hand, leading them both towards the door, where a woman in the plain dress of a housekeeper stood waiting for them.

III

A cold wind sprang up that evening, blowing towards Banon from the mountains; but in Louis' white drawing-room they could only hear its sounds in the trees at the top of the ridge. The leaping flames in the fireplace stained the marble mantel to a pale rose, and threw irregular lights across the deep red curtains. A single pair of candles burned on a table at the other end of the room; they were reflected in a high, silver-framed mirror. Sara, Andrew, and Louis sat in low chairs, turned towards the fire; their faces, flushed in its glow, were sometimes bright, then momentarily darkened by shadow, as the changing light played upon them. Occasionally Louis stirred to pile on a fresh log, and when the flames caught it, and burned high, Sara's hair and her silk gown took on a reddish tinge.

For a time now Sara had ceased to have any part in the conversation. She sat with her hands lying idle in her lap, her eyelids fluttering as she fought her drowsiness; the wind outside, and the crackle of the flames, were muted, matching the indefinite undertones of Andrew and Louis. She looked towards their host. This evening he had shed the sober clothes he wore on their arrival; now he was arrayed as splendidly as ever Sydney had seen him, in stiff brocade waistcoat, and the finest lace. The rings were back on his fingers, the jewels winking in the firelight as he twisted the stem of his madeira glass. He rested in his chair lazily, his feet, in silver-buckled shoes, were propped on a softly padded stool. Now and then, in his talk, he turned with a gesture towards Andrew—but mostly he gazed thoughtfully into the fire.

It was almost three years, Sara remembered, still looking at him, since he had perched on the veranda-rail at Kintyre and told her of what this house should be. That three years had been favourable to the colony, and kind to Louis. It was still governed by King, with whom Louis stood in particular regard, though it was generally felt that King's day would soon be over. A great deal of the time he was ill with gout, and, while he ruled well enough, his rule was not enforced severely enough to satisfy the needs of the Colonial Office. The power of the military was still unsubdued, and no amount of orders from Government House could wrest their privileges from them.

But King, even if ill, was not idle. He had a passion to regularise the affairs of the colony—to bring it into line as a typical English community. The idea of the girls' orphanage had matured, and the large house now confined its herd of unwilling young women. The *Sydney Gazette*—the colony's first newspaper—made its appearance under government sponsorship; exploration, with King's encouragement, continued steadily. The mountain barrier had still not been crossed, and the riddle of what lay on the other side was as yet an open question. But the secrets of the continent itself had slowly and painfully yielded to young Matthew Flinders's patient seeking. Under orders from the Admiralty, Flinders had commanded the sloop, *Investigator,* on a voyage to chart the coasts. He worked his way with infinite care from west to east, then south to north, from Cape Leeuwin to the Wessel Islands, proving, beyond doubt that New Holland and New South Wales were the one vast island. He had plotted and charted the vague shape which the old Dutch maps called simply *"Terra Australis,"* and was now on his way back to England with his beautifully-drawn charts, his painstaking logs. He went, cherishing the hope that the omnipotent Admiralty and the Royal

Society might adopt his suggestion that the island, in future, should be known by the name he had always given it in secret—Australia.

Governor King at last knew the extent of the domain over which he ruled; but the vastness of the hinterland troubled him not at all in comparison with the settled areas close at hand. The farmers were steadily pushing outwards; hemmed in by the mountains, they began moving south—farther, in fact, than King wished. It would now have needed an army of Government officials to keep land and farmers continually under inspection—and an army was precisely what King could not command.

The New South Wales Corps—locally known as the Rum Corps—was as great and as constant a source of trouble to him as his own gout. Officers and men, they incessantly harassed, disobeyed, derided, and ridiculed him, until he was almost ready to die from sheer weariness and disappointment. The Colonial Office was no help—it had little time, and even less money, to spare for his demands. Macarthur, whom he had sent back to England for court-martial for his duel with the Lieutenant-Governor, Colonel Patterson, had somehow managed to win the ear of authority. The samples of merino wool which he had produced from his own flocks had forced even the Colonial Office to take notice. Macarthur had promised that their problem-colony, forever begging money and supplies, would soon have an export that would fill the looms of the Yorkshire wool-spinners. His schemes had met with strong support and approval, and he was returning to Sydney, not in disgrace, but triumphant, with a large grant of the most coveted land in the whole of New South Wales—the Cowpastures district, where the herds of wild cattle, the property of the Government, ran. King raged when he heard the news; the troublemaker was returning with power increased tenfold.

The brief Peace of Amiens was over; England was now alone in facing the genius and organising might of Napoleon. The British people were committed to a long struggle, and, on receiving the news, already months old, King acknowledged sadly that the heads of Government in London would now have less patience than ever for their remote and unproductive colony.

But there was a threat of violence much nearer to hand than the future battlefields of Europe. Since Governor Hunter's time the Irish convicts had made their presence and their grievances felt in no uncertain way. There were continual rumours of a rising, and counter-rumours. A year after King's arrival a definite plot had been discovered; the colony panicked at the news that rough but effective pikes had been discovered in the hands of rebel convicts. King sent the ringleaders to Norfolk Island—and he was criticised for not having hanged them. The passionate outcry of the rebels died down to a murderous undertone.

Sara felt some pity for the worried, anxious Governor, whom she had learned to like—to even, in a sense, respect. For herself, and for Andrew, the years of Philip Gidley King's reign had been good ones. After she had been received at Government House, Andrew had, for the sake of the Governor's regard, withdrawn a good deal from the rum trade. But his prosperity no longer needed the bolster of the liquor sales, except in a nominal way. He withdrew, also, because his foresightedness saw the end of the trade. The Colonial Office would some day provide a Governor with the means to smash it, and all might not go well with the credit of those who engaged in it right up to the end.

And for Louis, too, Sara thought, the years had been good ones. King was generous in his land-grant; and generous in his friendship. Perhaps it was something of a relief to that harassed man to know that in Louis de Bourget he had found one prosperous farmer, whose money, he knew, for certain, did not come from illegal rum sales. Louis had never engaged in trade activity; that fact alone made him something of a rarity in that ring of business men. But, Sara mused, Louis had found the best of two worlds. He enjoyed an immunity from the rivalries of trade, and yet, from it, he made a direct profit. He and Andrew had joined forces to buy two more sloops for trade between the ports of the East. The sloops, *Thrush* and *Hawk*, had appeared only twice in Port Jackson during the two years of their trading, but, in that time, credits were beginning to mount up with Louis' agent in London, and Andrew had every reason to be well satisfied with his side of the deal. Latterly there had been talk of their buying yet another vessel for whaling expeditions to the Antarctic. It was Andrew who controlled these ventures, not by the power of money, but by his own initiative and driving-force. Louis was content to have it so—he rarely withheld his agreement when approached by Andrew in matters of policy; he could mostly be relied upon to shrug and profess no aptitude for business. The arrangement suited Andrew exactly; any partner-

259

ship in which he played a minor role would have been a brief and uneasy one.

But no such harmony existed in the business relations between Andrew and Richard. Richard had determined, from the very beginning, that he would be absolute master of Hyde Farm, and no suggestions or advice from Andrew, no matter how tactfully given, were received kindly. He was still very much in debt, and, though the farm was beginning to improve and pay its own way, the debt to Andrew increased year by year. The improvement continued, almost in spite of Richard's ignorance of farming— his duties in the Corps kept him in Sydney most of the time, and his overseer had a knack of rectifying his employer's mistakes without seeming to disobey his orders. But the mild prosperity of Hyde Farm only urged Richard and Alison on to fresh extravagances. Their house in Sydney was the hub of whatever gaiety was to be found there. Alison dressed and entertained far beyond her own small income and the salary of an army captain, and when money ran short with them, Richard applied once more to Andrew. But, in spite of the front she showed to the world, each time Sara saw Alison, she fancied that the delicately-shaped face had become a trifle paler, a shade more finely drawn. During the short winters Alison seemed never to be free from a disturbing cough, and the fierce heat of the summers sapped still more of her little strength. However, Sara reflected, for all that, Alison Barwell's vivacious charm never deserted her. If she were ill, her couch was always the place to hear the best stories and the tastiest gossip circulating within the town. Her wit was clever and sharp, and her house was the gathering-place for the unmarried officers of the Corps.

Of Richard himself, Sara knew very little these days. He attended to his duties with as much care as any other man of his rank, and when time allowed, he made the long trip up to his Hawkesbury farm. But there were tales always circulating of his incessant drinking, and he seemed to lack the will to stand out against Alison's expenditure. It surprised Sara that he could continue to ask Andrew for money; and that Andrew had not, long ago, wearied of watching good money go after bad. But it seemed that Andrew's contempt for the Barwells' extravagance was not greater than his desire to see his wife graciously received in their house. Formal calls were frequently exchanged between the two women. So long as Sydney continued to see and note these exchanges, Andrew turned a blind eye to Richard's growing debt.

It grieved Sara to realise how little knowledge she possessed of Richard's feelings and thoughts towards herself. Since the day they had quarrelled on the Hawkesbury Road she had never spoken to him alone. When his temper had cooled, he had taken her invitation, and called at Kintyre; he found her indisposed. At Glenbarr it was the same; unless Andrew was there when Richard called, Sara sent Annie to him with her excuses. Finally, he stopped coming alone; only on business with Andrew, or accompanied by Alison, did he ever put in an appearance.

Nothing—not loyalty to her husband, nor disgust over Richard's treatment of Jeremy—had ever quite stifled the feeling of dismay in her heart over his absence. She was forced to admit to herself that she missed him acutely, longing to write him the letter that would bring him back; pride, and a strong sense of prudence, always restrained her. He was constantly in her thoughts; she worried over him, wishing that Lady Linton's death might take them both back to London—and yet, with the arrival of each ship, she dreaded to hear the news. She had no peace or tranquillity from her decision not to see him alone again; he could still possess her like a guilty dream, reproach her with one quick glance in the midst of company, and drive her almost frantic by talking mildly of plans he had no intention of carrying out, knowing quite well that the tales would be taken back to her. In such small ways as these, Richard had his revenge on her.

It seemed that since the days that they had shared the school-room at Bramfield, Richard had possessed an unfair power over her—and he would never let it go. The thought oppressed her, and she turned from it wearily. Outside, the wind had risen, flinging itself against the walls of the house. She listened, and felt that the sound which, until now, had been remote and shut out, was suddenly mournful and close at hand. Despite the heat of the fire, she drew her shoulders together as if she were cold.

Always alert, Louis noticed her movement. He leaned forward in his chair.

"Sara, my dear! I have kept you overlong. It is selfish of me! You would like to go to your room now?"

She smiled faintly, and nodded, rising at the same time. Andrew also rose, and both men came to the door with her.

At a word from Louis to a manservant in the hall, the woman who had waited for them on the portico that morning reappeared, holding a candle to light Sara to her room. She was a Frenchwoman, Madame Balvet, about thirty-five and handsome, in a thin, rather sharp fashion. She had arrived from England three months previously, and acting under Louis' instructions, had come to Banon as housekeeper. She spoke very good English, and gossip knew no more of her than that she had been in service to a great French family before the Revolution. Sara eyed her with curiosity. Who was this woman whom Louis had brought over from France? Someone trusted? . . . Someone loved? A mistress, perhaps, before his marriage? Sara watched her warily as she strode along the passage; she seemed to have a look of pride and possessiveness in the house, but Sara was prepared to acknowledge that in this she might be mistaken.

The woman opened the door, standing aside silently for Sara to enter. Sara's eyes followed her as she carefully lit several candles in brackets and on tables. In their flare she examined in detail what she had noticed only superficially earlier. The room she was to occupy was furnished with a taste and sensitivity that betrayed—or was meant to reveal—Louis' intimate knowledge of women.

Sara woke when the first streak of light was grey at the window. It was a period of utter stillness—the wind had dropped, and it was too early even for the birds. Within the house there was no sound at all. It would be an hour yet before the dairy-hands stirred—longer before the faint bustle of the kitchen began.

Beside her, Andrew breathed quietly in his sleep. The gentle movement close to her own body was comforting and peaceful. In the darkness her hand went out slowly and touched his arm; she held it there for a few moments, then drew back. The rhythm of his breathing had not altered.

As she lay there in the stillness, she was suddenly reminded of her conversation with Louis on the veranda at Kintyre almost three years ago—the only time he had ever talked to her of his wife. With a feeling of dismay she recalled the words . . . "She was as cold as a splinter of ice." The words contained the crux of the reason why his marriage had failed. Probably, in his whole life, Louis had never woken, as she did now, to experience this feeling of tenderness and familiarity, the sense of protectiveness, and of being protected. Louis did not know the security of love in his marriage. The woman who should have lain beside him at this moment slept alone in her father's house, and his own daughter was a stranger to him.

Because of this, Banon must remain without its mistress. It was white and beautiful—and sadly empty. The woman who ruled it was not Louis' wife. With a sense of pity, Sara remembered Madame Balvet's thin, passionate face, her eyes that were not greedy or malicious, but watched over the running of the house with a look of brooding possessiveness.

IV

Louis' terraced garden was still unfinished, but a certain order had been brought into it, and even in its rough state it had a free sort of beauty, which Sara hoped it might retain even when smooth, English lawn replaced the tough grass, growing about in spiky clumps. A seat had been placed for her on the highest of the levels, and she took her needlework there on the fifth day after their arrival at Banon. Andrew and the three boys had come out with her, stayed by her some time to talk, and then wandered farther down the slope. Now and again she caught a glimpse of them as they broke from the cover of trees or shrubs, and their voices reached her, the children's high and shrill, Andrew's deeper. She smiled down at them, waiting to see them turn and make for the aviary; so far, they had ended each morning by a visit to the aviary, Andrew no less fascinated than his sons.

But Andrew, she knew, would not remain much longer at Banon. Louis pressed them to stay on—a month, six weeks. But idleness sat uneasily upon Andrew. He enjoyed Banon, he enjoyed Louis' company, and the card games that kept them from their beds until the small hours of the morning; but Sara observed signs of restlessness in him already. Louis' leisured world of elegance and peace was not his; he missed the bustle of the store, the constant journeyings between Sydney and Parramatta, the bargaining for livestock and corn, the gossip that was part of every business transaction. He had been away from it only a few days, and yet at dinner last night he talked rather wistfully of the possibility of mail arriving from his agents in London, and of the fact that there might be a cargo for sale, and he, at Banon, would be out of the bidding. Louis said nothing in reply to this, but he knew as well as Sara that the wilderness of the Nepean would not hold Andrew much longer.

There was a sense of remoteness here that the Hawkesbury,

even in the early days, did not possess. Here the soil would grow wheat finer and heavier than anywhere else in the colony, but the land was infinitely difficult to clear. Wherever the settlers had pushed forward to farm their claims by the river-banks, they had done so in loneliness, and with a steadfast will to ignore the silence and the immense tracts of bush about them. Here the natives still roamed in a half-wild state, scarcely touched by the white man's approach; the roads were not more than rough tracks, and civilisation had hardly begun its fight against the bush.

Sara had no pretence of interest in her needlework as she sat with the gentle spring sunshine full on her face. The paradox of Banon fascinated her—the creation of this, the loveliest and most unusual house in the whole of the colony, merely as a landmark in the wilderness. It faced the unknown, promising mountains like a grand, rather foolhardy gesture to the future of the country. Filled with wonder at the achievement, she turned back to gaze unbelievingly at the house: the long windows caught the sun with a dazzle strong enough to hurt her eyes.

It was the sound of a horseman on the drive that attracted her attention. Craning forward, she could see that it was one of Louis' overseers who had been sent to Sydney three days previously with orders for supplies. The sound of the hoofbeats carried to her on the air: but they were not clear, the birds were noisy, and the air was full of the sound of insects. A heat-haze was already rising above the mountains; by noon it would be too hot to sit out any longer. She watched the horseman idly; he took the path that led to the stables, and was lost from sight. Then her gaze returned to the mountains, and the river plains below.

She picked up her needlework again, and worked at it until, about half an hour later, she heard Louis' voice on the portico above her. He was walking slowly down its length in conversation with Madame Balvet; their tones were quiet and serious. Sara imagined, from his gestures, that he was giving his housekeeper instructions; she nodded several times, and then, with a final nod, accompanied by a decisive wave of her hand, she turned and went indoors again. Louis paced the portico a few times, his hands clasped behind his back. On the last turn he caught sight of Sara. He waved his arm, and then hurried down the steps and came towards her.

Something was wrong—his expression told her so instantly. At once her mind went back to the arrival of the overseer, probably

264

carrying mail from Sydney. Louis' walk was brisk; he brought an air of excitement and haste that usually was totally lacking in him. He moved Sara's needlework basket and sat down beside her, beginning to talk without preamble.

"There's news, Sara! Burke has brought mail from Sydney. By the by, there are several letters for Andrew—I must send someone to find him."

She shook her head. "Wait—not yet, Louis! Tell me first what your own news is."

"Something I had not expectcd to hear for many years yet." His voice was slower now, its crispness had faded. He was silent for a few moments, looking past her to the mountains. When his gaze came back to her, he was frowning a little.

"My wife, Sara, is dead. I have had a letter from my esteemed father-in-law, telling me in bald sentences that she died from a chill she caught out hunting."

Sara grasped at the sense of what he said, but she saw immediately that Louis' expression did not invite sympathy. She felt it would be hypocritical to offer it; there could be nothing but relief for him in the news of his wife's death. Relief, certainly—but, perhaps, also a trace of regret? There were so many things Louis might regret about this. He may have cherished an unexpressed hope that she would come, some day, to the colony; he may often have grieved over the beauty he had loved unwisely. Surely Banon hadn't been built without the hope of a son to inherit? But if these were Louis' thoughts, he kept them to himself, and his face told her very little. He had told her his news within an hour of receiving it, but it was clear that he did not expect her to probe his own feelings on the matter. Whether he was relieved, indifferent, or sorry, would obviously remain his own affair. She said nothing, fearful that any words of hers might intrude clumsily among his thoughts.

At last he said to her, "I'm angry, Sara!"

"Angry?"

"Yes—angry! My wife is dead, but Elizabeth, my daughter, remains very much alive. That blundering fool, her grandfather, thinks he can keep her from me."

He reached into his coat pocket, and brought out a letter. He unfolded it and laid it across his knees; Sara saw that the handwriting was thick, bold enough, but shaky, as if the writer could no longer control his pen with any certainty.

"Here . . . !" Louis pointed to the lines close to the end of the letter:

" ' . . . *Your daughter, Elizabeth, now eight years old, will, I presume, remain here with her grandmother and myself. From the reports I have of the colony, I must conclude that it is a wild and savage place, totally unsuitable for such a child as my granddaughter. Moreover, your roving life leads me to believe that you have no permanent home in which she may be properly received and brought up. Nor is there, I imagine, in New South Wales, any woman capable of instructing her in her lessons, needlework, music and painting.*
" '*I await, Sir . . .*' "

Louis looked up. "There it is, Sara! My daughter is the property of her maternal grandfather—too delicate a plant to be entrusted to this harsh manner of living, or to my irresponsible care!"

She had not known Louis as angry as this before. She said, "And what will you reply to him?"

"Reply!" With great emphasis he thrust the letter back into his pocket. "I'll reply in person—and I'll show him exactly whose property Elizabeth is."

Sara put a hand on his arm. "Louis, what do you mean?"

"I'm taking a passage to England in order to fetch Elizabeth. And then I'll bring her back to the country that in future will be her home."

"*Here . . . !* Are you mad?"

"Mad, Sara? If you had a daughter as well as three sons, wouldn't you keep her here with you?"

"That's different. If *I* had a daughter she would have been born here. She would be of the generation that *belongs* here, just as my sons are. She would know nothing of England, or the niceties of manners all little girls imbibe from the time they can walk. And in the end I would have to send her back to England, so that the accepted pattern of gentility could be imposed upon her."

"Elizabeth shall bring it here with her!" he said emphatically. "She shall have one of those females who run uncomfortable seminaries for young ladies to accompany her. And nothing— *nothing at all, Sara*—will be neglected in the direction of music,

266

painting, and sewing! If she is not precisely her mother's daughter, she will be grateful to me for taking her away from that cold barracks her grandparents inhabit.''

Sara shook her head doubtfully. ''Shouldn't you think again, Louis? You're angry now . . . but later you will see it differently. She is such a child still, yet . . .''

''But she is *my* child!'' he burst out. ''She will live in my house, and lead the life *I* have chosen for her!''

Angrily he rose, and stood frowning down at her.

''I am quite determined about this, Sara. The *Dolphin* is in Port Jackson—it was she who brought in the mails. I am going now to write to her captain to hold me a passage for the homeward trip. She goes directly back to the Cape, I believe. With favourable weather, in six months I shall be in England.''

Louis sailed with the *Dolphin* three weeks later. He went, leaving Madame Balvet in charge at Banon, and his business affairs in Andrew's hands, begging Andrew to find time occasionally to ride out to the Nepean, to report progress at the farm.

The harbour was white-capped the day he left, its green shores beautiful and aloof, as they had been the first time he saw them. He kissed Sara's hand, shook Andrew's firmly, and then made his way down the wooden steps of the jetty to the waiting boat. The wind whipped Sara's skirts about her ankles, and fluttered the handkerchief she waved. As he drew into the shadow of the *Dolphin*, he could distinguish Sara's red gown in the midst of the small crowd on the jetty.

Chapter Two

On a Sunday evening in March, 1804, Sara stood with Julia and Ellen Ryder on the veranda of their house. She bent and kissed Julia Ryder's cheek warmly in farewell.

''Take care of yourself,'' she said, in a low tone. ''Perhaps now that Ellen is back here to take charge, James could spare you to come to Glenbarr for a visit?''

''We'll see . . . we'll see,'' Julia answered cautiously. ''I've scarcely had time to get used to the thought of Ellen being back yet, and I very much doubt that the Bath seminary has trained her in the management of a colonial household. But, we'll see, my dear. Your Sebastian holds my heart-strings so firmly, I find it difficult to stay away."

Ellen, beside her, let out a little squeak of protest. "Oh, Mama, really . . . !

Andrew, standing on a lower step, turned back towards Julia. "I wish you could consider quite a long visit to Glenbarr. Sara will need some company while I'm away."

"Away . . . ?" she echoed. She looked questioningly at him. "I didn't know you planned a trip—is it to the East again?"

"Andrew," Sara said quietly, "is thinking about going to England. It isn't definite yet, but perhaps when the *Hawk* comes in again . . ."

James Ryder, who had been waiting with the carriage door open, suddenly spoke. "What's this about England?" He started to mount the steps again.

Andrew nodded. "I've had a notion to go for some time. The news about the way Macarthur's wool samples were received has set me thinking. He knows what he's doing, that man. He saw the future of this country was in wool long before any of us."

Ryder smiled faintly. "I wouldn't say you'd been precisely slow in following him, Andrew. Your own merino flocks are almost as large as his . . ."

"Ah, yes," Andrew broke in quickly, "but look how he's got ahead of me now. He knows the market for wool in England, and has made himself the most talked-of man in the wool trade there at the moment. Why, he got himself out of a court martial almost entirely on the strength of what he could do for the future of the trade in Yorkshire! I've got to get there as well, and convince these men that there are others producing wool, besides Macarthur."

"Oh, there's more in it than that," Sara said, laughing a little. "Andrew has heard the reports that Macarthur wrung a grant of five thousand acres from the Colonial Office for his sheep runs, and Andrew is after the same prize."

"Well, why not?" he retorted. "This climate is made to produce wool, and England needs every pound of it she can get. They've got the factories and the workers, they've got the market for their cloth—the merino wool from Spain comes in at the rate of five million pounds a year, and still Yorkshire wants more. I tell you there's a chance to make *real* money here! I have the ships to export the wool, I have the capital—or between Louis de Bourget and myself we could raise it. What I need is a substantial grant of land for pasture, and the contact with the leading wool-brokers. Macarthur believes that the time is coming when our wool will outsell the Spanish merino on the London market, and I think he's right.''

"If he's right . . ." Ryder began reflectively. "If he's right you'll stand to make a tidy pile of money, and money that goes on increasing as fast as your merinos breed.''

"If he's right,'' Andrew repeated, with a sideways look at his wife, "I'll build that other wing on to Glenbarr, and Sara shall stuff it full of silk curtains and white marble.''

Sara caught his arm and began to urge him down the steps towards the carriage. "If that day comes,'' she said laughingly, "I'll have a design of rams' heads in marble for all the chimney pieces in the new wing.'' Then she tugged more urgently at his arm. "But come—we keep Julia and Ellen in the cold.''

She hurried down the steps, James coming to assist her into the carriage. The two men shook hands, and Andrew climbed in beside her. James stepped back, giving the signal to Edwards, on the box above. There were calls of farewell from the two women on the veranda as the carriage moved forward. Sara waved; the pace quickened, and soon all she could see was the darker shape of the house against the night sky, and the lights that streamed from the hall and the drawing-room windows. Then the drive twisted sharply, and the trees cut off even the lights.

They were in darkness in the carriage, Andrew's face opposite her no more than a whitish blur. She felt sleepy and rather disinclined for talk. Two days previously Ellen Ryder had arrived in Port Jackson, in the *Lady Augusta*, after an absence of four years. The news had reached Sara and Andrew at Priest's, and they had driven over to the Ryders' farm that afternoon. Sara had not cared for the changes she saw in Ellen; the girl was fully a woman now, with all the self-conscious manners of one lately accustomed to the fashions of the Bath seminary, and the Twickenham house of her elegant aunt, Julia's sister. There was worldly knowledge in the way she greeted Sara, her former nurse, and a one-time convict; if she had dared, she would have snubbed her. But even two days back in the colony had taught Ellen that Andrew Maclay was not the man to forgive a snub to his formidable wife. So she dimpled and smiled, and consented to play the piano accurately and woodenly, to show off the polish of her English education.

The increased jolting of the carriage told Sara that the drive had now joined the road leading to Castle Hill and Priest's.

"What do you think of Ellen?'' she said to Andrew.

He stirred, as though he had been deep in thought, and was reluctant to give any consideration to the girl.

"Ellen . . . ? Oh—pert and pretty. I expect she'll improve with marriage and age."

That was all she could get out of him. She lapsed back into silence, prepared to doze through the journey to Priest's.

She was roused, stiff and a little cold—there was a trace of autumn already in the air—by Edwards's shout from the box. The carriage jerked to a stop, sending her sliding sideways in the seat. It was pitch dark on either side; as far as she could see, they were not near a house of any sort. There was no light anywhere, and, seemingly, no reason for stopping.

Andrew thrust his head out of the window. "What is it, Edwards? Why are we stopping?"

Edwards's hoarse old voice betrayed unusual animation.

"That light ahead, sir! I been watching it, I have. That be no ordinary light. That be fire!"

"Fire! Where?"

Andrew was out of the carriage in a second, and had scrambled up beside Edwards to get a better view. Sara, craning out of the window, could hear them clearly.

"We're not more than half a mile or so from Castle Hill, sir. That light be either the village, or the Govermnent Farm, where they keep the convicts."

"The convicts . . . !" Andrew's voice betrayed his own uncertainty. "Well . . . it's no more than an ordinary fire. We'd better go and see if there's anything we can do to help."

But Edwards cautioned him with a wary hand. "Be easy now, sir! It'll be better to wait a bit and see. There be much talk of trouble among the convicts, and maybe this . . ."

"Nonsense!" Andrew said. "I'm tired of hearing rumours of rebellion. All the talk never comes to anything. And this is nothing more than a barn that some careless fool has set alight. Come, man, we'll go on."

"Well, sir . . . just as you say. But I'd be a lot easier if you kept your pistol handy, now."

Edwards continued grumbling and muttering under his breath, as Andrew climbed down. In his jumbled stream of words, Sara distinguished "rebels" and "mad Irishmen" a number of times. Andrew opened the door to get in beside her again. Worried, she leaned forward and laid a hand on his arm.

"Don't you think we'd be wiser to turn back towards Parramatta, Andrew? If there's trouble . . ."

She was checked by Edwards's shout.

"Hold it, sir! There be someone coming! Someone with a lamp!"

Andrew stepped down on the road again. Leaning far out, Sara could see the wavering yellow light of a lantern far ahead of the carriage. Then the sound of footsteps reached them, the rhythm of someone coming at a half-run and occasionally stumbling. The night was very still and dark—dark, except for the reddish glow of the fire in the distant sky, and the lantern bobbing along close to the road. Andrew turned back quickly and groped in the place under the seat where he always kept his pistol when travelling. He took it out, cocked it, and waited. The three of them hardly seemed to draw a breath as they waited.

It was a woman's voice that reached them out of the darkness.

"For mercy's sake, wait for me!"

She burst into the circle of light cast by the carriage lanterns, breathless, half-sobbing. She wore a white nightgown, with a cloak flung carelessly over it. Her hair was black and long, tumbling in disorder about her shoulders. Her handsome, plump face was flushed from her running.

Sara gave a gasp. "Nell Finnigan! Andrew—its Nell Finnigan, from Castle Hill!"

Nell stumbled, and grasped at one of the spokes of the front wheel for support. Andrew took her arm and held it firmly. She leaned against the wheel, her head thrown back as she drew in huge gasping breaths. Andrew bent down, and gently forced the lantern from her clenched fingers. Edwards had scrambled from the box; he stood peering fixedly into her face.

When she had enough breath to speak, it was to Andrew she turned.

"There's a rising!" she cried, clutching him. "The convicts have broken out of the Government Farm, and burnt it! It's the signal for the rising they've been planning these past months. We must all get to Parramatta as quick as we can. We'll be safe there. They'll . . ."

Andrew shook her a little to halt her panic. "Tell me quietly, now. Tell me what you know."

Nell took another great gulp of air, and then restarted her story.

"Well . . . The first I knew of it was the bell ringing up at the

271

farm—the bell they call them in from the fields with. I was getting ready for bed, with my place shut and locked this hour past. Finnigan is in Parramatta, and I can tell you I was scared out of my wits. I looked out of the window and saw the fire—I knew about the talk of rising, so I hoped the bell meant a fire, and not that trouble was starting. Then the boys came pouring into the village, searching every house for food and ammunition. They've scarcely half a dozen muskets between them, though there seemed to be plenty of pikes—you know—the sort they make themselves.''

"Yes . . . yes,'' Andrew said impatiently. "But what happened when they got to Castle Hill?'' He gripped her arm too tightly, and she pulled away with a show of indignation.

"Here, mind what you're doing!'' She spoke roughly, but then her tone changed in an instant, as she recalled that she was depending on Andrew to get her safely to Parramatta. "If you'd been there at the time, you wouldn't be too clear on it either.''

She made an effort to be calm.

"Well . . . it was like this,'' she continued. "They came from the direction of the Government Farm—at the other end of the village. Most of them made for Carson's, the smithy. They were after the horses, of course. And probably they'd have more chance of a pistol or musket there. They kept away from the guardhouse—though there were only three soldiers on duty, and *they* couldn't have done much. I could see plainly enough that they were going into each cottage in the row, so I didn't wait for them to reach *mine*! I took a lantern, and away with me over the wall of my back garden! Some of those boys aren't exactly friends of Finnigan, you understand. I wasn't in much of a mood to see the things in my house pulled about—and I knew if I had anything to say, I'd be done for.''

She was clearly terrified, and Andrew gave a moment's thought to her neat little cottage, well-stocked with rum.

"How long ago did this happen?'' he asked.

She shook her head. "I don't know. I've been shivering in a potato field since I got away—no idea how long. Watching, you know, to try to see how many there were, and if they were using the roads. But it was too dark to see a thing—I could hear them, though. This is the start of the trouble, all right—and, believe me, there were more men in Castle Hill than came out of the Government Farm. They'd collected others. They'll try a march on Parramatta, I'll be bound. I doubt that the road between here

272

and Parramatta is safe. The news will spread like fire, and all the boys who've been sharpening their blasted pikes all these months will have them up from under the floorboards."

"Has anyone sent word to Parramatta?"

"How should *I* know!" she echoed. "I tell you, Mr. Maclay, you should have *been* there, and you wouldn't be taking it all so calmly. Maybe one of the soldiers went to Parramatta—I don't know. But, judging from the numbers of the boys, I don't doubt that Castle Hill has given them all they want for the present. Likely, they'll be spreading out to pick up more men, and whatever arms they have."

Andrew gave her an absent-minded pat on the shoulder, turning to Edwards.

"We'll have to go back to Parramatta—perhaps the news hasn't reached them there yet. Though, the trouble is, that the sound of the carriage on the road will give the convicts warning before we ever get near there. Yet if we leave the carriage and take to the fields, we'll not get to Parramatta before morning, and that'll be no use at all—we daren't delay as long as that. There may be gangs out on the road by now. But that's a risk we'll have to take."

As he spoke, Andrew was bustling Nell into the carriage beside Sara. She flung herself back on the seat, shivering, her cloak wrapped tightly about her. Andrew held the lantern high, until she settled herself; she seemed subdued, a softer, gentler Nell Finnigan than either had ever seen before. But her black eyes were still bold—her toughened, unsentimental nature faced their danger realistically; she might have fled from it, but she did not wilt at the thought of it.

Andrew drew a rug across her knees, but his last look, as he withdrew to close the door, was for Sara. The lantern light was soft on her face and hair; she gave him a faint smile—a small, private gesture of her confidence and trust. Then he stepped back and closed the door. The two women were in darkness again. They heard him climb up on the box beside Edwards.

The carriage rolled forward slowly—then with increasing speed. Soon Sara and Nell were rocking and swaying to its uneven rhythm. They were shut in the world of darkness, their faces indistinguishable to each other. Sara looked towards her companion, wondering. Was she afraid, when she no longer had the lonely road to watch, and the sounds in the fields to listen for? Sara was well aware that here in the carriage there was no

273

distraction from fear, and no limit to the imagination. Nell Finnigan was brave, she allowed. But could even Nell sit here long, and still not be afraid? Parramatta lay ahead, but on either side were the silent fields, the labourers' cottages, the convicts' huts that might easily have been the scenes of conferences that were carried forward by careful planners. Within a few hours the whole countryside would be aflame with news of the rebellion; muskets, pikes, axes—anything that would serve as a weapon— would be brought out, houses would be plundered, and horses stolen from the stables of employers. The cry of "Liberty!" would stir up the rebels again, as the night gave way to a revealing morning, when perhaps their hearts had grown faint, and their stomachs empty. These were desperate men, with only the flogging-post and the gallows ahead if they failed. Most of them had brought the spirit of rebellion from Ireland, had fostered it, and nourished its growth among their companions; to-night was the product of their efforts.

Sara grew cold with the thought of how many there might be to join the disaffected. Would the underpaid labourers join the rebels, with land and livestock promised as a reward? The hope of ultimate success was vague—but was it any vaguer when their friends and brothers had stormed Dublin Castle? Military discipline was lax, and all of them knew it. The danger lay in how quickly the word spread, and how many had pledged themselves, during these past months, to take up arms when it came.

The trees lining the road were like a solid menace to their safety. Occasionally they caught the glimpse of a light in a cottage, and wondered at it being there so late. There was no way of telling if the news of the rising was ahead of them on the road, or still behind them. They met no one, heard nothing.

In the darkness Nell stirred, tugging her cloak closer. "Well..." she said, her tone strong and clear. "I don't know how you feel, Mrs. Maclay . . . but, speaking for myself, *I'm* scared!"

With a rush of gratitude, Sara looked at the faint blur of the face opposite. If Nell Finnigan was afraid, then no one else need be ashamed of fear. Impulsively, she leaned forward to take the other's large, roughened hand; she pressed her fingers firmly round it.

"I'm afraid, too," she said.

Having admitted it, she felt relieved, but there was suddenly nothing more to say; their fear, acknowledged, seemed less terrible.

As they settled themselves back again, the carriage began a rather sharp descent; Sara leaned forward, and peered through the window. She recognised this spot, a place where the road plunged to ford a shallow stream; for the main part of the year it was dry, but now, above the rumble of the wheels, she could just faintly hear a trickle of water against a stony bed. The angle of the carriage levelled off as they splashed their way through, then tilted again when they started on the slope of the opposite bank. A shout rang out as they reached the top.

"Halt! Whoa, there!"

For the next few seconds there was mad confusion, wild cries, and men shouting, and over it all Sara heard Edwards's curse, and the cracking of the whip as he urged the horses forward. The carriage moved with a sudden lurch; Sara was flung back against the seat, and Nell, unable to save herself, fell on to her knees. The carriage maintained its progress for no more than half a minute. Sara knew from the way it was slowing down that their attackers were hauling at the horses' heads. At last they were jerked to a stop. Instantly the door was flung open; a man, unshaven, smelling vilely of stale sweat, thrust his head inside. He shone a lantern on the two women.

"Out!" he snapped, jerking his thumb over his shoulder. "This is as far as ye ride, ladies."

Furiously, without caution, Sara pushed against his shoulder. "Get out of here! Who are you, anyway?"

For answer, he caught her arm and tugged. He had twice her weight, and she was dragged forward suddenly, almost falling from the carriage to the road. Nell received the same treatment; her curses added to the noise and confusion.

"Take your hands off me, you filthy devils!" She stood with her feet planted wide, her arms akimbo, scowling defiance. "A fine bunch you are, I must say! A couple of pikes and an old musket between the lot of you. Do you expect to frighten Mr. King out of Government House with that?"

A nudge from one of the despised pikes silenced her.

Andrew and Edwards, down from the box by this time, moved close to the women. A circle of perhaps a dozen men stood about them, pressing forward, hemming them in. They were an uninspiring lot, standing their ground uneasily, and only the weight of their numbers appeared to give them any confidence. There seemed to be some doubt among them still as to which one was the leader; they looked from one to the other uncertainly. But Sara could find no reassurance in this. Seen in the light of the lanterns they carried they might be unprepossessing, but she was not, for a moment, blind to the fact that they were also desperate. The circle of dirty, unshaven faces filled her with horror. It was a face such as one of these that had pressed close to her own the night of the convict outbreak at Kintyre. So long ago, now, but she recoiled in terror as she remembered. She looked from each man to the next; they seemed a little awed by what they had dared, and, leaderless, they were far more dangerous than a disciplined troop.

One of the gang took the initiative. He moved through the group and faced Andrew. His only authority seemed to be the musket he held.

"There'll be no harm done to anyone who behaves peaceful-like." He spoke with a soft Irish accent. "We'll just have yer horses and yer pistol, now. And then we'll be lettin' ye on yer way. 'Tis a fair step to Parramatta for the ladies, I'm thinkin'. But like as not ye'll find some cottage on the way to give ye shelter."

Andrew, swiftly glancing about him, seemed in an instant to judge and weigh the temper of the mob facing him. Then he took a step back, at the same time thrusting his pistol forward menacingly. With the other hand he motioned to Sara.

"Get back in the carriage! Edwards—the box!"

Both Edwards and Nell made a movement to obey, but Sara stood still.

"Andrew, let them have what they want," she said in a low tone "They'll . . ."

"Do as I say!" he said peremptorily.

She drew away from him immediately. At his words, Nell, already on the carriage step, climbed inside. Edwards began to mount the box again. Sara hesitated, her mind numbed with apprehension and terror. Andrew stood quite still, pistol levelled, looking, each in turn, into the faces about him. She held her breath as she waited for his next movement; the blood was pounding in her ears, and she felt herself groping madly at the carriage door for support.

Andrew spoke at last. His voice was as cold as if he were addressing a group of troublesome children.

"You all know that hanging is the penalty for horsestealing and armed robbery. You know also that you haven't a chance of succeeding with this rising once the troops are called out."

Complete silence greeted his words. No one stirred in protest, and there was no movement among the gang.

"Now . . . !" Andrew continued. "Stand away from those horses. I advise you not to add further to the list of your crimes. I promise you it will go harder for you if you do."

The self-appointed leader fell back a step, uncertain and irresolute. He looked about him, seeking the opinion of his companions. There was an uneasy shuffling of feet, a low mutter rose from someone's throat. Above them a little wind stirred fitfully in the trees. It was a long minute of agony to Sara—the appraising of the desperate and yet fearful faces. In the intense quiet, the scraping of a boot against the ground was like the noise of thunder. The men wavered openly; their leader's indecision had reached them all.

A few more seconds, Sara thought, and Andrew would win.

Too soon, it seemed to her, he gave the signal.

She climbed into the carriage, craning her head to watch him. He put his foot on the step of the box.

"Right, Edwards!"

Andrew's sharp voice seemed to break the spell that lay over the group.

Someone shouted hoarsely from the back.

"Is it a man ye call yerself, Matt Donovan? Sure, it's not fit to lead a donkey, ye are!"

The men parted automatically as the speaker thrust his way through. He was a huge man; his ugly face was enraged and brutish. He looked directly at Andrew.

"Stand down, there! B' God, we'll have those horses, whether you like it or not!"

There was a general shout of approval from the men. Sara heard Andrew's voice rise above them.

"Whip them up, Edwards!"

The shot rang out before Edwards could bring down his whip. Terrified, the horses lunged forward; Andrew crumpled, and toppled down into the road. Sara heard herself give one piercing scream, and then she flung the carriage door open. She felt Nell's hands clutch frantically at her, but she broke free of them. Edwards was already hauling at the reins, and their speed had slackened. Sara jumped clear, holding her balance for a few seconds, then falling on her hands and knees into the ditch. All the breath seemed to have left her body from the force of the impact, but she scrambled to her feet again and started to run back to where Andrew lay. By the time the carriage had finally halted, she was kneeling on the road beside him.

The circle of convicts stood back from her, watching, muttering among themselves. They made no attempt to help her, and with her own hands she turned Andrew over on his back. The bullet had smashed his temple. He had probably been dead when he hit the ground.

They took the horses and the pistol, and left quickly—a quiet, nervous group now. Sara hardly noticed their departure, except for the sudden silence it left behind. She sat on the side of the road, holding Andrew's body, aware of nothing but the terrible stillness of the weight in her arms. Nell and Edwards held a whispered consultation, and then Nell came and crouched down in the dust beside them. Sara didn't feel her presence there until a warm tear splashed on her hand.

She raised her head and looked up incredulously at the other woman.

"You're crying . . . ?"

Nell dashed a hand across her eyes. "I didn't know him very well. He didn't take much notice of me whenever he passed through Castle Hill—but I liked him."

Sara bent until her lips brushed his quiet ones.

"I loved him," she whispered.

They sat there on the road, not talking. Presently, Edwards succeeded in detaching one of the carriage lanterns. With a few words softly spoken in Nell's ear, he set off in the direction of Parramatta.

II

The mainspring of the rebellion did not live out a full day. It died outside Toongabbie the next morning, in an encounter with a detachment of troops under Major Johnston. Cunningham, the leader of the rising at Castle Hill, was killed there, with sixteen other men, twelve were wounded, and thirty captured. The remaining two hundred and thirty took to the bush. Pitchforks, reaping-hooks, pikes, a score or two of muskets, and a desire for liberty, were not enough. Through the week they surrendered in bodies or individually—a ragged rebel army come to heel. When the news swept through the colony, small groups who were waiting to join up with the main movement quietly put away their arms. The rebellion was dead.

On the Thursday and Friday of that same week Sydney, Parramatta, and Castle Hill saw the executions of the ringleaders—among them Andrew Maclay's murderer. Some of the rebels went to the flogging-posts and the chain-gangs, others were exiled to Norfolk Island, or sent to that hellspot on the Coal River. His Excellency publicly commended the courage and actions of Major Johnston and Captain Abbott. Martial law, declared as soon as the Governor had received news of the rising, was revoked. The colony drew a sigh of relief, and prepared to settle back into its old routine. Even from the men in the chain gangs the spirit of rebellion seemed to have fled.

III

Sara leaned back wearily in her chair, her face turned towards the small fire that burned in the grate. Glenbarr's long drawing-room was still and quiet now. Early that afternoon Andrew had been buried. All day long this room had seen the coming and going of his friends and neighbours, even the Governor himself had paid his formal call. David, the eldest, had been there too, stiff and unnatural in his black suit, his child's face fighting exhaustion and the strangeness of living through ceremonies which belonged only to an adult world. Unconsciously, he had seemed to seek his father's support, and, not finding it, his expression had grown bewildered and half-lost.

Now they were all gone. The evening meal was over, David was in his bed this past half-hour, and Glenbarr had returned to its quiet. Jeremy was the only one who remained. He crouched on a fender-stool, his back to the fire, watching Sara's face, the movement of her restless fingers plucking at the rich black silk of her gown. Her hair was dressed smoothly back off her forehead, and, above the black gown, its fairness was almost white. He could trace the ravages of the past week in her face; there was a look of harsh experience written there, and shadows beneath her eyes that he had not seen before.

Suddenly she spoke; her voice was tired.

"Your sentence will expire this year—you'll be free, Jeremy. I have been thinking about you—about the future..."

He answered, a questioning note in his voice, "Yes?"

She looked at him directly then. "When you're free—when

279

the time comes—I'm going to ask you to stay. I want you to help run Kintyre and Priest's and the Toongabbie farm, as you've been doing.'' She stopped him with a wave of her hand, as she saw he was going to answer. "Yes, I know what you're going to say. You'll be free. You'll want to take land and farm for yourself. I'm asking one—two years from you, Jeremy. No more than that. Stay with me just that long. I'll pay you . . .''

"We'll not talk of payment just yet, Sara. There are other things.''

Her brows lifted. "Other things . . . ?''

He gestured meaningly. "You surely can't have decided to keep the whole lot on—the three farms, the store, Glenbarr? And what about the ships?''

"I mean to keep them all,'' she replied calmly. "They belonged to Andrew, didn't they? Don't they belong to his children?''

"But you're a *woman*, Sara! *You* can't do what Andrew did! It's beyond your powers—your strength, even,''

Frowning, she folded her lips. "Do you imagine, Jeremy Hogan, that I've helped Andrew build up his possessions all these years, without the thought of handing them over to our sons? Was there ever a single decision he made that I didn't prompt him? If I should sell the properties now—and the ships, and the store—the money is all that I'd have to give the children. And there is no sense of permanence in money alone. They need to know the feeling of possessing land. They've got to have possessions and roots. They'll forget Andrew—they'll never really know him—if they don't have the things that he built up around them. I want them—David, Duncan, and Sebastian—to look at Kintyre, and to know that it took more to build it than luck at a card-table, and a salvaged ship!''

He shook his head very slowly. "But you're a *woman, Sara!*'' he repeated. "Can you control all of it—the labourers of three farms, the captains of the ships, the store . . . ?''

"Yes, if you'll help me, Jeremy! Give me two years, and then I'll show them that a woman can do it. They'll doubt it at first—and they'll scoff. But I *know* that I can do it!''

"And what if I tell you that I believe it can't be done? What if I refuse to help you?''

For a moment she was taken aback. Then she said, levelly, "If you refuse, then I must try to do it without you.''

280

He sprang to his feet. "My God, Sara, you're heartless! You give me no choice!"

He paced the length of the room, paused, then swung round, and returned to face her.

"You've really made up your mind about this?"

She raised her eyes to look at him as he stood over her.

"How can it be otherwise, Jeremy? All these things *are* Andrew. How can I give them up? To lose them would be to lose him again—to lose him a thousand times over."

Her voice grew choked and stifled; tears were beginning to slide unchecked down her face.

"You, better than anyone else, know what Andrew has done for me. He took me from the hold of a convict ship. Because of me he settled here. Then he grew to love the place, and his heart was here. I'm as sure of that as anything I could be. I *must* hold together everything he's built up—keep it intact for our children. *They* belong to this country, and this is where they will see their father's achievements."

"And you're prepared to do it alone?" he asked quietly.

She nodded. "Alone—if necessary."

Then she bent her head, and he could see her shoulders heaving. She covered her face with her hands. Her next words were blurred and distorted.

"I didn't know it would be like this. I didn't think it was possible to feel so desolate—and lost. Andrew . . . ! Andrew . . . !"

Gently Jeremy put out his hand and stroked her bent head. He could remember clearly and painfully the first night he had ever spent under Glenbarr's roof—the night they had dined by candlelight off the packing-cases, and Andrew had strode across the bare boards, his face alight with the vision of the future. Then he had seemed indestructible, nothing was beyond the reach and scope of his energy and genius. Whatever he touched had been golden for him.

But now, four years later, the golden age was finished. And Sara's sobs were a wild protest against its going.

PART FIVE

***

Chapter One

For three weeks after her husband's death, Sydney saw nothing of Sara Maclay. Jeremy Hogan returned to the Hawkesbury without saying anything about her plans for the future; from Glenbarr itself there came no news. All that the servants could report was that their mistress spent her days with the children, walking with them on the South Head road, or down at the little beach; sometimes she took over the lesson hours from their tutor, Michael Sullivan, the young man who came to Glenbarr daily from his lodgings in the town. But Michael Sullivan was not to be probed for information. Richard Barwell appeared to know nothing either. From Annie Stokes came the report that Sara spent her evenings shut up in the room where all Andrew's business had been carried out. She gave orders for a fire there each evening, and Annie, always watchful, knew that it was often the small hours of the morning before her mistress took her candle and mounted the stairs to her bedroom.

For Sara herself they were weeks lived in a kind of daze; it was a period, not of trying to forget Andrew, but of rediscovering his mind, of tracing back the growth of every ambition and plan he had conceived during their marriage. Alone in the small, plain room she took down the heavy books that recorded each business transaction he had completed since the first land grant on the Hawkesbury. The store, the Toongabbie farm, Priest's . . . the first *Thistle,* then the new one bought in London, the purchase of *Hawk* and *Thrush* . . . the accounts of all of them were here, and copies of Andrew's instructions to his London agents. The hours spent here grew to be not only a process of schooling herself, but like a communication with Andrew himself. The records set down badly on paper were the framework of the life they had built up together. *". . . Store commenced business."* Back into her mind came that crowded, uncomfortable day, when the store had opened its doors for the first time. *"Purchase of farm at Toongabbie."* Those words represented Andrew's return from England, with the new *Thistle*—the period when Glenbarr had been building. Each line of his writing could be filled out with a hundred different details; they were bare notations of Andrew's vision and ambition, his belief in the future of the colony. It was like reading the intimate journal of the life she had shared. She gently touched the pages, and seemed to hear again his voice, eagerly explaining the possibilities of some new scheme he had in mind. Andrew had not possessed the soul of a poet, he had left no letters for her to weep over—but the careful entries were a tangible record of his love.

When the last of the account-books had been read and studied, she wrote to Louis. It was a long letter, containing the story of the convict rising at Castle Hill, and Andrew's death. In it she outlined her plans for carrying on his affairs, just as he had left them and, there and then, made Louis an offer for the outright ownership of the *Thrush* and *Hawk*—preferring, she wrote, to risk her own money, than to force him into placing their management into a woman's hands. She settled to wait, with what patience she could gather, for his reply. It would take, she imagined at least a year.

It was a morning less than a month after Andrew's death when David came running down the stairs to tell Sara that, from the schoolroom window, they had sighted the *Hawk* coming to anchor in Sydney Cove. Sara heard the news with a sense of misgiving; she felt that she was hardly ready for the problems that were ahead of her over the matter of the *Hawk*'s cargo, but she sat down immediately to write a note to the master, Captain Sam Thorne, bidding him come to Glenbarr.

The next day Captain Thorne waited upon her in the small room he remembered as Andrew Maclay's study. He had already determined what the outcome of this interiew would be—not for any money on earth would he remain in the employ of a woman-owner. He, Sam Thorne, was not accustomed to receiving polite notes, telling him the hour at which he might call to discuss the cargo waiting aboard. In his experience, owners had agents, or else they handled the business directly—and, by directly, he meant actually boarding the ship. Transactions with the owner were properly carried out over rum in his cabin—not in a drawing-room, sipping tea!

It was an enlightening two hours that followed. He sensed immediately that the woman who faced him across the table was not completely sure of her ground—but whenever he assumed authority not rightfully his, she had an uncanny knack of stripping it from him. She accepted nothing on faith, examining, one after another, each purchase and bill of sale, in a manner that, had she been a man, he would have considered downright insulting. She was nervous—he knew that very well; and yet she made no mistakes that would give him licence to point out that it was madness to believe she could, from this desk, and from this house, control the fortunes of three ships on the high seas.

The *Hawk* sailed from Port Jackson a month later, bound for London. In that time, Sara and Sam Thorne had reached an understanding. He still didn't approve of women-owners, and he still considered that she didn't know as much about the business as she laid claim to. But, by the same rule, she wasn't as ignorant as might be expected; and though a haggler down to the last penny, she was strictly fair and just in her dealings. They fought their battle, Sara and Captain Thorne, and the victory did not go completely to either one.

On the afternoon the *Hawk* left the harbour, Captain Thorne called at Glenbarr to take leave of the woman under whose orders he was to sail for perhaps many years.

She walked with him to the veranda steps.

"Well, Captain," she said, turning to him, "I hope you have a good voyage. And may God speed your return."

"Thank you, ma'am, I'm sure. And you may depend that I'll do my best for you. I'll see that those London agents treat you right."

"Yes, I know you will," she said quietly. She smiled, then, and extended her hand.

He went down the steps feeling that maybe Andrew had left his business to a head almost as shrewd and hard as his own.

In the town itself there was an outburst of curiosity when it was observed that Sara's first appearance after her husband's death was a visit, accompanied only by Annie Stokes, to the

Hawk. Then, when it was known that she had made her third visit to the vessel, the idea began to seep through the settlement that she had no intention of instructing the London agents to sell the three ships. People shook their heads, saying to one another what a great pity it was that Sara Maclay didn't realise when she was over-reaching herself.

II

Andrew's death ended the three-year-old quarrel between Richard and Sara. Although Richard called at Glenbarr several times during the following few weeks, he had not been admitted; then he came one day at the time when Captain Thorne was beginning to spread the news that he could continue to sail under Sara's orders, and he was not, as before, greeted with the reply that Mrs. Maclay was not receiving visitors, nor was he shown into the drawing-room. Instead, Bennett led him into the little room where he and Andrew had so many times talked over business matters. Sara rose from the desk to take his outstretched hand. He accepted the chair she indicated, and sat studying her—the set of her head above the high, black collar, the fine, pale face, and drawn-back hair. It was three years now since he had been alone with her like this—a long time in which to regret the words used to herself and Jeremy on the road to Kintyre, and to reflect on the qualities he had not seen before or appreciated. He felt an immense, but almost unwilling, respect for the woman facing him, this person who seemed to bear little relation to the girl he had known at Bramfield. In the three years of their separation he had learned her pride and spirit, the unbending determination he could no longer sway by a mere smile, or a lightly-expressed wish. He had no longer felt towards her any of the rash confidence of his first year in the colony. By Andrew's death, she had reached her full stature; he recognised it immediately, and he approached humbly and cautiously, almost afraid of her.

He didn't know how to talk of Andrew. He began clumsily, hesitantly.

"It seems...strange to see you here, Sara. Andrew always..."

She gestured vaguely—he couldn't tell whether in impatience—to have him come to the point of what he wanted to say, or whether it pained her to have Andrew spoken of.

"I know..." she said. "But what else should I do? I was not made to sit over a piece of needlework all day." She spread her hands on the littered papers before her. "There's enough occupation here for three heads . . . and it keeps me too busy to think."

But as she spoke, she rustled the papers nervously, and he did not miss the brightness of tears in her eyes. She spoke with quick jerking phrases, and he sensed that, for all her show of calm efficiency, she was afraid of what she had undertaken. He thought of the ship in the harbour, the captain who was accustomed to taking his orders from men like himself. Richard owned that, among women, Sara might be outstanding, almost formidable; but now she was entering into a world of men where only wits sharper than theirs, a need more compelling, a sense of opportunity more acute, would enable her to survive. A petticoat government was a precarious thing; she would need every last ounce of shrewdness and courage that Andrew had taught her to pull off what she was attempting. He looked again at her nervous hands on the papers, and he felt afraid of her.

He faced her directly.

"What I've come here to talk to you about concerns Andrew . . . I've come about the money I owed him."

She didn't reply, merely raised her eyebrows.

"I've come to assure you that it will be repaid, Sara."

"Repaid?" she repeated quietly. "Andrew didn't press for payment. It's not my intention to do so now."

"You don't see my point at all. There is a vast difference in owing money to Andrew, and . . ." his voice dropped, "owing it to you."

Her gaze left his face, and for a moment she stared down at the desk, at the writing materials laid before her. There was a maddening precision in their array, set out by Annie's careful hands.

"How do you mean to raise the money, Richard?" Sara said suddenly, looking up. "You don't mean to sell Hyde Farm?"

"No—not that. I'll keep Hyde Farm—no matter what happens. Lady Linton would advance the money if I wrote and told her the facts of the case."

She shook her head violently, holding up her hand to silence him. He thought, for a moment, that her face betrayed anger—a definite irritation at the very mention of Lady Linton's name.

"I don't want you begging money from her. I'm in no hurry . . ."

He cut her short, stung by her choice of words. Her father's arrogance and hauteur were still there, he thought, when she needed them. Since the Bramfield days, she might have learned prudence—but she was never humble. He watched her settling back with a greater show of confidence, into the chair that her husband had always used, watched her spread her hands on the desk and prepare to refuse the money of a woman many thousands of miles away, a woman who had long ago forgotten Sara Dane's very existence.

"I had no thought of applying to Lady Linton," he said quietly, "unless you wished to have the money repaid immediately. If you'll give me time, I'll find it myself."

"How?" she said. Her tone was gentler.

"I'll do what I should have done in the beginning. Expenditure will have to be cut—somehow. There must be ways and means of making Hyde Farm pay more. Alison and I should be able to live on far less than we do. Andrew went on lending us all the money we wanted. It was so easy—too easy—to continue taking it from him—but now we must put an end to that."

She listened eagerly as he began to talk, outlining plans he had for improving the farm, the ways in which he could cut expenses, of certain business deals which he had, from lack of interest, never entered into before. He was determined he would waste no more opportunities. The flow of his talk ran on, and she didn't check him. She knew perfectly well that he was building up an impossible ideal, he saw himself the man of energy and acumen he never could be. But to hear him talk in this way was to bring back to her the first few weeks after his arrival in the colony, and the months after he had acquired the farm. While she listened, she was able to imagine that their quarrel had never existed; their three years of near-silence was as completely forgotten as if it had not been at all. With brief nods and a question now and then, she encouraged him. If Richard achieved only half of what he planned, he would far outstrip any effort he had yet made in his whole life. She had no particular need of the money he owed, and its repayment was safely insured by Alison's eventual inheritance from Lady Linton, but she would not say a word to halt him. His pride had been touched, and he showed more spirit now than she had ever seen in him before. It wouldn't harm him, she thought, to learn at last how money was made, to watch every penny of expenditure to see if it couldn't be reduced to a half-penny. He would soon get used to wearing last year's coat, and choosing his wines with an eye to the price. For too long Richard had been unhampered by such necessities;

he would learn them now quickly, rather painfully, and be far better for having done so.

It was noon before he rose to go. They stood together wordlessly for a few moments, and then he bent and kissed her on the lips.

"Good-bye, Sara. It won't be possible to see you alone like this very often. But it won't be the hell it has been during the last three years—not again."

She knew quite well what he meant. It seemed that at last Richard had learned the prudence she had tried to impose upon him in the beginning. He knew now the smallness of the society to which they belonged, and the power of rumour and gossip. With a kind of wisdom and gentleness he had not possessed when he had first come to the colony, he was bowing to the inevitable.

She smiled at him. "We're fools if we haven't learned by this time that we can never successfully quarrel with one another. You and I were not made to quarrel."

Still smiling, she shook her head when he tried to kiss her a second time. Instead she took his hand and covered it with both of hers.

III

During the next few months Jeremy watched Sara carefully, concerned that the look she had worn when she arrived in the colony first, had returned to her face. Her eyes were cold, a little harsh; when she spoke, her voice was quick and brittle. He thought her afraid, unhappy, even tormented. She grew thinner, her beauty sharp and fine—something to touch a man strangely when he looked at her. And yet she herself seemed to be interested in no man.

Helpless to prevent it, he saw her driving herself to master the tasks it would normally have taken three people to do. Clapmore was promoted from his desk at the store to one in the room next to where Sara herself worked. He took notes at her dictation, toiled over long columns of figures, prepared letters to the London agents, and was general liaison between Sam and the people with whom she did business. The colony was learning the hopelessness of expecting to keep Sara Maclay out of any business transaction which she had made up her mind she wanted to enter. They didn't much like it, but in time accepted it, and almost learned to regard each communication from her as if it came from Andrew himself. Their acceptance of her part in the best of their commerce was, after a while, fairly good-natured—except for the fact that they were, whether consciously or unconsciously, waiting for the fatal mistakes to creep in, the false moves that would bring the structure crashing.

When Jeremy's sentence expired, Sara marked the occasion with a gift of cash and credits with her agents that staggered him. He returned it promptly, and rather curtly. She took it back, not at all embarrassed, shrugging her shoulders.

"You're a fool, Jeremy Hogan! You're free now, and you'll need the money—but, if you choose to be as stiff-necked as a mule, that's your own affair."

But he cherished the memory of the dinner she gave him at Glenbarr to celebrate his day of freedom. David was allowed to stay up later than usual to eat with them; the dining-room windows were open to the soft spring air, the wine was chilled and the candles shed a kindly light on the faces of Sara and the child. There was laughter between them, and some of the strain that now seemed to be Sara's habitual expression left her.

Suddenly Sara raised her glass, smiling at him down the length of the table. "To the future, Jeremy!"

He heard her words phrased ambiguously because of David's presence, and caught up his glass eagerly, as anxious as she was to toast his freedom. Fourteen years were gone out of his life, fourteen years since he had seen his home, or the things that had made his world—the pretty women, the gentle manners, the beautiful horses to ride to hounds with on sharp winter's mornings. It was all gone now, but so were the years of serving other men. He could not return to what he had known, but life here in the colony could be fashioned into something to his liking. He was his own master now. . . . Here he checked himself; he was not his own master while Sara chose to have him do her bidding. Telling himself he was a fool, still he drank the wine with her gladly.

The recollection of how Sara had behaved to him that evening had to suffice him for the future. He looked vainly for the return to life she had shown then; she was not so much being aloof with him, he thought, as withdrawn and preoccupied. It was almost as if, while she talked with him, her mind was already racing ahead to her next duty. He knew quite well how much she still relied on him, coming to him for advice, and even, occasionally, taking it.

But, it seemed to him, he made a useless effort when he tried to come close to her. Andrew was not dead, he thought, again and again—his ships sailed the high seas, his crops grew in rich soil, and Sara lived with his memory and a closed heart.

His freedom had brought little change to Jeremy's life. He divided his time between the Maclays' three farms—up early each morning, remaining in the fields with the labourers while the light held. Often at night, working over the account books in the silence of Kintyre or Priest's, he thought of Sara—probably similarly employed at Glenbarr—and he cursed her for the servitude in which she kept him. Occasionally he rode down to Parramatta or Sydney to find himself a woman, one of the easy ladies who sprinkled the streets after dark, decked in finery probably paid for by one of the soldiers of the Corps, or a farmer in town on a spree from one of the outlying districts.

But there was little satisfaction for him in this, thinking all the time of Sara, who shut herself up at Glenbarr, never admitting him unless Clapmore was there, or Annie paraded the hall. Sometimes he woke in the night, sweating from a dream of her, a dream in which her hair was twined about his throat, strangling him. He fretted and fumed under her yoke, and yet he could not break free of it.

As the months passed, her carriage was seen more and more frequently on the roads between the three farms; in all weathers she rode, a sober figure in her black, well-cut habit, on horse-back through the fields. She turned constantly to Jeremy at her side, commenting, sometimes praising—but ever more sparing of her praise than Andrew would have been. She was afraid to praise, he told himself—and always afraid that what she had taken on would in the end, prove too much for her.

IV

To Sara, the only real freedom from the sense of missing Andrew was complete absorption in her business affairs—absorption to the point where she was tired enough to sleep at nights, and tired enough to shut out the growing doubts that, alone, she could carry out her plans. A faint uneasiness grew in her heart as, each day, the complication of her work increased. True, the colony was getting over its surprise at her determination to carry on with Andrew's affairs, and she was becoming more adept at handling their diversity. The *Thistle* and *Thrush* had both put into harbour lately, and their masters had received her instructions willingly enough; she might well have been pleased with her success, but she began to sense all about her a growing coolness, a hardening in the attitude of those people who had cultivated her for Andrew's sake. In the weeks close to his death, she had shunned callers to Glenbarr, but, as the months passed without sign of the visitors that had once come to the house, she began to wonder if they would ever return. Where, she asked herself, were the women who had made her acquaintance, those who had followed the fashion set by Alison Barwell? Were they counting against her the fact that she was no longer the wife of a prominent free settler, but merely a prominent ex-convict? She met them only on Sunday mornings when she took the children to the service which the Reverend Samuel Marsden conducted in the temporary church beside the place where the new stone one was building. Each Sunday when they had been in Sydney she and Andrew had always attended the services here, and their walk back to Glenbarr had been slowed by the number of people who had stopped to speak to them. Now Sara walked there with David and Duncan beside her, and her acquaintances, hurrying to be there on time, seemed to go by without noticing her. They sat on the hard, wooden benches to listen to Mr. Marsden's haranguing; the convicts dutifully crowding in at the back; they sang hymns rather tunelessly without the help of an organ. Afterwards they filed out, spreading about the rough building as if this were the conventional English churchyard, except that their ears were always listening for the bell that didn't ring. No one moved away until the Governor and Mrs. King had left; there were bows and curtsies, and often in the past Andrew and Sara had been among those whom the Governor had elected to stop and speak to. Now Sara stood with the boys among the crowd to watch the Governor go—watched also as Alison Barwell went by with scarcely more than a sketchy bow in her direction. She noticed that the bows and nods of the other women were growing more than a trifle perfunctory. They told her plainly enough what Sydney thought of a woman who didn't spend the first year of her widowhood sitting quietly in her own drawing-room.

As the time went on, she knew almost without doubt that whenever she travelled to inspect the farms, or visited the store or the vessels in the harbour, her movements were marked and criticised. With a kind of helpless dismay she felt her position slipping back to what it had been when she had first returned to Sydney from the Hawkesbury.

The one real satisfaction in that lonely, bewildering year was the change in Richard. As he and Sara had agreed, they did not see each other, except for chance encounters in Sydney's streets, or at the store. But an undeniable intimacy grew up between them, established on the slender basis of his occasional letters to her, and the short interview they had when he came each quarter with an instalment to pay off against the debt he owed.

The card games at the barracks saw Richard hardly at all these days; as often as he found time, he made the long trip to Hyde Farm; there were no more tales of his drinking. Alison no longer gave her evening parties, and, although she was as exquisitely turned out as ever, she wore last year's gowns—and it was noticeable that there was no more wistful talk of what Mrs. Barwell was expecting from London with the arrival of the next ship. Richard even made a hesitant attempt to engage in a little trading on his own account. He was not very successful—he had no heart and less skill for the day-to-day struggle for the profits from the rum trade. In Richard, ambition had been fired too late; energy alone could not compensate for the shrewdness and cunning he had never learned. Sara, watching him closely, seeing him work as he had never done in his life before, knew that the rewards of his labour were slight. The sum of money which he paid her each three months represented the ruthless cutting of his personal expenditure rather than his increased profits. But it would have wounded his pride to let him know she realised this; if his dress these days was more modest, and she heard that he had sold his thoroughbred mare, she had more discretion than to mention it.

She welcomed his rare visits alone to Glenbarr. She settled eagerly to hear of his improvements at Hyde Farm, and encouraged him in the idea of expansion, knowing that she did so as much for the pleasure of listening to him spin his web of dreams, as for the sake of the future prosperity of the farm. It was far too late, she knew, for him to achieve half the things she desired for him; but, in his altered spirit and outlook, she found the slow emergence of a personality less selfish, and less self-centred.

When occasionally he wrote her—in a strange mixture of business and personal matters—she read and folded the letters many times over. And without letting herself consciously acknowledge her reason for doing so, she kept them all locked together in the drawer of the desk where she worked.

The months wore on slowly, filled with a sameness that dismayed her a little when she paused to consider it. In her periods of leisure she found that her own thoughts were dull companions. Jeremy was far away—at Toongabbie, Priest's, or Kintyre. Richard was self-banished. Her children were too young, and Michael Sullivan too shy, to provide the sort of conversation she craved. Not all her multiple affairs gave sufficient outlet to her energies. And the arrival of each mail found her searching eagerly for a letter from Louis.

Chapter Two

"Will we soon be there, Mama?"

Sara turned to look at Duncan, sitting across from her in the carriage. His mouth had a sticky rim round it from the cake he had just finished eating; he spoke cheerfully enough, but he looked tired, and his clothes were dusty and crumpled. On the seat beside Sara Sebastian was asleep; she supported him with one arm, the other leaned along the ledge of the window, bracing her body against the jolts of the rutted road. Annie, sitting next to Duncan, was nodding drowsily. Of the five, David seemed the only one with enough energy to watch the road that wound its way by the river.

"Yes, darling. It's not far now—not more than a mile."

David glanced across at her then. "This is the place we visited before, isn't it, Mama? Before Papa died?"

His tone suggested that the visit eighteen months ago was already lost in distant memory. Banon was a place he could only vaguely recall.

"Yes," Sara said. "Don't you remember, David—and you, Duncan—the white house above the Nepean? And the aviary—you remember the aviary, surely?"

"Yes . . . I remember." Duncan spoke uncertainly. He did not much care for moving outside his familiar orbit. "But when are we going back to Kintyre, Mama? I like Kintyre best."

"Perhaps after a week at Banon, we'll go to Kintyre."

"Why are we going to Banon? Monsieur de Bourget won't be

there—he's still in England." David swung his foot discontentedly. Like Duncan, he showed no great enthusiasm for the unfamiliar. Kintyre was their love, the place that, even more than Glenbarr, meant home to them. He seemed rather impatient with the thought that Banon was holding them back from the delights of the Hawkesbury farm.

"Well . . ." For a few seconds Sara was at a loss for words. "Well, before Papa died, he promised Monsieur de Bourget that he would ride out to Banon from time to time, to see how it was being kept while he was away. Papa only managed to go once—and now it's more than a year since anyone visited the house or farm. As Papa was Monsieur de Bourget's partner in a number of business matters, I thought I should go in his place."

David nodded, and seemed satisfied. He turned his head again to stare out of the carriage window.

It was a day late in March, 1805—a year since Andrew's death. Autumn was creeping gently upon the landscape; Sydney had yet hardly noticed it, but here in the higher country the nights would be sharp with frost. There had been no rain for a week, and the dust rose from under the horses' feet. All around them the afternoon was silent and hushed. Sara was surprised at the change in the countryside since she had last travelled the road to Banon. There was now much more evidence of settlement. Rough tracks led left and right to farmhouses hidden in the trees; whole blocks of ground were cleared for agriculture, and cattle grazed within enclosed paddocks. They were close now to the Cowpastures district—the rich land on the other side of the river, where the wild Government herds had bred from a few strays since Phillip's time. No one was allowed to enter the area without official permission, but there was no real order enforced, and settlers who wanted fresh meat apparently hunted there at will. This was still a part of the country to which the hand of authority reached only uncertainly.

To Sara, the remoteness of Banon was, for the time being, a relief and a blessing. She had looked to it as a refuge, the farthest part of the settled areas to which she could go. In panic, almost, she had fled from Sydney, bundling children and boxes into the carriage, clinging desperately to Andrew's promise to Louis as a pretext for this escape to the quiet of the Nepean. She craved the silence and the peace, the unfamiliarity of Louis' house. There, alone and undisturbed, she could think around the situation, grown now so much in magnitude that she could no longer ignore it. It had reached a new height in Sydney three days before, sending her, with undignified haste, to seek the solitude of Banon. She knew that, within the next week or so, she must make some sort of decision regarding her own future and her children's; she wanted to be free to make it away from associations with Andrew, away from any memories of the past which might influence her. The thought of Banon brought a feeling of great calm.

At the window, David had suddenly stiffened. He craned forward, and then knelt up on the seat to get a better view. Annie put out a restraining hand, but he shook it off.

"There's the house, Mama! I remember it now! Look, Duncan!"

Sara also leaned forward, glad of the sight of the white columns and the terraces. She eased Sebastian's weight a little on her arm. Earlier in the day a messenger had ridden ahead to announce their coming to Madame Balvet; she had evidently set one of the servants to watch the road, for, as the carriage began climbing the slope to the house, the housekeeper's black-clad figure appeared on the portico. With her one free hand, Sara straightened her bonnet and tried to brush the dust from her gown. As the carriage halted, Louis' housekeeper came down the steps; despite the servant standing by in attendance, it was she herself who flung open the door.

"Welcome to Banon, Madame!"

She spoke warmly, reaching forward to lift the sleeping Sebastian from Sara's arms.

II

For the next two days Sara worked constantly, leaving the children to Annie's supervision, and immersing herself in the affairs of Banon. Her activity gave her no time to think on the problem which had sent her fleeing from Sydney; she was concentrated fully upon the business in hand. First, mounted on one of Louis' horses, she inspected every section of his farm, noting the condition of the crops, the livestock—and saying little. She listened to the slightly nervous talk and explanations of the two overseers—she listened, and treated it all with the same degree of reserve that would have been Andrew's, or Jeremy's. Then she closeted herself with them for a full day while the account books were gone through. These had been as honest as might be expected from two men left to their own devices for over a year. Her experienced eye on the figures told her that no questionably large sum of money had been spent on any one item. She knew quite well that the pair had not run the farm in Louis' absence without a thought for the lining of their own pockets, but that was to be expected. Louis had known before he left that he would have to pay in extra, unspecified ways for the services of men as experienced in farming as these two. Sara realised that she must accept the accounts without undue investigation. At the end of their long day together the men went off, touching their caps, relief stamped plainly on both their faces.

On the third morning of Sara's stay Madame Balvet came to her and insisted that she should inspect the house. Rather unwillingly Sara accompanied her; it had never been her intention to question the Frenchwoman's housekeeping; and she found it embarrassing to stand silently by while the linen was counted out, and checked off against a list. The storeroom accounts were in meticulous order—every pound of flour, every side of bacon recorded and accounted for. Gradually Sara began to see that, far from being reluctant to display the storeroom, the linen cupboards, the servants' pantry, Madame Balvet was actually eager to do so. This was an indirect form of boasting, a desire to show off a perfect piece of work. The inspection went from drawing-room, with its delicate china ornaments, and the furniture that had been dust-sheeted until Sara's arrival, to the bare cleanliness of the scullery-maid's bedroom—Madame Balvet pausing always to draw aside curtains, open drawers, and point out the fierce polish of the floors. She turned expectantly to hear Sara's praise. It was given in a rather astonished fashion, but without stint. The Frenchwoman appeared satisfied; a look of pride and pleasure came to her face.

When it was over, in a kind of ceremonial fashion, they drank tea together in the housekeeper's room at the back of the house. Sara watched the other woman's deft hands at work with the silver teapot and the spirit-lamp. They performed the ritual with care and ease.

She accepted the tea, and stirred it thoughtfully.

"You don't find it too lonely here, Madame Balvet? The distance from Sydney is so great . . ."

The Frenchwoman shrugged. "I am busy, you know. There is not time to be lonely. There is always much to be done.

Monsieur de Bourget will find I have not been idle during his absence.''

Watching her face as she busied herself with the cups, Sara was startled to see the expression there. It was an unguarded look, telling her how completely, even from the distance that separate⁴ them, Louis still dominated this woman.

III

Wearing a loose, silk wrapper, Sara sat before the fire in her bedroom at Banon, holding in her hands a sheet of paper, and reading over the half-dozen lines she had written.

"Cher Louis . . ."

She tapped quietly on the edge of the escritoire. She had meant to write him a full account of everything she had seen and heard at Banon in the past three days, while it all was still fresh with her; but even these few lines already had a tired air about them, an air of half-interest. Once more she dipped the quill in the ink, wrote a few more words, and then laid it down again.

It wasn't about Banon she wanted to write.

For the past week a single thought had turned itself over and over in her mind. Thrust into the background while she had worked over the farm accounts, it now reasserted itself, and demanded her attention. It had first come into her head at the same time that she had had positive proof of the weakening of her position in the colony since Andrew's death. The leading families had given what sympathy they thought her due, and were now prepared to forget her. And along with her, her children also.

David and Duncan, now eleven and nine years old, could no longer be entirely sheltered from the knowledge of the struggle every ex-convict fought against the stigma of his conviction. Even political offenders, like Jeremy Hogan, did not escape it. The prominent free settlers, and the officers of the Corps, had banded themselves into a tight little circle which no one who had sailed into Botany Bay for his crimes could hope to break. Through her marriage to Andrew, and her friendship with Alison Barwell, Sara had been accepted there. But with Andrew's death, his power ended, and now she was being pushed surely and quite definitely into the other camp—the emancipists, who stoutly claimed their own place in the colony's society, but who were steadfastly ignored by the ruling clique.

She had had this fact brought home sharply a week ago. Invitations had been issued for a birthday party for the eldest son of Captain Taylor of the Corps. Andrew had done a fair amount of business in London on Captain Taylor's behalf, and David and Duncan had always been prominent guests at young John Taylor's earlier parties. This year no invitation arrived at Glenbarr—and Sara knew none would be forthcoming. David knew it also. He had made only one mention of the fact, briefly, with an elaborate shrug of his shoulders. But before he turned away, Sara glimpsed the bright tears standing out in his eyes, and tears he refused to shed in front of her. Her heart ached for him—so young, and yet already understanding that his mother's past would not be forgiven her, that it would be laid on him and on his brothers.

"It doesn't really matter," he said. "In any case, I've always hated John Taylor. And I love you, Mama."

Duncan would be the next, she thought, as she slipped her arm about her eldest son's shoulders—if indeed he hadn't already realised vaguely that there was something about his mother that was unlike other women. She recalled the day when they had returned together from the township, dirty, with torn jackets, and David trying to wipe away congealing blood from a cut on his forehead. Both had refused to give any explanation of the fight—though Duncan had seemed bewildered, and looked frequently to his brother for guidance. David had hustled him out of the room before he could say very much. Sara had watched them go with disquietening thoughts.

That night she had paced Andrew's study in nervous recollection of the empty, lonely year that was past. Her position in the colony was ambiguous. There had been no invitations to any of the parties or receptions held during that time—and she admitted now that she had gone on desperately believing that this was out of consideration for her mourning. But there was no mention of invitations in the future, nor had one come from Government House for more than twelve months. Another year without social acknowledgment from Mrs. King would mean the end of the position Andrew had won for her in the colony.

The realisation of this had driven her, early the following morning, to write a letter to Madame Balvet, announcing her intention of bringing the children on a visit to Banon. But the inspection of farm and house was over, and now she must face her problems.

She touched the thick paper before her uncertainly. If she

accepted the situation as it stood, she told herself, her sons would grow up in an unhappy position midway between the emancipists and the officer-clique. And whom would they marry—the daughters of ex-convicts? They would, in time, fight Andrew's battle all over again; however little real thought they gave to it, unconsciously they would hold her responsible. Sara had no intention of being pitied by her own sons.

With sudden impatience she ripped the sheet across, screwed it up tight, and threw it into the fire.

"*Cher Louis . . .*" she wrote for a second time.

If only Louis would return—there was her salvation. Louis would come back to Banon, wifeless, and with a young daughter to take care of. No man remained for long in such a position. He must be made to marry her. If she were the wife of a free settler again there would be no need for David to pretend that he hated his friends, in order to spare her feelings—or for him to instruct Duncan in the things he must not say to her. Louis could do all this for her—if he would.

She frowned heavily over the words on the paper. This year of waiting had so far brought no letter from Louis. It was quite possible that he had married again in England; it was even possible that he no longer wanted to live here in New South Wales. Many things were possible, and the power of Madame Balvet must not be overlooked. The idea had taken only a week to grow in her mind, but already it possessed her utterly. Louis must return—and somehow be made to marry her.

"Louis! Louis . . . !" she whispered. "Why do you not come back?"

She thought with a kind of helpless rage of the distance separating them—the distance and the time. She realised uneasily the diverse influences which might be at work on him; other women would find him attractive, either for himself or his fortune; he might be beguiled by the ease and luxury of life in London; he might hesitate now to bring a young daughter to the loneliness of Banon. A dozen different things might combine to keep him away from her. She looked savagely down at the paper in her hands. Even this would take six months to reach him—and perhaps by then he would no longer care for the news of Banon.

The sense of her own inactivity infuriated her. She thrust her chair back abruptly, and began to pace the room. How did one influence a man at thirteen thousand miles distance? How did one, in the dull, hard-working life of the colony, compete against

the brilliance of London society? Did Louis remember her in
fashions that were outmoded, as the mother of three children
who always seemed to crowd about her? Her conversation lacked
the lustre of the drawing-room—and she did not possess the
mysterious quality of Madame Balvet. She pressed her hands
together as she paced. What could she do? Only write Louis that
his farm had been inspected with the ruthless efficiency Andrew
had taught her. She paused. Perhaps efficiency was not what
Louis looked for in a woman. Would he have preferred a
charming bewilderment?

She halted before the fireplace, her hands locked tightly
together.

"Andrew would have known what to do," she said aloud.
"He would have known how to handle Louis."

There appeared nothing incongruous to her in the idea that
Andrew would have bent his mind to this problem of Louis.
Marriage to the Frenchman, if it could be achieved, would be a
business proposition, a move which Andrew himself would have
approved. It would be a step taken to safeguard the interests of
his sons, to hold together the possessions he had built up, until
they were old enough to take them over from her. Andrew would
not easily have forgotten his own fight against her position as an
ex-convict, and the ways it might affect their children. He would
have been prepared to go to even these lengths to protect their
interests. She thought of Louis, his dark, thin face, and his air of
worldly wisdom. Comparing him with Andrew, she wondered if
it would ever be possible to love him deeply, apart from being
attracted by him—and she wondered if he would ever love her.
She thought Louis had the passion of love, but not the tenderness;
his knowledge of women would be wide, but superficial. Probably many had interested him for a time, but she doubted if any
one woman had ever wholly possessed him, absorbed him. Louis
would never sit at any woman's feet to take her orders. He was
an individualist, unpredictable; his emotions not to be trusted
completely, even in marriage. He was unbiddable, uncertain—
and somehow she must get him back to New South Wales.

Suddenly she dropped into the low chair before the fire,
balancing on the edge, and holding her hands to the blaze. The
heat scorched her face, yet she savoured the warmth which
seemed, momentarily, to take away her fear and doubts about the
future.

Then she cupped her chin in her hands. How would Jeremy

behave if she married Louis? Jeremy loved her; he worked with the purpose of three men because of that love, and the love he had had for Andrew. Many times during the past year she had thought about Jeremy—thought regretfully that his position was no better than her own. He might love her deeply, but his love would not benefit her children. Jeremy, who, after Andrew, was of greater worth than any man she had known, was an ex-convict like herself. Did he ever think of asking her to marry him? That much she never knew. He seemed to understand every thought in her head, the motive for every action; he knew all her harshness and cruelties, as Andrew had never done. It was always Jeremy who had pointed out her failings, forcing her to live up to his idea of what Andrew's wife should be. With no illusions about her, yet he still said he loved her.

Slowly, she shook her head at the thought. There must never be an exchange of love between herself and Jeremy. Emancipist and emancipist. . . . If she married again it must be to pull herself upwards, to regain what Andrew had won for her. Marriage to Jeremy would be going over completely to the opposite camp; that was not to even be considered. In ten years from now, her sons should not have to regret the follies their mother had committed.

But she was well aware that Jeremy had the qualities she would never find in Louis. Jeremy was devoted and loyal, with sometimes an unnameable tenderness in his voice when he spoke to her. For her sake he was working himself half to death on three farms that would never belong to him; all these years he had helped build up a fortune in another man's name. She supposed that she had loved Jeremy, in a fashion—not as her love for Andrew, nor for Richard—ever since the night of the convict raid on Kintyre. Perhaps it went back even before that, but her jealousy and suspicion had masked any love she might have felt. If it were possible . . . She shut her thoughts off abruptly. Jeremy was an ex-convict.

She rose and walked back to the escritoire. The blank page with its two written words stared up at her. She felt a sudden weariness and contempt for herself at the realisation of what she would do to Jeremy, and what she would do to her own feelings. She must presently sit down and write to Louis, calculatingly telling him how diligent she had been in his interests, convincing him in unwritten words how diligent a guardian she would be to his child. She knew she didn't in the least want to mother this unknown daughter of his, but that was part of the bargain she had made in her own mind.

She sat down again and picked up the quill. The trouble was that the bargain did, so far, exist only in her own mind. Louis was thousands of miles away, beyond her reach, beyond her influence. She gave a quick sigh, and then she began to write.

For more than an hour she wrote, and was still writing when she heard the sound of horses and a carriage in the drive beneath her window. She looked up at the clock; it was after ten, and no one travelled so late without good reason on the lonely Nepean road. Puzzled, she went to the window and drew back the curtains. The carriage had halted some distance away; there was a confusion of voices and sounds as servants called to each other and one of them scrambled to the roof to untie the boxes. Suddenly, in the light of the lanterns they had placed about, she recognised the figure of the man who stood talking to Madame Balvet. He turned and leaned into the carriage, and when he faced the light again, he was carrying a child in his arms, well wrapped in rugs against the cold March night.

Louis had come back to Banon!

Sara waited only long enough to see that no woman alighted with him, and then she let the curtain fall into place.

She hurried across the room, the draught of her passage sending the sheets of her letter swirling. They came to rest on the carpet with a gentle rustle. With her hand on the door-knob, ready to rush out into the hall, she paused, and turned back. Deliberately she walked to the dressing-table, bending close to it, examining her face carefully. Would Louis think she had changed? Had she grown older since he left? To her own eyes she didn't look any different, but how would he see her compared with the cherished pale complexions of London? From a drawer she brought out powder, and flicked it across her face, anxiously peering at the result. Her hair had already been loosened and brushed for the night; it hung over her shoulders, the same bright colour he would remember. She looked at it with satisfaction, and at the slimness of her figure, which the wrapper revealed. Then she went to the cupboard and took down another wrapper. It was sea-green silk, and Andrew had once said it was like her eyes.

Before she left the room she tore the pages of the letter in two; the pieces burned merrily on the fire. She watched them with a flush of excitement on her cheeks. The letter need never have been written. Louis had come back—alone.

The hall candles had all been hastily lit. The front door stood open to allow the manservant in with the boxes. The wind blew down directly off the mountains, and Sara shivered as she paused to take in the scene. Louis and Madame Balvet stood close together, talking excitedly in French; the child had almost disappeared into the depths of a high, winged chair. Her hood had slipped back, revealing black hair, and waxy white skin. Her eyes were closed; she took no notice of the bustle about her. Sara started forward.

Louis turned at the sound of her footsteps. Immediately, he came towards her with both hands outstretched.

"Sara!"

He wasn't changed. His tanned skin was as tightly stretched as ever across the prominent cheek bones; he had the same quick, light walk. He was smiling, and at the same time half-laughing.

"Come, Sara! No word of welcome for me?"

She took his hands tightly in her own. For a moment she found it difficult to speak; she had the sensation of tears pricking at the back of her eyes, and her throat was dry. She was disconcerted; she had not expected his return to affect her in this way. The eighteen months without sight of Louis had made him almost a stranger in her own mind. It was a relief beyond anything she had imagined to find him still familiar, still as he had left the colony. But there was an added familiarity. Crossing the hall, it seemed to her, for perhaps just a second, that she was moving forward to greet her own father. Here was the same thin, dark face, the lean body. Sebastian Dane might also have laughed in just this way.

"Louis!" she cried, in a low voice. "Of course, I welcome you! No one more than I. But this is so unexpected..."

He shrugged. "Am I to wait about in Sydney until you give me permission to come to my own home? We arrived back two days ago, and they told me at Glenbarr that you had gone to Banon. I told myself, 'Louis, there she is—taken possession, as always. She is ruling like a despot at Banon, while you kick your heels here in Sydney. Go and surprise her! Rout her!'"

He bent and kissed her hand. "And here I am!"

She smiled delightedly. "Never was defeat more welcome. I shall retreat with all possible speed and grace."

"Oh, but no, Sara! I shall have to have a few days to get used to seeing you, before I let you go back."

Her eyebrows shot up. "A few days...! I can't stay so long here alone."

"Let gossip make what it will of your staying here," he said shortly. "Are you not my business partner? And are you not...But, enough of this!" Laughingly, he tugged at her hand. "We chatter too much. Come, I want to present my daughter to you."

She was led forward to the winged chair. A middle-aged woman who was obviously a nurse stood diffidently waiting orders. Madame Balvet was there before them, touching the child on the shoulder to rouse her. Dark, sleepy eyes opened, and looked up wonderingly at Sara.

"Elizabeth," Louis said quietly, "this is Mrs. Maclay. You remember I told you about Mrs. Maclay's three little boys you should have to play with?"

For a few seconds the child stared uncomprehendingly. Then with an effort she collected her wits, and began to push herself forward in the big chair. She rose on unsteady legs, and started to sink in an uneven curtsy. Sara's hand stopped her.

"I'm glad to meet you, Elizabeth," she said gently.

The child did not answer, merely turned her eyes down to the floor. Her little white face looked pinched and cold, and she plucked at her cloak in a gesture of shyness.

Sara turned slightly. "Louis...?"

He nodded, signalling to his housekeeper. "She is so tired, ma petite! She has had too much travelling, too much excitement, after all the months of the voyage. In the morning..."

Madame Balvet stooped and lifted Elizabeth up into her arms. From her new height she regarded them solemnly.

"In the morning," Sara said, "you shall meet the three little boys. One of them is just your age."

For a second it seemed that Elizabeth would smile. But she nodded, with a quick jerk of her head, and then settled down against Madame Balvet's shoulder. Sara and Louis watched her as she was carried away. The nurse trailed behind uncertainly.

"I hardly know what to make of her," Louis said softly. "She's still shy with me, even after all the time we've been together. Precocious, I suppose, in ways—and I didn't mend matters there, for I spoiled her shamefully in London. I'm convinced she wasn't happy in that great barracks of a house in Gloucestershire, and yet I can't truly say she seems happy away from it. She might be better here. She rides, of course, as if she had been born on a horse—as she very nearly was. Her mother's nature is in her in parts.''

"Does she look like her mother?''

He smiled. "That's the one characteristic of her mother's I had hoped for—and Elizabeth has it in abundance. She will be a beauty.''

Then he touched her shoulder affectionately. "But let us not stand here, Sara! Come with me into the dining-room—Madame Balvet is sending food there.''

Sara sat with him while he ate supper, her fingers curling about the stem of the glass of wine he had poured her. Madame Balvet insisted upon waiting on him herself. She came and went with trays, two spots of unaccustomed colour showing vividly on her cheeks.

Louis talked rapidly as he ate—disjointed scraps of news, and questions thrown at Sara.

"England is at Nelson's feet—but most of them don't care for Emma—Bonaparte had his Grand Army camped on the cliffs of Boulogne.''

"Invasion?'' Sara asked.

He shrugged. "Nelson is there, anyway.'' Then he pointed a chicken leg at her, laughing. "But should the good people of England become too frightened of invasion, there's always the scandals of the Prince of Wales to divert them. Mon Dieu, how that man spends money! He lives, in what is presumed to be domestic bliss, with Fitzherbert—who, happily, has the Pope's brief to tell the world that she is truly married to His Royal Highness. Poor Princess Caroline is always in trouble of one sort or another—but the people who loathe the Prince rally about her.'' He gave an exaggerated shudder. "What atrocious taste she has! My belief is that she could have kept him faithful, more or less, if someone had taken the trouble to show her how to dress. He could hardly be expected to live with such a guy.''

He finished his wine, and pushed the empty glass towards Madame Balvet to be refilled.

"I made the acquaintance of the Barwells' Lady Linton,'' he said. "She still entertains the Prince occasionally. She's prodigiously fat. Always seems to wear purple, though I can't imagine why. Her complexion is the colour of an orange moon.''

Sara smiled at his expression.

He finished his meal, and turned directly to the housekeeper.

"The box I showed you, Madame—the small one—I should like it brought here."

She nodded, and left the room.

Louis turned back to Sara. "I saw John Macarthur several times when I was in London. He's pining to be back here. I think he's expecting to return fairly soon. The court martial, of course, was all in his favour, and I don't believe our unhappy Governor has come out of the affair very well. Macarthur has a plausible tongue, but the samples of merino wool he brought did far more to win him favour than any other thing. He comes back with a grant of land in the Cowpastures."

"Wool . . ." Sara murmured.

"What did you say?"

"I said, 'wool' . . . Wool will be more important to this country than anything else. Macarthur has seen that all along. Agriculture will not expand beyond our own needs, but wool will make our fortunes abroad."

"Always the business woman, Sara! You have not altered, my dear!"

She lifted her head, and her colour heightened a little.

"And why not? What else is there to occupy me here? I haven't any gossip of the Court, or of Nelson's mistress, to beguile you. Treat me kindly, Louis!"

"Then give me some of your own news—quickly!"

Her eyes darkened a trifle. "I had been writing you a letter when you arrived this evening. It was mostly news of Banon . . . But all that can wait till tomorrow. There is one thing, though, which I'm sure will interest you. They say the Governor has had reports of Matthew Flinders. Do you remember him, Louis—the young lieutenant who sailed in the *Investigator*, to map the continent for the Admiralty?"

He nodded. "But, of course! What of him?"

"He set out for England in the *Cumberland*—by the route through Torres, to the Cape. He put into Ile de France for repairs, and the news is that the Governor there, General Decaen, is holding him as prisoner of war."

"The man must be mad!" Louis said thickly. "Flinders was carrying a passport for a voyage of scientific exploration from the French Minister of Marine himself. Mon Dieu, what a return for the hospitality and sanctuary Governor King gave the French expedition, when they came under Baudin! There must be something more to this, Sara."

306

"Flinders' charts and maps," she said, "... they're all with him on Ile de France. You know what that means, Louis. If he is held there any length of time, Baudin will publish his own account of the voyage, and the explorations he made for France. And then Flinders's discoveries may be discredited."

Louis shook his head slowly. "So purposeless ... so stupid! Was he married?"

"Yes. Three months before he left England, in 1801. Apparently he was bringing his wife, but at the last moment she wasn't allowed to sail with him in the *Investigator*. And now she must wait until Decaen decides to let him go."

He fingered his glass, moving it round in a circle, and watching the wine gently tilting. "These men of science—what sacrifices they make for their mistress! Here is young Flinders, with logs and maps that are exquisite models of skill and patience, cooped up on Ile de France—and a bride of three months waits for him in England! Which of them, I wonder, does he love the better? Which would he sacrifice ... ?" Then he looked up. At a tap on the door, Madame Balvet entered, followed by a manservant, carrying an iron-bound box on his shoulder.

"Thank you," Louis said. "Put it there, by the fire."

He addressed the housekeeper. "Elizabeth—is she in bed now?"

The Frenchwoman nodded. "The nurse has attended to her. I imagine she sleeps already."

"Excellent! She will be better in the morning. Poor little one—she is so tired."

Madame Balvet cleared the last dishes from the table. She hesitated before the wine and the two glasses. Louis shook his head. "No, leave them."

She made no reply, and did not raise her eyes to either of them while she stacked the tray with dishes. She handed it to the manservant, lingering for a minute or two longer—purposeless lingering, which Sara quickly noticed. Then she left, closing the door noiselessly behind her.

Louis leaned forward to refill Sara's glass; his action was slow and deliberate.

"Now, Sara ... we can be peaceful. The voyager has returned to his own fireside, and the clamour of Europe fades! I am glad to be back—far more glad than I would have said was possible

307

five years ago." He paused there. "And you, my dear . . . ? How has this past year gone with you?"

She hesitated, looking sideways into the fire, twisting her glass nervously. The wine was dark; she moved it to see the play of the firelight through it, struggling to find the words to talk to him. He sat opposite, silent. She would almost have preferred his light-hearted mood of banter. There was no sense of peace here, as he had suggested. Suddenly she thrust back her chair, half-turning to the fire. Her movement shook the table, and a little of the wine spilled.

"This past year, since Andrew died, has been—damnable," she said. "Oh, you must be able to imagine how it's been. I'm occupied and busy from the moment I wake in the morning, until I go to bed again—and it all feels as if it's to no purpose. What point is there in the life of a woman who lives as I do now, when I remember what it used to be?" Her voice had dropped, and she kept the side of her face turned to him. "I'm a successful business woman, I'm the mother of three children, but, with all that, I'm lonely. I go out and inspect the farms, and I'm pleased—but who is there to share my pleasure? I buy a new gown, but it's black, and there's no one to care how I look in it."

She swung round, looking at him passionately. "That is not a woman's life, Louis—that is just existence! I grow inhuman and withdrawn. I feel it myself, and yet I can't prevent it."

Then she sank back in the chair. "They hung Andrew's murderer as high as the rest of the rebels, but justice gives me so little comfort. It cannot give me back the reason why I was content—happy—to work as I did. Now I busy myself in the affairs of my sons, but I have no heart for it."

He nodded, his hands resting on the arms of his chair. "This is all so true—and I can offer you no comfort. I have thought of you often, Sara, since I had your letter. Andrew's death brought me back here sooner than I planned—as soon as I could find the ship to take me. I suffered for you, but somehow I felt I was merely hearing news I had known in my heart for a long time. You and Andrew were too perfectly matched, too lucky. Everything was yours—and no thought stirred in either that didn't find its counterpart in the other. Heaven can well be jealous of such happiness. Mon Dieu, how others must have envied you—as I envied you!"

He lifted his hands expressively. "Well, it's gone now. Don't weep for what is gone, Sara. You're a greedy woman if you cannot be grateful for what you've had.''

She stirred restlessly, frowning. ''That is not enough to make me stop wishing for that time over again. Have you no heart, Louis?''

He smiled thinly. ''I have a heart—but it doesn't overflow with pity for you. You have been lucky, my dear, and luck doesn't last for ever. I grieved for Andrew, also—I know I shall miss him in a thousand ways. I cared for him as a friend, more than any man I have ever known. But he is dead, and, at some time, there must be an end to one's grief. Be glad for what you have had, Sara, and forget your self-pity.''

A look, half of surprise, half irritation, crossed her face.

''Self-pity . . . ? No one has ever suggested . . .''

''No. No one has suggested it, because everyone is too afraid of you. Only I myself am not afraid of you—myself, and possibly your overseer, Jeremy Hogan. Though even he, I doubt, would dare suggest such a thing to you. Oh, I knew exactly how you would pattern yourself to widowhood. I thought about you so often, and I believed I knew you well enough to see how it would be. And I fear that I was right.''

Humbly now, she said, ''Tell me!''

He began slowly. ''I knew you would fling yourself into Andrew's affairs—and work yourself to death in the mistaken notion that you were assuring the future of your sons. You would shut the world out of Glenbarr, and at the same time give it a model of how a widow should behave. You would make-believe that your heart was buried with Andrew, denying and holding back your own vigour and spirit—which you'll never succeed in stifling. You could lose the whole world, Sara, and you'd still remain yourself. Tell me, am I right? Isn't this what you've done?''

She answered thoughtfully, without looking at him, ''You could be right. But I haven't learned to look at it in this way.''

''Then it's high time you did. A year has gone since Andrew was killed, and you're not a woman of so little courage that you can't learn to live without him more successfully than you've done in the past. I expected more from you than this—and yet somehow I knew how well you would play the role your notions of respectability set you. Mon Dieu, Sara, you are not like the other gentle, simpering ladies of the colony, who must sit in their drawing-rooms and knit. You arrived here in a convict-transport. You have learnt harder lessons than those others will ever know; life can't now give you worse than you've already had. Why try to pretend that Andrew's death is a blow from which you'll never recover? This is false to yourself—wrong!''

"Enough, Louis!" she burst out. "You've said quite enough! I won't stand any more of it."

"Enough, then, it is!" His eyes were crinkled up with teasing laughter. "You sat there so meekly through it all, that I began to think you had indeed changed since I went away!"

Unwillingly she smiled also, though still annoyed and bewildered by what he had said, and yet unable to resist his mood. She felt his amusement at all her ideas of conventional behaviour, and she resented his parody of her position at Glenbarr. But there was rough justice in his remarks. No one, in recent years, had dared to recall to her her convict past, or to draw such sharp contrast between herself and the colony's other prominent women. He was right in saying she would never suffer again as she had during her imprisonment and the voyage in the *Georgette*—but only he would have dared to reason in this way, to trace the influence and effects of such experiences through her whole life, and because of them, pronounce judgment on her present behaviour. She thought on and around the subject, and she was forced to admit to herself that he was also right in saying that she was false to her true self in this effort to preserve the conventional aspects of widowhood; the young Sara of the *Georgette* would have scorned such practices, would have mocked the older Sara for pretending like this before Louis.

She smiled across at him now, quite broadly, thinking of how, ten years ago, she would have flung herself back into the business of rearranging her life to complete satisfaction after Andrew's death. In particular, she would not have given Louis the picture she had displayed of herself in the last half-hour. Too many years of comfortable, secure existence had dulled her wits, she told herself. Realising this, she suddenly relaxed completely, laughing, the strain wiped from her face.

He leaned forward again.

"You encourage me now," he said. "I thought the time would never come when it would be appropriate to present my gift."

"Your gift . . . ?"

He had begun to search in his pockets, and at last brought out a ring of keys.

"I pictured you languishing in your black gowns, Sara—and in the little time I had to prepare before we sailed, I found something for you which I hoped might bring you to revolt against them."

With this he rose and put the key he had selected into her hand, motioning towards the small chest.

"I should like you to look at it," he said.

She dropped to her knees before the chest, her fingers trembling slightly with excitement as she fumbled with the lock. It was well-oiled, and it sprang back easily. She was madly impatient.

Behind her, Louis said, "At great inconvenience, my dear Sara, I've kept it with me in my cabin. I was determined that this was one thing the sea-water would not spoil."

She was lifting out quantities of soft paper, scattering them on the floor about her; then she came on a loose, calico wrapping, and underneath it, the sheen of satin. She laid reverent hands upon it, bringing it up slowly to catch the light of the candles and the fire. It was a ball-gown of the deepest blue, with clusters of small pearls sewn into its folds—a gown to take her breath away. She sat back on her heels, looking at it.

She was silent for so long that at last Louis spoke.

"I presumed upon our friendship in choosing this for you. A personal gift, you'll think—even an intimate one. Perhaps a set of books for Glenbarr would have been more suitable. But if you'll accept this, you'll show me that you are the woman I believe you to be—that you . . ."

"Wait, Louis!" Her voice was harsh.

Quickly, with nervous fingers, she turned the shining gown around, holding it against her body, fitting it close to her. Its colour swam before her eyes, its richness—and it was like a challenge to her. She recalled the hour she had spent before Louis' arrival, the painfully-written letter, the frustration of believing him beyond her reach. He was so necessary to her plan and her purpose. Should she now try to carry him forward on the mood of their hour here together? Faced with this sort of situation Andrew himself would not have hesitated, nor, ten years ago, would she herself have hung back. She had good reason to curse the caution and prudence she had acquired. Why should she not reach out to what was well within her grasp, to secure it before other influences attempted to take it away? Was he teasing her with the intimacy of his gift?—he was capable of teasing her for many months yet, and Madame Balvet would always be there in the background. If she had the courage, she could end the doubts here—and within a few minutes.

"Louis . . . ?"

"I am listening," he said quietly.

Still on her knees, she twisted until she was facing him, the gown pressed against her.

"Louis . . ." She repeated his name slowly, conscious of holding back the next words.

Then she looked up at him fully. "Would you marry me, Louis?"

He dropped to his knees beside her, gently taking the gown from her grasp and flinging it across the chest. He put his hands on her shoulders, looking at her.

"Do you realise what you have said, Sara? Do you know what you have done?"

"I suppose . . ."

"No supposition, this!" he said firmly. "You *have* asked me to marry you."

His arms went about her, and he pulled her body in close to his. When he kissed her it was in a calculated fashion, as if he had known how he would do it. And yet she sensed that he found little satisfaction in it. His kiss was not an answer to her question—it might yet be another piece of provocation. She started to draw away from him.

He didn't release her, as she expected. He looked searchingly into her face for more than a minute. There were faint lines puckering his forehead, a look of inquiry. Then it faded, to give place to a gradual smile. The corners of his mouth twitched, and straightened themselves, as if he pulled them back before she should notice. Holding her by his left arm, he reached behind her to take the two cushions from the large chair that faced the fire. They made soft, dull thuds as they dropped to the floor. Carefully he caught her up in his arms, and laid her like a child with her head upon the cushions. She made only a slight motion to rise, and then her lips met his again. This time his kiss was not calculated, nor had she thoughts to analyse it; it gave her an exquisite sense of warmth and life, and the deepening feeling of discontent, which had hung upon her for so long, was stifled. It was deadly quiet in the room, and she heard, with a sharp, gratified pleasure, the sound of their breathing close together. Her hand moved slowly upon the roughness of his face, caressing it, and telling herself that the emptiness which had surrounded and oppressed her through these last months would be there no longer.

At last he drew back from her. She turned her head upon the cushions to watch him. He lay full length on the hearthrug beside her, leaning on one elbow, his chin resting in his hand.

"I thought," he said quietly, "that it would take you many, many months to speak to me like this. In Sydney they told me how it was with you—shut up there at Glenbarr, and never venturing out except for business. I knew I should never ask you to marry me while you persisted with that parody."

Suddenly he pointed a finger at her. "I was determined that I would make you want me, Sara. I would make you confess that you were tired to death of living alone—that your own passion would force you to make this demand of me. I swore—yes, I swore I would marry no woman who gave herself to me with a show of reluctance, even if to give herself the desired cloak of respectability. I will not live with this pretence you try to maintain. You will marry me because you *want* to—and not after a decorous interval of courtship, either. It must be quickly, so as to give the gossips nothing to say but that we did it because we wanted each other, and not to suit our mutual conveniences. In a month, perhaps—yes, I will send you away from Banon tomorrow, and in a month we shall be married."

"A month . . . ?"

"That is not too soon, Sara—because we need each other."

He leaned over towards her, brushing his lips against her hair, which lay tumbled in a dishevelled mass.

"You are so beautiful with the firelight on you," he said. "Your skin is warm, and I am tired of the marble-white English skins. Your hands are strong and possessive, Sara, and I have imagined their touch on me all these months past. I am filled with a mad longing to kiss your throat, and yet I hold back for the pure pleasure of looking at it. Oh, beauty . . ." His voice was barely a whisper.

He put his head on the cushion beside hers, his lips almost against her cheek. But he was content to rest there only a few moments. He shifted his body closer to hers, and, leaning over her, he gathered her up tightly in his arms.

Chapter Three

Five days after the notice of Sara's coming marriage to Louis de Bourget appeared in the *Sydney Gazette,* Jeremy presented himself at Glenbarr. Unannounced, he opened the door of the study where she was working, filling its frame with his bulk, standing silently until she turned to see who had entered.

Her startled glance took in his dishevelled clothes, and beyond him, in the hall she could glimpse Annie Stokes, wringing her hands in her habitual, nervous gesture.

Jeremy closed the door with a bang. He took a few steps towards Sara, extending a crumpled copy of the *Gazette.*

"This reached me yesterday," he said. "Is it true?"

She looked at him coldly. "If you refer to the announcement of my marriage—yes, it is true."

In sudden fury, he twisted the paper between his hands.

"God in heaven, Sara! Have you gone out of your mind? You can't be serious about this!"

"I'm perfectly serious. Why should I not be?"

"But you *can't* marry him! *Not* de Bourget!"

"And what objection have you to him?"

"None—in any position other than that of your husband. There were never two people less suited to live together. Think of it, Sara! I beg you to think again before you do this."

His tone had softened, and she looked at him in a more kindly fashion. The dust of the roads had gathered thickly on his clothes and boots; his black hair, hanging on his forehead, was damp with perspiration. A far cry, this, she thought, from Louis' elegance; yet it was very familiar, and, after a fashion, beloved to her. She had never learned to look at Jeremy without recalling the first years at Kintyre, the happiest time of her whole life.

"Tell me, Jeremy," she said gently, "tell me why you think I should not marry Louis de Bourget?"

The tension left his body somewhat as she spoke; the hand holding the rolled, crumpled paper dropped to his side. For a moment he seemed bewildered; slowly he walked across to the desk, bringing his fingers up to rest against the edge, and leaning towards her.

"Does one cage together two animals of a different species,

314

Sara? Does one try to wed happily two people of utterly dissimilar character, purposes, and thought? Louis de Bourget's mind and outlook is European—more than that—it belongs to France before the Revolution. To you, this colony is home, and the life, however crude and rough, is the shape of better things to come. To de Bourget, the colony is a refuge from all that he finds uncongenial in his old world. Although he may not consciously see it in this fashion, to him, the convicts here are like the peasants of France. There is a great wealth to be won from the soil, and at the expense of their labour. A new-born France, is how he sees it. It's a country where the laws of privilege and wealth hold good, where all power is in the hands of the few, and there exists a level of society even lower than the French peasant.''

"Careful, Jeremy!" she said. "These surely are the sentiments which earned you your passage to Botany Bay in the first place.''

He waved her words angrily aside. "Never mind the colour of my political sentiments! Listen to me, Sara! How can you possibly marry de Bourget, when he doesn't know one particle of what you have experienced here? How can he ever know the person you were once—the girl that Andrew brought to Kintyre? And can you, for the sake of his position, and his ideas of how his wife should behave, leave behind everything you and Andrew created together? Will you sell the store, the farms, the ships? Are you content to sit over your needlework all day? Because, if I am any judge of Louis de Bourget, that is precisely what he will expect of you!''

"How blind you are," she retorted angrily. "It's to keep the store, and the farms, and everything else I have, that I am doing this! Have you thought of that, Jeremy Hogan? Have you remembered that it isn't easy for a woman to carry on these things entirely by herself? Each time I give an order, or handle a transaction it is resented, because it is not backed by the authority of a husband.''

She drew in a swift, deep breath, feeling the furious colour spring to her cheeks. Her anger was beginning to match his own.

"And what of my children? What is to become of them? You know the emancipist problem as well as I do. Since Andrew's death I have been merely an ex-convict, and nothing more. My sons have been treated accordingly. Is it fair to bring them up to

315

face that situation, and the knowledge that they are not accepted by the people they would wish to know?''

"Your sons are also Andrew's sons," he said firmly. "Not one of the three will be a weakling, unable to fight his own battles. They'll make their way wherever they choose, and there'll be no barrier they cannot cross if they so wish. At least, give them the chance to do it themselves—don't impose upon them the worse burden of a stepfather who is at odds with his environment, who will sneer at the commerce and trade which Andrew taught them to look on as their world. Would you give them thoroughbred horses and soft hands—and have them grow up not knowing a spade from a plough?''

"My sons need a father," she said sullenly. "And I . . . I need a husband.''

Perspiration was breaking out on his forehead; his hands, pressed against the desk, trembled slightly.

"If it's a husband you want, Sara—then, marry me! Surely I'd fit that role better than Louis de Bourget?''

Her mouth dropped open; the colour mounted again rapidly in her face, until her cheeks were two patches of scarlet.

"You!'' She choked over the word.

He looked at her steadily for some moments, his eyes narrowing as they concentrated on her face. The perspiration stood out in beads on his forehead; he put up one hand and wiped it impatiently, his eyes never leaving her. Then, quite abruptly, he leaned still further forward until his face was within inches of her own.

"No! That wouldn't do for you, would it, Sara? I'm merely another ex-convict. By marrying me you'd be hopelessly ruined, and your children also. But you'll marry this Frenchman without counting whether or not he loves you—or whether you love him. If you searched the whole world you wouldn't find a man less like Andrew in every way—and yet this is the man with whom you choose to spend the rest of your life. Are you going to buy your way into pompous little receptions at Government House with this wedding? Would you rather your sons were bathed in viceregal smiles—or that they turned out men like Andrew?''

Suddenly he slapped his open hand down on the desk.

"Damn your mercenary little soul, Sara! You're not worth any man's regard!''

He drew back, his expression frowning and dark.

"Well, go ahead, marry your Frenchman—but you've lost

316

your overseer! I'll be damned if I'll slave out my guts to provide more gowns for Madame de Bourget to wear to Government House! Farm your own land in future! Do what you like with it—it's no longer my concern. The day you marry de Bourget, you can stop sending your instructions to me—I won't be at hand to receive them.''

"Jeremy!' she said faintly. "You wouldn't leave! What would you do . . . ? Where would you go . . . ?''

"I'll be occupied using my time to my own advantage,'' he said shortly. "You've had enough of my life—from now on it will be my own.''

She jumped up quickly. The papers on the desk fluttered briefly, and subsided.

"Wait!'' she said harshly. "Wait, Jeremy! You can't leave me like this . . . !''

He stepped back from the desk. The crumpled newspaper he had held fell to the floor.

"It's high time you learned that you can no longer say, 'Do this,' and 'Do that,' and expect to be obeyed. You seem to forget that I'm free. I do what I want now—and that includes telling you that I'm finished with you. I'll bring the farm accounts up to date, and send them here to Glenbarr. There'll be no need for us to meet again.''

He turned and strode to the door; he opened it, and then, after a pause, his hand fell away from the knob. He wheeled around, fumbling in his pocket.

"I'd forgotten . . . I called at the Ryder Farm on the way down. Mrs. Ryder asked me to deliver this note.''

He crossed the room and laid a letter on the desk. He took no further notice of Sara, nor did he bang the door as he left. Outside, she could hear him calling to Annie for his hat. Listening carefully, after a few minutes she heard the smart clop of horse's hooves in the drive.

Only then did she reach for Julia's letter. She tried to control her rage as she broke the seal.

"My dear Sara,

"I trust that in time you will be able to forgive me for writing as I do now. Believe me, I do so only in the hope that you may pause to consider what you are doing in committing yourself to marriage with Louis de Bourget.

"My dear, can there be any real happiness in this for

either of you? Are you content to give up all you and Andrew have built since the beginning of the colony, to retire to Banon? Or has Louis de Bourget decided to give up Banon to suit your interests? I sincerely hope that you are not attempting to compromise between the two ways of life—for I see the result only as confusion and unhappiness . . ."

Angrily, Sara read to the end. The whole letter was Jeremy's words over again, though less forcefully expressed. When she reached Julia's signature, she crumpled the paper in her hand, screwing it into a tight ball and letting it fall to the desk. Damn all of them! she thought. They thought they knew what was best for her—they thought they could bid her carry on as she had been doing for the past year, and that she would meekly do as she was told. They strove to see, Julia and Jeremy, a bent in Louis' character that would run contrary to her own, a difference of purpose that would give them no peace together. She clenched her hands in defiance.

There had never been any intention in her mind—and she didn't believe there was in Louis' either—of selling the farms or the store. He knew that they were not hers alone, that they belonged to her sons. When they had discussed them, he had suggested bringing an experienced manager out from England to run the store, and perhaps two farmers, with their families, to help Jeremy. Naturally, after their marriage, Louis would expect more of her time than she was at present able to give—but she felt that he would be patient until her London agents could find such people as she needed.

Suddenly, to her intense annoyance, tears began to slip down her cheeks. She brushed at them with the back of her hand, but could not check them. They were wrong, Julia and Jeremy, and whoever else was disposed to think as they did. She would show them all what Louis was prepared to do for her sake—and what she would do for his. They were not children, either of them, unused to the ways of the world; they had much to give each other, much to contribute to marriage. Louis knew that she meant to hold every part of Andrew's property intact; he had agreed to marry her knowing that. So much for Jeremy's rage and scorn! So much for Julia's cautious warnings!

And still the tears could not be kept back. She was forced to face reality, and the fact that Jeremy was gone. He was gone to the sort of freedom he had not known for fifteen years. She preferred not to recall that he wanted to marry her—the person of Jeremy did not weigh up evenly with the other considerations against him. He was free of her now—free to do exactly as he pleased. But the future without Jeremy was bleak and somewhat frightening. Very slowly she began to unfold and smooth out Julia's letter again; it was difficult to read, with the blur before her eyes.

II

Until the day she was married, a little more than a month after Louis' return from England, Sara expected a message, or a visit, from Richard—but none came. At first she waited eagerly, and then became resigned to the fact that here was another who anticipated disaster from her marriage, or who was too jealous to even acknowledge the necessity of this step she was taking. After giving the situation some thought, she was able to shrug away her dismay; she should have expected no better from Richard.

She and Louis were married on a morning in April, with no one but the Ryders, Sara's three sons, and Elizabeth de Bourget to witness the ceremony. David, Duncan, and Sebastian were quiet, but, on the whole, Sara judged, they were well content. They remembered Louis, and his constant visits, when Andrew had been alive, and to them he was a liked and trusted friend. But on Elizabeth constraint and uncertainty were plainly visible. Occasionally Julia, who had deliberately placed herself near Louis' little daughter, touched her arm soothingly. The child was obviously bewildered by the whole situation, and she seemed to be glad of the attention Julia gave her.

That night Glenbarr blazed with lights. The rooms were filled with the scent and colour of flowers; in the dining-room long tables were loaded with food—Louis' French cook had come from Banon to prepare the supper, and it was something that would be talked over for many weeks after. Polished silver gleamed, and the wine stood waiting. White-gloved servants from Banon glided through the rooms, lighting the last candles. Bennett stood in the hall, magnificent in a hunting-green livery of his own design, directing his helpers. The carriages began to roll up the drive in their numbers for the first time in over a year.

Sara stood beside Louis to receive their guests. She wore the blue satin gown he had brought her from London; her hair was elaborately dressed, her tanned skin lightly powdered. The gown might have graced a Court function; it was too magnificent for a place like Sydney, but it gave her satisfaction to wear it and have Louis look at her as he did. He tapped his foot a little on the floor as he waited—in his brocade coat and powdered hair he looked more Gallic than ever in the midst of these English faces. People streamed in, their glances quizzical, their eyes ready to notice and to criticise. The Abbots came, the Macarthurs, the Pipers.... Smiling, Sara graciously took the hand of each in turn. The Pattersons, the Johnstons, the Campbells, the Palmers, all presented themselves. So many of these people were, at one time, Glenbarr's frequent visitors, but had been absent since Andrew's death. She knew that many of them did not approve of her any more now than they had done formerly, but, as the wife of Louis de Bourget, they were obliged to receive her back into their circle. In the midst of all the gaiety her thoughts went to the little bush wedding in the Ryders' house twelve years ago, where the only colour in the scene was not the silks and satins of the women she saw here tonight, but the scarlet tunics of the few officers of the Corps that she and Andrew had been proud to welcome as their guests. She recalled the work and love that had gone into the preparing of the rough, unfinished house on the Hawkesbury, and the happiness she had known there. And then she visioned Banon, white, and elegant, and cool.... She *would* be happy again, she told herself. They were wrong, the people who believed this marriage would be a disastrous one. She thought of Jeremy, who to-day would have taken the last of his belongings away from Kintyre. Silently her lips formed his name. The faces passing before her swam in a blur.... William Cooper's dull, kindly one; Julia's anxious and searching; a young, laughing girl's, whom she did not recognise. She turned from them and her disturbing thoughts, and sank into a deep curtsy as the Governor and Mrs. King arrived.

Finally, Captain and Mrs. Barwell were announced. They came forward unhurriedly. Alison was exquisitely groomed and gowned in peach-coloured brocade, but, for all her beauty, looking as frail as a piece of glass. Richard, splendid in dress uniform, was sullen and ungracious. He bent over Sara's hand kissing it, but as he straightened he did not look into her eyes.

And later it was said of Richard Barwell that he disgraced

himself that night, and shamed his wife, by being noticeably drunk.

III

Sara and Louis went to Banon immediately after they were married. The countryside was quiet in the dried-out browns of autumn; the house above the river plains looked as settled as if it had been there always. It was no longer a raw, white gash on the landscape, but sunk back, and warm against its hill. The days were golden and full of sun; at night they burned wood fires late, and Sara drew from Louis his memories of the months in England. Europe seemed far away, almost a dream; tales of the London ballrooms, and the games of faro that lasted through the night, might quicken her imagination, but close at hand her own affairs were absorbing and rich. For almost four weeks she was lazily content.

Madame Balvet was no longer there to disturb the contentment. Her successor was a soft-spoken Irishwoman, who listened with deference to Sara's instructions. Madame Balvet was lodged in Sydney, waiting for the first possible passage back to England. The Frenchwoman's real position at Banon was never explained or discussed; Mrs. Fagan slipped into the role of housekeeper as quietly as if there had never been a change at all.

When Sara's idyllic month was almost up, the first disturbing news found its way into the peace of Banon. Clapmore was ill, and the overseer, newly engaged to run the Toongabbie farm, had been killed by a falling tree, as his men worked to clear more land for pasture. Louis tried vainly to soothe her agitation, and, at last, rather unwillingly, agreed to go back to Sydney with her. During the journey she noticed he was often silent.

She found that that month with Louis was to be a pattern of their married life. He made it quite clear that he wanted her at Banon; as often as possible she travelled up from Sydney, diligently organising the whole retinue of children and servants to come with them. But she always went with a backward glance to all she had left undone in matters concerning the farms and store. Clapmore was well again, and a new overseer had been found for the Toongabbie farm. But, even together, they could not greatly relieve the pressure on Sara herself. Clapmore, though conscientious, had not the authority necessary to deal with the questions that required her attention; the overseer, an emancipist, drank too much, and was too free with the men. At best, they—Clapmore and the three principal overseers—were poor substitutes for Jeremy Hogan.

But she stifled her frustrations and went to Banon whenever she could—and Louis' good humour returned. A week or two they would spend there, while Louis toyed with his farming, smiling indulgently to see Sara immediately assume control of the overseers and labour. He was amused by the children; he seemed to enjoy taking their lesson hours out of Michael Sullivan's hands. Outside the huge, bright room at the end of the portico, that had lately become the schoolroom, Sara often paused to listen to Louis' voice repeating Latin verbs; very soon she noticed that her sons had ceased to pronounce their few words of French with an Irish accent. The happy sound of their laughter, Louis' mingling with it, reached her constantly.

She found that it took time and great patience to adjust herself to marriage with Louis. He was not as easily commanded as Andrew had been, or as easily pleased. He expected much from a woman; once, he had breathed the heated, over-civilised atmosphere of the Paris salons, and the gaze he now turned on a woman was forever coloured by those years. She strove to please him in a hundred different ways—her costume must be immaculate and appropriate from early morning until they retired late at night; she ordered gowns extravagantly, and they were far too many and too magnificent for the society of the colony. But Louis always dined, even when alone, with great ritual and elegance, and her own toilette must match it. She slipped into the habit of speaking French with him, and in their long talks together she learned that her conversation must never touch more than passingly on the subject of crops or trade. These did not amuse, or even interest him much, and were hardly matters to be introduced over the dinner table, or in the drawing-room. Louis talked as her father, Sebastian, had once done—bringing to the inevitable sameness of the gatherings they attended a whiff of a sophisticated, cultivated world. She was hard put to keep pace with him.

His challenge excited her. Physically and mentally he drained her energy, and still stimulated her—at times to an almost unbearable pitch—able to make love to her, even across a room, by a mere change in his expression, or the tone of his voice. So completely did he absorb and fascinate her, that she began to fear she might lose the struggle to keep her own personality intact.

322

He was capable of great passion and great tenderness; she sometimes wondered uneasily if her preoccupation with him might succeed in ousting her own ambitions for her sons. A battle of wits and strength developed between them; they played at it laughingly in the brittle, clever fashion that was Louis' way, and yet they were deadly in earnest.

The periods they spent together at Banon were always too short. News would reach Sara of trouble at one of the farms, or at the store, and then she would fume impatiently until she could be on her way to attend to it. In swift succession the *Thrush*, *Thistle*, and *Hawk* returned to Sydney, and on each occasion there was no possibility of dealing with the business of their cargoes from the remoteness of Banon. The procession of carriages and baggage started back to Glenbarr once again, and Louis' expression was thunderous.

As usual, Captain Thorne came to see her at the house.

"My compliments on your marriage, ma'am," he murmured, bowing over her hand. "Doubtless, marriage suits a woman well— but, I'm thinking that, if you're to run your ships successfully, you'd best be wedded to your desk."

His gruff old voice went on.

"Monsieur de Bourget, I recall, was part-owner in your late husband's day. He'll assist you now, surely?"

Louis made no excuses for refusing to have any part in Sara's business dealings.

"I have no intention of turning myself into a slave," he replied shortly. "And it will be better for you, Sara, the sooner you realise that that is precisely what you are making of yourself."

Their disagreements were fairly constant, but not serious, until Louis learned that she was going to have a child. He wanted to take her to Banon, and force her to remain there until the child would be born, the following May. This step she had foreseen, and dreaded; she begged him to remain at Glenbarr. They bitterly fought the question for two weeks, and then Louis finally gave in. She knew quite certainly he believed that, by continuing to refuse his help, she would reach a stage where there was no alternative but to part with some of Andrew's property.

"Sell it, Sara!" he urged. "Sell it! There's no woman alive who can manage all you attempt, and give proper attention to her children. You'll kill yourself—and break my heart."

"I can't sell—nothing belongs to me," was her only reply to

this. "If I leave the farms and the store to look after themselves, they'll go to pieces—the ships' masters will trade just according to their own inclinations. And then what has become of the value of my sons' investments?"

"Oh . . . !" This turn of the conversation aways made him furious. "You talk like a shopkeeper!"

"That's precisely what I am, of course!" she retorted.

In the midst of their quarrelling, her thoughts constantly turned to Jeremy. If only Jeremy were at hand to entrust with all this business—his knowledge of farming was second to none in the colony, his shrewd eye would run over the store accounts in a few hours. But Jeremy was gone completely now; he had bought a farm on the Hawkesbury and reports came to her that the young, and rather pretty, woman who had been assigned to him as housekeeper was very obviously living quite happily with him as his mistress. As long ago as the days of the first *Thistle,* Andrew had, as a gesture of gratitude to Jeremy, invested a small amount of money for him in the cargo; with every voyage the profit had enlarged, and by the time of Sara's marriage to Louis, he had gained control of enough money to buy the mortgage of Theodore Woodward's farm, four miles from Kintyre. He lived there now, with sixteen labourers, and the young convict woman, whom gossip reported variously from downright plain, to beautiful. Sara shrugged her shoulders at the news, and tried to remain unconcerned.

From Richard there was no sign or communication—except the quarterly instalment paid off against his debt, which he now always handed over to Clapmore. Occasionally Sara met him with Alison in various Sydney drawing-rooms, and twice he attended a reception at Glenbarr. But his face was no more expressive than dull, pleasant William Cooper's might have been, as he bent over her hand. If he appeared in the store to make a purchase, it was always at a time when it could be safely reckoned she would not be there. One day, as she set off with David to walk from the store back to Glenbarr, she saw him directly ahead among the crowd that thronged the dusty street. It was a terrible moment when she realised that he had deliberately turned down a side street to avoid her.

Elizabeth de Bourget could not be counted among the difficulties that clouded this first year of her marriage to Louis. The three boys plainly delighted in their little step-sister; she had the makings of a coquette, capricious, wayward, and charming. For the first weeks she was shy, and rather bewildered by the demands made upon her by this new country, and by her step-mother and step-brothers, but her confidence increased as she came to realise the security of her position, and was petted and fussed over. She rode, as Louis prophesied, as if she had been born on a horse; she delighted in showing off, urging her pony to feats which even David did not attempt. She didn't seem to hold any resentment against Sara; Louis himself was a person only a little less new in her experience, and she never appeared to connect either of them with her own mother. As the months went by she was not more diffident than her step-brothers in claiming Sara's attention and love. Sara herself often pondered the situation with vast relief and satisfaction.

At the end of February, 1806, the procession of carriages and baggages once again set out from Glenbarr. Sara had finally given in to Louis' demands that she should rest until the birth of her child, in May. Banon, she had argued, was too far away, and, instead, suggested going to Priest's. Louis countered this by pointing out that the farmhouse at Priest's was too small to hold themselves, the four children, the tutor, and the servants; his unspoken objection to the place was that it was too close to the centre of Sara's activities to give her the complete rest he knew she needed. In the end they compromised on Kintyre—almost as remote as Banon, but connected by better roads with Parramatta. Louis listened to her arguments about getting a doctor and midwife quicker, if she needed them, and at last agreed.

The final concession she wrung from him was a digression on the journey to visit Priest's, and the Toongabbie farm. Her heart warmed at the sight of the two farms, thriving, prosperous, bearing the marks of Jeremy's care. With a touch of excitement she pointed out to David and Duncan the increase in the merino flocks. At the last counting there were altogether more than twenty thousand sheep in the colony, and the triumph of Macarthur's merino strain was beginning to turn the thoughts of the farmers to overseas markets.

"They need the wool in England, David," Sara explained, as she stood with him, Duncan and Elizabeth, leaning together on the fencing of the field where the Priest's merinos grazed. "England can never be quite certain of getting all the merino wool she needs from Spain. And the quality of the wool Spain sends isn't always as good as what we produce here, even now."

She shielded her eyes from the sun, and gazed across the paddocks, dried and brown by the length of the summer.

"This climate and pasture seems to suit the merino. In a few years we'll be producing a grade of wool that will fetch better prices in London than any of the Spanish stuff."

Elizabeth had hauled herself up on to the first rail of the fence for a better view of these creatures, on whose backs money was literally growing. They seemed unnaturally large by comparison to the sheep she had seen grazing in the quiet pasture of the English shires.

"But if the flocks keep on increasing like this, Mama," David said, putting his hand on Elizabeth's shoulders to hold her more firmly in her position, "where will we put them? I've heard Mr. Macarthur say there'll not be enough land."

Sara gave him a sideways glance—he was twelve years old, and he was beginning to advance beyond a child's acceptance of farming just as it appeared to the casual eye. She had seen him often with books on botany and agriculture; to Louis' amusement he had started to ask what prices the wheat and wool had brought.

Sara said thoughtfully, "We need another man with Matthew Flinders's spirit, Davie. We need someone to find a way over the mountains. There's sheep country beyond them—most people are certain of that. When we get over the mountains, there'll be plenty of room."

Chapter Four

As the dusk came down on the Hawkesbury, it lent a dark, sinister appearance to the swollen flood-waters, which, since the beginning of March, had swirled and lapped, inch by inch, to forty feet above the normal height of the river. At the dining-room window, Sara paused to look at the desolate waste before her, at the stretch of water where Kintyre's lower fields had been, at the currents and eddies, which she judged must roughly mark the submerged trees lining the opposite bank.

The flood was seasonal, but this time it had not come with a spectacular wall of water, sweeping down after heavy rains in the mountains. Its approach had been gradual and relentless. For a whole month the farmers living in the valley had woken to the

326

pounding of rain on the roofs, and day by day the Hawkesbury had crept higher. There had been a brief halt; the level fell a little, and then resumed its advance. Livestock was shifted, and houses abandoned; families moved into the farms of neighbours who inhabited higher ground. The water still rose. In some places the settlers tarried too long, and had to be taken out of their lofts, and off their roofs by boat. The rescue work was confused and unco-ordinated; there were reports of drownings. Sara had spoken to soaked, dispirited farmers, whose tales never varied—livestock drowned or strayed, houses under water, haystacks swept away.

From Kintyre's windows they could see, in the centre of the flood-water, a vicious current, which seemed to follow the original course of the river. In the last three days they had watched it tell its own tale of destruction. Sometimes a horse struggled frantically against it, trying to gain the bank; it carried the swollen carcases of cattle and sheep; haystacks rode it merrily, until dragged down into miniature whirlpools; the liberated furnishings of flooded houses sailed past—rocking-chairs, pictures, oak tables. The rain was ceaseless, monotonous—dreary grey skies greeted them each morning, and showed no signs of breaking. An odour of decay hung over the river; there were decomposing bodies of animals caught in the branches of the few trees that remained above water; snakes and enormous, ugly lizards were cast up, and taken on again as the level rose. The air was sour with the smell of mud and rotting crops.

Sara turned wearily from the window and went back to her task of sorting out the clothes which lay in bundles on the long table. Kintyre had not escaped the reach of the flood, although she knew, almost certainly, that the house itself was safe—Andrew had built it well above the level of the traces left by past floods. But the haystacks were gone and some cattle, not yet counted, wese missing. The outhouses down at the bottom of the slope had disappeared five days ago. For consolation, she recalled the sheep, safely penned in tiny, improvised stockades in the muddy fields at the back of the house. It was not pasture land up there, and there was no grazing for them. The sheep, along with the penned-up cattle, had to be hand-fed. They stood desolately in the rain, complaining loudly to the unrelenting sky. The horses in the stables were restless for want of exercise.

She finished roughly sorting the clothes into their appropriate groups. All through the colony there would be an appeal for

327

clothes and blankets for the families forced to abandon their homes to the flood. Kintyre had already taken in its own share of the refugees; when the river had risen so sharply three days ago, four farmers, who were settled on low-lying ground bordering the Maclay property, brought their wives and families for shelter. The men themselves went back immediately to continue with the work of rounding up cattle, and saving some of their household goods. Two of the wives, waiting only to deposit their children with Sara, and give a garbled account of their losses and the destruction throughout the whole of the valley, left to go back to help their husbands. The two women who remained, Susan Matthews and Emily Bains, occupied the sitting-room exclusively, passing the time lamenting their misfortunes, and offering thinly-veiled criticisms of the hospitality Sara gave them. The children of the four families, seven in all, shared the veranda with Elizabeth and the three boys. They had each been forbidden to move beyond it, and they fretted at the restriction placed on their liberty. They played, quarrelled, resorted to blows frequently; their howls and laughter had been part of each daylight hour for the past three days. It could have been much easier, Sara thought resentfully, if either of the women had taken them in hand—but there seemed little hope of that. The six convict servants, which the four families had brought along with them, were determined to enjoy their unexpected spell of leisure. Cramped together, they filled a small sitting-room, gossiping ceaselessly, and making no attempt to help Annie Stokes, or Bess and Kate, Sara's other two servants—and no orders to do so were forthcoming from their mistresses. There seemed to be a spirit among the refugees urging them to give as much trouble as possible; Sara guessed that in their years of struggle on the river, they must often have envied the good fortune of Kintyre's owners, and now when they found themselves planted here they made their presence felt in no uncertain fashion. The house was bedlam; it was cold, disarranged, and strewn with rough mattresses. The muddy tracks left by the children's boots had stained the rugs, their fingermarks were visible on all the walls. And along with that, the unending sound of the rain had pitched their nerves near to breaking point.

Sara left the dining-room and made her way down the darkening passage in the direction of the kitchen. Many times in the past week her thoughts had gone to Jeremy, wondering how he had fared through this period. He was fortunate that the site of the farm he had bought was as favourable as Kintyre's own. His predecessor, old Theodore Woodward, had been one of the first settlers on the Hawkesbury, and, with an eye to Andrew's sound choice, he had had the pick of the high ground. She supposed that, like them all, Jeremy's crops had suffered, even if he had managed to keep his livestock intact. She wished that there might have been some news of him—that he himself might have come to inquire how they were at Kintyre. But there was little likelihood of that—his house would be as crowded with homeless people as her own was. She was conscious of a stab of annoyance at the thought of Jeremy's young convict housekeeper playing hostess to a swam of refugees.

She entered the kitchen and went to the long trestle table, which had been set up there for the children's meals, to light the lamps. In the scullery beyond, Bess and Kate washed dishes and gossiped. Annie closed the oven door with a blackened cloth, and turned to speak to her mistress.

"Them, ma'am," she jerked her head in the direction of the sitting-room, "are eating their heads off—and in such comfort, too, if you please! This is the second baking in three days. If the rain don't soon end, we'll not be able to feed them."

Then she laid down the cloth and came closer to Sara. "Why, ma'am, you're as pale as a sheet!" Her thin, wrinkled face was screwed up in consternation. "Been overdoing it . . . that's what! I just wish the master was here to see that you rested proper—you coming near to your time, an' all!"

"Yes, Annie," Sara answered soothingly, bending over the lamps once more. Hardly an hour of the last three days had gone by that she had not breathed a sigh of thankfulness that Louis was *not* at Kintyre. Ten days ago he had left for Sydney, when a message arrived from Clapmore that the *Hawk* had returned from India. With a shrug of his shoulders, Louis had prepared to go and meet Captain Thorne in his wife's place, good-humouredly joking about the high commission he would demand, Kintyre was lonely without him. Sara had expected him back within two weeks, but, when the rains brought the level of the water always higher, and with it, the crowd of women and children from abandoned homes, she began to hope that the flood would delay his return indefinitely. It was impossible to imagine Louis amid this chaos, or to believe that he would be willing to share the communal meals. To see Louis marooned by floods at Kintyre would be bad enough, but marooned along with chattering, quarrelling women and eleven children was unthinkable.

"Perhaps it's just as well he isn't here, Annie," Sara added. "With all this . . ." She didn't finish the sentence, but her gesture indicated the confusion of the house, the noise that never ceased while the children were awake.

Annie paused a moment, and Sara read in her face a look of mingled amusement and dismay at the thought of Louis' fastidious elegance among all this disorder.

"Ah . . . perhaps you're right, ma'am." Annie threw a shrewd glance at Sara. "But don't you fret . . . We'll have them out of this in no time now, and then you'll be able to rest—as you should be doing."

As she spoke, Annie's eyes swept the long table, laid with places for the children's supper. "Well, we'd best be calling the young rogues in now, and have done with this business." Then, in dismay, she clapped a hand over her mouth. "Begging your pardon, ma'am. I wasn't meaning Miss Elizabeth or your three."

"That's all right, Annie. It's difficult to distinguish these days. But, yes—call them in. Perhaps they'll be quieter when they've had something to eat."

Annie turned and raised her voice. "Bess! Go and bring the children indoors. And see if you can keep them quiet! My ears are fit t' burst with the noise they're making."

Bess came to the doorway, wiping her hands in her apron.

"I thought one of them other lazy sluts was supposed to keep order. Like a circus—that's what this house has been like since they all came. It's not right . . ." She went off down the passage, still muttering.

Sara pretended she didn't hear. She couldn't blame Bess, or anyone else, for feeling resentful. These other women had descended upon them like locusts, taking food and shelter without a word of thanks, expecting to use Kintyre as if it had been an inn. Sara flushed with irritation to think of their ingratitude. Moving the sheep and cattle had meant a great amount of extra work; the stockades had been hastily improvised, and each man on the place did the work of three to keep the livestock within bounds. Even Michael Sullivan had left his pupils, and was working every daylight hour with the convict labourers. But indoors eight women sat about idly all day, not even making a gesture to help with the cooking. Sara did not dare to voice a protest; the story would be wildly distorted, and, years from now, it would be flung up in her face that she had been chary of hospitality at a time when every house above water along the river had been regarded as a natural refuge. She could only hope, along with Annie, that they would soon be left in peace.

She took a loaf of bread from a side table, and began to cut it. She glanced across at Annie, briskly dishing out meat and vegetables, and envied the speed and energy in her movements. Her own body felt heavy and sluggish; she looked down at it with a frown of distaste, and tried to drape her long shawl more becomingly. The seven weeks ahead of her until the child would be born seemed endless. This pregnancy had been much more irksome than the earlier ones; the time had passed slowly, and yet it had been crowded with the effort of attending to her business affairs, and still meeting Louis' demands that she should rest. Louis waited patiently for the child's birth. He was tender to her, considerate, and quiet—not talking much about the child, but she knew that the extra attention he gave to the running of Banon was given with the thought of a son to inherit it. She glanced down again at her ungainly body, and prayed, for Louis' sake, that it would be a son.

The children came crowding in then, pushing a little in the doorway, and looking expectantly towards the table. Elizabeth was in the middle of them, a flushed, wild expression on her face, a frill torn from her hem. Sara could not help a smile when she saw her; Elizabeth's prim manners had slipped noticeably, and now she claimed her place at the table without any hanging back, her manner plainly announcing to the others that Kintyre's wide kitchen belonged to her and her step-brothers. Her gestures were unmistakably Louis'.

A slight, red-headed son of Sam Murphy's smiled up at Sara as she placed a plate before him.

"We caught a snake, Madame de Bourget. Killed it, too! It was *this* long . . ." His arms stretched to their fullest extent.

Her nose wrinkled in disgust. "Horrible things! I'm glad you were quick enough to kill it, anyway. They're . . ." She paused, her tone growing suddenly serious. "But where did you find it, Timmy? It didn't come on to the veranda, surely?"

He hung his head, glancing sideways at David, with a look of appeal.

Sara turned to her eldest son. "You didn't leave the veranda, David?"

331

"Well," he said contritely, "the snake was only a *little* way off, Mama. We thought it might come up later when it was dark, and get into the house."

Sara flushed slightly. Her fear made her speak sharply. "But I've told you you must never go near a snake. This may have been a deadly one. And besides, you promised that none of you would leave the veranda."

She turned from him, glancing quickly down the table, to where Annie was seating the last arrival, Tim Murphy's seven-year-old sister.

"Annie—where's Sebastian?"

The old woman's head flew up. Swiftly her eyes skimmed the two rows of children, and then came back to Sara's face.

"Well . . ." Annie ran her tongue over her lips. "He don't seem to be here . . ."

Sara said to David, "Was he with you when you killed the snake?"

He wrinkled his brow in an effort to remember. "Yes . . . I think he was."

"How long ago was this?"

David bit his lower lip. "I'm not sure, Mama—not long before Bess came out."

Annie called to the two convict servants in the little adjoining room, all her anxiety in her voice.

"Bess! Kate! Have you seen Master Sebastian?"

They came into the kitchen; they shook their heads solemnly. Sebastian was a favourite with them both, and the concern on their faces was real and unassumed.

"Lor' ma'am," Kate began. "I ain't seen Master Sebastian since he was in here at midday. One of them others," she nodded in the direction of the six women in the sitting-room, "was supposed to be keeping an eye on the children."

Sara looked about wildly. "But he must be somewhere! Kate . . . run outside again and call him. Take a lamp with you. Annie, we'll go through the rooms. He's probably in the sitting-room with the others. Quickly . . . !"

Ten minutes later they were all back in the kitchen. Susan Matthews and Emily Bains had now joined them, and the convict women stood together in a nervous group. Sara and Annie had given up their futile search of the rooms; Sebastian was not anywhere in the house. They turned expectantly as Bess and

332

Kate came in, having completed a tour of the outside of the building.

"Well . . . ?" Sara demanded.

Her hands twisted and gripped each other. The children had stopped eating, and they also turned to stare at Bess and Kate. In that slight pause, with every sense straining for their answer, Sara noticed absently as if part of her mind functioned quite separately from her anguish, that a small boy, no older than Sebastian himself, whose name she couldn't remember, hadn't been given his supper yet. He had no eyes for what was going on, but stared at the plates of the others with an aggrieved air.

Kate spoke. "It was no good, ma'am. We called and called. He's nowhere around the house."

Sara let out a sharp breath, "Oh . . . !"

Annie touched her arm. "There . . . ! Don't you take on, ma'am! He'll be with the men—yes, that's where he'll be. I'll just take a lantern, and step across to the stables. And Bess and Kate can find their way down to the men's huts. Without doubt he's there—with all he's told not to go near them. The men, ma'am, they encourage him to come. We'll find him yet somewhere down there, hand in hand, with Mister Sullivan. And if he's still not about, Mister Sullivan and Trigg will organise the men with lanterns. You'll see, they'll have him in no time."

While she was speaking, Annie gathered up her shawl, and took a lantern. Bess and Kate prepared to follow her. By this time the short dusk had deepened into night. With the fading light, except for a few jobs in the stables, the men would be finished their work. The convicts' huts stood behind the house, also on high ground, and well above water. The emergency stock-pens had been erected in the space between.

Sara went to the doorway with Annie. They could see a dim light in the stables, but the rain curtained out everything else. With a sick terror Sara faced the emptiness of that black space before her. The restless livestock were moving about unseen; she could hear their stamping, and the shifting of their bodies. The light from the stables was friendly, but, down the slope from the house, the water was rising steadily. She could only think of Sebastian's ceaseless curiosity; day after day, he had questioned her about other floods on the Hawkesbury, begging to be allowed to venture out as far as the water had advanced. He was only six years old, and to him the flood was a great adventure—never a danger.

She shivered in apprehension. "Hurry, Annie! Bess, Kate, hurry . . . !"

When the bobbing lanterns disappeared into the darkness, Sara turned back dispiritedly to the kitchen. She walked to the table and began to attend to the children. A plate was handed to her to be refilled; she poured milk from a jug into two mugs. Surprisingly, Susan Matthews and Emily Bains had fallen to their share of the serving. They both wore frightened expressions, and seemed to walk lightly on their toes, as if any noise on their part was out of place. The twisting, nodding heads of the children were a blur before Sara's eyes; she heard nothing that they said. Sebastian's dark little face, his eager voice, seemed to be all around her. Already the bread was gone from the platter she had filled; she reached for the knife and began cutting again, but her thoughts were with Annie, and Bess, and Kate, as they made their way towards the huts. If they didn't find Sebastian there . . . In her heart she didn't believe they would. When he left the veranda he would have wandered, not towards the back of the house, as they suggested, but down the slope in the direction of the water which had held his fascinated attention for the past week. She thought of him, tall for his six years, but with a slight, wiry body that used its energy in quick bursts. If he should have fallen and hurt himself, out of earshot of the house. . . . She flung the knife down with a clatter; she knew she couldn't endure another five minutes of inactivity.

"David, I want you to come with me," she said. "I'm going to have just another look around the outside of the house."

Nodding, David slipped from his chair.

Susan Matthews threw Sara a startled glance. "Mercy, Madame de Bourget! You're never thinking of going out! Why, the men will be here in a few minutes, and they'll spread around and find him. He can't have got far."

With steady hands Sara lit another lantern. "I'll be quite safe, Mrs. Matthews. I won't go more than a few yards from the house. When Mr. Sullivan gets here, tell him to come out to me."

"Yes . . . but . . ." Susan Matthews clucked her tongue despairingly. "I think you shouldn't go. Your husband wouldn't like it—not as you are now . . ."

Sara took no notice. "Come, David—we'll go out by the front. You can show me where you killed the snake."

As she made for the door, Duncan stopped her.

"Mama..."

"Yes...?"

"Can I come with you? I know where we left the snake."

She shook her head, giving him a swift smile. "No, darling. You stay with Elizabeth."

Then she took David's arm. Together they left the kitchen and walked along the passage to the front door. On the way Sara stopped to collect a coat for David, and to pull a warm cloak about her own shoulders. The sound of the rain greeted them more strongly than ever when they opened the door, the pelting, monotonous sound that had hardly ceased for the past week. In the lamp-light the boy's face was serious. He stared into the darkness ahead, with a bewildered, fearful air.

Suddenly she bent to look at him more closely.

"What is it, my love?"

His lips quivered, and then straightened. "Sebastian...He's the youngest, and you always said that I must look after him. He's only a baby...and if he's lost, it's my fault."

She put the lantern down on the veranda, and squatted—awkwardly, because of the heaviness of her body—before him. She placed her hands on his shoulders, and looked into his eyes.

"Darling...it's no one's fault. One of Mrs. Matthew's women was to have stayed with you on the veranda. If she'd done as she was told, this would never have happened. No one expected you to...Oh, Davie, don't look like that! We'll find him, pet!"

Then she leaned forward and brushed his cheek with her lips. She rose, taking up the lamp again, and pulling her hood into position. On the top of the steps she paused, reaching to take David's hand in her own.

The ground was churned into soft mud. She carried the lantern low, and placed her feet carefully, feeling them sink with each step. The night was as black as pitch; the rays from the lamp only revealed endless pools of water lying on soil already too saturated to absorb any more. Farther down they could hear the roar of the swollen river.

David tugged at Sara's hand. "Over here, Mama!"

They found the snake, half-embedded in the mud. For a few moments Sara stared at it, then looked around her helplessly. The lights of the house, dimmed by the curtain of rain, gave her her

335

bearings. From here, the carriageway followed the slope sharply down to join the road that linked Kintyre with the neighbouring farms. She hesitated, remembering how close the water had come to the road when she had last seen it. She drew the cloak closer about her, and took a tighter grip on David's arm.

"We'll just go a little way farther. He may be quite close. He may have fallen and hurt himself."

Suddenly she swung the lantern high, flashing it over the sodden ground.

"Sebastian! Sebastian!"

Her voice was weak against the noise of the rushing water and the rain. She moved forward as quickly as the soft mud would allow, zig-zagging across the width of the carriageway, swinging the lantern to see as far beyond it as the rays of the lantern penetrated.

"He'll never hear me!" she cried despairingly. "Call with me, David. Now—together!"

"Sebastian . . . !"

No answer came back to them from the rainy distance. They moved on a few yards.

"Sebastian . . . !"

Sara could feel a tight dryness in her throat, that made it difficult to produce any kind of sound. Gusts of wind swept the rain into their faces, and the lamp flickered uncertainly. Quite desperate now, she noted the force of the wind. It would increase the strength of the currents; trees that had weathered other floods would go if it continued; houses would move off their foundations. The thought of that rushing, swirling water, choked with debris, made her frantic. She clutched David's hand for comfort.

"Oh, Davie . . . ! We've got to find him!"

They reached the boundary of Kintyre's land, the place where the carriageway joined the road. Sara peered ahead, but could see nothing. Here, the rush of water was unusually loud and close. She hesitated fearfully, and then plunged forward a few steps, holding the lantern high.

Suddenly David stopped still. He pulled hard at her hand.

"Mind, Mama! The water . . . It's covered the road!"

Cautiously she took another step, and David advanced to keep pace with her. The swaying light revealed the edge of the water, a black, ominous line, that eddied and lapped almost at their feet—its constant movement hinted at the force of the currents building up behind it. Sara stood dejectedly. On both sides of

336

this point the road dipped lower, one part of it running through a group of boulders, which had been blasted with gunpowder to let the road pass. The land rose again a little farther along, the beginning of the high ground on which Kintyre stood. The road wound about its base, and there, she knew, it would be several feet under water. The realisation of this frightened her badly. Never before had the flood waters reached this level; for the first time she began to fear that the house itself might be threatened.

"Just a little farther, David, and then we'll go back. There may be news of him at the house." She had to shout to be heard above the wind.

They began to trace their way carefully along the edge of the water, their feet finding precarious holds on the slope. They continued for about a hundred yards, until they were among the scattering of stones that marked the beginning of the group of boulders. They climbed a little higher, and the noise of the water carving a path through the boulders was much louder. At last she stopped.

"We must turn back," she said. "They'll have to know that the water is much higher. We should be ready to leave the house."

As she swung round, the light fell on a vividly white object, lying against a stone. They both saw it at the same instant, and moved forward with a rush. David bent and picked it up.

"It's Sebastian's wooden horse!" he shouted.

He handed it to his mother. Taking it from him, her feelings were a mixture of fear and relief. It was Sebastian's favourite plaything—a wooden horse, painted white, and splashed with irregular patches of black, carved for him by one of Kintyre's convict labourers. A frayed piece of red cord served for a bridle, giving it the gay, jaunty appearance which had so attracted Sebastian.

Clutching the little horse to her, Sara lifted the lantern again. "He *must* be somewhere about! We can't leave now. . . . If we go back the water may rise farther. Sebastian. *Sebastian*!"

David's voice echoed hers. *"Sebastian!"*

He lunged ahead of her. With a furious energy he skirted around the boulders, shaking the tufts of scrub that grew between them. Sara struggled to keep up with him, lest he should disappear beyond the arc of the light she carried. They pushed their way steadily up the rising ground. Sara's breath was soon short with the effort; she drew in great gulps of air, steadying herself with her free hand against the rounded stones.

"Sebastian . . . !"

They were beginning the descent of the other side when she felt the first pain. It went through her body like fire and then was gone. She took a further few steps before she fully realised what was happening; she shivered with fear at the thought. The pains were starting—a full seven weeks before the time. A choked little cry came from her lips, and she stumbled against a boulder.

"David . . . wait! I can't go any farther," she panted, as he returned to her side. "I must go back to the house."

"But, Sebastian . . . ?"

She shook her head. "It isn't any use. I can't search any more. The others will have to come back. Let me lean on your shoulder, David."

A vague comprehension dawned on him. He took the lamp from her hand, and raised it higher, peering into her face.

"Mama, you're ill! Mama . . . ?"

"Yes, darling—but I'll be all right. We must go back now."

He drew nearer to her, slipping his arm about her waist, and pushing his body close to her side to support her weight.

"Lean harder on me, Mama! You're not leaning on me at all!"

They started down the way they had come, but Sara's steps were less certain now. She was conscious of the desperate need for haste, and yet her body couldn't be urged to the effort she required of it. Determinedly she clung to the wooden horse, pressing it close to her, like a talisman. She stopped abruptly, as yet another spasm of pain gripped her. Longingly she pictured the comfort of Kintyre, and at the same time was torn with anguish at the thought that Sebastian might be somewhere close by, and needing help. But pain and weakness were beginning to blur every other feeling; she forced herself to concentrate on placing one foot carefully before the other. Now her whole body was bathed in sweat, and her wet cloak clung to her icily. She began to lean on David more and more, though aware that his child's strength couldn't support her much longer in this way. Then, at last, her judgment clouded with the effort of resisting the waves of pain, she let her foot slip on a loose stone. David clutched frantically as she was flung forward, but he couldn't hold her; she pitched heavily against a boulder. It broke her fall, and she managed to remain upright; but the breath was knocked out of her body, and her will to fight the increasing pain had evaporated. She clung to the boulder, the side of her head pressing against it, sobbing wildly.

Then David's fingers roused her, plucking urgently at her cloak.

"Walk, Mama...! I can see a lantern. It'll be Mr. Sullivan. Please do try to walk, Mama!"

He swung the light he held high above his head to attract attention. A shout reached them thinly through the rain. Sara opened her eyes only long enough to make certain that the flickering lantern ahead was coming towards them, and then she sagged gratefully against the rock.

Again David plucked at her cloak. "It's all right now, Mama. There's *two* men! It's Mr. Sullivan..." He tugged violently now. "Mama, look! It's Mr. Hogan!"

Sara turned her head weakly. "Jeremy? Jeremy, *here*...!"

Blackness was crowding in on her as she felt herself lifted into Jeremy's arms.

II

At sunrise Annie came wearily into the kitchen; with Bess and Kate she began to prepare breakfasts for the men who, headed by Jeremy and Michael Sullivan, had spent most of the night searching for Sebastian. There was little conversation between the women as they moved about, handling dishes and pans quietly, so that the sounds did not reach the other parts of the house. A pale sun streamed through the windows, touching kindly Annie's wrinkled, worried old face. Now and again she paused to wipe her eyes on her apron, and to give a loud sniff which could be heard across the room. During the night the flood had reached its greatest height, but before dawn the wind died and the rain stopped. This morning the floor of the convicts' cookhouse was six inches under water; presently the tired, hungry men would come trooping in for their meal. For once Annie had no thoughts of the mud they would track across the kitchen floor.

She paused as a shadow darkened the doorway, and turned to find Trigg and Jackson, the second overseer, there.

"Well?" she demanded eagerly.

But Trigg shook his head. "The last of the men are back— there's no trace of Master Sebastian. I've had a word with Mr.

Hogan and Mr. Sullivan, and they say we're all to have a few hours' rest, and then to start again. The water will be lower by that time..." His voice trailed off dismally

"Mercy on us!" Annie cried, the tears springing to her eyes. "There's hardly hope now for the poor little lamb... and him so bright and full of fun." Once more she raised the corner of her apron.

Jackson nodded. "Aye, he was that, all right! A real favourite with the boys, was young Master Sebastian. I've never seen them set to anything with such a will as they did last night. Ah, well..."

Then his eyes wandered to the table with its places already set. Annie, interpreting the glance, dropped her apron and moved briskly to the range. "It'll not be more than a minute now..."

Trigg and Jackson took their seats, their heavy movements betraying the fatigue of the long night in the rain.

Suddenly Trigg twisted round to Annie.

"Any news of the mistress yet?"

She looked up. "Lord, yes! I've been so taken up with Master Sebastian that I didn't think to tell you. Four hours ago—a girl. A little scrap of a thing—but she seems strong enough, and it looks as if she'll live. She has black hair, and she's the living image of her father."

"The mistress...?" Jackson asked.

Annie frowned doubtfully. "I just couldn't say... She had a terrible time, poor soul. Not like the others, this one weren't. She hasn't perked up at all, now that it's over. Not sleeping either—just lying there with her eyes open, and asking all the time about Master Sebastian. Lord, how I wish the master were back! Can't say how long it'll be before he gets through, with the water come as high as it has."

Then she set their plates before them, and there was silence again in the sunlit kitchen.

"If you could just rouse her in some way, Mr. Hogan," Emily Bains said anxiously. "She doesn't seem to want to have the baby with her, and she takes no notice of anything I say..."

Jeremy nodded, finished the low-voiced conversation that had taken place outside Sara's bedroom. He stepped forward gently, and opened the door.

The large room was flooded with light; the curtains fluttered softly by the open windows. Sara lay in the simple, white-canopied bed, her eyes opened wide, staring up at the cloudless sky. There was a frightening stillness in her body, a sense of waiting. Her face and lips were colourless; her hair, drawn back and thickly braided, lay across the pillow. Low at her throat a ruffle of cream lace showed, and round her shoulders she wore a fluffy blue shawl. The room was immaculate; it gave no sign of the chaos of the night before.

"Sara!" he said softly, closing the door.

She turned her head towards him, half-raised it, and then let it fall back again.

"Jeremy! What news . . . ?"

He looked at her steadily. "None . . . not so far. All the men are back now. They're having a meal and a few hours' rest, before they start again."

"Oh . . ." The hope that had sprung to her eyes was gone as quickly as it had come.

He walked to the bed. "Sara . . . Sara! Don't look like that! There's a chance that we may yet find him. Now that it's daylight . . ."

"Daylight, yes. But you won't find him—not now." As she spoke she turned again towards the windows. Her face was haggard in the strong light; the look of stillness and brooding had returned to it. He gazed down at her, acutely conscious of his helplessness to rouse or stimulate her. She was as chill and cold as stone lying there. He moved noiselessly and came to stand at the foot of the bed. Now he could see her clearly, and for the first time he noticed that close to her side she clutched the white wooden horse, with its worn bridle of red cord. She gripped it possessively, as if afraid it might be taken from her. In the same way, he remembered, she had clutched it when he had found her last night, refusing to give it up.

"Sara," he said gently.

Her eyelids fluttered, but she didn't speak.

"Sara, you haven't seen your baby yet—your daughter."

She twisted her head on the pillow to look at him.

"My daughter? But I have lost Sebastian. He wasn't much more than a baby, either. Look, Jeremy, he took a toy with him when he went—that's how much a baby he was still." And with her fingertips she stroked the chipped side of the horse.

Suddenly she put her hand across her eyes. "Oh, Jeremy!" she cried out. "Come here . . . ! Come here, quickly!"

He went to her side, bending over her. Her fingers sought his hand, and gripped it feverishly.

He dropped to his knees beside her.

"Sara . . . !" he breathed.

"I couldn't believe it when you came," she said, her voice hardly more than a whisper. "I remember thinking that I needed you badly, but that you were miles away."

His lips brushed her fingers clasped round his hand.

"I came when I knew the water was rising," he murmured. "I heard Louis was in Sydney—I thought you might need help,"

He laid his cheek against their locked hands, and they were both silent. He could hear her quiet breathing close to his ear. The coldness of her hand terrified him; he drew it closer to his body, and tried to press some warmth into it. Her eyes were closed, and he had a moment of agony wondering whether she might lose consciousness. But then she opened them fully, looking straight up at him.

"I'm so glad you came," she said faintly. "I don't believe Sebastian can be alive now. But your being here helps me to bear it. Stay here at Kintyre awhile. I'm so lonely with all those others. You'll stay, won't you, Jeremy?"

He bent over and kissed her quietly on the lips.

"I won't leave you, Sara," he said.

III

The baby, Henriette, was three days old before Jeremy at last made up his mind that he must leave Kintyre and return to his own farm. He was anxious about his livestock; although penned on high ground, the enclosures he and his men had built were rough and temporary. And the thought that, at the highest of the flood level, his store huts had probably been a couple of inches under water, worried him considerably. As the water went down there would be plenty of work—debris to be cleared, carcases to be burnt, cramped livestock moved and turned out to pasture again. Along the whole of the Hawkesbury valley a gigantic effort would be made to wipe away the traces of the disaster, and every man was needed on his own property. He felt badly at having to go, leaving Kintyre in the hands of Michael Sullivan. The young schoolteacher from Cork was a good lad, Jeremy thought, but more at home with history books than dealing with the aftermath of a flood. He hoped that Trigg and Jackson might both exert their full energies now, and, not for the first time in the past three days, he wished it was Andrew Maclay's return they awaited—not Louis de Bourget's.

Sebastian had not been found. A disheartened search was still going on, up and down the river—but there was no longer any hope held that he might be alive. Sara grieved for her little son, but seemed to have taken comfort from Henriette at last. Perhaps, Annie had suggested to Jeremy, when Sara pressed her face against the tiny head, with its fuzz of black hair, it was Sebastian she was reminded of. She lay in the white-canopied bed, the baby asleep by her side, but she seemed to care nothing for what went on outside her room. She ate little, and said little, except to constantly ask for news of Sebastian.

David and Duncan were saddened and downcast; Elizabeth questioned the men frantically—where was Sebastian? Why didn't they find him? But after three whole days of searching, even Elizabeth grew silent.

By the late afternoon of the third day, the water was down enough to allow Jeremy to make the journey back to his own farm by horse. He was preparing to leave, standing on the front steps giving last instructions to Trigg, when he caught the sound of horsemen on the road below. He watched them as they trotted quickly up the slope—Louis de Bourget, and the surgeon, D'Arcy Wentworth.

Trigg took the bridles of the sweating horses, and Jeremy went forward to greet the two men.

He looked hard at Louis. His shirt was dirty, its ruffles limp; his boots were caked with mud, days old; his coat appeared to have been soaked through several times. Jeremy concluded that he had been caught by the flood at some point along the river, and like every other available man, had turned out to help move the livestock to higher ground. He looked tired and worried. By now he would know of his daughter's birth and Sebastian's disappearance—not more than half an hour ago Jackson had set off from Kintyre with one of the farm carts loaded with children and supplies of food and clothing. They were being taken to the Talbots' house—Kintyre's nearest neighbours to have escaped the flood. The offer to take them had come as soon as the news had spread of the state of affairs at Kintyre. If Louis had not known before then, he would certainly have heard from Jackson on the road.

Jeremy had a few moments in which to wonder how he would

be received by Louis. He had not spoken to the other—he had done nothing more than glimpse him once in the street, in Sydney, since his return from England. There was no way of telling how Sara had reported their last meeting to her husband, or what her explanation had been for his giving up the management of the three Maclay farms. Louis, gay and charming, but with the temperament and ideas of the French nobility, might regard his presence here, at this time, as damned impertinence. He was capable of walking past without a glance, and going straight into the house.

But Louis approached him, his hand outstretched. He was unshaven, and he had the look of weariness common to them all for this past week.

"I was relieved when Jackson told me you were here, Hogan," he said. "You will have been a great comfort to my wife."

Jeremy gripped the other man's hand warmly. "I have achieved nothing, so far. Sebastian is still . . ."

Louis cut him short. "I have news of Sebastian—this morning."

"What is it?" Jeremy said sharply.

"His body has been found—about six miles down river. He was caught in a tree on the Sutton farm—they found him when the water went down. They recognised him, of course, and Mark Sutton passed the news to Captain Pierce, who sent a messenger after me. I have told Jackson to go on to the Suttons' after he has delivered the children. I told him I would return myself, as soon as I had seen my wife."

They looked at each other steadily—Sebastian had stood in almost the same relationship to them both. He was Andrew Maclay's son, and, they both suspected, Sara's most loved child. Because he was the youngest, he had been closer to Louis than his brothers, and Elizabeth had given her heart to him. Jeremy realised that had Sara's child been a son, Sebastion's death would not have affected Louis so greatly. But there was a sense of desolation in his bald words, and Jeremy was conscious, for the first time, of feeling sympathy for Louis.

"Could I not . . . ?" He shifted uneasily, wondering how much he dared presume on his past association with the Maclays. He looked carefully into Louis' dark face. "I should be glad to go immediately to the Suttons myself, if you would like that."

A touch of warmth came to Louis' eyes. "That is kind of you—but you have your own farm, and there must be much

344

work to be done..." He finished, lifting his shoulders a little, "None of us have escaped in this flood."

Jeremy was momentarily inarticulate. Then he said, "I have known all the Maclay children since they were born. I should be grateful if you would permit me..."

The other nodded. "Of course. Go now—I will follow as soon as I am able." He added, so quietly that Jeremy could scarcely hear what he said, "Sebastian must have his friends to bring him home."

By this time Wentworth had unstrapped his saddlebags. Trigg still held the horses' heads, and Annie and Bess had come out on the veranda. Both women looked expectantly towards Louis, as if they somehow sensed that news had arrived. He glanced up at them. There were no glad faces to greet this homecoming—this, the first time he would see his daughter.

"And now, Hogan," he said, "I must go and tell my wife that they have found Sebastian."

Slowly his gaze moved along the veranda, until it rested on the windows of Sara's bedroom. He had the look of a man who is afraid. Silently Annie and Bess made way for him as he mounted the steps.

Chapter Five

On a morning of September, 1806, the de Bourget carriage waited for a long time before the open door of Government House. Edwards sat on the box, blinking in the sunlight, and every now and then raising his head to sniff the fresh, sharp smell of the wild flowers, which for a week had been appearing in a quiet, half-vague fashion to announce the spring. The old man stretched his legs to their fullest extent, grateful for the hot sun which gave him such relief from his rheumatism, but still feeling unaccountably disgruntled at what he saw about him. He sadly missed the English springs, the sudden breaking-out of the young green on tree, hedge, and hedgerow, after the long months of nakedness. It was his private opinion that spring in this country of evergreens was no spring at all.

His eyes brightened with the prospect of a gossip as he noticed a man, carrying pail and a twig-broom, come slowly round the corner of the house. He climbed rather stiffly down off the box, laid a gentle hand on the bridle of the nearest horse, and waited for the man's approach. He and the newcomer, Simon Brand, had shared many a pot of ale in Costello's, while Government House gossip had been bandied about; but he had not seen the other for some time past, and he was eager for news.

"Good-mornin' to ye, Simon, lad!"

"Good-mornin', Tom! It's a fine sort of day we're havin'."

"It's that, all right, Simon."

Brand ran a speculative eye over the carriage, noting the shining paintwork, the rich, fresh upholstery.

"The Frenchman has business with the Governor?" he said casually.

Edwards shook his head. " 'Tis the mistress I'm driving." He winked, laughing a little. "Nothing but the best for His Excellency—so the master's own carriage was ordered."

Brand spat reflectively into the neat, clipped shrubs that lined the drive. "Well . . . let me tell ye, a fine carriage'll not make old 'Bounty Bligh' think any better of her. He's not in love with any of the moneyed folk in this colony, because he knows fine well they got it from rum. I tell ye, Tom, that man'll stir up a power of trouble in this place, before he's through. An honest man, Tom, but harsh . . . Let me tell ye . . ."

He came closer, taking out his tobacco pouch and offering it to Edwards, at the same time giving a careful glance in the direction of the windows of the Governor's study. Then, with heads close together, the two men fell into a low-toned conversation.

For the past six weeks the new Governor of New South Wales had been the constant subject on the lips of most of its citizens. On King's request to be relieved of his position, the Colonial Office had appointed yet another seaman, Post-Captain William Bligh, whose name, sixteen years earlier, had swept through naval circles and beyond them, with the story of the mutiny on the *Bounty*. "Bounty Bligh," they called him now, and his name was a symbol of a feat of courage and navigation unequalled in the annals of sailors. With eighteen of the *Bounty's* crew he had travelled nearly four thousand miles in an open boat from Otaheite to Timor; he made this journey in a bare forty-one days, across almost uncharted seas. Bligh was a brave, just, and careful captain . . . but made of stern, unimaginative stuff, which invited mutiny from men who had passed six months in a Pacific idyll on Otaheite, and had then been forced to give up their native mistresses, and sail with Bligh and his cargo of bread-fruit for the West Indies. But he had piloted his small boat safely to Timor, and now the world knew him as much for his splendid seamanship, as for the mutiny which Fletcher Christian had led.

Later, he had been, unhappily, involved in the mutiny at the Nore, and the tale of his tyranny spread; he had fought magnificently under Duncan at Camperdown, and Nelson at Copenhagen. He proved himself courageous, resourceful, efficient . . . but the legend of the cruel discipline of the *Bounty* died hard. He was a victim of his own passion for perfection; as stern with himself as with other men, he was condemned as humourless and arrogant by those who didn't take into consideration his integrity and his tenderness towards his family. Sixteen years later the world still judged this man on the disastrous voyage of the infamous *Bounty*. It was a ghost that would never be laid. The little colony of New South Wales had awaited his coming with apprehension; unless the temper and disposition of "Bounty Bligh" had softened considerably, he was not the man to do no more than make feeble protests against those who ignored orders from Government House.

"It's for all the world as if he were back on his own ship, Tom," Brand said. "He's up at the crack of dawn every morning, ordering this one and that one about. An' just when you think he's safely at his desk, there he's standing right before yer eyes, wanting to know why the path hasn't been swept." He considered a moment, finishing slowly, "But I reckon as I like him, for all that . . ."

Then his eyes went back to the carriage. He said reflectively, "Now, what business do you suppose Madame de Bourget could have with old Bligh? She ain't been abroad much these days . . ."

Edwards looked squarely at his companion. "I reckon what business the mistress has with the Governor is *her* business, Simon. But yer right about her not being abroad much these days. It's gone six months since the little 'un, Master Sebastian, was drowned in the Hawkesbury flood—but she don't seem able to forget about it for a minute. Poor lady—she were hardly finished wearing black for Mr. Maclay, when she puts it on again for the young master. She don't go nowhere, except to attend to business at the store, or one of the farms. I reckon Monsieur de Bourget don't like it much, either. They have words sumtimes, I'm told, about her wearin' herself out. The master—he's not the one to take kindly to her givin' half her attention to summat

347

else. But that's summat he ought t' seen before he married her. She's not likely to change for any man, she isn't.''

Simon's expression encouraged him. He took a deep breath, and prepared to launch out on another stream of gossip of the de Bourget household.

In deference to his caller's sex, the Governor had not waved Sara to the usual seat on the opposite side of his desk. Instead, he had indicated the tall winged chair before the fireplace. She settled herself gravely, spread her skirt a little, and gave him plenty of time to take up what must have been a familiar stance, with his back to the grate.

So when she raised her head, she found "Bounty Bligh" looking down at her, his sharp eyes bent upon her with a questioning interest. His black hair was grey-streaked, and he had the thickened figure of middle-age. But he was somehow saved from the pomposity which his commanding attitude might have given him. In the slightly arrogant fold of his lips Sara recognised something of her own characteristics. She reminded herself that this man would have need of authority and arrogance, as well as courage, to bring eighteen men in an open boat across four thousand miles of sea.

Civilities had passed between them when Sara entered the room, and now Bligh shifted his weight slightly from one foot to the other as he waited for her to announce her business. His term of office was only a few weeks old, but the details of Sara de Bourget's history were known to him well enough. He looked at her carefully, trying to decide if it were the quality of ruthless ambition alone which had brought her to her present position in the colony. But it was said of her that she was an excellent mother, and Bligh—the father of six daughters—had a strong respect for any woman who discharged the duties of motherhood creditably. She puzzled him, for all that—fitting, as she did, into no definite category within the colony's society. He knew that in the early days her first husband had been active enough in the rum trade, but had ended his connection with it about the time of King's arrival. She herself was an emancipist, and yet had married a man who was known to have no truck at all with emancipists, a Frenchman who farmed as a gentlemanly recreation, and who did not soil his hands with trade. It was an enigma which interested Bligh—the business woman married to the elegant dilettante.

He noted her black gown, and her lack of ornaments, recalling then what King had told him of the death of one of her children in the flood six months before his arrival. Apart from the brief morning call she and her husband had made upon him to pay their respects, he couldn't remember having seen her at any of the gatherings he had officially attended. Her hands lay folded in her lap; instinct told him that, in a woman of the sort who faced him now, they should have been quiet, still hands. Instead they twisted nervously.

He spoke at last, feeling that the silence couldn't continue between them any longer.

"Is there some way in which I can be of service to you, Ma'am? Some matter . . . ?" It was a foolish statement, he knew, leaving him open to a direct request from her. The more money these people had, the more they seemed to demand privileges from the Government. He had not come to this country to pamper to such as Madame de Bourget, but to curb their power.

She answered him firmly, as if she at last knew what she wanted to say.

"There's nothing I want to ask of you, Your Excellency, except your discretion."

"My discretion, Ma'am? I don't see . . ."

He frowned, suspecting her next words. No one came to Government House to ask for nothing—and this woman certainly hadn't the appearance of a senseless flipperty-jibbet. The histories of the previous governors of the colony had taught him to be immediately wary of what he did not understand. If the Frenchman thought he could send his wife, a figure for sympathy in her mourning, to wheedle something from him, then both of them were mistaken! He drew himself up to his not-very-commanding height, and waited for his visitor to continue.

"I have come to see you about the grain which I have held at my Toongabbie and Castle Hill farms since the harvest."

"Yes?"

Bligh's voice had an edge to it which he hoped would be very much apparent. He sensed what she was about, and he believed he had her measure taken. She knew, as did everyone else in the colony, that grain was desperately short as a result of the flood on the Hawkesbury. To try to relieve the situation, Governor King had sent ships to India for provisions, but, as yet, none of them had come back to Port Jackson. In the intervening months the reserves of grain had dwindled alarmingly, and, for the first time in many years, the days of famine and rations returned. As the stores of grain went down, the prices asked by those who still had it to sell, rose. Bligh's mouth twisted as he watched Sara. So this was what she sought from him—she was about to offer the large stocks of grain he knew she held, at a price even higher than any farmer had yet got from the Commissary. She had waited until the Hawkesbury settlers were feeling the true pinch of hunger—until no Governor, unless he were completely heartless, could any longer remain oblivious to their distress—before she threw her produce on to the market. On top of that she had the audacity to ask his discretion in the matter! He felt his rage mount at the sheer coldbloodedness of it. She sat looking at him calmly, this woman who was prepared to bargain for high profit on a flood which had taken her own child's life.

"It was, fortunately for me," she said, "an extremely good harvest at both farms."

His voice broke in coldly. "Might I remind you, Ma'am, that the Commissary is the proper person to make your offers of grain to. And might I also remind you that he is authorised to offer no prices above those I have already stipulated."

Sara rose to her feet swiftly, colour staining each cheek.

"You are mistaken, Your Excellency; I came to *give* my grain, not to sell it."

He stared at her steadily. The quiet ticking of the mantel clock was suddenly loud in the silence which had fallen between them.

"To give it, Ma'am . . . ?" he said slowly.

'To give it, Your Excellency," she repeated.

The high colour was still in her face, but she spoke evenly. "I have recently returned from a visit to my Hawkesbury farm . . . and I have seen the distress for myself. Most of the families there cannot possibly afford the price of flour, and their own crops are gone. The children . . ." Here she halted, not trying to fill in the details for him.

He nodded. He locked his hands behind his back, and the gaze he turned upon her was both questioning and reflective.

"There is no need to tell me, Ma'am," he said quietly. He paced the length of the hearthrug, and then turned back to her, flinging his arms wide in a gesture that conveyed his own distress and anxiety. "I have not long returned from my own tour of the Hawkesbury, and I have seen the need of the smaller farmers for myself. The plight of the children would touch the hardest heart. But," he added, "there are those in this colony who know too well that the possession of a heart does little to further their business interests.''

He shrugged, as if trying to shake away the thought. Then he questioned her directly.

''Madame de Bourget?''

''Your Excellency?''

''Why are you doing this? Why should you *give* your grain, when others every day force the price higher?''

She ran her tongue over her lips. ''I think I've already made that clear, Your Excellency. The distress . . .''

He gave a snort. ''My dear lady, I may only have been in the colony a short time, but already I am well acquainted with the histories of most of the prominent citizens—yours, and your late husband's among them. Do not be offended if I venture to suggest that your past transactions seem hardly compatible with this offer.''

Sara frowned, and seemed to fight for control of her voice.

''Your Excellency—let me remind you also that my past business transactions have very little to do with the fact that my youngest son was drowned in the flood which caused this scarcity. In choosing to make this offer, for once I am not acting as a businesswoman. And that is the reason I ask for your discretion. I have no desire to have it gossiped about all over the colony—I should infinitely prefer to be known still as a businesswoman.''

He bowed slightly. ''Certainly, Ma'am. I will give my instructions accordingly . . .''

''Then,'' she said, ''I will let you have the details of the grain, and when it can be delivered. Perhaps you would pass them on to the Commissary . . . ?''

Bligh looked at her fully. He was touched and affected by her simplicity and dignity—and more than that, he was impressed by the discipline with which she kept her emotions under control on an occasion when most other women would have been weeping. Even to ''Bounty Bligh'' she was formidable as she stood there, and somewhere within him there was not only the warming thought that her grain would be a stop-gap to the famine for at least a short time, but also the surprisingly comforting realisation that where he had looked for an enemy he had found a friend. Here was one, he thought, among the circle who controlled trade, whom he could feel was not working directly against him.

He knew she could well afford her gift—and yet the fact that she had made it was precious balm to him.

But while he was pondering her action, she had drawn back a few steps from him, and seemed on the point of leaving. He raised his hand in a gesture to detain her.

"Pray be seated again, Ma'am. There are many things I'd dearly like to discuss with you . . ."

But she was already sinking into a curtsy.

"If Your Excellency will permit . . . some other time."

She rose and turned, walking swiftly to the door. She was gone before he had time to take more than a few paces. It was then that he realised that she wasn't any different from other women, after all. As she curtsied, he had seen tears in her eyes.

II

On the afternoon following Sara's visit to Governor Bligh, the spring weather had turned suddenly to rain. In the schoolroom at Glenbarr she stretched her feet comfortably on a footstool before the fire, and turned her tapestry-frame to catch the light from the window. Duncan sat at a small table near her; his tongue hung out slightly as he concentrated on building with elaborate care a house of cards. Occasionally he gave a sigh of exasperation as one card slipped, and the whole structure came down. David sat on the other side of the hearth with a book.

Sara selected a different silk from her workbasket, and glanced at Elizabeth, who stood looking over her shoulder. "It's better to avoid using too much of the one . . ."

Then she paused. The schoolroom door opened, and Louis entered. David glanced up from his book, a smile breaking on his face. Duncan gave a soft groan as his card house collapsed in the sudden draught.

Louis pulled a face of mock tragedy. "I promise you I'll build it up again, Duncan. They used to say there was no more gentle a hand at cards in the whole of France than mine!"

He stooped then to kiss Sara's hand, and bent to receive Elizabeth's kiss on his cheek. He pulled playfully at one of his daughter's black curls.

"I hope you are paying proper attention to all these lessons in needlework," he said. "I promised your grandfather you should lack none of the feminine arts."

Sara nodded in Elizabeth's direction.

"She does very well, Louis," she remarked dryly. "The other day I heard Annie telling her that she had fingers as quick as a monkey's. No doubt it was meant as a compliment..."

But she broke off and raised her eyebrows questioningly, as he bent over her again to hand her a sealed package, which he had drawn from his coat pocket. She took it, turning it over to read the inscription.

"What is it?" she asked, puzzled.

He shrugged. "Open it, my love. As I came up, a messenger arrived with it from Government House. Viceregal letters are never to be ignored, and when they come from such an impatient man as Bligh, then they obviously demand immediate attention." He drew Elizabeth down on to the footstool beside him, while Sara, with knitted brows, broke the seals and began to read.

Her eyes ran down the bold script.

> *"...I acknowledge receipt of the details of the grain which you purpose..."*

Then followed more comments about the grain, and Sara's arrangements for its delivery. The business being dealt with swiftly, the tone of the letter changed. She began to read more slowly.

> *"...Those settlers' families who will benefit from your gift, Madame, will never know of your generosity, and can never have the opportunity to thank you. Their present distress touches me sorely and I, of all the colony, am the only person who may make some suitable reply for them. Therefore, I trust that you will accept a grant of land which I have in mind, close to your husband's present property on the Nepean River, and adjoining the Cowpastures District. This land is for you and your children, for however long..."*

Tears misted before Sara's eyes as she struggled to read on to the end. Bligh wrote that he knew of her interest and success in breeding merino sheep, and he understood the area to be particularly suited for pasture. This was a direct reference to the fact that John Macarthur, to the Governor's extreme annoyance, had chosen his grant of five thousand acres in the Cowpastures itself. Through the concise, rather stiff phrases, there ran a spirit of goodwill and humanity. Sara felt herself warm to this irascible, unimaginative man who was so touched by the plight of the Hawkesbury settlers—who would, without any public display, seek to reward her with this magnificent gesture, because she had lightened the burden of feeding them, even in a small way. A more subtle man would have found a less obvious way of showing his gratitude—or would have waited some months before making this offer. But Bligh was a sailor, and one not noted for his tact. This was the largest single grant of land, apart from the one which the Colonial Office had given Macarthur, that she could ever recall. The legend that had built "Bounty Bligh" into a tyrant great enough to provoke mutiny did him a grave injustice—but possibly the small settlers were the only ones who would never know it.

Sara smoothed the papers, and handed them to Louis.

"Governor Bligh has been more than generous," she said quietly.

His expression, as he read, grew gentle and reflective. Then he looked across at her, a faint smile on his lips.

"His generosity is not undeserved, my love," he said, folding the letter and handing it back.

Duncan slid off his chair, coming round the table and standing beside Louis' elbow. "Will Governor Bligh be coming here, Mama?"

"I don't think so, dear. He's extremely busy."

Duncan's mouth pouted in disappointment. "I wish he would. I want to ask him all about the mutiny."

Sara shook her head. "I think it would be better not to, Duncan. Perhaps it's something he doesn't care to talk about."

David put down his book. "The voyage from Otaheite is the best story. He'd talk about that, wouldn't he, Mama? Lieutenant Flinders said it's the greatest piece of navigation ever known." As he spoke his blue eyes were full of dreaming; he had the look of a boy in love with the vivid colour that adventure wears. "Did you know, Mama, that Lieutenant Flinders once sailed as midshipman with Captain Bligh? That was after the mutiny, of course."

Sara sighed "Poor man . . . The mutiny will never be forgotten, I'm afraid. How it crops up every time his name is mentioned!"

Elizabeth turned to her father, and tugged at his coat sleeve. "Tell me about the mutiny again, Papa! I like the part where . . ."

"No!" Duncan cried. "Tell us about the boat voyage! I want to hear that again!" He sat down on the footstool beside Elizabeth, wriggling to make room for himself.

Louis laughed at the upturned faces. "You must, in fairness to the Governor, remember that he did other things besides survive a mutiny and a long voyage in an open boat. He once sailed with Captain Cook, and he was second in line to Nelson at Copenhagen. After the battle, Nelson called him on board the *Elephant* to thank him . . ."

As they talked, Sara, with a nod to Louis, rose and left the room quietly. The even monotone of his voice followed her down the stairs. Bennett, passing through the hall, eyed her as she made her way to the study. Scurries of rain still beat upon the window-panes; the sky had grown darker with the heavy clouds. Here there was no fire, although one was already laid in the grate. She shivered a little in the chill of the room, and then she lit the candle on the desk.

Spreading out Bligh's letter, Sara read it through again. Here, in this bold script, was the title to land that Andrew had planned to go back to London to obtain. This was what he had dreamed of—pasture in that fertile valley for the flocks of merinos he had envisaged. How the paradox of this gift from Bligh would have astonished him—Bligh, the stern champion of the small farmers, willingly increasing the holdings of one who belonged to the land-owning class, because his heart had been touched. She found herself again wondering at the humanity of this man of the *Bounty* legend.

She opened the top drawer of the desk to take out a map of the Nepean and Cowpastures district. But here she paused, her hand wandering down to the bottom drawer. It was locked, and for a few seconds she tugged at it impatiently. Then she searched for the key among the others she carried. She inserted it quickly and turned the lock. The drawer was empty, except for an object wrapped in a dustsheet of plain, white calico. She drew it out, unfolding it carefully on the desk. Sebastian's painted wooden horse still bore the mud splashes of that night she had found it on the hillside above the road. She set it on its feet, and leaned back in the chair to look at it. The red cord bridle was limp, but the little horse still wore the air of battered jauntiness with which the Kintyre convict had fashioned it.

She touched the frayed cord gently, and then her gaze went to Bligh's open letter. Her stiff lips started to form words soundlessly.

"Sebastian—he never saw you, my darling. But because of you, he's given me what Andrew wanted. No matter what happens, I'll never let this land go..."

She reached eagerly for the map, and sought the approximate area that Bligh had indicated. She traced it roughly with her finger, noticing its closeness to Banon, wondering when and how it would be possible to get hold of the land which lay in between. A few small farmers had holdings there, but in time they might be persuaded... Her thoughts ran on into the future.

"I'll call it 'Dane Farm'—that's for Sebastian and my father."

Chapter Six

Bligh's rule in New South Wales came to an abrupt end on a day in January, 1808—the twentieth anniversary of the foundation of the colony. It was a year and five months since he had taken office.

He had come to the colony determined to carry out his duties as ruler, but he had been unable to beat the factor that had worn down his predecessors—the army. So long as he could not control the Corps he was virtually powerless; he was thwarted and frustrated at every step by its officers. Without their support, the edicts issued from Government House were just so many scraps of paper. The quarrels between Bligh and the Corps deepened and grew bitter with the months—but it was Macarthur, now a private citizen, who finally brought them to a head. In protest against what they said was a wrongful imprisonment of Macarthur for a slight offence—which Bligh had ordered—the officers then in Sydney, headed by Colonel Johnston, marched to Government House to arrest the Governor. With them went three hundred of the Corps in military formation, and a band playing *British Grenadiers*. Half of Sydney's dusty population trailed behind, like small boys off to a circus.

This was a far cry indeed from the mutiny off Otaheite, but when Bligh, wearing full dress uniform and the Camperdown medal, prepared to meet them, he knew that the mutiny he faced now was no less serious. He was placed under house-arrest, and in Sydney's streets that night many cheered openly for Macarthur and Johnston and others, less openly, pondered the possibility of Bligh's eventual triumph. The "Rum Corps" had had its hour of rebellion—and already some of its members were beginning to fear the day of final reckoning.

II

"This is treason, Sara! The whole regiment is in open rebellion! They've arrested and humiliated Bligh—the King's representative! *Mon Dieu,* how do the fools hope to escape the consequences?"

In the darkness of Glenbarr's veranda, Sara could hardly distinguish Louis' face. The warm summer night was alive with the song of the cicadas; something about the intimate, throbbing rhythm of their chorus always excited her, but to-night all her attention was on Louis. He paced a few yards down the veranda, his head turned to watch the lights of the township. Then he came back, standing close to where she leaned against a pillar.

"Bligh will not forgive easily," he said, his tone reflective now. "And when the time for the courts-martial comes, no one will be allowed to forget that it was the King's representative they rebelled against. Twice in his lifetime it has happened—only his sort of pig-headedness could invite mutiny twice."

He looked down towards the township again, where that day he had been among the crowd that had witnessed Johnston's march on Government House. He had returned to Glenbarr scoffing and indignant, contemptuous of the heavy-handed way Macarthur had chosen to rout his enemy. His French mind deplored the lack of finesse in the plans, the victory that gave Macarthur nothing more than a breathing-space in which to prepare a defence of his act. It was so easy, Louis had said, to take a Government by force of arms—but to take it by arms, as Macarthur had done, and then try to make it legal, was wholly laughable. Whitehall might be six months away by sea, but eventually its decisions would be made known—and Louis felt they would not be in Macarthur's favour.

He put out his hand and touched Sara's shoulder lightly. "Macarthur will try to justify himself, my dear—he and Johnston both."

She stirred, and drew near to him. The white frill of lace at his throat was sharp in the darkness; always when she could not see his face, his voice became strangely dominating and she listened more to the sounds than the words.

"They will start to gather together their friends, Sara. They will send round documents which we will be expected to sign—documents expressing our heartfelt gratitude that the colony is freed of a tyrant. We must not be here to sign them! Bligh himself might be finished, but government still remains—and one does not put one's signature to treason!''

"Where . . . ?'' she said slowly. "Where shall we go?''

"As far beyond Macarthur's reach as we can get. We'll go to Banon. And we must be diplomatic about this. It will not do to be unfriendly towards that gentleman either—because until another governor is appointed, it isn't very hard to guess who'll reign as king here. This is a time when we must both walk a middle-line, my dear—and it can best be done from the distance of Banon.''

"For how long?''

He shrugged. "Who knows . . . ? Does it matter . . . ?''

He raised his other hand and gripped her shoulders firmly. There was a faint light from the stars—just enough to let her make out the smile that had come to his face. Louis, she knew, was well aware of the power of his smile. The quality of his voice turned a journey to Banon into an adventure they alone shared; he could suggest excitement where none existed.

"There's nothing to keep you here, Sara. Now that you have good overseers for the farms, you don't have to visit them so regularly. Clapmore could run the store blindfolded—besides that, he wants to get married, and I think it would be a graceful gesture if you let him have the empty rooms above it. You don't expect any of the ships back for six—perhaps nine—months yet. Why shouldn't we have the peace of Banon while we can?''

She moved restlessly. She didn't want to go. The raw, ugly little town of Sydney had to-day grown in stature by its act of rebellion; it had suddenly expanded to a full, vigorous life—if, perhaps, not the right kind of life, then exciting, just the same. She wanted desperately to stay and watch its struggles at first hand; but Louis' shrewd predictions were not to be thrust aside. There would be more trouble yet, and she would certainly be expected to declare herself for or against Macarthur—and either decision would be a dangerous one. Her eyes went to the cluster of lights of the township, and then towards the harbour, where the pale starlight had given the water a cool, silvered look. The exotic splendour of Banon did not compare with this world—this place of half-beauty, half-ugliness. Banon was lovely, remote in its river-valley, but her heart urged her to stay here among this bustle and intrigue and worldliness.

"You would be on hand when the first merino flock is brought up to the new property, Sara. You've always said you'd like to be there for the first lambing season at Dane Farm..."

He broke off as the soft clop of a horse's hooves in the drive reached them. They both peered into the darkness, but could make out nothing but the vague shape of the horseman who had reined to a halt before the front door.

"Hello, there...!" Louis called out.

The man turned his head, staring in their direction; then he urged his horse forward at a walk across the lawn, apparently indifferent to the way its hooves would cut up the turf. He halted at the border of the flower-bed beneath the veranda.

"Richard!" Sara breathed.

Her hands gripped the rail nervously. Richard had not come willingly to Glenbarr since her marriage to Louis. At the time of Sebastian's death he had written to her—a letter that was no mere formality, words from his heart, for her eyes alone. Apart from that, the only communication from him was the quarterly instalment paid on his debt. But Richard himself—his thoughts and plans and ideas—had vanished from her life as completely as in those other years following their quarrel over Jeremy. No, his sudden appearance here, mounted and half-lost in darkness, was like a return from the dead. Her hands against the rail had begun to sweat.

"I must apologise for bursting in upon you like this..." Richard said. His voice was like a young boy's—half-eager, half-truculent.

Louis said coolly, "We are delighted, of course. My only regret is that your horse cannot be accommodated in the drawing-room, otherwise you would be most welcome to come inside."

"I've just ridden in from Parramatta," Richard said, ignoring Louis' remark. "I came as soon as the news of the rebellion reached us there."

"It is most considerate of you," Louis replied. "But we're in no danger, I assure you. Governor Bligh is the only one who might have felt the need of your support today."

"I haven't time to bandy words with you, de Bourget!" Richard burst out impatiently. "It was chiefly on Sara's account I came!"

"What is it, Richard?" she said quietly.

He leaned sideways in the saddle, the tone of his voice dropping again, becoming low and earnest. "I'm on my way to the barracks—I wanted to talk to you before I became involved in all this mess. There are some of us in the Corps who think we're well rid of Bligh—and some who don't. But the one thing we are all agreed about is that, although Johnston may have taken over the Government, it's Macarthur who'll give the orders. He'll be in charge until they send someone out from England to arrest him. Perhaps he'll have a year—perhaps longer. But his time is limited—he'll have to make the most of it. And, believe me, he *will* make the most of it!"

Louis spoke, interrupting smoothly. "But what has this to do with my wife, Barwell?"

"Simply this . . . Macarthur will try to involve as many prominent people in the colony as he can. He'll need support when they call him to give an account of himself. But for the meantime, those who side with Bligh won't be much in favour with Macarthur and Johnston. It's a tricky business."

"Well . . . ?"

Richard addressed himself directly to Sara. "It's bad enough for those who have to be involved in this—like myself. But for you, it's unnecessary . . . if you stay out of Sydney. I came hoping to persuade you to stay away for a few months—longer, if you can manage it."

Sara said gently, "Thank you, Richard. It was kind of you to think of coming."

"It's not a matter for thanks!" he returned sharply. "I came because this business is far more serious than perhaps it looks now. It may affect your future in the colony, Sara—under the next Governor, or Bligh himself, if he is reinstated. Johnston may offer land grants to win supporters like yourself. I hope you won't be tempted . . ."

"I'll remember what you've said, Richard," she replied. "I'm very grateful for your warning."

He nodded. "Well, then . . . good-night to both of you. They're expecting me back at the barracks."

He saluted stiffly, wheeled his horse, and set it at a canter straight towards the low hedge which bordered the lawn. Clods of earth flew up as the animal jumped. They listened to the sounds of the hoof-beats fading into the distance.

Louis ended the silence between them. "I expect Barwell is

too old to be taught some manners. Or perhaps he likes the dramatic figure he cuts as he ploughs up the lawn."

"I hardly think he noticed what he was doing," Sara murmured soothingly. "He is more upset about today's trouble than I would have expected..."

Her voice trailed away wonderingly as Louis turned to her, and suddenly raised his hand to touch her cheek softly. With his forefinger he began to trace the line of her jaw; finally he tilted her chin, so that she was forced to look straight at him.

"He is like an eager boy in his love for you, my Sara. He is either all passion, or all coldness. He leans over backwards to display his indifference to you—but when he thinks he can help you, he is here like a knight to his lady. He is so young and foolish, and always will be."

Sara jerked her head to break from his grasp.

"You think Richard loves me? How are you so certain?"

"Because, my darling, any fool could have seen it years ago—and I have never been exactly a fool."

His hands went about her shoulders possessively. He bent until his face was close to hers.

"And now, my love, I hope you are doubly convinced that we must go back to Banon."

She hesitated a moment, then nodded. His lips found hers in the darkness, and he held her close against him. She closed her eyes, and tried to forget the tumult in her heart at the sound of Richard's voice.

III

The de Bourgets and their family stayed at Banon for almost two years. During that period the rebel administration changed hands several times—from Johnston it was passed on to Lieutenant-Colonel Foveaux, and, on Colonel Patterson's arrival from the settlement at Port Dalrymple, he reluctantly took over what remnants of authority remained. Macarthur and Johnston left for England in March, 1809, to answer the charges against them. In the same month Bligh was released from his imprisonment, and allowed to sail in the *Porpoise*. He had given his promise that he would return immediately to England; but, as he regarded any promise made to a rebel government as no promise at all, he headed for the Derwent River, in Van Dieman's Land, and waited there for the help which he expected from the unhurrying Colonial Office.

Each in their turn, the *Hawk, Thistle,* and *Thrush,* put into Port Jackson, and for a few days Sara and Louis came to Sydney to see their captains. Whenever they appeared in the town they were almost swamped under the wave of gossip and scandal which greeted them; if the evidence of the Sydney drawing-rooms was to be believed, every member of the rebel administration was engaged in a race to determine who could make himself the richest in the limited space of time in their hands. Seventy-five thousand acres of land had been parcelled out, and the Commissary was wiped clean. But these favours were paid for by a signature on the documents which supported the rebellion. The commerce of the colony had the feel of over-ripe fruit about to fall. It did not need Louis' urging to convince her that she was better away from Sydney while no authorised governor ruled there.

She was anxious over the state of affairs at the store and the farms. Clapmore was doing his best with the harrowing conditions of trade; he managed well enough as long as the de Bourget ships kept him supplied with cargoes. But Sara had given him instructions that on no account was he to buy from anyone within the colony itself, even if it meant that the shelves were to stand empty for months on end.

"Don't give them the prices they're asking," she said to Clapmore. "Shut the store, if you have to!"

Clapmore struggled on, facing the hundred-and-one decisions that formerly Sara had made. She was worried about him, but she felt that she dared not remain in Sydney for spells of any length.

On brief visits to Priest's and the Toongabbie farms she saw evidences everywhere that her absences were far too long. At both properties she gave orders for repairs to house and out-buildings, but was never able to wait to see them carried out.

She had no worry over the management of Kintyre. Since the time of the flood disaster, it had been almost completely in Jeremy Hogan's charge. His practice of riding to Kintyre to look over the stock and discuss the crops with Trigg—as they had done together in the old days—had begun during the months following Henriette's birth, when Sara had remained there, still ill and too weak to make the long journey back to Sydney. By now it was an established custom—and Louis had insisted that

Jeremy be paid a proper commission as her agent. A letter from Jeremy, giving details of the property, reached her at Banon every few weeks; at times when she was worried about conditions at the other two farms, the letters gave her a picture of Kintyre's acres, as prosperous and as trim as if Andrew himself had been there to attend to them.

But she found that Banon was the refuge from the troubles of the colony that Louis had meant it to be. The valleys and gorges had a haunting, faintly mysterious beauty; it was possible, within a few miles' ride of the house itself, to go well beyond the reach of any settlement; across the river the wild government herds roamed unchecked. Great storms of rain came down from the mountains, but there were long days of sun and perfect stillness, when Sara felt herself becoming part of the silence that surrounded them. She let the peace of those uninterrupted months close over her, like a blanket that smothered all other thoughts.

Louis himself wore an air of contentment. He rode every day with the children, or with Sara alone, and as time passed she felt that his attachment to Banon became more and more a decisive factor in his life. He seemed to desire nothing more than to remain there undisturbed. Under his hands the gardens were becoming a place of exquisite and carefully informal beauty; occasionally, with two or three of the men, he made excursions into the foothills of the mountains, bringing back young flowering trees to plant among the eucalypts and Norfolk pines surrounding the house. He added a library to store the books that arrived for him by every ship.

A governess, Miss Parry, was brought out to take charge of Elizabeth; she was a prim, softly-spoken young woman, whom Louis mimicked outrageously. Elizabeth still had lessons from her father and Michael Sullivan, and went reluctantly into Miss Parry's charge for music, needlework, and painting. Every morning from the drawing-room came the airs of Mozart and Handel, executed efficiently enough, but woodenly. Elizabeth's greatest passion in life was still her pony, and, latterly, her small half-sister, Henriette, had begun to interest her. Henriette was very much Louis' child—with an assured charm which already she had learned would get her most of the things she wanted. To Sara, it was still something of a wonder to see the way Louis treated his little daughter—he adored her, and spoiled her shamefully, delighting in her precocious, baby French. Always remembering the tragedy of Sebastian's death, Louis engaged a

363

nursemaid solely for the care of Henriette; this woman had instructions never to let the child out of her sight for a moment. Sara wished she had the courage to step in and put an end to the dominance that Henriette exerted over the entire household at Banon, but she was never free of the thought that Henriette had to take the place of the son Louis had hoped for, and he should be left to spoil and indulge as it pleased him.

With each month that passed, David and Duncan became more absorbed in the routine of life at Banon. David was growing into a shy and withdrawn adolescence—much too prone, Sara noticed, to spending his time ranging through Louis' library, or riding off alone along the bush tracks. He seemed content to be led by Duncan—Duncan, who talked enough for them both, who had Andrew's sense of opportunism, and a boisterous love of fun. But in their interest and knowledge of farming they were equal; they knew that Dane Farm, in the coveted Cowpastures district, was to be theirs some day, and they followed its progress with interest. Two or three times a week they rode there with Sara to inspect the clearing and fencing; they knew almost as much about the breeding of the merino as their mother; they were familiar with the prices fetched for sheep and cattle at every stock sale in Sydney and Parramatta. As Sara saw them both, week by week, shed their childhood a little more, she pondered the question of sending them to school in England . . . and, week by week, she put the decision off. Next year they would go, she promised herself . . . next year.

At the end of December, 1809—almost two years after the rebellion against Bligh—news reached Banon that Lieutenant-Colonel Lachlan Macquarie, the newly-appointed governor of the colony, had reached Port Jackson, in the *Hindostan*. With him in the *Hindostan*, and in the accompanying storeship, the *Dromedary,* were the soldiers of the 73rd Regiment sent out to replace the rebellious Rum Corps. By placing the Commandant of the regiment in the governorship, the Colonial Office was making it abundantly clear that it would stand for no more of the quarrels that had waged incessantly between Governor and Military since Hunter's time.

With this new governor came the hope of peace within the colony, yet Sara packed for the journey to Sydney with a strange reluctance. These past two years had given to her a life of tranquility she had never known, and previously had hardly looked for. Almost she dreaded the return.

Chapter Seven

A haze of dust rose into the hot air above the Parade Ground, on New Year's Day, 1810. The population of Sydney had put on its best clothes, and in a holiday spirit had turned out to hear the reading of the Governor's commission. Beside the splendid new uniforms of the 73rd, those of the New South Wales Corps were faded and rather sad-looking; but the Corps presented arms as smartly as their fellows. The guns of the Battery on the point roared, the echo sounding back off the hills on the North Shore. A freely-perspiring military band played the National Anthem.

Sara, sitting in the carriage with Elizabeth and Henriette, noted, with a smile she kept carefully hidden, the respectful fashion in which the crowd uncovered its heads as the Great Seal was displayed on the Patent, by the Judge-Advocate. Tall hats and cloth caps were removed with equal alacrity; there was nothing here to indicate that this was the same crowd who had greeted the overthrow of the King's authority so enthusiastically only two years ago.

> "*George the Third: To our Trusty and Well-Beloved Lachlan Macquarie...*"

In the closeness of the carriage, Elizabeth fidgeted with her bonnet, trying, Sara guessed, to keep her face shaded so that the freckles wouldn't appear on her nose. But Henriette, almost four now, was unnaturally still, her eyes fixed in a long stare of concentration. She was fascinated by the spectacle before her. Never, in her short life, had she seen anything to equal the red and gold splendour of the uniforms; to her, the roll of the drums and the royal salute from the Battery were awe-inspiring. She seemed to have forgotten the irksomeness of her many petticoats under the India muslin dress. It amused Sara that Elizabeth, while paying no attention to the ceremony, thoroughly enjoyed looking pretty in a gown that was having only its second wearing.

Louis, standing beside the carriage, wore a slightly bored expression on his face—an expression which, whether intentional or not, plainly said that this little display of vice-regal pomp impressed him not at all. He shifted his hat to the other hand while the Judge-Advocate's voice droned on. The midday heat was intense; the crowd swished irritably at the flies that settled on faces and arms. Beside Louis, Duncan nudged his brother frequently, and, stretching on tip-toe, made many whispered remarks. Sara managed to lean down quietly and touch his shoulder with her parasol. He turned around, grinning impishly up at her, and then cocking a quizzical eyebrow at Elizabeth's discontented face.

The Governor finished his address, and again the guns roared from the Battery, and from the ships in the harbour. The drums started, and once more the band struck up the National Anthem. The tension in the crowd relaxed.

Louis opened the carriage door with an air of impatience. *"Mon Dieu,* how they love their little ceremonies!''

He didn't make it clear whether he referred to Governor Macquarie's party, or to the eager, gaping population.

As he was about to step into the carriage he halted, his head turned sideways, staring into the crowd which had broken its lines and begun to drift.

"Here's Jeremy Hogan!'' he said.

Sara leaned forward. Jeremy came towards them, smiling, his hat still in his hand.

"Jeremy!'' she cried, delightedly. "What brings you here? I thought an occasion like this wouldn't bring you down from the Hawkesbury—not even if the King himself..."

Her words were lost in the enthusiastic greeting of the two boys. Even Elizabeth stopped looking bored and smiled charmingly.

"Sometimes an Irish fit of sociability falls on me,'' Jeremy said, shaking hands with Louis. "I suddenly see myself growing dull and rusty in my wilderness, and then I think I must go and drink in some of the cultivated talk and habits of our great metropolis. They tell me there's even to be fireworks to-night—now, fireworks are something I never could resist..."

Louis was urging him towards the carriage. "Then you'll not be able to resist coming back to Glenbarr. Eat dinner with us, and we'll see if we can't persuade you to stay on. This evening we're having a bonfire and fireworks of our own to celebrate the coming of the Lord's anointed.''

Sara saw the broad smile that immediately crossed Duncan's face as he listened. "You're hardly respectful, Louis...''

"Nonsense, my dear!'' he laughed. "I hear the text of the

sermon the Reverend Cowper will preach is, 'Arise, anoint him; for this is he!'"

As he spoke he climbed into the carriage behind Jeremy, taking no notice of the wail of protest Elizabeth set up when she realised what the extra crowding would do to her muslin frills. Before he closed the door, Louis turned to the two boys.

"David, you'll make your own way back, won't you? There isn't any room in here now."

David nodded eagerly, "Yes, of course . . ."

Duncan, as soon as he heard Louis' words, waved his hand gaily, and charged off through the crowds towards the place where the band was still playing. David swung round to follow him.

Louis watched them with a smile. "That, I imagine, is the last we'll see of the pair of them until they're hungry and tired enough to want to come home."

He sat down and leaned back, and the carriage rolled forward. Its progress was slowed by the line of chaises and carriages ahead. Sara swished her fan to keep off the flies, staring at the throngs of people on foot, listening to them shouting and calling to each other. The soldiers on the Parade Ground had been dismissed, and they were now mingling with the crowd, their red uniforms notes of solid colour among the light cottons and muslins of the women. A pretty girl, hanging on the arm of a corporal of the 73rd, stared, with mildly envious eyes, into the de Bourgets' carriage, then her escort bent and said something in a low voice, and she looked up at him laughingly, forgetting the silk and the velvet upholstery that had caused her envy a few seconds ago. It was a Sunday afternoon, and yet the place had none of the decorum of a Sunday about it. The dust rose under the feet of the crowd; the heat and the noise made Sara's head ache, and set her thinking wistfully of the cool of Glenbarr.

Jeremy was doing a wickedly malicious little paraphrase of the sermon he imagined the earnest Mr. Cowper shortly afterwards delivering in St. Phillip's, greeting the new Governor as the Saviour of the colony. Louis, shaken out of his boredom, was highly amused, and lay back chuckling quietly. He had, true to his character, refused to join the small throng of people who had pressed forward immediately to be presented to Macquarie. He and Sara were invited to attend a reception at Government House later in the week, and it did not suit him to be one of the line waiting in the hot sun to be presented before the eyes of Sydney's interested population.

As the two men talked together Sara had time to examine Jeremy carefully, and to note the changes which the last years had brought to him. He was accustomed to his freedom now; his ease sat upon him naturally, his speech and humour no longer constrained, as when he had been Andrew Maclay's convict overseer. His coat was smartly cut, and his linen impeccable; he was stamped with the prosperity of the Hawkesbury farm. She saw, with some alarm, the streaks of grey in his black hair, and she realised then that he was, after all, forty-two, or perhaps forty-three, and his years in the colony, save the latter ones, had been hard and wearing. His face had a deep tan, and his skin was hardened by the weather. But he had the assurance of a man who is at peace with his world; she doubted if he often turned his thoughts backwards to Ireland. Fourteen years' penal servitude separated him from the man he had been there—a young man with a taste for women and good horses. He was confident of his future, and could shrug his shoulders at the memory of a sentence imposed for sedition. It had left no mark against his character; here, in the colony, he was free to rise as high as he wished. While Sara stared at him, she found herself thinking of the convict woman who was his mistress, and wondering if he would ever marry her.

That evening the entire de Bourget household, guests, children, and servants, stood around the huge bonfire that Edwards and Ted O'Malley were tending. At a smaller fire, Bess and Kate took turns at slowly turning a pig on a spit. The smell of roasting meat was heavy on the air.

Elizabeth, standing close to her father, gave a shrill squeak as a rocket shot into space, exploding in a shower of pink stars. The whole of the township was dotted over with the lights of the bonfires that burned to welcome Governor Macquarie. From a dozen different points that Sara could pick out and name, a series of fireworks coloured the night sky—from Captain Piper's garden, from the South Head, from the Parade Ground, from the ships in the harbour, from Dawes Point. Sydney had never looked so beautiful—the darkness hiding its ramshackle buildings, and a new moon over the water. Twenty bonfires glowed in the warm summer night.

Sara, lost in all the beauty about her, started a little at a light touch on her arm. Jeremy was beside her. He spoke in a low voice, which she could scarcely hear above the crackle of the flames.

"I've been trying to talk with you alone all evening, Sara."

She smiled, glancing at him. "Was it important, Jeremy?" Then her eyes went quickly back to Duncan, who had jumped away from a cracker which Edwards had let off almost under his feet.

"Important, I think, to you," Jeremy said quietly.

She turned to him, her smile fading. "What is it?"

"I wondered if you'd yet heard the news about Richard Barwell?"

"What news?" she said sharply. "What do you mean?"

"A letter arrived on the *Hindostan*. Lady Linton is dead. She has left Alison her fortune, of course. I heard this morning that Richard has been making inquiries about a passage back to England."

"For them both?" She struggled to keep the note of panic out of her voice.

"Yes, Sara—both."

"Well . . . thank you for telling me, Jeremy. I'm glad you were able to tell me before anyone else did."

Her lips quivered as she spoke, and the sudden tears blinded her. The bonfires, and the children's excited cries, belonged to another world. Sydney's hills, dotted with lights, swam before her gaze. Touching Jeremy's arm, she stepped back a few paces from the fire, grateful for the darkness which hid her face.

II

Glenbarr wore a drowsy air as Sara looked at it from across the lawn. It was mid-afternoon, and in most of the rooms the shades had been drawn against the direct sun. A fierce light came off the harbour, and Sara, turning occasionally to glance towards the bay, had to shield her eyes against the glare. Nothing stirred about the house; David, Duncan, and Elizabeth were at their lessons with Michael Sullivan; Louis had ridden down to the township to supervise the unloading from a ship of some pictures which had been sent from England for Banon. Beside her, Henriette was sitting in the swing, which the nursemaid, Fanny, was pushing in a dreamy fashion. The rhythmic creak of the ropes was a gentle, lazy sound on the warm air. The child's blue dress floated softly as she swung to and fro. From the direction of the stable came the distant sound of buckets clanking together; not even a suggestion of a breeze blew up off the water to stir the branches of the group of Norfolk pines under which they sat.

Now and then Henriette spoke, and Sara answered her absently; but the heat made them both lethargic. Sara's sewing lay on the ground beside her in a basket, but she had made no attempt to take it up. It was six days now since the reading of Macquarie's Commission, and, although the settlement was still carrying on its round of celebration, the heat, increasing day by day, was taking the energies and tempers of Sydney's inhabitants. Sara rested her back against the trunk of a tree, listening to the buzz of the insects about her; she stared across the lawn, which was turning brown after weeks without rain, to the drive, and she strained to catch the first sound of the horseman she expected.

But it was Henriette who saw Richard first. For the moment Sara's attention was distracted by the appearance of a fishing boat in the bay below the garden; Henriette's voice recalled her sharply.

"Here's someone coming, Mama!"

Sara turned quickly. She recognised the scarlet uniform of the Corps, but Richard had come on foot. He walked up the drive slowly, and, even at a distance, there was a dejected look about him that touched her strangely. A little nearer he halted, staring across at the group under the dark pines, and raising his hand to shield his eyes from the sun. The quivering heat-haze rose between them like a curtain.

Sara got to her feet.

"May I come too, Mama?"

Sara shook her head. "No, Henriette. It's time you went upstairs for your rest. Just ten minutes longer, Fanny, and then you can take her in."

"Very well, ma'am," Fanny said thankfully.

Sara stepped out from the shade of the trees, and began to walk across the dry lawn towards Richard.

Two days ago Richard had sent a note to Sara, asking if he might come to see her at Glenbarr. The note put an end to her hours of questioning and wondering since Jeremy had told her of Lady Linton's death, and the Barwells' plans to return to England. She had replied, telling him to come at a time when she could be quite certain Louis would be away from the house. And then she had settled to wait, her mind unnaturally clear and calm. She knew what Richard would say to her, almost knew the words he would use. This would be the unsatisfactory ending to the relationship that had existed between them since the day they had talked together on the little beach below the garden. For ten years their lives had run parallel—a time of being very close to one another, of love and tenderness, interspersed with quarrels and estrangements. This was not the feeling they had known for each other in the Bramfield days, when they had thought of love with children's minds; this feeling had brought Richard across the world to be at her side, and had given him ten years of frustration and bitterness.

She knew all this was coming to an end as she walked across the lawn towards him. She came up close to him, and put her hand into his.

"I'm glad you've come, Richard," she said.

He nodded, but made no reply.

She plucked at the sleeve of his tunic to lead him forward on to the veranda. He followed her up the steps, and along to the french window following into the drawing-room. As she passed through into the room beyond, she caught the flutter of Henriette's dress, like a pale blue flower under the lofty pines.

At all but one window the shades and curtains were drawn against the sun, and the room was dim. There was a cool look to the wax polish of the floors between the rugs, and the clean white walls. But flowers that had been put in fresh that morning were already fading in the heat. Many changes had been made in this room since Sara's marriage to Louis, but, in feeling, it was essentially as it was the first evening Richard and Alison had come for dinner. He looked about him carefully as he entered, and Sara guessed that the same thought was running through his head.

He stood by the mantelpiece, one hand resting on it, his gaze fixed on her face as she sat down on the sofa near him. His eyes wore a brooding look as they followed her movements.

"I suppose you've heard my news, Sara?" he said.

She nodded. "I imagine most people have heard it by this time."

He spoke hesitantly. "Then . . . you don't mind me coming here . . . like this? It's five years since I've been here to see you alone . . . five years, Sara!"

Suddenly her composure deserted her. Her mouth worked nervously; she stretched out her hand to him.

"Oh, Richard! Richard! If you hadn't come, I don't know how I could have borne it!"

In an instant he was with her, crouching on a low stool at her feet, both her hands clasped tightly in his own.

"My darling, Sara! I won't let go of you! There isn't any need for us to be apart again. Somehow I'll make Alison stay here . . . She must stay, if that's what I want!"

She bent until her face was against his forehead; she moved gently, and her lips brushed his cheek.

"Oh, hush, Richard! Hush! No more of it! This is what we said to each other ten years ago—and it didn't do any good, to either of us."

He pressed his face closer to her shoulder.

"God!" he said, in a low voice. "What a mess I've made of everything! You don't have to tell me that I behave like a child, Sara—I know that I do! And yet I can't help myself. I can no more stop loving you than breathing. But we've been nothing to each other all these years, but a constant torment."

With gentle hands she stroked his hair. "Don't blame yourself, my dearest. There's no blame . . ."

Abruptly he flung his head back, so that he was looking at her directly.

"But there *is* blame! Through my stupidity I've ruined Alison's life and my own. She's not happy—she's not been happy since . . ."

"But Alison loves you!" she protested. "You are her whole world—she doesn't see beyond you."

"That's what she would have everyone believe," he said. "That's what she made *me* believe. Oh . . . she loves me all right. There's no doubt about that. She loves me in a way I don't deserve—there's room in her heart for nothing else. But she also knows and understands me far better than I thought."

Sara was frowning. "What do you mean?"

"I mean that my loving, adoring wife has known what I felt for you since the first evening she met you."

"Richard . . . !"

"It's true! When the letter came to tell us that Lady Linton was dead, I told Alison that I wanted to stay in the colony. I tried to convince her that, with money in my hands, I could make much more money—as Andrew did. She told me then."

"What did she tell you?"

"She said that she wasn't having any more of the colony. She said she had been bored from the very moment she set foot in the place—and tired of the dull, stupid receptions, of seeing the same people every time she went out, of hearing the same talk. It appears that every year she's stayed here, it's grown worse and worse. And then . . ."

"Yes . . . ?"

He ran his hand distractedly across his face.

"Then she talked about you, Sara. She recalled to me the night we first came here, and then almost every other meeting we've had when she has been present. She remembers how we each acted, and what we said. Step by step she built it up, and put it to me. She made me see what I had done to her life, and yours. I have been useless to you—*she* pointed that out—it would have been much kinder and better if I'd left you in peace."

"And Alison . . ." she said slowly. "She kept silent all this time . . . and she still stayed with you, knowing what she did? Why?"

"I've already said that she loves me more than I deserve. I am not good enough—either for Alison, or for you, Sara. But she still loves me. It shames me to think of the way I've treated her—and you."

She said reflectively, "A long time ago, when I first heard that you and Alison had come to Sydney, I remarked to Julia Ryder that at last the colony would have a real lady to fuss over. At the time I said it, I didn't mean it generously, because I hated and feared the very thought of Alison. Now, when I think of her knowing of our love all these years, and yet being silent, I'm shamed also. She is a far greater lady than I believed."

His grip on her hands tightened. "It was a strange thing, seeing the wife I'd always dominated suddenly take control. She didn't cry, Sara—she didn't cry at all over the love I'd given you uselessly, and which she'd wanted for herself. But I hadn't heard the worst of it even then."

"The worst of it?" she said, alarmed. "Richard, what . . . ?"

"A few months ago D'Arcy Wentworth told her she hadn't much more than twelve months to live—perhaps more if she took a sea voyage. She hadn't talked of this to me because she knew there was no possibility of leaving the colony until her aunt died. But now she has the money, and she'll go. Her lungs are diseased. You've seen her yourself, Sara—she's like a shadow . . ."

He thrust his head against her shoulder again. "So . . . whether I want to or not, I can do nothing else but go back with her to England. If I've made her wretched all this time, then at least I owe her the last year."

Then he let go of her hands, and his arms went around her.

"Oh, Sara! Sara, what can I do? I'm lost without you—and yet I can't stay."

She cradled his head against her breast, her arms holding him tightly. "Dearest, go with Alison. You'll find some sort of peace away from me. We're no good to each other—we torture and destroy, both of us. I have Louis and the children, and I will be happy here. And you—in London, when you have money, you will find distractions. That's your world, Richard. That's where you belong."

"Do I really belong anywhere in the world without you, Sara? Ever since we were children . . ."

His words were stilled abruptly as she bent over him and kissed him on the lips.

"There is nothing more to say, my dearest. I love you, always. Just kiss me, Richard, and let this be our goodbye."

Slowly he rose to his feet. He pulled her up to him, and gathered her into his arms.

"Oh, Sara! Sara! What shall I do without you?"

She put her arms about his neck, and as they kissed she could feel the hot tears on her cheeks. Already she had the sense of him having gone beyond her reach.

III

Richard and Alison sailed from Port Jackson, in the *Hindostan*, at the beginning of May, 1810, with the rest of the disbanded New South Wales Corps. To Sara, the period of waiting for their going seemed endless. The *Hindostan* and the *Dromedary* were to travel back to England together, but they had first to be victualled and repaired. The round of farewell parties dragged on, and the months passed slowly.

Bligh, who had returned to Sydney in the leaking old *Porpoise*, too late to be reinstated as Governor, was also to sail in the *Hindostan*. His enforced stay in Port Dalrymple had sharpened his temper, and the delays seemed to give him a perverse delight.

He and Macquarie had hated each other on sight; Bligh's presence in Sydney was a perpetual embarrassment to the new

Governor. At the end of April, he gave a ball and a fête in his predecessor's honour, to speed him thankfully on his way.

Sara was nervous and unable to rest while the two ships remained at anchor and she knew that Richard had not yet embarked. She suggested to Louis that they should return to Banon, and he, understanding her unease, made arrangements immediately for their departure to the Nepean.

She was at Banon, in May, when the news reached her that the two ships had at last left the harbour.

The knowledge that Richard was finally gone gave her a peace that helped cover her feeling of solitude and loneliness. Now there could be no more shared memories of the Romney Marsh—there was no one who might ever mention her father's name. Richard had taken with him the image of the young Sara Dane.

IV

Governor Macquarie had small liking for the state of affairs in which he found the colony when he arrived. He knew exactly into what shape he wanted to mould the small world he ruled, and he set about it with determined energy. The dilapidated buildings of Sydney annoyed him—he visioned them replaced by solid, prosperous-looking stone; he wanted better roads, and he got them, paying for them by constructing turn-pikes. A new hospital was started; St. Phillip's Church was finished and consecrated. Macquarie's energy touched everything; it reached everywhere.

Offered the example of his own lavish hospitality, the social life of the colony blossomed. It was fashionable to take picnics along the newly-finished South Head Road, and to make an occasion of Sunday morning church-going. There was a regular promenade in the evenings in Hyde Park, to the music of the Regimental Band; private parties and balls—always overcrowded with the officers of the 73rd—punctuated the weeks. A race-course had been laid out in Hyde Park, and the annual Race Week, in October, became Sydney's greatest social event. On the other side, the fierce, bawdy, often grim life of the town persisted, but in three years Macquarie had pushed it back to its own district—known as The Rocks—and confined it to the convict barracks. He liked and encouraged the veneer of genteel and polite society, and society, such as it was, rewarded him by a determined effort towards elegance.

But there was another quirk to the Governor's character less to the liking of the colony's élite; he had a curious partiality for emancipists. He favoured them whenever possible, and encouraged them to mix in the social junketings. But he was not as strong as the traditions which excluded the emancipists. He might bid them to dine at Government House, and appoint them to committees—but he could not force their entry into the drawing-rooms of the officer and merchant class. When His Excellency pointed out the degree of acceptance Sara de Bourget had won, he was gently reminded that all emancipists were not fortunate enough to marry men too powerful, too well-born, and too wealthy to be snubbed.

For Sara the three years following Macquarie's coming were, on the surface, tranquil ones. But she had to learn gradually an acceptance of the fact that Richard was gone; beneath her calmness there was a sense of loss. He had been so small a part of her daily life since her marriage, and yet she had known as much about him as local gossip knew—had seen him quite often at the gatherings they both attended, and had sometimes spoken to him. But with his going even these familiar things were gone. No one spoke of him any more, and there was no excuse for mentioning his name. Hyde Farm had changed owners twice in that short time, so that not even there had he left a permanent mark. Richard had never belonged at the heart of the colony's affairs, and the colony forgot him quickly.

By this time, Louis was reconciled to a life passed half at Banon, half at Glenbarr; Sara no longer went to the store, but merely looked over the accounts when Clapmore brought them to Glenbarr. Nor did she ride so often to Kintyre, Priest's, or Toongabbie; Jeremy Hogan still had the greater part of the control of Kintyre, and the overseers of the other two farms were efficient enough, in their fashion. She had learned by now that she must pay the price of lower profits from both, if she was to have peace with Louis. She was not over-anxious about the fall in the profits from the farms; she looked on this time simply as a period of waiting until David and Duncan were old enough to take charge themselves, and when their own ambition would make it unnecessary for her to exert herself. With each year the acreage of cleared land at Dane Farm was increasing, and the merino flocks spreading wider. The *Hawk*, *Thistle*, and *Thrush* carried, on every voyage, a substantial cargo of her wool to the

London market. At times Louis still called her a shopkeeper, but she was amused to notice that his former contempt was missing from the title.

It was at the beginning of 1812 that she received her only letter from Richard. He wrote simply and quite briefly, telling her of Alison's death, at Lady Linton's house in Devon. She was saddened by the news. Poor Alison! she thought—she had loved so futilely. Richard was unworthy of such love, and yet Sara knew so well that it was as natural to give it, as it was to breathe. She wondered about his life now, and pictured him, surrounded by the London gaiety he had always leaned towards, left in possession of the fortune Alison had not been able to spend. She tried to make herself believe that Richard would be happy now, in the new wealth and freedom he had found.

Chapter Eight

There were lights and an air of bustle through the whole of Glenbarr as Sara mounted the stairs to her bedroom, on the last night of 1812. Below, she clearly caught the sound of the servants' voices, chattering in the hall, on their way to the kitchen; here, close at hand, she sensed the excitement and the careful dressing that went on behind the closed bedroom doors. Glenbarr was gay; it wore a festive look. She paused at the head of the stairs, and glanced about her. The balustrade was hung with garlands of Elizabeth's fashioning, and bowls of wild flowers, in great masses, stood in every corner. In the dining-room, the supper tables were laid; the drawing-room was prepared for cards, and sofas lined the walls for those who preferred simply to gossip.

Suddenly the excitement communicated itself to Sara herself; she picked up her skirt and half ran along to the window at the end of the landing. This window overlooked the garden at the side of the house, where a marquee had been erected for the dancers. It was brightly lit, two sides open to the warm night, and to the view of the harbour. The sky was clear; later there would be a moon. She stood still and listened, and even above the voices of the men as they put last-minute touches to the decorations, and the scrape of a fiddle from a solitary member of the orchestra, who sat on a wooden box by the entrance to the marquee, playing a tune for the benefit of himself and two gardeners, she could hear the gentle murmur of the water on the rocks below. The tune went on—one of Tommy Moore's lovely, sentimental ballads, which she hummed to herself as she stood there. Then the mood changed—a lively Irish jig this time, with a touch of laughter in it. She could not recognise the man seated there, silhouetted against the light, but she knew she listened to a cry from the heart of an exile. The gardeners moved off, and for a few moments there was nothing but the sound of the water as a faint accompaniment to the tune on the fiddle.

She swung round at a step beside her. David had come out of his bedroom, and was walking towards her with a smile.

"Not dressed yet, Mother?"

She shook her head. "It doesn't take me as long as Elizabeth. I'm no belle—besides, I've been doing it for many more years than she has!"

"Elizabeth won't outshine you, for all that!" he said, and suddenly leaned forward and kissed her on the cheek. "You're still the most beautiful woman in the colony—and what's more, you know it!"

Sara laughed, reaching out to take hold of his hair and pull it. Then her hand dropped. "I can't even do that, can I? You're much too immaculate, David."

"And that's the way I mean to stay!"

She looked at him with satisfaction. He was nineteen, taller even than Louis, handsome, with his fair hair above the blue coat he wore. He had grown into a thoughtful, quiet young man, but Sara felt that she was very seldom able to reach into his mind and discover what he believed in. She had his love and loyalty, but not his confidences. David was, in a small way, a perfectionist—he attempted nothing that he was not sure could be well and efficiently completed. He had left Michael Sullivan's care now, and was preparing to take over some of the management of Priest's. He seemed happy enough with this, contented—and yet she was afraid that his enthusiasm had no passion in it; he seemed to be doing this because there was nothing else for him. He shot and rode well, he was polite, charming, anxious to please—and yet he constantly wore a slightly aloof air. He shared their family life readily enough, but always seemed relieved when the time came for him to make one of his solitary trips to Priest's, or one of the other properties. She knew quite well that David loved her, but he had never given her his heart completely. She felt a vague disquiet whenever she looked at him searchingly, especially this evening—handsome, and suddenly appearing older than his nineteen years; he so completely lacked the passion that had been Andrew's, and which Duncan possessed in such abundance.

But she shook off the feeling, smiling and tapping him lightly on the cheek with the palm of her hand. "Don't you worry, I won't disarrange you. Although I can imagine the flutter of feminine hearts . . ."

She broke off as a door was flung open noisily farther along the passage. Duncan came out of his room, grinning broadly.

"How do I look, Mother? Am I all right?"

"You look splendid, Duncan—magnificent!"

He flushed a little with pleasure, and smoothed an imaginary crease in his trousers. Looking at him, Sara was touched. His coat was far too brilliant a red—Louis, she knew, would privately deplore it—but it was Duncan's own choice, and he was happy in it. He had a graceless rather untidy charm about him, and a confidence that allowed no difficulties to stand in his way. The whole household adored and waited upon him; he had a heart for gossip, and he had friends in every possible level of Sydney's widening population. He rode his mare and sailed his skiff in the harbour with a reckless, heartwarming fervour. In Duncan, there was nothing of his brother's touch of introspection.

Sara reached automatically to smooth the ruffles at his throat.

"Mother, will you be sure to save a dance for me?" he said. "I've been practising with Elizabeth, but she says on no account am I to dance with anyone but you and herself or I'll disgrace us all."

"I'll be proud to dance with you, my dear."

In the hall below, the clock began to chime. Sara looked at her sons in alarm.

"I must go . . . or I'll never be dressed and ready to dance with anyone!"

Again she picked up her skirt and hurried along the passage. David looked after her affectionately; but Duncan was absorbed in pulling his new coat into a better position.

II

Sara was almost finished dressing when Louis came into the bedroom. He walked slowly across the floor and stood behind her, for a few moments studying her reflection in the mirror. Then he bent towards the dressing-table and drew from its case the necklace of sapphires, which he had given her two years earlier. When he fastened it about her throat, by contrast to her stiff, ivory brocade gown, its colour came to sudden life. He smiled, brushed his lips briefly against her shoulder, and then strolled over to the window.

"The garden looks attractive," he said.

She nodded, remembering how it had looked when she had stood at the window on the landing outside. Small coloured lanterns had been placed to mark the edges of the lawn and the drive; they had been lit now, and glowed softly in the darkness. A sense of expectancy had fallen on the house and garden; they waited for the sound of music and laughter, the voices of couples who would walk arm in arm across the lawn.

"But the mosquitoes will plague to death anyone rash enough to venture out," Louis added.

Sara glanced over her shoulder at him, but he still stood peering out, his hands clasped behind his back. From the way he spoke she knew that he was merely making conversation, while his mind turned over some other thought. But she waited, knowing that, in his own time, he would tell her what it was. She looked at herself again in the mirror, rearranging the set of a curl in her hair.

"It will be scorching by noon tomorrow," he said, glancing at the cloudless sky and the moon that was now beginning to appear over the harbour. "Just the sort of day to put everyone in a thoroughly foul humour for the Races. I have an uncomfortable certainty that I'm not going to beat David for the Magistrates' Purse."

"That would be a pity," she said slowly. "Perhaps it would do David good to be beaten at something. I think he's almost afraid of the race, in case it proves to be an occasion on which he will fail to achieve what he wants. He's a shade too successful at most things. It's not good..."

"Oh, a race..." he said, shrugging, "I think it needs more than a race to shake David."

A hint of impatience in his tone made Sara turn quickly. Behind his back, Louis' hands clenched and unclenched rhythmically.

"What do you mean, Louis?" she said.

380

He wheeled round. "I'm not just talking of David. It's all the children . . . Duncan, and Elizabeth, and even Henriette."

Puzzled, she frowned. "I'm afraid I don't understand. What's wrong with them?"

He flung his hands in a gesture that indicated his uncertainty.

"I'm not at all sure. But I can't help feeling that it's a great pity there *is* nothing here to shake them occasionally. They've seen nothing . . . This party tonight, for example . . . To their minds, it represents the very peak of elegance and fashion—because they don't know anything better. They live, more or less, at the top of their world—and they're inclined to forget that it's a very small one."

She turned gravely back to the mirror. "You're right, of course," she said, her eyes meeting the reflection of his. "But what is to be done about it? Whenever I've talked to David about his going to England, he has always said he prefers to stay where he is. It's too late for school, I know, but . . ."

"School! That's not where he'll learn what life in England is like! David is just the right age for London. He is old enough to enjoy it—and young enough to absorb it."

Sara noticed that her hands were trembling slightly as she reached to pick up her long gloves. "And the others . . . ? What of them?"

"They need it, just as he does. Elizabeth is seventeen, Sara. She will fall in love with some young subaltern here from the regiment, without ever knowing that any other sort of men exist."

She raised her eyebrows. "I trust you're not forgetting, Louis, that, in England, marriages for girls are not arranged quite in the same way as they are in France. Elizabeth should be allowed to choose for herself. And if she wants to stay here to marry . . ."

He held up his hands. "*Mon Dieu!* I'm not suggesting an arranged marriage for her! I hope—and I feel quite certain she will—return here to the colony to finally settle. Because this is where she has been happiest. But she should know, while she is still young enough to make a choice, what sort of face the rest of the world wears!"

Sara fumbled clumsily with her bracelet, struggling to fasten it over her glove.

"You suggest the three should go, then?"

In the mirror she watched him cross the room to her. He stood behind her chair, tenderly taking her shoulders between his hands.

"Let all of us go, Sara."

Startled, her hand flew to her throat.

"All of us! You and I also . . . ?"

"A year or two. No longer."

"But . . . To leave Glenbarr . . . Banon . . . I don't think I want to do that, Louis."

"But why not? Must you be forever chained here? I'm beginnning to think that you need a glimpse of the outside world quite as badly as the children do."

She made no reply. Her head bent forward, and she began to pluck at the ospreys in her fan. Louis' fingers on her shoulders tightened a little.

"Sara . . . my darling! What is it?"

Suddenly she flung back her head and her eyes met his directly in the mirror before her.

"I'm afraid!" she said passionately. "That's what's wrong with me! I've been in this colony for twenty years and I'm afraid to move outside of it. Here, they all know my story and they've stopped whispering over it long ago. I have my own place here—and you ask me to leave it, and go and face the gossip in London? You want me to hear my past raked over and over for all its juiciest pieces? Once, Louis, you reminded me that I arrived in the colony in a convict transport—and you said I'd never again suffer like that. It would be possible to make me suffer in a much worse way. If you . . ."

His thick brows came together. 'Hush, Sara! You let your imagination run away with you! Who is there in London to make you suffer? Truly, my dearest, you're looking at the whole matter in the light in which Sydney would see it. Tell me, who will point to your life and say that you have cause for shame? London has long recognised what Sydney is afraid to acknowledge—that there were many travesties of justice in the sentences of transportation. To those who know your story, you are guilty of nothing more than a childish prank. Have you forgotten the sophistication and cynicism of London? You have position, money—London cares for little else. It would be a happy thing for England if the Prince himself were surrounded by people as guiltless as yourself. Can you not believe that?"

"But that's not all!" she said, shaking her head, as if to thrust aside the reassurances he offered. "The children themselves . . . !

What makes you so certain that they will want to go? Elizabeth, maybe—but will David and Duncan want to go? If David refuses, I can't force him. It would be natural if he wanted to stay here now that he has begun to take over the farming. I can't believe that he will leave it readily."

"Ah, Sara . . . children are never the creatures we like to believe they are. You and Andrew built your fortune from a rough farmhouse on the Hawkesbury—but you can't expect your children to cherish their possessions as you have done. They haven't had to work for them—and they don't remember much about the time before their father was a man of importance. You'd like to think that it is love of Kintyre that makes their hearts beat—and that they couldn't leave it, or any of the other places, for a year or two. But you are wrong. To them, the things they own are an established fact—something they've always had, always waiting for their return. When a new side of life is offered them, it's not in their nature to refuse."

She fingered the sapphires nervously. She said quietly, "Louis, what makes you so sure of all this? How do you know what they will feel about it?"

He pressed her shoulders back until she leaned against him. She could feel the stiffness of his brocade waistcoat on her bare flesh. He bent over her slightly.

"I know—because I asked them, Sara," he said.

"You . . . Without asking me first!"

"Don't be angry with me, my love. I knew quite well that you'd be afraid—and I wanted to forestall that fear with every argument against it I could summon. I asked them, because I had to know before I spoke to you about it. Sara, they *need* to get away from this place, so that they can come back to it gladly. How can they appreciate what they've always lived with? How can they be expected to realise the peace you and I have found here, when they've known nothing else? It's for their sakes that I want this trip to England. But they need you with them."

Miserably she clenched her hands. "It won't be as easy as you make it sound! Once they get a taste of London life, they'll despise this one. They won't want to come back—and all the work of these years will go for nothing. I've struggled to keep the farms and the store working, so that they should be ready for them to take over. Give them a year of London's gaiety, and they'll want to sell up what they have here. Oh, Louis, don't you see that?"

"Do you have such little faith in their attachment to this place, Sara? My only thought was to convince them that, by comparison, their lives here were full and satisfying. You can't possibly believe that they will never want to make the voyage. Let them go now . . ."

He broke off at the sound of running footsteps in the passage outside. There was a knock on the door. He released his grip on Sara's shoulders, and stepped back a little.

"Come in!"

The door burst open immediately, and Elizabeth stood there. She wore a gown of soft, white silk, that seemed almost the colour of her skin. This was her first ball-gown, and her father had decreed that it be completely simple, with none of the elaborate trimmings she had yearned for. Sara looked at her and smiled. Louis' choice was a triumph; Elizabeth was radiant and beautiful in it.

"You look wonderful, Elizabeth!" she said admiringly. "You're a picture!"

"Yes . . ." Elizabeth gave an excited little laugh. "David and Duncan have just said the same—though Henriette seemed to think it was too plain, when I went to the nursery to show it to her. She didn't actually say, but I expect she would have preferred something in a bright red. Duncan had paid her a visit before me, and his new coat was much admired by our young despot."

She stepped into the room, and twirled before them.

"Papa, do you like it?"

"I do indeed, my darling. I'm extremely proud of you."

Then Elizabeth's gloved hand flew to her mouth in alarm.

"Mercy, I'd forgotten to tell you what I came up especially for! The first of the guests has arrived. It's only old Mr. Bridie. He made straight for the supper-room, and didn't seem to notice that you weren't down yet. He *walked* here—that's why you didn't hear the carriage." Her tone implied complete mystification over people who walked, when they might just as easily have ridden.

She turned to leave them, but paused, looking back slowly.

"Papa . . . have you talked about it yet?" she asked hesitantly. "I mean . . . you promised to speak to Mama this evening."

"Yes Elizabeth—we've discussed it."

The girl's face lit up. "Is it settled, then? Are we to go?"

"It's not completely settled," Louis said. "Not yet."

384

Suddenly Elizabeth ran to Sara's side. "Please, Mama, say we can go! I'm longing to see what London is like—and to see the country. If I could just once hunt with a Midland pack, I'd be happy. Imagine how terrible it would be to grow old and fat without ever having ridden to hounds!" She brushed a fleeting kiss on Sara's cheek. "Do think about it—and say we may go!"

Then she turned and fled. They could hear her calling to David as she ran down the stairs.

Sara stood up, smoothed her long gloves over each arm, and opened the osprey fan out to its full width.

"It seems," she said, looking at Louis, "that my mind is being quite firmly made up for me."

A slow smile spread across his face. Leaning forward, he kissed her lightly on the temple.

"I've always thought I should enjoy the chance of showing you off to London, my love."

He offered her his arm, and they left the room together.

III

A sense of bewilderment and disappointment crowded in upon Sara all through the party. The guests arrived, and she greeted them smilingly, but always thankful when each one passed on, and she was spared the effort of making further conversation. The rooms filled with voices and laughter; music floated faintly from the marquee, where, as usual, the men were too numerous, and young subalterns—not so much out of politeness, but simply because they had the urge to dance—danced with grandmothers, three times their own age. The women were surrounded by admiring little groups, and Elizabeth, for whom nothing that evening could possibly go wrong, insisted upon splitting her dances in half, to fit in all her partners. She was the complete coquette, without a trace of shyness, and a flush of excitement on her cheeks. David, when he came to ask her to dance, got a laughing refusal; but when the Governor presented himself, she rose demurely and curtsied. There was no thought in her head of splitting this dance!

At last, when all but the few late-comers had arrived, David came to where Sara stood with Louis in the hall. He smiled, and offered his arm.

"Mother has had enough now, don't you think, sir?" he said, looking at Louis. "If people arrive as late as this, they don't deserve to be welcomed. I propose to take her to the supper-room for something cool to drink. And then perhaps she'll dance with me.''

Louis nodded, glancing about him. ''And I must go and find Mrs. Macquarie . . . David, do you suppose I'll have to join a line of officers waiting for the favour of dancing with the Governor's Lady?''

He wandered off into the drawing-room, straightening his gloves, and searching each sofa and card-table in turn.

In the supper-room, David led Sara to a chair and brought her a glass of champagne. It was chilled, and she sipped it gratefully. He talked lightly to her, criticising some of the more pompous guests, describing, with impudent exaggeration, the florid details of the gown worn by the wife of one of the colony's most prominent citizens.

''. . . purple, Mother—with large yellow bows! Truly, even the natives have more taste!''

Then he hurried away from Sara's side to bring a chair for Julia Ryder, who had just entered on the arm of William Cooper. He called to Bennett for more champagne, and he went off himself to attend to the serving of some food.

''David does you great credit, Sara,'' Julia remarked, nodding in his direction.

''Indeed, Madame de Bourget, your son is known throughout the colony as a young man of the *most* graceful manner!'' William Cooper murmured this with heavy flattery.

Julia interrupted briskly.

''I hope this rumour of your going to England is true. The children all need it, Sara. They shouldn't grow up in this colony without a notion of what the rest of the world is like. They'll be better for it—all of them. You yourself have earned a few years of leisure, and so has Louis. You can't expect a Frenchman not to get restless sometimes for the sort of life he's known once.''

Sara smiled, making a non-committal reply, and thankful when David returned and insisted upon taking her to the marquee to dance.

''I think I must have been the very last person to know of this visit to England,'' she said to him as they stepped out on to the veranda. ''In the minds of everyone here, I'm sure we're already packed and almost gone. And I hadn't heard a whisper of it until a few hours ago!''

"Oh, Elizabeth has been talking," David said. "She's so excited about it."

They walked across the grass in silence. They paused at the entrance of the marquee, watching the intermingling of the scarlet uniforms with the more sober coats of the civilians, and the soft colours of the women's dresses.

"How gay we all are these days!" Sara said. "Twenty years ago there wasn't a piece of silk in the whole colony as fine as the most commonplace gown here tonight." She spoke absently, as if the memory was something that did not, even remotely, touch David. Then she drew closer to him, and her voice changed.

"How badly do you want to go to England, David? Louis says he has talked to you about it. And I want to be quite sure you are not agreeing just to please him."

He turned and looked at her directly. "I want to go, Mother—very much. And it isn't to please anyone but myself."

Then he led her forward to join the dancers.

Sara found the same reaction from Duncan when she opened the subject of the trip to England. She had a few minutes' conversation with him after they finished their dance together. It had grown almost breathlessly hot, and they strolled to the edge of the lawn, where the coloured lanterns marked the flowerbeds.

"There's so much I want to do in London, Mother," he said eagerly. "I'd like to take some fencing lessons—and go to one of the riding-schools. And there's the playhouse . . . You know, they say if one rides in Hyde Park in the afternoons, you'll see almost all the swells . . ."

She smiled, and patted his hand. "I'm sure you do. Do the—swells—mean very much to you, Duncan?"

He frowned. "Not a great deal. But I'd just like to *see* them."

The hours were long and tedious to Sara until the last couples reluctantly left the marquee, the card-tables and sofas emptied, and the carriages rolled down the drive. They had toasted the New Year in at midnight, when a piper from the regiment had solemnly strode the lawn, his thin, eerie notes drifting across the garden to the silent guests. Two natives, fishing by the light of the moon in the bay below, heard the piping, and were convinced that it was the wail of an evil spirit. Like shadows, they slipped away in their canoe.

The Governor and his party had left at two o'clock, but it was dawn before the general exodus began. The servants went slowly about extinguishing candles; the coloured lanterns along the lawns flickered feebly in the growing light. The supper-tables were being cleared.

Arm in arm, Elizabeth and David climbed the stairs, laughing together over something Duncan had said. Elizabeth's dark eyes had the fixed look of tiredness about them, but her feet moved as lightly as they had done at the begining of the evening.

"We're going to England . . . ! To England . . . ! To England. . . . !" she sang, as she mounted the last few steps to the landing. The words, in her sweet, high voice, were a stab at Sara's heart.

IV

She laid the sapphires carefully in their case, and sat looking at them, not attempting to begin undressing. She no longer fought her disappointment and fear. They would all go to England—that much was certain now. Since Louis first spoke of it early in the evening, she had been waiting for a denial from the children—at least from David. She was counting on his enthusiasm for the work he was doing at Priest's being great enough to fight the attractions of London. It was difficult, looking at the impeccable David this evening to remember that he wasn't much more than a boy yet. Louis was right, she thought, wearily. She expected far too much from both her sons—she expected them to know, as if they too had been through it the first years of struggle on the Hawkesbury. In time, she told herself, they would learn their own lessons about the price they must pay as owners of property—but they would not be the same lessons as she and Andrew had learnt. Perhaps, after all, a trip to England was what they needed to teach them the value of their possessions here.

She sighed, closing down the lid on the sapphires. Rightly or wrongly, she was committed to making the voyage now. As she kicked off her slippers, she noticed that at last a faint breeze was stirring. But it would probably be gone when she woke again, and the sun beating harshly against the side of the house. Then she remembered that, in the afternoon, she would have to take her place with the crowds thronging Hyde Park, to watch Louis and David race for the Magistrate's Purse. She slipped off her stockings, wriggling her toes, and relishing the softness of the carpet beneath them. She wished she were at Kintyre, or Banon—

anywhere that would excuse her from the dust and heat of the Races in a few hours' time.

She was sitting up in bed, sipping the glass of cold milk that Annic had brought, when Louis opened the door and came in quietly. He wore a long, dark red robe over his nightshirt. He moved rather slowly as he came towards her.

"*Mon Dieu!* How old and feeble I must be growing, when a few hours' dancing fatigues me!" He flung himself full length on the bed, lying on his back, with his hand beneath his head. "And to think I was fool enough to say I'd ride against men as young as David tomorrow."

"Today," she reminded him.

"Today—so it is! I'll not be fit to climb on a horse by afternoon, much less race." Suddenly he rolled over, propping himself on his elbow to look at her. "I have it, Sara! We must invent a serious malady—a fever that keeps me abed, and you must stay to nurse me. I shall lie in a darkened room all afternoon, away from the heat and the noise of those yelling fools. I . . ."

Then a smile crept across his face.

"What is it?" she said.

"I was thinking . . . that it would be pleasant if you could lie beside me."

They laughed together, and she reached out to pull his hair, much in the way she had done with David earlier. He jerked his head away, catching hold of her wrist.

"I shall have to subdue you, Madame! You grow undutiful and insubordinate! In fact, I think an afternoon would be well spent . . ."

She put the glass down quickly, and clapped her hand over his mouth. "Enough! I'll have respect . . . !"

He bit at her fingers until she was forced to withdraw.

"Respect, is it? That's the trouble—you've always commanded too much of that. I remember . . ."

"Remember what?"

"I remember the first time I saw you, in the cottage of the amiable Nell Finnigan—who, incidentally, has become monstrously fat of late. Never get fat, Sara—it's so unbecoming!" He pulled himself closer to her. "When I first saw you, I said to myself, 'Ah, here is a woman of great passion!'—and I was driven quite wild by the sight of you. But, *Mon Dieu*, you were so

389

wrapped around in your respectability! When you left I remember lamenting that this was New South Wales and that civilization had not yet touched its shores."

"What do you mean?"

"It's simple! If this had been Paris, or London, after a little wooing, there would be every chance of you becoming my mistress. But, alas, it was New South Wales—and what could I do but wait until I could marry you!"

Abruptly he reached up and caught her shoulders, pulling her down off the pillows.

"It has been worth even marriage to have you for myself," he murmured, as he kissed her. "And once married, I was glad the ways of the civilised world hadn't yet caught up with the colony. I have the most uncivilised notion of keeping you all to myself."

V

Sara was standing at the rails with Elizabeth and the usual attendance of young officers, watching the finish of the race for the Magistrates' Purse, and she saw clearly everything that happened. She saw the dog break suddenly from the crowd and dash madly on to the course as the first horses galloped towards him. Louis was fourth, on the outside, and almost on top of the dog before he saw it. His horse started, swerved violently, and fell; Louis was thrown heavily. Directly behind, the next three riders, unable to pull up, rode straight over the top of them both. Another horse went down in the general tangle, but the rider got to his feet immediately, and began to limp towards Louis.

As soon as all the horses were past, the screaming crowd broke past the barriers and raced forward. Sara closed her eyes tightly, and turned away. She leaned back against the rails for support.

They told her later that Louis had broken his neck in the fall. The surgeon said he had probably been dead even before the first of the other horses had reached him.

Chapter Nine

The storm had broken at about seven o'clock, coming at the end of a day of murderous, stifling heat. For two hours now it had rained without pause—rain that slashed against the houses, and turned the streets into soft mud. In the east the lightning still flickered, followed by cracks of thunder, but the worst violence of the storm was past. Out at sea it raged yet; it had a devilish fury, and the waves pounded the headlands at the entrance to the harbour. The township was deserted; its odd, untidy buildings seemed to huddle together before the onslaught of the rain. One moment they lay in darkness, the next they were suddenly bathed in the eerie blue flash of the lightning. There were pale lamps here and there, and the taverns were crowded out; but the streets were deserted. Sydney had the unreal look of a toy town—the mushroom houses had sprung up wherever they pleased along the crooked, winding streets; the shipping tossed about in the bay like a child's boats—and the sea ran wild at its very doorstep.

In a room above the store that still carried Andrew Maclay's name, Sara watched Clapmore begin to take down some rolls of material. She watched him listlessly, feeling unnaturally weary, as if the long day of heat had drained her energy, and the storm coming at the end of it had no power to stimulate her. She had left Glenbarr as soon as the storm was past its height, and had driven alone to the store. She had come straight to this room upstairs, leaving Edwards huddling into the doorway below, refusing to come inside. A young stable-boy held the horses, shivering, she imagined, half with fear of the lightning, and half from the rain, which, by now, must have soaked him through. The decision to come here at this time of night had been forced upon her by the fact that Louis had been dead only two days, and she had no intention of shocking the town by letting herself be seen driving abroad so soon. In the darkened store Clapmore had cautiously answered Edwards's knocking, holding a lantern high, and then quickly throwing back the bolts as he recognised the carriage and its occupant. His red-headed wife came from the back room to bob a curtsy, murmur her appropriate words of sympathy, and then disappear. Clapmore, as soon as Sara told him her errand, went hurrying before her with a lamp, up the stairs to the storeroom above.

"I'd have brought them myself, if I'd only known, ma'am," he hastened to assure her.

"Of course, Clapmore—I know. But there's been so much to think about all day, that I had no time to send a message. When the storm broke this evening I was too restless to stay in the house. I thought this was a good chance . . ."

He nodded, setting down the lantern, going to the shelves and flinging back the dust-covers. For almost fifteen years now he had worked for Sara, and he would just as soon have questioned the coming and going of the seasons as her movements. If she had cared to visit the store at midnight he would have received her, knowing that she had had good reason for what she did.

He brought the rolls forward, laying them, side by side, on the big centre trestle table. The black material glimmered dully in the light of the lantern. Sara fingered it . . . black silk, black satin, black bombazine. All of it black, like the draped windows at Glenbarr, like the gown she wore now, and the bonnet. Clapmore spread out more and more of it, until she began to feel that the whole of Sydney could have taken this wretched stuff and gone into mourning for Louis de Bourget. There were gowns for herself and Elizabeth to be made from it, shawls, cloaks . . . Suddenly she could bear the sight no longer. She turned and moved swiftly away to the window.

Clapmore stared after her. "Why, ma'am . . . !"

She didn't speak. She gripped the edge of the sill, staring out across the deserted wharf, which the store overlooked. Beyond that, in the darkness, were the tumbled waters of the harbour. With the rain she couldn't even see the navigation lights of the ships. For a few moments she gave herself up completely to her sense of desolation and loss. It didn't matter to her what Clapmore might be thinking. For the two days since Louis' death she had been unable to give way to her feelings; there was always Elizabeth to remember, and Henriette. She had determined that they should not be saddened more than was necessary by the sight of her own grief. But she wasn't disturbed by Clapmore's presence; he was hardly more personal than the furnishings of the store itself. She didn't care that he might see the tears glistening on her cheeks. He had known her since her first years in the colony, he had known her life both with Andrew and with Louis, and he was not so unperceptive that he couldn't guess at her misery and anguish. Louis' death had left her dazed; she found it almost impossible to believe that he was gone. Louis had possessed her body and soul; he had very nearly succeeded in winning her away from the things she had believed she could never put aside—the farms, the ships, the store. For the last two years she knew that she had been madly impatient for David and Duncan to reach the age when they would take full control of their possessions, and her time would be free to devote to Louis.

He had been a demanding, exacting and selfish man, but he was stronger than she; he had bent her will to his own, as no one else had ever done.

She sensed the patient attitude of Clapmore, standing by the table with his sober black rolls. It was a good thing, she thought, that he was not a woman, who might have come forward with mawkish, feminine sympathy; who might put a flabby hand on her shoulder and offer her platitudes Louis himself would have abhorred. Men always understood better about these things. If she wanted to weep alone by the window, that was her own affair, and he had the good sense to know it. She wanted Louis back—and she felt that Clapmore would know that too—she wanted his conversation, his habit of being amused at the things this small world took so seriously, she wanted back the elegance, the charm, and the passion that had been his. He had added to each day a spice of excitement and of pleasure, and she must somehow learn not to expect them any longer.

She hoped desperately that her tears would not turn into the kind of sobbing that had racked her last night, because even Clapmore couldn't be expected to stay where he was and not try to do something to help. She didn't want to be rude to him.

Above the noise of the rain she hadn't heard the voices below the window, where Edwards and the boy waited; the sound of the knocker hammering against the door was shockingly loud and sudden. Clapmore turned in a startled fashion, as if he expected the unknown caller to come straight up the stairs. He seemed to be rooted were he stood.

"Better answer it, I think," Sara said quietly, "But there's no need to mention to whoever it is that I'm here."

"Oh, no, ma'am, certainly not." He took up the second lantern, and ran lightly down the stairs.

Hastily Sara wiped her eyes. She straightened her bonnet, and walked quietly—so that whoever it was below would not hear her footsteps—to the landing. She heard the rasp of the bolts being thrown back. Then a rumble of thunder in the distance blotted out the first words spoken between Clapmore and his visitor. She leaned farther over the banister to listen.

Clapmore's agitated voice reached her. "...Madame de Bourget is not here, I tell you! You've made a mistake. Mr. Hogan."

"God damn you, I'm not such a fool as all that! I went to Glenbarr, and her son himself told me she had come here. Now I find her carriage at the door, and Edwards..."

"Jeremy!" Sara called. "Jeremy, I'm here!" She started down the stairs. "Wait, Clapmore, I'm coming!"

The two men came through the store and stood looking up at her. She was greeted by Jeremy's truculent face, and Clapmore's slightly aggrieved one.

"I was only obeying Madame de Bourget's orders, Mr. Hogan. I'm sorry if you..."

His voice trailed off. Sara, giving him a quick glance, realised that he probably loathed being in the position of having to offer some sort of apology to Jeremy Hogan, an emancipist, while he, Clapmore, had come to the colony a free man.

"Thank you, Clapmore," she said, as she reached the bottom of the stairs. "I'll call you when I'm ready, and you can bring the rolls down here."

"Very well, ma'am," he said, withdrawing.

Sara waited until he had closed the door leading into his own quarters before she motioned Jeremy to follow her back into the main room.

Half an hour later they still faced each other across the space of floor where the shadows leapt with each flicker of the single candle. Outside the low growl of the thunder continued, and the lightning flashed occasionally. Sara stood erect, twisting a handkerchief between her hands; Jeremy leaned against the long counter, his arms folded and his sodden greatcoat flung back from his shoulders. The pattern of rain on the windows was like the ceaseless tapping of many fingers; every now and then they heard the stamp of the horse's hoofs, and the scrape of Edwards's heavy boots as he took a turn along the length of the sheltered store-front. His shadow, thrown through the big windows by a light in the house diagonally opposite, marched across the floor between them. It fell on the kegs and barrels, the cheeses, the scales; it darkened the rolls of calico and cotton, the sides of bacon, the piles of boxes. It was almost like the swing of a pendulum between one and the other.

"So that's how it is, Sara," Jeremy said, breaking a long silence.

"Yes," she said, flushing slightly with annoyance at his tone. "That's how it is!—as you put it."

The shadows marked the heavy frown he wore.

"I can't believe it," he said. "I can't believe that you'd be so crazy as to throw up all you have here for some mad whim."

394

"I've told you till I'm weary of telling you, Jeremy, that this is no mad whim. Louis wanted it—and I fought him over it until he made me see how necessary it was for the children. And as for throwing up what I have here—that's absolute nonsense! A year or two, and then I'll be back. David and Duncan will, I hope, come back with me gladly, because by that time they'll know that their lives here hold something more worthy of love and labour than England can offer them."

"And you, Sara—what of yourself? What will England have for you?" His voice had a rough edge to it, although he kept it low.

"For me? Very little, I think, Jeremy. I must be with Elizabeth of course, and then . . ."

"Yes?"

"I want to be on hand to prompt the return as soon as David and Duncan begin to think of it. They forget so easily. . . . They'll fritter their time away, and the memory of Kintyre and Banon and Dane Farm could grow very faint if I were not there to keep bringing them up."

Jeremy regarded her in silence again. Then his eyes left her, and watched Edwards's silhouette moving across the two curved windows. Outside, the Maclay name-sign creaked a little in the wind; the candle fluttered wildly as a sudden stronger gust forced a draught under the door.

At last Jeremy spoke, turning to look at her. "Why don't you tell me the truth?"

She stiffened. "What do you mean?"

With a loud, smacking noise he crashed one fist into the other. "Oh, damn you! Do you think I'm taken in by your sentimental notions of going to England just to be with the children? You may often have forced me into doing things I didn't want, Sara, but you've never yet succeeded in hoodwinking me!"

Angrily she took a step towards him. "Tell me exactly what you mean, and stop this quibbling!"

He was breathing heavily. "You're going to England because of that fool, Richard Barwell. Isn't that it? You've always wanted him, and now he's practically yours."

She almost recoiled before his words. "How dare you say that to me! How dare you say it when Louis is only dead two days!"

He tugged at his coat, dragging it back on his shoulders.

"I think I'd say anything to you . . . now that I know what is really in your lying little soul! God, when I think of how long

I've tried to believe that you were different! I made excuses for the way you behaved. I told myself that you acted as you did because the hardships of your life had taught you to look after yourself first. When you came to Kintyre, I hoped that Andrew's love for you, and the way he worked to give you the things you wanted, might chip away some of that crust of self-love. You assumed a softer façade, but you didn't really change—not ever! For years I've pretended to myself that you've altered—but you haven't. Here you are, now, planning to have yet another prize that you've always hankered after!''

"Don't you preach to me, Jeremy Hogan!" she cried passionately. "Don't you set yourself up to be *my* conscience! Anyway, what do you know of women like me? Haven't you always told me that you were brought up among women who had soft voices and slept in soft beds? Don't you come here like a twice-a-year parson and tell me what I must do, and mustn't do! You think you know me through and through—you've always thought that—but I'm telling you right now that you couldn't even begin to understand what sort of woman I am. You've only known two kinds—the kind who played the piano in your mother's drawing-room, and the convict strumpet you're living with now! And I'll tell you something else . . . I'm sick to death of having you order me about—I'm sick of your moralising and your preaching! Ever since I've known you it's always been, "Sara, you must do thus, and thus!' Or, 'Sara, Andrew would expect you to do this, and this!' And all the time you've been rotten with jealousy because I didn't fall into your arms when you wanted me. Long ago, at Kintyre, you confessed that to me . . . and I've never forgotten it.''

"Be quiet!" he snapped. "You're talking like a streetwoman!"

"Do you think I care about that? Listen to me, Jeremy. I don't have to ask anyone's permission for what I'll say or do. *Do you understand that?''*

She flung out her hands. "Oh, I've many reasons to be grateful to you, many reasons—and I'll not forget them, either. But my gratitude doesn't give you the right to tell me how I'll behave. From the day Andrew died, you've tried to tell me how to live my life. Well, I haven't lived it as you wanted—neither has it turned out to be the disaster you predicted. I've had a pretty full life—but if you had your way I'd still be sitting over my needlework, weeping for Andrew. Louis knew the sort of life

I wanted—and *that's* why he married me. Do you understand now?"

He picked up his hat and riding-crop.

"Yes. Certainly I understand—very clearly."

"Well?" she demanded.

He walked up close to her, and stared into her face.

"I understand it all so clearly, that I'm going out of here and I'll marry the first presentable woman I can find. The only thing I'll ask of her is that she has no ambition, and no thoughts beyond her own fireside. I want her to be meek and pliable and biddable. She'll be, in fact, as different from you, Sara, as it's possible for a woman to be. Because, if you're sick to death of me—then I can tell you that I've had my belly and guts full of you, and I hope to God I never lay eyes on your kind again!"

Then he turned and strode across the floor, cramming his hat on his head, and flinging open the door. Edwards, leaning against it staggered back wildly, clutching at a large keg to keep his balance. The door closed with a mighty crash, setting an assortment of frying-pans, hanging from the ceiling, swaying and tinkling. Edwards stood with his mouth open a little, staring up at them dumbly.

"Mr. Hogan has gone, Edwards," Sara said, unnecessarily. "You'd better go and tell Clapmore he can come out now."

PART SIX

Chapter One

Sara opened her eyes slowly to the sight of her familiar bedroom in the house in Golden Square, on a morning in June, 1814. Every morning for six months past she had awakened with just the same sense of expectancy, as if this day, above all the others, might have something different about it. But within a few moments the feeling of disappointment and indifference had fastened upon her again. The room was dim with the drawn curtains, and she had no idea what the time was, but already the sounds of the London day had begun to penetrate—the street cries, the rumble of heavy carriage wheels, the shrill voices of servants gossiping together as they swept the area steps. These were the sounds with which she had grown familiar but never resigned to—and each morning they struck her ear as if for the first time. She stared up at the silk canopy above the bed, and knew that her resentment was entirely unreasonable; she wasn't any more pleased with herself being forced to admit it. With an almost savage movement she reached out and pulled at the bell-cord.

As she lay waiting for the hurrying footsteps to come in answer to her ring, she thought of the day ahead of her. It wouldn't be much different from most other days—there was correspondence to be attended to, perhaps a visit to her shipping agents, a drive in the Park, and then to end it a party in Lady Fulton's house, in St. James's Square. She would hardly be in bed again before dawn. Until a few weeks ago she had been quite willing to accept this routine, hardly questioning it, because it was new to her, and, in its way, exciting. The sharp contrast between the London she now inhabited, and the London of the cheap lodging-houses in and about Fleet Street and the Strand, which she had known with her father, was somewhat of a balm for the boredom and impatience she sometimes felt. To rent one's own London house, to keep a carriage and good horses, to have liveried servants on the box when one drove in the Park— all these things, the marks of belonging in a fashionable world, would have seemed no more than an idle fairytale to the young child who had served as a dressmaker's apprentice an almost forgotten number of years ago. She remembered that child vividly, and she remembered how her mind, sharpened by the need to scrape some sort of living from Sebastian's precarious earnings, had seized upon every opportunity towards advancement, and, as quick as a monkey, she had seen her chances and taken them, until the day Sebastian's debts had finally forced them into the coach bound for Rye. Now Sara herself was a respected patron of one of the most fashionable of the dressmakers, but, unlike most of the other patrons, she had a curiously naive habit of paying her accounts promptly. She had a strange feeling sometimes, that the young Sara was at her elbow when she attended receptions and parties, giving those same appraising glances to the furnishing of the houses, and the smartness of the carriages in which the guests arrived, and the quality of the clothes they wore.

She turned over in bed and sighed. Once she had taken a chaise—hired, because the servants would have wondered at their mistress's errand if she had ordered the carriage—and driven to Villiers Street, off the Strand. She took it all in carefully—the tall, narrow houses, the street-pedlars, the dirty children, the dogs. This was the street Sebastian had told her she was born in; but it evoked no particular sense of familiarity. She didn't stay long—the young Sara seemed to have deserted her at the crucial moment—and a richly-dressed woman in a waiting chaise excited too much comment in that outspoken neighbourhood. She returned to Golden Square with the feeling that she had lost something definitely precious to her.

A trim, middle-aged maid tapped softly, and opened the bedroom door. She went directly to the windows and drew back the curtains, the clear, bright sun of a summer morning flooded in.

"It's what you might call a fine day, ma'am."

"Yes, Susan," Sara returned indifferently. She sat up to take the light shawl the woman had brought for her shoulders, and then the comb, which she ran through her hair

She took the breakfast tray and rested it across her knees. "The children . . . ?" she asked. "Are they about—or have they gone out already?"

"Mr. David and Miss Elizabeth are still here, ma'am. I believe Mr. Duncan has gone, though. And Miss Henriette has just begun her lessons."

Sara nodded, and waited with an unaccountable impatience for Susan to finish her fussing, and be gone. They exchanged a little more conversation about clothes for the day's programme, and then she was left alone. She sipped her coffee thankfully.

It had been easier than she believed to slip into her present position in London. Louis was more than accurate in his estimation of what London would have to say of her. She could not, of course, escape the tales that were told of her past, but she soon found that there were many people among the smart set who were not anxious to look beyond her obvious wealth, and were then willing to cultivate her society. She knew well enough that most of her new acquaintances—the people whose invitations she received to dinner and receptions—did not belong to the top bracket of the circles in which they moved, but she weeded them out, and accepted the most attractive. To all but the royal circles, elegance and wealth seemed to be the only arbiters of one's acceptability, and in these two factors Sara held her own. Stories of her convict origin, naturally, circulated; but shrewd guesses had been made at the extent of her fortune, the half-forgotten history of Louis de Bourget revived, and the power of money had, in many minds, turned her from a convicted felon into the innocent victim of a judicial blunder. On most occasions she was very well received; she was admired, and made much of. Bligh, now a Vice-Admiral, and living in Lambeth, came to call on her; he seemed delighted to see her again, and, in his embarrassed manner, expressed deep sympathy over Louis' death. He took her to visit his friend and patron, Sir Joseph Banks, who, as president of the Royal Society, wielded an immense influence. To Banks, Sara was something of a colonial oddity, and she appeared to amuse him; but more important, she had brought back with her Louis' meticulous collection of botanical specimens, and, for the sake of possessing them, Banks—the scientist before all else—was prepared to receive her into his house. Those who met her there were soon given the information that she had been pardoned, instead of serving her full sentence. Sara had good reason to remember, in those first months, that she had once done something to earn Bligh's gratitude.

Richard Barwell had played his own part in introducing her to the fashionable world in which he moved. He was now in full possession of Alison's fortune, had taken a town house on the edge of Green Park, and was leading the sort of life to which he had always seemed eminently suited. On his return to England from New South Wales, he had joined Wellington's army in Spain, and he carried the glamour of that successful campaign about with him—added to that, he had a reputation for gallantry, earned by a shoulder wound which would not respond to the treatment of the army surgeons, and was responsible for his being sent back home. He had been one of the great Wellington's soldiers, and he wore the distinction with becoming—but, Sara suspected, not very sincere modesty.

Richard had greeted her, on her arrival in England last November, with undeniable enthusiasm, coming to Portsmouth to meet her, and later in London helping in her search for a house. The Golden Square house had been finally rented through a friend of his—a Lady Fulton, sister of an earl, and wife of an Irish peer, who never himself appeared in London, and whose estates were squeezed dry to meet her expenses. The house belonged to a cousin of her husband, and Sara shrewdly guessed that Lady Fulton was herself collecting a commission on the rent. In a practised, skilful fashion she assumed a proprietary air towards Sara, and more especially towards Elizabeth. With a full knowledge of what was happening, Sara found herself paying for the parties and dinners Lady Fulton gave to introduce Elizabeth, David, and Duncan to suitable friends. In a way, this relationship between herself and Anne Fulton pleased Sara. There was no pretence that, in other circumstances, they would have been friends; it was simply that they were useful to each other. Anne Fulton had important connections, and for the sake of having some of her debts paid with de Bourget money, was quite prepared to use them. She was a friend of that exquisite grandmother, the Marchioness of Hertford, the *confidante* of the Prince Regent. Sara had once attended a reception in the house in St. James's Square, when the Marchioness arrived unexpectedly with the Prince. They had strolled around, played cards, eaten supper, laughed and gossiped with some of the guests, then, just before they left, the Prince had indicated to Lady Fulton that he wished Madame de Bourget to be presented to him. Something of the fabulous story London society had woven around Sara had been whispered to him, and his bulging blue eyes were full of amusement as he questioned her about the colony, which, he said, seemed to be quite beyond the reaches of the civilised world. He was unpopular, hated by many, but his taste in the elegant and graceful was unsurpassed in Europe, and the fact that Sara de Bourget had found favour with him, even for a brief five minutes, was commented upon and remembered. With faintly-flushed cheeks she withdrew from his presence reflecting that, in some circles, the cut of one's gown and the arrangement of one's hair seemed to matter more than the sentence of a judge in a court of law.

The months of winter advanced to spring and summer, bringing the news of Wellington's great victories north of the Pyrenees, the capture of Paris by the allied armies, Napoleon's abdication, and his imprisonment on Elba. Europe drew a breath of relief, and settled down to long-drawn-out quarrels over the spoils of war. But to London, this June, came the Czar Alexander of Russia, and the King of Prussia, attended by their victorious generals, on visits of state. London's welcome to them was wild and exuberant. The very height of the season's shows were the official entertainments given to them, but in a lesser degree the whole capital celebrated. The Czar was mobbed whenever he appeared; crowds waited all night in the streets to glimpse him. With equal fervour they hissed the Prince Regent's carriage when it passed by.

Sara put aside the tray and lay back on her pillows. It was exciting to even breathe the air of London this summer, but she was appalled to find how weary of it she'd grown—all the endless round of drives and dressmakers, dinners and entertainments. It seemed so purposeless as she faced each new day of it.

Her thoughts were interrupted suddenly by Elizabeth's appearance, after a brief tap at the door. She entered with a rustle of silk, and wearing a new bonnet. She came to Sara's side immediately, and bent to kiss her.

"It's a perfect morning," she announced. "Just about as warm as a spring morning at home..."

"Home?" Sara said.

"Don't tease," Elizabeth answered, wrinkling her nose. "You know what I mean. It's the sort of morning when I long to be riding at Banon."

Then she stood and surveyed the remains of the breakfast, and began to pile butter on the last piece of toast. "How is it," she said, biting into it, "that you manage to get the only unburnt toast that comes out of the kitchen in the morning?"

"I probably ask nicely for it," Sara answered casually.

Elizabeth flung herself down in a chair, licking her fingers. "I don't think I want—to go to Lady Fulton's party this evening," she said.

Sara's eyebrows went up. "Oh . . . ? Lady Fulton says she's particularly asked some young people she thought you'd all enjoy meeting."

"Oh . . . them!" Elizabeth gave a shrug of exasperation. "I know their sort. Young men who won't look sideways for fear of spoiling their neckcloths. And besides . . ."

"Besides what . . . ?"

"David says he's not coming. I'd counted on him being there. When I run out of talk with these silly creatures I count on him being about to help me."

"Well . . . you should know David well enough by this time," Sara said as casually as she could manage.

Elizabeth fingered her dress, straightened the set of her bonnet and looked down at her slippers, carefully avoiding Sara's eye. In the past months Sara had been made aware of her stepdaughter's growing attachment for David, and had been equally aware that David treated her as he had always done, with a mixture of affection and playfulness. She grew afraid as she considered the situation that could develop between them; she knew Elizabeth's nature well enough—she had all of Louis' passion and possessiveness, and a formidable determination to have what she wanted. All through the months here Sara had watched her, and saw her keep her head amidst a surge of flattery and attention that would have made most other young girls breathless. In a few years Elizabeth would inherit the first part of the fortune Louis had left to her—a fortune swollen by the careful investments of his London agents. She had a spirited beauty about her that attracted attention wherever she went. Sara knew that Elizabeth was fully aware of all this—and the fact that, if she wished it, she could make a titled marriage here in London. She was aware of it and at the same time she seemed to understand that it was of very little use to her. For so long as David remained unimpressed she seemed to take little pleasure in her money and her pretty face.

That face now wore a sadly discontented look under the pale yellow bonnet. She twisted on the chair and sighed, looked at the clock, and bent to make certain once more of the smooth fit of her stocking. Sara felt that in some way she was failing Elizabeth. She had spread before her all the things she imagined a young girl delighted in—gave her clothes and an unstinted round of entertainment. But it was obviously not what Elizabeth wanted. Soon after her arrival in England she had gone on a visit to her Gloucestershire relations. Since it was winter, she had bought two magnificent hunters, and had expected to remain until the end of the hunting season. After four weeks she was back in the house in Golden Square, and there had been none of the exhilaration about her Sara had expected. She had little to say about her hunting, and less about the relations. She had come back quietly, flinging herself into an extravagant orgy of clothes-buying which Sara guessed as a futile compensation for whatever had gone wrong. Later David mentioned casually that Elizabeth had written to him from Gloucestershire with an invitation for him to come and hunt also, and he had refused it.

"About this evening..." Sara began again. "Did David say why he wasn't coming?"

"No... he merely said he didn't think Lady Fulton would be offended so long as *I* went. It seems there's something else he prefers to do!" And as she spoke, Elizabeth's hands gripped the edge of the chair tightly, and she scowled.

"Well... you don't *have* to come," Sara answered reluctantly. "I expect I can make excuses for you both."

"Good! Well then, that's settled," Elizabeth said briskly.

Suddenly Sara wanted to smack her—to drum into her a few of the manners that Louis would have expected from her. Louis would never have stood such behaviour in a young girl, and Sara knew she should put a stop to it somehow. But Elizabeth was not her own daughter; she had a mind and temperament which only Louis himself could have dealt with successfully. Then she looked again at the other's miserable face, and repented of her impatience. In the uneasy silence that fell between them, Sara wished she could have gone and put her arms about her—but in her present mood Elizabeth would have resented it furiously.

With relief Sara listened to the footsteps in the passage, and then her feeling faded as David tapped and put his head round the door.

"Good-morning, Mother."

He walked round the side of the bed, seating himself on the end of it and eyeing the tray. "I see Elizabeth has got here before me and finished the toast."

"Since you all make such a habit of coming, I can't think why you don't have breakfast here and be done with it. Where's Duncan?" she added, in the same breath.

"Riding in the Park," David said carelessly. "I must say he chooses a very unfashionable hour for it."

"Oh . . . you make me tired!" Elizabeth burst out. "Duncan is the only one of us who has the sense to go when there's room to ride. There's such a crush in the afternoons—and still everyone continues to go. As stupid as sheep!"

"My dear Elizabeth, if you want to call yourself a sheep you may, but I . . ."

"Oh, hush!" Sara cried. "Really, I shall have to ask you not to come in here unless you can stay ten minutes without quarrelling. It's too childish . . ."

David leaned over and patted her hand. "What a nuisance we are to you . . . and yet if you banished me from this room I should feel obliged to do something desperate."

Sara looked from one to the other with a sick feeling in her heart—from Elizabeth's discontented face to David's bland and non-committal one. She was brought up sharply against the realisation that they had both altered alarmingly since their arrival in England, and she felt that long ago she had lost control of the situation. They were growing like everyone else in London—fed on a surfeit of pleasures until they were too tired and bored to care what became of them. Look at them now, she thought angrily—sprawling here, both of them, in her bedroom, at the time in the morning when they should have had other things to occupy them, picking at one another irritably, and yawning as they looked at the clock. At Gilmour, or Banon, such a thing could never have happened. In the colony David's time had been fully taken up with his own duties, and, in a lesser fashion, so had Elizabeth's. She wished desperately, as she looked at them, that they had never left New South Wales. Six months here had very nearly succeeded in ruining both of them—and in a further six months they'd hardly be fit to return to the colony, even if they wanted to. Look at David—the decisions he made these days were over matters no more important than the cloth his coat should be made from, or which of his invitations he would accept, and which decline. Occasionally he went on visits into the country to the homes of acquaintances he made, and when he returned Sara questioned him fearfully, wondering if he was becoming too attracted by the life of the English country gentleman. Was he beginning to think of his life in the colony as too dull and too hard-working by comparison with what he saw here? It was a bitter thing for her to have to question whether any son of Andrew's might be fighting shy of work.

Until this time she had been reluctant to admit what a disappointment David was proving—but this morning, coupling him with Elizabeth in her thoughts, she saw it more clearly than ever before. She wondered if it was her own fancy, or was he beginning to adopt the languid airs and speech fashionable among the young dandies; did he care more now for the fold of his neckcloth than for what was happening to Priest's and Dane Farm? Where was the ambition she had hoped to discover in him? He seemed all too content to accept the world as it was, instead of striving to shape it more to his own liking, as Andrew had set out to do. If this was what money did to one's children, she thought bitterly, then it would have been better if they had never moved beyond the first modest prosperity of Kintyre.

And yet, in his very aloofness there was power. It would only need him to say firmly that he intended to go back to the colony, and Duncan—and probably Elizabeth—would follow him unquestioningly. This was one matter in which Duncan was still too young and unprepared to take the lead. David had the power to change it all—and yet the weeks went by and he said nothing, did nothing.

"Are you driving this afternoon?" Elizabeth asked her idly.

"I thought I might go around to Fitzroy Square to inquire how Captain Flinders is . . .

David straightened, looking at her directly. "Flinders . . . ? Not Matthew Flinders, Mother?"

"Yes. I've run him to earth finally . . . They've moved so often it's been like a paperchase to follow them."

"What's the matter with him . . . is he ill?"

"He's dying, David—dying of a disease they call 'the gravel.' He's in pain the whole time, and only half-conscious these past weeks. And there's very little money . . . He's kept himself alive just to see his book through the press, and I begin to doubt now that he'll live to see a finished copy."

Elizabeth's face wrinkled with concern. "Oh . . . how sad! Is he married?"

Suddenly David broke in. "Yes...I remember now. He *is* married. He used to talk about her—Anne, her name was, and he had married her only about three months before he sailed in the *Investigator,* God...how many years ago can that be? I was a child then."

"It must be about thirteen years ago," Sara said thoughtfully. "Poor Flinders...! As you say, David, he left almost as soon as he married Anne, and he didn't see her again for more than nine years. That was the time he spent charting the coast of New South Wales—and the six and a half years as prisoner of the French, on Ile de France."

"The book of the voyage...?" David said. "It's completed, you say?"

Sara nodded. "Two volumes and an atlas. But they've stolen his greatest pleasure, even from that. He called it *A Voyage to Australia.* But they've insisted it should be retitled *A Voyage to Terra Australis.* If ever anyone deserved the honour of naming the continent it's Flinders, but it seems even that is to be taken from him."

"Australia..." Elizabeth murmured. "How soft it is..."

"Whom do you mean by 'they'?" David burst out. "*Who's* stopping it?"

Sara shrugged. "The Admiralty, the Royal Society...Sir Joseph Banks is against it, and his word seems to be law where Flinders' book is concerned."

David frowned heavily. "So...the Great South Land belongs to the Admiralty, does it? And the man who mapped it counts for nothing. He's given his life to putting their blasted continent on paper, but he's not permitted to name it..."

He got to his feet, and strode to the window, his hands clasped behind his back rigidly. "It's the same stupid sense of official-dom that ruins everything in New South Wales. The Colonial Office is ten...fifteen years behind the most progressive of the settlers, but still sheafs of restricting orders keep coming from Government House. Control...Control...keep everyone bound in tightly. Look at the question of the sheep. The colony could send England every pound of merino wool she could use, if only they'd give the settlers as much pasture as they need."

"But they're expanding all the time, David," Sara said.

"Expanding...!" he repeated. "Timidly pushing a few miles to the north and the south! The Colonial Office won't spend any money, and so we're all doomed to stagnate on the edge of the country, until the sheep and cattle eat us out of pasture. I tell you, it's damnable!''

If Sara had dared she would have smiled for the pure joy of hearing him talk like this. Not for months had he been roused to such a degree, and it seemed weeks since he had even mentioned the colony. She began to wonder if perhaps this very point he raised was the reason for his disinterest. Had he begun to lose hope in the future of the colony? He had been given land that was already cleared and prosperous, and it was not sufficient for him—the quiet, dull farms needed no gust of energetic planning to help them. With the exception of Dane Farm, they were well run and paying good profits while he was still a child. She wondered if he truly believed the picture he had painted of the future—the population and livestock growing within the limits of their coastal strip, until there was not room for them all.

''The mountains, David . . . Have you forgotten that a way has at last been found to cross them?'' she said quietly. ''Surely you can't have forgotten all the letters we had about Blaxland and Lawson going off with D'Arcy Wentworth's son, and finding a way through.''

''Of course I haven't forgotten,'' he said impatiently. He turned to face her, and he looked angry. ''And I've been waiting ever since to hear more of it . . . but there's been nothing. All right . . . I know Charles Wentworth found a way through the mountains, but we had that news last January, and there's been not another word since. It's a nine days' wonder. And what is the Government doing about it? Precisely nothing. Charlie Wentworth says they saw excellent country from the ridges——But do the Colonial Office direct that a road be made, so that settlement can begin?—not they! It would mean that a little section of the community would move out beyond the control of Government House, and that would never do. Shall I quote the *Sydney Gazette* to you, Mother, on the subject of the discoveries of Messrs. Blaxland, Lawson, and Wentworth? It called their trek a 'trackless journey into the interior,' and described the country they saw as one 'which time may render of importance and utility.' That's the enthusiasm of the Government for you! That's the reason why men like Flinders must break their hearts and their bodies over official stupidity.''

He scowled. ''I tell you it makes me sick to think of it.''

Then he became aware of Sara's startled expression, and his own features relaxed. ''I'm sorry, Mother. I didn't mean to shout." He gestured expressively with his hands. "I think I must have a walk and get rid of some of my ill-humour."

He looked down at Elizabeth. "Since you've already got your bonnet on, you might as well come with me. It'll do you good. I notice you're not much in favour of walking these days."

She got to her feet eagerly. "Yes—of course I'll come!" With misgiving, Sara watched the slow radiance that had begun to shine on her face.

II

Richard Barwell's carriage came to a halt before No. 14 London Street, Fitzroy Square. The sun of the June afternoon was not kind to the mean-looking street, with the rows of shabby brown houses, the paint peeling and chipping from most of them. Farther along a family was moving out; their rolled bundles of mattresses and linen were displayed in their poverty to all the world. The children who made the thoroughfare hideous by day with their increasing noise, had gathered about the removalist's cart, fighting and tumbling over the shabby furniture standing on the pavement. But the arrival of the smart carriage, with the liveried coachman and footman on the box, attracted instant attention, and with whoops they descended upon it to watch for the occupants to alight.

A saucy imp of a girl, about ten years old, wearing a soiled mob cap, came close to the door and peered in.

"Well . . ." she announced to her companions. "If it isn't the Czar of Russia!"

Shrieks of laughter greeted this remark, but the rest of the children stood shyly back, retreating even farther as the footman climbed down off the box and went to pull at the ancient door bell. After some time a neat, tired-looking woman appeared. Richard opened the door of the carriage and got out. The woman crossed the pavement towards him.

"Good-afternoon," he said. "I've brought Madame de Bourget with me—we've come to inquire about Captain Flinders."

The woman peered uncertainly into the carriage, but as Sara got down, her expression altered. "Oh, yes . . . I remember," she said. "You're the lady who's come before to see the Captain and Mrs. Flinders. Well . . . I shouldn't go up now if I were you. Mrs. Flinders, poor thing, came down ten minutes ago, and said that he was sleeping at last. She left the little girl with me, and stepped out for some air.''

"How is Captain Flinders?" Sara asked.

The woman shook her head. "Bad, Ma'am—bad! Now that the book's off his hands at last, he's sort of given up. He doesn't seem to know what's happening to him half the time with the pain, and the doctor doesn't do any good. Terrible, isn't it," she observed, "what diseases these sailors pick up in foreign parts?"

Sara nodded. "Well . . . thank you. We'll not disturb Captain Flinders, then. Perhaps you'll tell Mrs. Flinders we called?" As she spoke, she took the covered basket which the footman had lifted from the carriage, and handed it to the woman. "Mrs. Flinders may find these useful.''

"Oh, yes, Ma'am . . . And who shall I tell her came?''

Sara turned back. "Oh . . . tell her Sara de Bourget and Captain Barwell.''

The woman nodded, repeated the names, stumbling a little over Sara's, and then stood with the basket in her hand to watch the carriage go.

As they turned into Fitzroy Square, Sara touched Richard's arm. "Would you mind if I didn't come with you to the Park, Richard? It's stupid of me, but I don't think I can face the crowds. If there's the least chance of the Czar driving out, they'll be there in their thousands.''

"Certainly—I'll tell Simmons. Where would you like to go? Shall we drive through Marylebone or Primrose Hill?''

Sara shook her head. "I think I'd prefer to go back to Golden Square. Hearing about Flinders has left me in no mood for idling away the afternoon. In a way, Richard, I'm glad we couldn't see his wife. I feel almost as if I'm insulting them by handing over my basket. Flinders deserves so much better treatment from the Admiralty—and yet they're so short of money that they can't refuse even such things as my miserable basket. This morning David . . .''

Richard put his head out of the window and gave the coachman directions to return to Golden Square. He settled himself back against the seat again.

"What was that about David?''

"He was talking about Flinders so wildly this morning. I had never realised before that he felt so strongly about the mismanagement of these affairs. He ranted on about the way the colony was being run—shouted at me. One would have thought he hated it.''

''Perhaps he does—have you ever tried questioning him about it?''

Sara shrugged. ''It's as easy to question David as to question the Sphinx. He's self-sufficient—far too much so. Except when he has one of these outbursts, he's my pleasant-mannered, smiling son, and one can never even guess what's going on in his head. He never speaks of it, and yet I feel his discontent growing with each week we have been here. Elizabeth too—they're so restless, and dissatisfied.''

''Could you be to blame for that, Sara?''

''I?—in what way?''

''Your own discontent, my dear. It's a very catching malady.''

She twisted around to stare at him closely. He sat where the sun came fully on his face, showing the lines that were now deep about his eyes, and the grey in his hair—the streak above the old scar on his forehead was pure white. But he still had the bronze of the long summers in the colony, and his spare-framed body seemed scarcely to have thickened at all since the Romney Marsh days. He was remarkably handsome, and despite the stiff shoulder, which was the legacy of the Spanish campaign, he moved with grace and ease, and still sat a horse superbly. For Richard these days life was a gracious and pleasant affair; his good humour was boundless because there was never anything to disturb it. He had been welcomed back to the drawing-rooms of his old acquaintances with a warmth that might have turned anyone's head; he merely smiled and accepted his popularity with a modesty which he must have known was intensely becoming to him.

Altogether, Sara thought, he was such a man as women fell in love with by the score—the born charmer and favourite. But he was a disappointment to most of them in the fact that he was by temperament too lazy to pursue flirtations once they threatened to become serious. With all this dangled before her eyes, Sara couldn't understand why she didn't marry him. He had wanted that, and kept pressing it, almost since the day she had arrived in England; for one reason or another she had never answered him finally. He had joked good-humouredly about her avoidance of the question. But then, he could afford

411

to be good-humoured and patient; his life spread before him like a long golden afternoon, and there seemed little need for hurry when dalliance was so pleasant. No longer full of impulse, he seemed content to wait. She wondered if perhaps it was his very contentedness that disturbed her—it was almost as if loving her had become a habit which he couldn't take the trouble to shake off. She knew well enough that if she had not appeared in London as a widow, he would eventually have married someone else. It was not in Richard's nature to live long without the absorbed attention of some woman. But she *had* appeared, and there was enough of the passion of long ago left to them to make him ask her immediately to marry him.

For six months she had hesitated—and each day that passed in which David made no mention of returning to the colony brought her closer to agreement. She knew she was going through the phase in which the unobtainable—suddenly put into her hand— was not, after all, so desirable All her life she had loved Richard, and she loved him still. But in more than twenty years she had learned to analyse that love, and to know precisely how strong it was. It was not any longer the consuming force it had been for the young Sara, nor could it ever again cause her the anguish she had suffered when he had first come to New South Wales. It could not be weighed against her love for Kintyre, for Banon, and Dane Farm. But her feeling for Richard had its undisputed place in her life, and one that she could never deny.

She held Richard off, and waited for some move from David. If he was going to disappoint her, and treat his inheritance with indifference, then she would take the consolation which marriage to Richard could give her. She envisaged the life that lay before her—in the small and elegant town house and the Devon estate. In that, and in Richard himself, there would be enough distraction to ease the pain of watching David turn into an absentee landlord.

Yet, she was equally certain that if David had suddenly declared, with any degree of enthusiasm, that he was going back to the colony, she would have gone with him gladly, and Richard would have assumed once more the role in her life that he had always played.

She knew well enough what he meant when he called her discontented.

412

"Discontent?..." she repeated the word slowly, not quite knowing how to meet his charge.

He stirred, and leaned towards her; stretching out and taking possession of her hand quite firmly. "Sara, you must know what causes your restlessness. You won't settle your future, and you play about with your own emotions and mine like a child with a toy. Why don't you marry me quickly and put an end to this indecision? Once you've made up your mind there won't be any place for restlessness."

She shook her head. "Not yet, Richard ... not yet. I must give David more time—and Duncan and Elizabeth."

"More time ... time?" he echoed after her. "What are you talking about? If you're thinking of settling their futures out of hand before you marry me, you're making a great mistake, Sara. You just can't seem to see that they're no longer children, and they make their own decisions. Why do you hold on to them like that? Let them go free—they won't thank you to wait your own happiness on their convenience. If you would once settle your own life, you'd find they'd quickly enough settle theirs.

"If David wants to go back to New South Wales—then let him," he added. "Duncan also. Elizabeth will, of course, marry here. What is there all the fuss about, Sara?"

"But you don't understand ..."

"No, I don't," he agreed. "I don't pretend to understand your attitude towards them. Whether they stay here or return to the colony, they're well provided for. They cause you no worry— and you're free to marry any time you want. Besides that—I'm growing more than a little impatient."

"I'm sorry, Richard. I'll try to decide about it soon."

He smiled as if he were humouring a child's whim. "Very soon, I hope, Sara. A long and leisurely wooing is pleasant enough, but I must watch that I don't become rather ridiculous by my very faithfulness. After all, we've wooed each other for the greater part of our lives. Isn't it time it came to an end, my dear?"

The carriage turned into Golden Square, and she withdrew her hand from his gently.

"Yes, Richard. Very soon."

The footman flung open the door with a flourish. Richard got out first and handed her down, waiting with her until her own front door was opened.

413

She took her leave of him feeling as if she had made an escape.

III

David came to the head of the stairs as Sara entered the hall. Something about the changed expression of his face as she glanced towards him halted her; slowly her hands reached up to the ribbons of her bonnet.

"David . . . what is it?" she said quietly.

"We've been waiting for you, Mother. Could you come into the drawing-room?"

She nodded, and with the ribbons dangling loose, hurried up the stairs towards him. He smiled at her, and she could sense the excitement about him, but his face was serious enough. Inside the drawing-room Duncan got to his feet when she appeared, and Elizabeth, who had been standing by the window, turned and came towards her.

"Mr. Macarthur's been here, Mama. He's just left—we thought you'd be back from the Park much later."

Sara laid aside her bonnet. "Macarthur? I'm sorry I missed him. What news does he have from the colony?"

Macarthur had become an occasional visitor at Golden Square, though the servants had strict instructions never to admit him if Admiral Bligh happened to be calling at the same time. The court martial which had cashiered Johnston after the rebellion had been unable to try Macarthur. He could be tried only in New South Wales, and he knew that Macquarie had instructions to prosecute him, and that there was no hope that he could escape the verdict of guilty. Therefore he remained eating his heart out in self-imposed exile, and through letters from his wife and colonial contacts in London, vicariously living the life he longed for again. Sara often shook her head over the sight of his energies wasted on such trifles.

"Plenty of news," Duncan burst out. From a side-table he picked up a letter, and brought it to Sara. "This is from Mrs. Ryder, Mother—it came by the same ship that brought Mr. Macarthur's mail. He's wildly excited about it—Macarthur is, I mean. He came straight round here directly he'd read his letters."

Sara began to break the seals. "But *what* is it?"

David straightened from his leaning position against the man-

414

elpiece. Sara's hands dropped nervously into her lap as she
looked at him; never before had David appeared like this—with a
light of passion and excitement in his face that might have been
Andrew's own. His cheeks had a pinched-in appearance, the
corners of his mouth pressed in firmly to a thin line. She drew in
a sharp little breath, and half-rose from her seat.

"Well . . . *what is it?* Tell me!' "

"The mountains, Macquarie sent Surveyor Evans to follow
Lawson's route across them. He went down into the plains on the
other side and travelled a hundred miles beyond the point
Lawson reached."

"The land . . . what's it like?"

"As good . . . better than the best on the coastal side of the
mountains. Like laid out park-land—grass three feet high, and
none of the barren patches that occur on the other side. They
went on for as long as their supplies lasted, and they could see
no end to the fertile country. No sign of the desert that people
predicted."

Duncan tapped her shoulder impatiently. "Read Mrs. Ryder's
letter, Mother. She probably talks of it."

Sara smoothed it out hastily, and the stiff crack of the paper
was the only sound heard in the room. She skimmed the first
pages, which were a collection of small items of news she knew
their impatience would never permit her to read aloud. Finally
she came upon it—Julia's reference to Evans's expedition. With
a feeling of wonder she noticed that her hand was shaking as she
began to read.

> "We are in a great state of excitement here over the
> expedition which the Governor sent to follow Lawson's
> route over the mountains . . . No doubt remains now that
> they have been crossed, and that the fine land beyond
> extends far beyond the place Evans reached . . . The Gazette
> published Evans's report on the journey. I have it by me as
> I write, and I quote Evans's statements. '. . . this soil is
> exceedingly rich, and produces the finest grass . . . the hills
> have the look of a park and grounds laid out; I am at a loss
> to describe this country; I never saw anything to equal
> it . . .' People say the new country teems with game, and
> Evans caught enormous fish in the westward-flowing river
> which he followed.
>
> "There are authoritative reports that the Governor does

*not mean to hesitate over the construction of a road. They
say that it will be no more than a year before the country is
opened up for settlement. This surely is what we have
dreamed of all these years, Sara. James and myself, of
course, will not leave Parramatta; we're far too old for
such pioneering now. This new country is for the young
ones . . ."*

David broke in suddenly. "There—that's it! The road! That's
everything. Without the road the land's as useless for settlement
as if it had never been discovered. Think of it—grass three feet
high. What flocks we'll be able to run on that!"

Sara ran her tongue over her dry lips. "Does that mean
. . . you want to go back, David?"

"Back? Of course I'm going back. I tell you, Mother, that I
mean to have my own land now. Something that no one but
myself had ever worked on—in ten years one could make a
fortune from wool—twenty years one would be a rich man."

"What . . . what about the other properties?" Sara said weakly.
"Don't they count for something?"

He gestured impatiently. "They do very well, but with them I
should only be following the same old routine that Father worked
out years ago. They belong to the old pattern when agriculture
was as important as sheep. When I get my own land I don't
mean to grow more than I need for myself—over the mountains
it's *sheep* country."

Suddenly Duncan smacked his hand resoundingly against his
thigh. "By God, David, I'll race you for it! Give me that ten
years and I'll show you who's the best sheep farmer in the
colony. Ships to take the wool to the London market . . . as much
land as one wants for the flocks. By God!" he said again, "this
is something worthwhile."

Sara gave a nervous little laugh. "To hear you both talk, one
would imagine the farms on my side of the mountains amounted
to nothing more than a few acres for growing vegetables."

David turned, and answered her quietly. "It's not that at all,
Mother. Everything that you and Father have achieved will give
Duncan and myself the money to start in the way we want. But
that achievement is still *yours*. If I slaved my guts out for the
next forty years I would never believe that I had done anything
with those farms. They were yours from the beginning, and they
always will be. We're not ungrateful—Duncan and I. But there's

no crime or ingratitude in wanting something of one's own. I want more satisfaction from life than merely holding together what you've created. Beyond the mountains there's a whole continent—and it will belong to those who go and take it!''

She nodded, and looked down at the letter again. But she wasn't reading it. Back into her mind had come the recollection of that bright morning when the *Georgette* had prepared for departure from Table Bay. Then Andrew had used words almost the same as David's. He had started with a few pounds' worth of credits, and livestock won at gambling. David and Duncan would have far more than that—but what mattered was that they were willing to start before the first rough cart-track over the mountains had become a good road. Like Andrew, they wanted to go and find their lands, to settle for themselves where their flocks should pasture.

Vaguely she heard Elizabeth's voice break in.

"I mean to come back with you—you can't leave me here." David and Duncan wheeled round at her words. Almost together they answered her.

"Of course you'll come with us!"

Again Sara sought the place in Julia's letter. She felt a choking sensation in her throat as she found the paragraph.

> ...*this soil is exceedingly rich...I am at a loss to describe this country. I never saw anything to equal it...*

IV

"This finishes it, Richard," Sara said as she laid down her cards. "I've lost quite enough to you already."

He smiled broadly. "I never mind your being in debt to me, my dear. It gives me an incredible feeling of superiority. Besides, after we've had supper I'll give you the opportunity of winning it back."

She shook her head. "I said 'finish,' and 'finish' it is! In any case after supper I want to talk to you—seriously."

A mock expression of concern spread over his face. "I tremble. When you're serious, you're a very formidable woman."

He made the remark lightly, and she joined in the laughter that followed, but as they ate supper together, it kept returning to irritate her. Of course, Richard was right. To attempt to be serious over anything but cards in a gathering like this was futile.

Lady Fulton's house was thronged with a fashionably dressed crowd, some of the women still displaying the jewels they had worn for the occasion of the Czar's visit with the Regent to the opera in the Haymarket that evening. They had brought with them the fantastic story of Princess Caroline's arrival, a laughable figure in her diamonds and rouge. She had caused acute embarrassment to her husband, the Regent—in which the Czar had seemed to take malicious pleasure—and had been wildly applauded by the audience. It was a story that the whole of London would know by morning, and it made a delicious morsel for supper-time gossip.

But presently Richard caught her hand and led her towards the door of the supper-room. "I can see plainly enough, Sara, that my efforts to amuse you don't meet with much success. You had better come and tell me what has happened since I left you this afternoon to cause that expression. It isn't becoming to a beauty to keep frowning so."

He took her along the hall, and opened the door of a small room that Annie Fulton used in the mornings. It was the only room in the house, so far as Sara could judge, that hadn't been decorated to the last inch of space; with its collection of odd furniture it achieved an air of peace and intimacy completely lacking elsewhere. Richard indicated a small sofa for her to sit on, and he drew up a fat, padded stool for himself.

"Now . . . this tale that you must tell," he said. "What is it?"

She began uncertainly. "We had a visit from John Macarthur this afternoon . . . and a letter came from Julia Ryder."

"Yes . . . ?"

Telling him wasn't easy, but by degrees she built it all up—her fears over what David would decide about his inheritance, and his ability to influence Duncan in the same way. She told him of the months of unease when the conviction grew stronger that he would never return to the colony, or, at best, return unwillingly . . . her sharp sense of disappointment, the frustration of searching for a sign of enthusiasm and never finding it. Then at last the news of the crossing of the mountains, and the change it had wrought in him.

Richard gave her a hearing in silence, patiently listening while she groped for words to describe the scene in the drawing-room in Golden Square that afternoon. He regarded her thoughtfully, the points of his dark eyebrows almost meeting as he wrinkled his forehead.

418

"And what you're going to tell me now is that you're going back to New South Wales."

She nodded.

"You're making a mistake, Sara. You can't tie them to you like that. They'll resent it—and hate you for it. If they want to build their own new worlds they should be left to do so themselves. Let them at least make their own mistakes."

"I've no intention of following them into their bright visions beyond the mountains." She shook her head. "There's quite enough on the coast side to occupy me—and I think they won't be averse, now and again, to learning something about farming when they visit Banon and Kintyre. But my decision doesn't really concern them, Richard. It belongs to me. I knew quite certainly this afternoon—whether the mountains had been crossed or not—that I couldn't remain here any longer. There's an itch for power in me that will never be satisfied by what England can offer. I grow stifled here and breathless. I'm so cluttered by people and traditions that I live in mortal dread of tripping myself up. And none of this I had the courage to admit until this afternoon."

Richard patted her hand rather absently.

'You'll think me a very faint-hearted suitor, Sara, that I don't go on my knees and beg you to stay. In fact, to be truthful, my dear, I'm not sure that there isn't some relief for me in this. One so often wants what is bad for one and I think that may be the case with me. You're not my sort of woman, really. But because I've wanted you since I was a boy, it's now become a point of pride not to admit my own mistake. You've still too much energy and spirit for the sort of man I've grown into. I begin to suspect that in old age I'm going to turn into a rather pompous bore, and I'll need some cosy, comfortable wife who won't mind in the least. I suppose Alison suited me far better than I knew."

A smile spread about Sara's lips.

"This is hardly what I expected, Richard—that I should refuse your offer of marriage, and find you not more than mildly disappointed over it."

He gave a short laugh. "I'm not going to say I'm sorry—at least we can be honest with each other now. It will do you good to have a little set-back—you've always had men to adore you, and I don't doubt there'll be others in the future. But I can't tell you truthfully that it will break my heart if I don't have you to disturb my comfortable, pleasant life."

She threw back her head and laughed. Puzzled, he watched her for a few seconds, and then their own ludicrous position struck him. He began to laugh also; he reached forward and took both her hands, and pulled on them, so that they both rocked a little.

"Oh, Sara...Sara! That's what I shall miss when you're gone. The cosy, comfortable wife of my imagination will never be able to laugh with me like this!"

While she still laughed, he leaned forward and kissed her fully on the lips. Her arms went about him in an embrace, and the laughter was stifled by the kiss.

They were still in each other's arms, when Lady Fulton opened the door. She took in the identity of the occupants in a glance, and stepped back swiftly.

"Do forgive me," she murmured as she closed the door.

Richard released her slowly. "How very tiresome! She'll talk about it, of course...and when they discover that you're not going to marry me, I shall be pitied by the whole of London as the disappointed lover."

V

The first light of the summer dawn lay on Golden Square when Sara returned to it that morning. A heavy-eyed manservant admitted her; she paused on the step for a brief moment to salute Richard, standing still by the carriage. Then the door swung to with a gentle click, and the hall was dim once more. She took the lighted candle the manservant held, bade him goodnight, and started up the stairs.

In her bedroom it was dark; she set the candle down on the dressing-table and moved to the windows to draw back the curtains. The soft grey light flooded in; she stood looking down into the square. In a few months this house and this square would be part of her memories of an interlude—memories edged with gilt and parcelled together neatly.

"I'm going back..." she whispered aloud. "I'm going back."

That cruel, austere country had won David, Duncan, and Elizabeth, as surely as it had won her. It demanded a strange and compelling loyalty, and tolerated no other loves. One loved it, or hated it...but was never indifferent. And once loving it, one could have little patience for the claims of other places. People like Richard hated it—and it was harsh with them. From her,

420

who loved it, it had taken Andrew, Sebastian, and finally Louis. Impartial ... severe ... and lovely when one learned where to look for its beauty.

She sighed, and stretched to relax her taut, excited body. A faint little wind stirred above the housetops. She stepped back from the window and turned around.

Across the room she could see her reflection dimly in a tall pier glass. She tilted her head a little, and stared critically. Then she began to walk slowly towards it. When she stood before it she stretched out her arms and gripped the frame. Slowly she began to examine what she saw—her face with the hair drawn back and dressed elaborately, her shoulders and neck which the cut of the high-waisted gown revealed, her slim body behind the straight, stiff fall of the brocade.

"Sara ... Sara Dane," she said quietly to the reflection. "It's time you started to remember that you'll soon be old."

Then the corners of her mouth curved into the beginning of a smile. "But you've some time left yet."

ABOUT THE AUTHOR

CATHERINE GASKIN was born in Ireland, grew up in Australia and, after spending eight years in England, married an American and settled down for ten years in New York. She and her husband then moved on to St. Thomas in the Virgin Islands where they lived for two years, and they now make their home among the Wicklow Hills in Ireland.

Catherine Gaskin has now written seventeen bestselling novels; *The Summer of the Spanish Woman* is the most recent, and she is now working on her eighteenth.

PATRICIA MATTHEWS' LATEST BLOCKBUSTER!

EMBERS OF DAWN

In the fiery afterglow of the Civil War, Charlotte King was penniless, her only possessions a ravaged farm and a cache of prized tobacco. Two men kindled her dreams, ignited her ambition, fired her passions—and torn between their love, Charlotte fought to see her beloved South reborn.

Don't miss any of these Patricia Matthews' bestsellers!

☐ *TIDES OF LOVE (22809-9 • $3.50)*
☐ *FLAMES OF GLORY (01415-3 • $6.95*
  ($7.95 in Can.))—A large format paperback
☐ *EMBERS OF DAWN (23107-3 • $3.50)*
  On sale April 15, 1983

Buy these books at your local bookstore or use this handy coupon for ordering:

Bantam Books, Dept. EM2, 414 East Golf Road,
Des Plaines, Ill. 60016

Please send me the books I have checked above. I am enclosing $_____ (please add $1.25 to cover postage and handling, send check or money order—no cash or C.O.D.'s please).

Mr/Ms _____

Address _____

City/State _____ Zip _____

EM2—3/83

Please allow four to six weeks for delivery. This offer expires 9/83.

"The most honest, deeply felt book about contemporary women that I know."
—Elizabeth Forsythe Hailey,
author of A WOMAN OF INDEPENDENT MEANS

THREE WOMEN AT THE WATER'S EDGE

by Nancy Thayer
author of STEPPING

Graceful; warm, richly humorous, the new novel by Nancy Thayer is the story of a mother and two daughters, three unforgettable women confronting today's world—and discovering what really makes life worth living.

Buy THREE WOMEN AT THE WATER'S EDGE at your local bookstore (on sale February 15, 1983) or use this handy coupon for ordering:

Bantam Books, Inc., Dept. WE, 414 East Golf Road, Des Plaines, Ill. 60016

Please send me _____ copies of THREE WOMEN AT THE WATER'S EDGE (22749-1 • $3.50). I am enclosing $_____ (please add $1.25 to cover postage and handling. Send check or money order—no cash or C.O.D.'s please).

Mr/Ms_____

Address_____

City/State _____ Zip _____

WE—1/83

Please allow four to six weeks for delivery. This offer expires 7/83.

HISTORICAL ROMANCES

Read some of
Bantam's Best
in Historical Romances!

☐ 23286	**Sara Dane**—Catherine Gaskin	$3.50
☐ 23028	**Windborn**—Victor Brooke	$3.50
☐ 23058	**Yankee Stranger**—Elswyth Thane	$2.95
☐ 22657	**The Store**—M. Pearson	$3.95
☐ 20821	**Cajun**—S. O'Brien	$3.50
☐ 22581	**Dawn's Early Light**—	
	Elswyth Thane	$2.95
☐ 12168	**Bayou**—S. O'Brien	$2.50
☐ 20609	**Black Ivory**—S. O'Brien	$2.95
☐ 20404	**Providence**—E. Green	$2.95

CLAIRE LORRIMER

☐ 13992	**Chantal**	$2.95
☐ 20765	**Mavreen**	$3.25
☐ 20542	**Tamarisk**	$3.50

REGENCY ROMANCES

☐ 20479	**Lady's Maid**—Nella Benson	$2.25
☐ 22922	**That Wilder Woman**—	
	Barry Kaplan	$3.50
☐ 23129	**Bridal Journey**—	
	Dale Van Emery	$3.50

Bantam Books, Inc., Dept. HR, 414 East Golf Road, Des Plaines, Ill. 60016

Please send me the books I have checked above. I am enclosing $_____
(please add $1.25 to cover postage and handling). Send check or money
order—no cash or C.O.D.'s please.

Mr/Mrs/Miss _____

Address _____

City _____ State/Zip _____

HR—3/83

Please allow four to six weeks for delivery. This offer expires 9/83.

THE LATEST BOOKS IN THE BANTAM BESTSELLING TRADITION

☐	22749	**THREE WOMEN AT THE WATER'S EDGE** Nancy Thayer	$3.50
☐	23028	**WINDBORN** Victor Brooke	$3.50
☐	23026	**CAPRICE** Sara Hylton	$2.75
☐	22924	**PUBLIC SMILES, PRIVATE TEARS** Helen Van Slyke w/J. Edwards	$3.95
☐	23554	**NO LOVE LOST** Helen Van Slyke	$3.95
☐	23071	**A RAGE TO LOVE** Liz Martin	$2.95
☐	22846	**THE DISINHERITED** Clayton Matthews	$3.50
☐	22838	**TRADITIONS** Alan Ebert w/Janice Rotchstein	$3.95
☐	01415	**FLAMES OF GLORY** Patricia Matthews	$6.95
☐	22751	**A PRESENCE IN A EMPTY ROOM** Velda Johnston	$2.50
☐	22577	**EMPIRE** Patricia Matthews w/Clayton Matthews	$3.50
☐	22687	**THE TRUE BRIDE** Thomas Altman	$2.95
☐	22704	**THE SISTERHOOD** Michael Palmer	$3.50
☐	20901	**TRADE WIND** M. M. Kaye	$3.95
☐	20833	**A WOMAN OF TWO CONTINENTS** Pixie Burger	$3.50
☐	01368	**EMBERS OF DAWN** Patricia Matthews (A Large Format book)	$6.95
☐	20921	**TANAMERA** Noel Baker	$3.95
☐	20026	**COME POUR THE WINE** Cynthia Freeman	$3.95
☐	20664	**THE GLITTERING HARVEST** Maisie Mosco	$3.50
☐	22719	**FROM THE BITTERLAND** Maisie Mosco	$3.50

Buy them at your local bookstore or use this handy coupon for ordering:

Bantam Books, Inc., Dept. FBS, 414 East Golf Road, Des Plaines, Ill. 60016

Please send me the books I have checked above. I am enclosing $_____
(please add $1.25 to cover postage and handling). Send check or money order
—no cash or C.O.D.'s please.

Mr/Mrs/Miss_____

Address_____

City_____State/Zip_____

FBS—3/83

Please allow four to six weeks for delivery. This offer expires 9/83.